The Captive Dove

John Ouellet

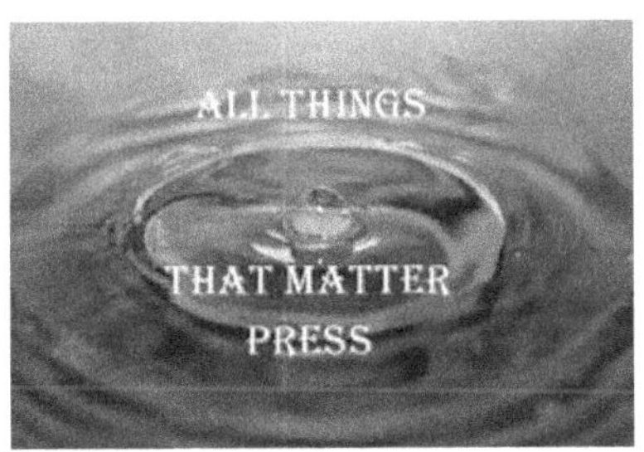

The Captive Dove

This is a fictionalized account of actual events and people.

ISBN 13: 9780989403245

Library of Congress Control Number: 2013953016

Cover design by All Things That Matter Press

Back cover image by Steve Ouellet

Published in 2013 by All Things That Matter Press

This book is dedicated to the strength and perseverance that is Joe, Sue, and Yamma.

To my wife and children, all I do I do for you.

In addition, I want to express my appreciation to you, the reader, who has invested in me a most precious commodity, your time. I hope I've earned it and that you enjoy this journey.

ACKNOWLEGEMENTS

I received a call from a colleague with whom I had spent years working an undercover investigation. He had read several of my writings, to include short stories in St Anthony Messenger. When Special Agent John Moran called me excitedly with the background which eventually became this book, I was elated but overwhelmed.

"You can write this," he said after he gave me the outline. I wasn't so sure. I had a three-month assignment in Iraq. I knew the desert and some words. I could visualize scenes. But this setting was Palestine and the story was real.

Joe is John's brother-in-law. He had known him for decades. But it wasn't until that summer when Joe casually told John of his childhood in the West Bank and how he found himself stranded in the Six Day War. I am beyond grateful to John for believing in me as a writer, for sitting with Joe for hours and writing down the story. He confessed to not being able to follow it all and so provided a cassette tape of Joe's telling, as well.

When I bogged down, which was often, I corresponded with both Nasser (Joe) and his sister, Sureia (Sue). In a flurry of writing a novel, I forgot that the essential story was their memoir, and the details of those years were often cruel and punishing. Though the pain of those days haunt them still, they not only permitted me to include such particulars, they encouraged me.

To you both, thank you for allowing me to trespass into those early years. And for helping with the tedious details concerning foods, housework, chores, school, daily topics of conversation between children there and then, for this is what the story is eventually about, children growing up amidst the madness.

I never met either of you during the writing of this book. I never spoke to you. To be honest, I never listened to that cassette tape. Call it a novelist's phobia but I had the visions of the characters I wanted to populate the novel. Still, having your input as I wrote was worth a thousand Wikipedia queries.

Sue, you were there chapter-by-chapter with your critiques and encouragement. The photographs you provided were essential in helping me establish place and as a constant reminder that this really happened to real people.

Readers, many details are true, many are not. I apologize to those who know better than I the politics, people, language, history and the land of which I wrote. Criticize my missteps there if you must, but please understand my intentions in telling a story with this universal truth: children don't deserve any of this.

To Phil and Deb Harris of All Things That Matter Press: I don't know where this book will go from here, but thank you for bringing it this far.

The Captive Dove

Anne Brontë
(1820-1849)

Poor restless dove, I pity thee;
And when I hear thy plaintive moan,
I mourn for thy captivity,
And in thy woes forget mine own.

To see thee stand prepared to fly,
And flap those useless wings of thine,
And gaze into the distant sky,
Would melt a harder heart than mine.

In vain, in vain! Thou canst not rise:

Thy prison roof confines thee there;
Its slender wires delude thine eyes,
And quench thy longings with despair.
Oh, thou wert made to wander free
In sunny mead and shady grove,
And, far beyond the rolling sea,
In distant climes, at will to rove!

Yet, hadst thou but one gentle mate
Thy little drooping heart to cheer,
And share with thee thy captive state,
Thou couldst be happy even there.

Yes, even there, if, listening by,
One faithful dear companion stood,
While gazing on her full bright eye,
Thou mightst forget thy native wood.

But thou, poor solitary dove,
Must make, unheard, thy joyless moan;
The heart, that Nature formed to love,
Must pine, neglected, and alone.

CHAPTER 1

Last week in a trade magazine I came across a story on the man I was now going to see. It was an article I normally would've skipped over but for a slab of grease that stuck it to the classified section I was scouring for a freezer chest. The uniqueness of the name made me stop. After reading further, I was sure.

I told my wife it wasn't a good time to be leaving. She agreed, but shrugged. "When is?" she said.

"The restaurant," I said.

It'll be fine, she told me. I had come to doubt whether I'd ever be the man she deserved. So many times I had tried and failed. Still, many times I *hadn't* tried and failed. I was coming to terms with the failures. It was the efforts that were crushing me. This time, I felt deep inside I had the chance to make it work. But yes, she was right again. When is there a right time?

I met him on June 8, 1967, and saw him only once after. That last time being thirty years ago. Both occasions were matters of life and death. The first time being mine; the last time being his.

Then, he was tall and thin with a protruding chin and deep set eyes. The photograph of him in the magazine bore little resemblance, but for the smile. He was wide and full now, with a gray beard. He was neatly tailored in a blue suit. Back then, he smiled seldom, but it was one I wouldn't forget.

He had done well. He had worked hard, created a successful business, invested wisely, and donated generously. He raised four children. His wife, a slight, petite thing with slouched shoulders stood behind him. I wanted to meet her. I wanted to see his children. I wanted to see a son who was tall and thin with a protruding chin and deep set eyes who smiled seldom but with purpose, and say thank you.

When I read the article, I knew I had to go. But there was another man who came to mind. Though the three of us had spent no time together, our lives were linked by those two meetings all those years ago. In my heart, it was right for him to join me.

I called the only person who knew his whereabouts. Nearly fifteen years ago I drove him across the Illinois River to dump him off in Peoria, not caring if I ever saw him again. I took the deserted road beneath the bridge as I was instructed, pulled into the riverfront parking lot and waited. It was two in the morning, late January. The snow squeaked, but other than that, there was no noise and no movement. I killed the engine. The silence grew.

The last time we met, before that ride, was not pleasant. I surmised by his silence on the three-hour drive he remembered it the same way. Several times I wanted to break the silence, but my pride wouldn't allow it. I don't believe he ever felt the need to speak to me.

Lights hit my rearview mirror. Before the car pulled into the lot, he was out the door with his duffle bag. There was no good-bye. He got in the car and was gone.

I expected it would be the last I saw of him. I'd make the exchange and he'd be dragged out to some forlorn desert town where, if he was lucky, he'd live out the rest of his life in peace.

"Sabaah al-khair, Johara," I said. She sounded happy, but guarded, upon hearing me.

I explained my call, that there was to be a memorial service next week for a very good man. She asked how I knew him. I told her. "And why should Rasul go?" she asked. I didn't know how much she knew about the relationship between the three of us, but I felt an obligation not to discuss it with her.

"He won't go with you," she said.

"I know."

"He's still angry."

"He owes many people his life."

"Such as it is, he'll tell you."

"That's his concern now isn't it? Measuring the days?"

"He's always measured the days."

"He was wrong, you know."

"But not always. And he doesn't believe he ever was so there's no use in you telling him that."

"It's time you stopped protecting him," I said.

"I'm protecting you both, Joe. I'll call him to—"

"No," I said. "Don't. I don't want him denying me. It's time for both of us to talk."

She gave me his address. It was against her better judgment, she said, but as always, it must be Rasul's decision.

He hadn't been driven into the desert. He hadn't even left Peoria. He was living in a plain house in a plain neighborhood east of the Central Illinois Railroad. Here, he was invisible amongst invisibles. He came and went with no one to give a damn. Almost fifteen years later, I'm back looking for him. Now, as then, I'm on a mission for a man whose time with me should have remained inconsequential. But as he once told me, things change, and I've changed with them.

CHAPTER 2

My story begins in the land my father called home. Palestine. It's not my home. Mine is Chicago where I've raised two daughters and have a wife I treasure above all else. She knows my story, and during my bouts with fear and what my doctors have labeled severe depression, she holds me and understands. It's how I know I am not insignificant in the universe. I choose not to be and my wife won't allow it. I sometimes fear that I've come to this conclusion too late for my children. They grew up with a man who dispensed of yesterday like spoiled food, who cared little for the pattern being woven about him. But time may change things. I can only pray it does.

Did I say it begins in Palestine? Of course it begins much earlier, the moment it begins for all of us, and isn't that a glorious thought? That though our paths are as varied as seashells and as numerous, one creation is indistinguishable from another.

I've at last found a bit of success and contentment as the owner of a breakfast and lunch shop on the South Side. It's a rundown building which my wife and I have renovated. The first month it was broken into. Twice. There was a third attempt while I was camped inside. I was able to get a shot off when they came in and I think I grazed one of them.

This is our fourth business venture, all in the food service industry. I love food. Cooking, eating, and serving. My friends say we should work for someone, let them take all the risks. We'd rather not. I think I enjoy the risk as much as I do the food.

It was 1964 and my parents were sending me to Palestine with my Siidi, my grandfather. I had no idea where Palestine was. My brother told me it was far away. I thought maybe down past West 71st Street. At six-years old, that was as far as I had ever gone.

I'm known by Joe, but my given name is Nasser, Nasser Khudayer. I was just out of kindergarten and looking forward to going to Earle Grammar School. I was looking forward to the new TV shows coming up that fall: *Voyage to the Bottom of the Sea, The Addams Family, Bewitched, Flipper, Daniel Boone.* My best friend, Franklin, just got a round pool in his backyard, one with a metal deck that went all around the outside and even had a place to sit and eat sandwiches which his mother forbade us to do because it would attract squirrels.

I knew nothing about the old country. I didn't care. I was an American and had learned early how to handle the slings and arrows that were those cruel names like, "sand nigger" and "camel jockey." I was taught to turn around and ignore them. If it was an adult, I was told, they were ignorant. If it was a child, they knew no better. Most times I followed those rules, but on occasion, when I knew I could take the kid and get away with it, I let loose with my legendary haymaker that never missed its mark.

Even at my age I understood that the names, though hurtful, were American names meant for American Arabs. I accepted them as readily as I did the names I heard for the Italians and the Chinese and the Irish and the Hispanics and the Blacks. Never did I have a desire to run past West 71st Street to escape them.

My father was from Palestine and raised by strict Muslim code. Siidi was my mother's father. He was of Palestinian descent. He married a woman from Nicaragua where they raised my mother with touches of Islam and Christianity. My parents weren't a match that would have worked well in either country, but it worked well enough on the South Side.

They had the same trials and tribulations of any household of the 1960's which left little time for waging battles over religions. They were far too busy working and handling five kids ranging from age seventeen to me, their last born.

Actually, by the time I was six it was just three of us. A sister died of influenza shortly after I was born so I didn't know her and no one talked about it. I do remember another sister who was killed by a hit-and-run driver. She had just turned sixteen. Though her killer was never caught, there were suspicions it was a boy in the neighborhood who took his father's car that night. He was only fourteen. The windshield was smashed the next morning and kids said there was blood and hair on it. I never saw it and the car disappeared that day.

Topics such as religion and ancestry were as commonplace in my house as an unoccupied bathroom and my father prayed devoutly in his Arabic tongue. I didn't understand the Salaat. I didn't understand the words or gestures. To me, it was a mournful wailing. I stayed in the corner, away from my ghost-like father who stood and bowed and knelt while gripped by a thing I knew nothing about. "Allahu Akbar, Allahu Akbar, Muhammed al rasul Allah." *God is Great, God is Great, and Muhammed is the messenger of God.* It was terrifying while fascinating.

And though I neither knew nor cared a single M&M about the politics of the Middle East, my father loved his Palestinian people. He wrote regularly to Presidents Kennedy and Nasser. He also wrote to Nikita Kruschev and Fidel Castro for their intervention. He was sure the FBI was tapping our phones for this, so small creaks and groans in and around our house became somewhat of an Anne Frank-concealment mission. After I came back from Palestine, this self-appointed duty didn't stop as he wrote steadily to Presidents Johnson, Nixon, Ford, and Carter.

The trip to Palestine was his good idea that Siidi fully endorsed. Siidi was a merchant who left the Middle East for Nicaraqua at forty. I was never told of the connection he had to that other side of the world. My sister surmised, probably foolishly, that he had met his wife while she was on a humanitarian mission to Palestine. Deeply in love, he fled with her back to her country to escape his arranged marriage. This made some sense in the fact he hadn't returned to Palestine since.

I figured my Siidi to be about eighty. It was not the way to discuss such things as age or familial relations with children. But using eighty as a yardstick, I suspected he left Palestine in about 1925 to avoid the European Zionist movement which was calling for Palestine to be made a permanent Jewish settlement. Of course this theory I came about decades later. At the time I left for Palestine, crazy love made as much sense to me as anything.

I didn't know Siidi well. I saw him on his bi-annual trips to the house, but I was young and he traveled often to see other relatives and friends when he came. He arrived for good after his wife passed away and just prior to our journey. My mother's Spanish descent did nothing to endear her to her father's family, or endear my grandfather for that matter. After his many years away from Palestine, he was probably no longer wanted there. But now it was time for him to go home, before it was too late.

Though he walked slowly and with a cane, I knew him as a very vibrant man who told tales of South America and Palestine with great clarity and the precision of a scholar. He spoke only Spanish and Arabic so my mother interpreted them for me. I figured the stories were meant to persuade me to go willingly. Looking back, I knew they were more than that to him. They were lost memories.

I became engrossed in those memories. If there were true-life stories of war ravages and beheadings and tortures in his day, he gave me no indication. Much to do with my tender years, I suppose, but something more, for in his eyes and in his voice there came a serenity. My favorite was *The Captive Dove* who is caught in a hunter's net and freed by a mangy rat who gnaws through it. A passing raven, so impressed by the rat's good deed, wants to befriend him. The rat will not hear of it. "I am a vile, repulsive, germ-carrying rodent," he says, "whom you would be better served without."

But the raven is insistent. He tells the rat that what he desires most, the rat possesses. The two join in friendship. Very soon this friendship grows to include other incongruous creatures: a gazelle, a pheasant, and a turtle. It is the gazelle who next falls into a hunter's snare. Again, the rat gnaws while the others work alongside to free her. The slow turtle cannot move fast enough and is caught in a second snare. Ignoring further danger, the rat gnaws once again as the friends work feverishly to distract the hunter.

"Ahhh," the rat says to the raven when they are safely away, "I understand now. It is my long, sharp teeth you desire from me." The raven cocks its head. "No, my friend, many have teeth. But in you, self is forgotten."

Ikwhan al-Safa, Siidi called it, Brethren of Purity. To willingly sacrifice for your brother, he said, is to defy all the evils and vices of the world. To him it was a philosophical compass; to me, it was a swashbuckling tale of danger and intrigue. I couldn't wait to get to Palestine.

For my own parents, I suspect there was a more urgent matter, to save us from the streets. As my grandfather's life was running out, so, too, was my childhood. My oldest brother, Daa'ood, we called David, was seventeen and already lost to the gangs of the South Side. I don't recall the gang's name, but I remember my mother flipping out over the leather jacket he had stashed under his mattress. It had a sweet motif of a black and gray rose on the back, spots of scarlet blood dripping from the petals. She put it in her closet to show dad when he returned from work. I wasn't supposed to see it but I did. "That is sooo cool," I said. My enthusiasm shocked her more than the jacket itself.

David didn't deny his involvement with the bloody rose gang, but he did his best to explain it away as a civic group of some kind. My parents were not impressed. And, it seemed, that in order to afford the jacket he earned his own money. Mom and dad knew he didn't work, but fell shy of asking him how he came up with the funds. They had all the facts they could handle for the moment. So at six, it was only a matter of time before I would follow David's path. It seemed they had more faith in the powers of the mean streets than they did in their Salaat.

My fourteen-year old sister, Sureia, whom we called Sue, was to go with us. This did not sit well with her. She was about to enter high school. She was well-grounded, intelligent, ambitious. She loved learning and wanted to be a teacher, perhaps a college professor. Math and Science were her interest, but really, she was well versed and intellectual in many topics. She had a beautiful singing voice, doing all the Top 40's of the day. And folk songs, mostly, Peter, Paul, and Mary, Joan Baez stuff. You couldn't tell her from Mary Travers.

And I often heard her reciting poetry with friends on the front stoop at night. Allen Ginsberg and William Carlos Williams. I once listened from my bedroom window as she recited *Howl* in its entirety to a throng of friends. Passers-by were stopping to listen in. I didn't understand the thing then; I don't understand it now, but like all of them, she had me mesmerized.

So off we went in the summer of sixty-four, just as the White Sox swept four straight from the Yankees and were creeping up on them in the standings. The Beatles were coming to the Amphitheater. Lennie Borskey's father bought him a four-foot boa constrictor. Me and three other kids finally managed to get the steel grate off the sewer in Lindblom Park. The stuff I knew of my sister was what I glimpsed from the corner of my six-year old world. Of Siidi, I knew cute animal stories. We were three strangers going somewhere strange. None of it made sense to me, yet I was anxious to get there.

CHAPTER 3

Why is the sky so high? So the birds don't bump their heads.

A joke I heard in kindergarten. I thought about that as the jet climbed forever, leaving me to wonder if it would ever come down or disappear into the sky like I had seen so many freed balloons do. I looked around and no one appeared worried so I kept my fears to myself.

The trip took nearly ten days as we went from Chicago to New York to London to Germany. At each stop I asked if we were there yet. We spent several days in London and overnight in Germany with Siidi's friends.

It was the longest ten days of my life. I couldn't imagine the world being so big. We spent endless hours over Lake Michigan, then Sue told me it was the Atlantic Ocean. Siidi slept a good while on the flight. I played with the belt on his keffiyeh to pass the time until I pulled it out and the keffiyeh fell into his lap. He gave me a displeasing look and mumbled something.

He was always mumbling something. It being in Arabic or Spanish, I couldn't know if they were prayers or curses or just ramblings of an old man. Neither I, nor Sue, spoke anything but English so except for ordering food in London, we were usually left out of conversations. It made it all the lonelier. Home was so far away. I realized now that that was how it would be for us in Palestine. It hadn't occurred to me that I wouldn't be able to speak to anyone. And, not only would I sit in the house without speaking or understanding, I would sit in school without speaking or understanding, and walk the streets. How could I learn if I didn't know the language? This new venture was becoming as overwhelming as the skies I was lost in.

I cried. Not out loud but softly, when the lights of the rooms or plane went out. What were my parents thinking? Certainly they knew better than to send me away like this. When I told my friends I was going they asked if my whole family was moving. I said it was just me and Sue with my grandfather. They didn't get it. When they traveled it was with family during summer vacations. And they didn't go away with grandparents; they went away to visit grandparents. I began to see this was not an ordinary way of life and my early sense of excitement gave way to confusion.

The airport in Jerusalem was much like the airport in Chicago. It was immense and busy and noisy. Siidi had us sit on a bench at the baggage claim area while he made a phone call. I was wearing my navy blue blazer and black fedora. I was a short, pudgy boy and my legs dangled from the bench. Dark-haired women reached down to pinch my cheek while men doffed their hats to me. A woman gave me a bag of milk chocolate coated wafers which Sue and I shared while waiting.

We were picked up by the husband of Siidi's niece, Abdel El Karim, who greeted Siidi with a generous hug and kiss, referring to him as El-Hajj Mahmud. He spoke a few phrases of English which was a great comfort to me. But he was mostly aloof as he drove the black Mercedes at incredibly high speeds. He was dressed in a black suit that was covered in a mist of dust from the desert sand. He was tall and dark and wore a thick mustache. But for the mustache, he looked like so many of the businessmen I saw in Chicago.

We were going to Dayr Ghasana, Siidi's village in the West Bank. It was a quiet ride. Siidi sat in the front, mostly taking in the sights that rolled past us. Sue and I did the same in the back. I was surprised not to be hearing the same kind of chatter between Siidi and Abdel as I had heard in London and Germany. There it was non-stop, serious talk that made the men nod and bow their heads. But here, Siidi seemed to have nothing to say. Perhaps he was looking at the land with the same attachment he had when reciting in his stories. It didn't occur to me that he was as much a stranger to Palestine and Abdel El Karim as I was.

It was over an hour drive. Just outside Ramallah, Abdel pointed to a palace belonging to King Hussein of Jordan. Jordan, he explained proudly in five words or less, was the nation that ruled Palestine. Even at six that made an impression on me. The word "ruled" to me meant those stories about kings and queens and witches and dragons; the evil king who ruled the ill-treated peasants and tossed poor boys into dungeons. I developed an immediate dislike for this King Hussein and the magnificent palace the poor Palestinians had to build for him. I wondered if Abdel El Karim was one of those builders, but he looked too rich in his black suit and Mercedes to have been tasked into such labor.

Perhaps he was a close friend of this King. I was determined to keep quiet on the subject of King Hussein during my stay.

Past Ramallah, the roads became dusty and the landscape bleak. The back of my brother's leather gang jacket had more color. Abdel pointed out the front window and announced, "olive trees." There were many groves of them on the hillsides. We passed rows of them in front of houses and even lining the streets the way oak trees did in Chicago. Some were mere bushes while others were thick, burly Halloween structures with gnarled trunks and jagged limbs that would have terrified me on a windy night. I didn't connect the trees to olives until Sue exclaimed that she loved black olives. I hated olives and spent many Sunday dinners picking them out of my portion of the family salad.

There were continuous clouds of dust. So bad in one tiny town that Abdel had to reduce his speed considerably. He said a dust storm had just blown through. I now had the sense of a true desert. It was stifling to look across. The car had air conditioning so we could keep the windows up, but everywhere outside people moved about bent and slow with scarves covering their faces and heads. There was still a stiff wind that whipped their robes like struggling bird feathers. They seemed to be going about their day; walking with bags of groceries, children my age playing some game with a stick and a soccer ball, and some men were even chatting casually at a gas station.

An old man was having a terrible time corralling his sheep that must have become lost in the storm. The entire road was blocked as they ran in a figure-eight circle. The herder was old. His robe was tattered. The wind played him like a kite and flogged the sheep into a mad frenzy. We were the fourth car in a line that was backing up quickly. The three cars in front emptied so there were now about ten men, women, and children dashing in wide circles to contain the dumb animals. I pulled myself up and peered over the hood. It looked rather like a game. There were three kids about my age who were having a ball. The women clapped madly at the sheep. The men gathered sticks to thrash at them. Others from behind us ran around our car to join in while Abdel leaned on the horn in anger. I was embarrassed to be sitting there uselessly.

Finally the road cleared and Abdel roared around the cars and people. We were climbing the side of a mountain. I had just witnessed the poor quality of roads through the desert; I could only imagine their condition as they wrapped around a mountain cliff. I wasn't wrong.

They were narrow and rocky. I closed my eyes most of the time and squeezed the armrest. Sue was nervous, too. Whenever I looked over at her she was peering around Abdel to see what was coming ahead. I didn't have to look. I knew. It was one quick turn after another. And always a sharp drop on our right. I was a daredevil. Always highest up the tree, riding the handle bars of my bike, first one down the toboggan run at Swallow Cliffs, but this was insane. The time I dared mimic Sue to get a look, we practically scraped a man and his kids on an ox cart. They didn't flinch and Abdel never slowed. Very confident or very crazy is all I could think. That, and when the hell was the mountain going to end?

The ride down was less harrowing. The speed remained outrageous and the cliffs as steep, but the view of the valley below was breathtaking. It was still colorless desert but now so vast. "Ghasana" Abdel announced, alerting us the village was down there somewhere. I was overjoyed for our trip to be finally ending, yet terrified of the life that was to come.

CHAPTER 4

Palestine, religion's perfect storm. It is the place Abraham entered into a covenant with God for the salvation of the Jewish people. Here, too, God's promise to Abraham through his son, Isaac, was fulfilled by Christianity. To Abraham's other son, Ishmael, God promised twelve princes who would become a great nation which is Islam.

Would it have been so hard to have sent Abraham on his epic journey in different parts of the world so these seeds could have been cast thousands of miles from each other? Why did God impart such vast differences between the three religions rather than petty variations? What God would throw three angry brothers into a locked room to fight to the death?

Of course, these were the ramblings of an angry young boy whose mind could not grasp the purity of such a storm. I did not comprehend that there exists events created outside our control which could not be changed, only accepted. I've been told this is a fatalistic outlook on life, to which I can now reply, to believe man is the beginning and the end is our most fatal flaw.

***

When the great Muslim leader, Saladin, recaptured Palestine following his siege of Jerusalem, he rewarded those faithful to the cause. His staunchest ally and fiercest fighters came from the Bani Zeid tribe. To them, Saladin granted the towns of Dayr Ghasana and Beit Rima,

Dayr Ghasana is historically known as the home of Jeroboam, King of Israel's ten northern tribes. Jeroboam was a protégé-of-sorts of the great King Solomon, but he lost favor upon Solomon's death and had to wrestle the kingdom from Solomon's son, Rehoboam.

He is forever known at the "King who made Israel sin" by erecting twin golden calves at either end of the southern kingdom in Judah, then instructing his people to abandon Solomon's Temple in favor of worshipping at one of the twin calves. Hardly an auspicious heritage to put upon a town. Still, not as horrific as the labeling an entire nation the persecutor of the messiah.

The mountains we traveled were the northern slices of the Hebron Hills whose southern sisters made up the ancient highway traveled by Abraham, Isaac, and Jacob. In these hills David made his home until conquering Jerusalem. Adam, Eve, Sarah, Rebecca, and Leah are said to be buried in the Cave of Machpela in Hebron. King Herod built a temple over the cave. All this, lost on a young boy sweating profusely in a blue blazer and scared out of his mind he wouldn't survive the mad ride.

We made it down the mountain and drove a flat stretch for about ten minutes. I was squirming and tired of the ride but feared what lie ahead. Abdel turned to Siidi and smiled. He put his right hand on Siidi's shoulder and shook it. Siidi nodded contentedly. He was home.

Dayr Ghasana was a real village, about fifteen hundred people, mostly farmers and merchants. The buildings looked to me like white and gray boxes, the kind we used to make out of playing cards. They even leaned that way. I found out Dayr meant monastery, but I never saw one. I was assured by my cousins it was there at one time but was buried by sand and no one had discovered it yet.

The village was shades of beige and green. Olive trees were everywhere. And fig trees. I loved Fig Newtons with the soft cookie, but the idea of scraping out the insides and eating it had no appeal to me. Olives and figs growing in streets like acorns were not promising for a fat kid with a legendary sweet tooth.

We stopped in front of a cinder block structure that was to be our home. It seemed that the entire village had come out to greet us. The Mercedes skidded to a stop in the dirt drive and kicked up so much dust the crowd instantaneously disappeared. When the dust settled, they hadn't moved. Abdel got out and the silt settled on his black suit. It was a bizarre scene, Abdel holding court with the curious neighbors and anxious cousins.

We three waited in the car by design, or lack of knowing what else to do. Abdel spoke to the throng for a long time, waving his arms and pointing back at us. Kids were leering around him to see us. There were a dozen or more. I had no idea which ones were his. Mama told us we'd have cousins to welcome and play with us. She didn't know how many; neither did dad.

Kids are like animals when meeting someone new. While an adult will go on about how well you'll get along, kids know better. Adults aren't really concerned about what happens once they leave the room. As long as no blood is spilled, they feel the entire process was a success. But their casual introduction quickly becomes your battle lines.

I studied those kids intently. Their leering and my studying was nothing more than sizing each other up. In a strange way it gave me comfort, knowing that I wasn't dealing with something entirely foreign; that even half-way around the world kids want to know if they can kick your ass.

They dressed like kids back home during summer vacation, in jeans and T-shirts. They were scruffier, which I mistook for meaner. But it was from daily living out here, and it would soon become impossible to dismiss me as one of them by mere looks.

Abdel came back to the car and opened Siidi's door. He spoke to him as Siidi slowly slid out without looking back at us. I guess he expected us to follow, which we did begrudgingly. One-by-one the neighbors came up and greeted Siidi. "Hajj Mahmud," they addressed him as the men and boys kissed him on each cheek. Although he was bent and crippled, Siidi looked very regal amongst them, like a king. It was more the way they responded to him than the way he acted.

Sue and I were next. The greetings weren't so formal. They were like those back home when seeing aunts and uncles. As I said, I was overweight when I arrived. The men and woman tugged at my cheeks and patted my stomach. They spoke to us in Arabic and very quickly, and their faces became a blur that day. Siidi disappeared inside the house as people wandered away, sorting out our cousins from the others.

There were four of them. It took several days but I figured them out, making only occasional mistakes in identity. Faid was the oldest son. He was sixteen and pretty much weary of me as soon as I arrived. He would stare blankly at Sue but didn't say a word to her for the first month we were there. I thought he was mentally retarded but found he was enrolling in college soon to study engineering so I gave him the benefit of a doubt. He creeped Sue out, and, though he tried, she wouldn't stay in the same room alone with him. Even when there were several of us together, she would make an early exit, giving any reasonable excuse she could devise.

Johara was fourteen. She was very receptive to us that first day. She spoke English well enough to get through mundane conversations. She was eager to learn more in the way of culture and slang, the Beatles and The Rolling Stones, miniskirts and hot pants, the Twist, and Andy Warhol. I was very fond of her. Looking back, I recognized her as my first love.

Of course, her interest in all things western had been her darkest secret. Whisperings late at night and walks to school became something of international spy talk between her and Sue. She asked questions incessantly to the point Sue would at times need to treat her as she did Faid.

I was not privy to those conversations. I was young and a boy and suspected of turning snitch to her parents or worse. It was further distance I did not need. I caught Johara in her bedroom doing the Mashed Potato to *Sawah,* an Abdel Halim Hafez song. I couldn't help laughing. The dance was idiotic to begin with; watching it done to Arabic cadence was cartoonish. Instead of being angry at me, Johara broke down into hysterics, too. It was a moment that was a great salvation for me.

Then there were sons Adli, eight, and Gamal, seven. Gamal was the boy I caught eye contact with while sitting in the car. "Anta Sameen," he said to me when the adults were gone. Adli and Faid laughed. I joined them from embarrassment. It was when I saw Johara give them a sour look that I knew I was the object of ridicule. She interpreted it delicately for me. "Healthy," is how she said it. Regardless of the language, I was well acquainted with the theme.

Siidi's turning away from us and into the house was a signal to me. Not only was I a stranger, I was an ignorant one with no compass, no guidance. Siidi was more one of them than one of us. Not by his disregard but by the nature of things. He was old, nearer to death than to life, and he was re-entering into his world while I was departing mine. I wondered furiously during these first few moments if my parents had lost their minds sending us here with him. I was in a village that turned out en masse to meet me, yet I never felt lonelier or more lost in my life.

CHAPTER 5

Then I met Yamma.

Her real name was Amineh, the faithful one. She was my mother's cousin and Abdel's wife. She was Yamma, meaning mother, to their four children. For those nearly three years, she was my yamma, too.

She wasn't there when we arrived. I sat with Sue and the cousins around an old oak table in the cramped kitchen. It was terribly cluttered and equipped with worn out appliances. Least I thought so. We had just thrown out an old stove back home and bought a new yellow and green Frigidaire Flair. All the neighborhood mom's came over to see it like it was a new baby. This one, the one's my cousin's had, looked worse than the one we threw out. And the refrigerator was dirty and stood crooked on cracked floor tiles. The counters were just tables pushed together, and the food boxes, cans, and bottles sat out like books on a library shelf.

It was hot with all of us just sitting there. I had these visions of doing this forever, just sitting and sweating. Gamal and Adli were jabbering in low voices and punching at each other. Johara rested her head on the table. She stared over at me with ghost eyes. Faid stayed for a few minutes but left when his father went into the other room to talk on the phone and chain smoke Lucky Strike cigarettes. I could see Siidi through the window as he walked attentively in a grove of olive trees in the backyard.

Yamma came in like a wisp of spring air. She was carrying an overflowing paper bag under her left arm, and with her right pulled a small black wagon loaded with boxes into the kitchen. Though it was stifling, she wore a long dress and a long-sleeved sweater. It wasn't a traditional hajib. These were rags, really, but very clean, always clean, and her skin was concealed whenever she left the house. She had yellowed teeth that were large and rounded. Her eyes were dark. The bags under them were heavy and pronounced. Her cheeks sagged and the skin at her neck hung like wilted lettuce. Yet when she saw us and smiled, with that huge wondrous joy that overwhelmed the congested room, she was an angelic apparition come to my rescue.

She dropped the bag and the wagon handle abruptly as she ran to us. She was a big-hipped woman who moved as much side-to-side as she did forward. But she could move quickly. Sue knew enough to stand and so deflected the force of her charge. I sat dumbly as she caught me in her thick arms and carried me up as effortlessly as she did the grocery sack. It was a bear hug tighter than I have ever known. It threatened to squeeze the tears out of me. I loved her forever from that moment.

She scattered the rest of them outside, telling Johara to stay. She called into the back room for someone named Khaal. Abdel poked his head around the corner, still on the phone, squinting in annoyance, the Lucky Strike dangling from lips, a scruffy version of James Dean. Yamma motioned for him to get off the phone. She bustled about the kitchen with the groceries in a way that made her look quite manic. I was rarely to see her slow down. Besides occasional help from Johara, she was on her own for the cooking, cleaning, shopping, gardening, and caring for the goats and chickens. I helped when I could. It wasn't the work I enjoyed as much as being around this woman who had no reason to be so caring and giving.

Khaal is the name for a maternal uncle. So it was Khaal Abu Faid, meaning maternal uncle, father of Faid, the first born son. Johara explained that that was what we were to call him from that day forward. And Siidi would be El-Hajj, a term of respect for elders who had made the pilgrimage, or hajj, to Mecca. I was amused to learn years later that Siidi never made it to Mecca but made no attempt to dissuade the homage.

I sat there the rest of that first day. Sue went off with Johara to her room. I watched Yamma making pita bread. She spread open her arms to indicate the kitchen. "Matbakh," she announced. I smiled. She rolled her hands back to herself, indicating she wanted me to join in. "Madbar," I said softly. She laughed. "Mat baakh," she said slowly. I was closer this time, and more comfortable with her and my response. She bobbed her head vigorously. "Good, good."

She held up each ingredient as she announced its Arabic name. When I listened to normal Arabic conversation, I swore the entire language was made of up no more than a dozen words. It was spoken so fast and shrill. But I was learning to enjoy the sing-song rhythms of it.

She pointed to the bowl of flour. "Ahjiin," she announced grandly and implored me once again to join in. Holding up a saltshaker, "Melh," she said slowly. She filled a measuring cup with water. "Maa." I would forget the word as soon as she turned back to the work counter. She took a large spoon. "Mil'aqah." Then "Ajaana," as she worked the yeast into the flour. It was fun learning from her that way.

Gamal and Adli came back inside. Really, they were no different than American kids in that I knew right away they had been up to something they shouldn't have been doing. They eyed me suspiciously then turned to Yamma. Yamma asked them several things to which they had no answers. She ordered them to their rooms. Adli puffed out his cheeks at me and extended his thin waist, waddling as he passed me. Yamma caught it and smacked him across the back, hard enough to make him wince.

For the rest of that day I followed her everywhere. She seemed to enjoy my company. We were good for each other that way. She was lonely as she went about her chores which were many and never ending. She waved at neighbors and talked to goats and chickens. But her day seemed empty for a reason I could not then understand, though I had a profound awareness of it.

My own mother must have had similar days when all of us were at school. All of us were at school. She cooked in the back of a restaurant. I went with her one day when I was sick and couldn't go to school. She scurried about for hours without lifting her head one time. Home, she'd do the same but for no money. Like Khaal, my father would spend days without having a multi-sentence conversation with her. But unlike Yamma, she had no goats or chickens to talk to.

I felt empty, too. After dinner, Yamma went to her room. Johara took Sue to a friend's house. I hadn't seen Siidi since he was walking in the olive grove. I was left to sit with Faid, Gamal, Adli, and my uncle. Faid and Abdel had nothing to say to me. I was to sleep in the same room as Gamal and Adli who seemed to genuinely despise me.

To further set my six-year old nerves into hyperdrive, Johara explained that Sue and I were to start attending school the next week. It took us nearly an hour to comprehend that message. Johara spoke rapidly to us about school, some words in English, some Arabic, some by gestures. I gathered from all of this that there were old buildings, large athletic fields, field trips, and at least one tall, skinny teacher with glasses who walked with drooped shoulders and bored them by reading from text books.

She was obviously excited and anxious to begin. Sue seemed so, too, but I expected that. As for me, riding and walking and being bullied by my two older cousins, who would no doubt be with friends, which would beget more bullying, was a slow death. And at school, more bullying. Bullying in a language I couldn't understand wouldn't make it more palatable. Really the opposite because it hurts when kids talk about you and you don't know what's being said. Like when Paul Colontoni whispered to everyone in our class that I was sent to the office because I peed my pants. Only I didn't know he was telling kids that and it wasn't true. I forgot my milk money and Sue was bringing it to me. But, of course, it was too late by then to defend myself.

I would be put in a corner away from other kids. Not because I was making farting sounds like Rusty Symanski, but because I was stupid. But I wouldn't be stupid, just in a different place where I didn't understand anyone. I could count to one hundred with only a few mistakes, and I knew the alphabet and how to spell some words. I knew all my colors. I knew the capital of Illinois was Springfield, not Chicago like most kids thought. If the teachers here asked me I could show them I wasn't stupid. But what did they care about Illinois, or how to count to one hundred in English?

Throughout the night my head ached with this stream of consciousness that was overcome with fear, apprehension, confusion, and anger. I didn't know why I was sent here. What started out a great adventure had rapidly become a nightmare. And what is worse than a nightmare you can't wake up from?

I had heard Siidi's stories. I saw my father in prayer. I heard his calls to Allah. But that was their world. I knew nothing of this side of the world, their side. It was less than two weeks ago I was in Chicago where I belonged. I was supposed to be going into the first grade at Earle Grammar School. Didn't anyone care about that?

I knew nothing of Islam or olive groves. I didn't care. I'd never care. I'd walk half a mile behind my cousins to school. Maybe I wouldn't even show up. If I did, I wouldn't answer any questions, even if I got to understand what they were saying. I wouldn't call Abdel "Khaal" or Siidi "El-Hajj". I wouldn't eat olives. And if Adli or Gamal kept it up, I'd smack them with my haymaker. I put one upside their friends' heads, too.

In an odd show of hospitality, Gamal afforded me the bed by the window. He made sweeping gestures with his hands to indicate a breeze. I didn't fall asleep until very late. Gamal and Adli talked in low whispers, yet loud enough to let me hear. And they snickered a lot. God, how I learned to hate them for that, especially Gamal, whose laugh was through his nose like he was blowing it in thin air. Funny how those first weeks I couldn't understand a word they said, yet I understood all of what they meant.

I was awakened in a fright by the growl and clawing. It sounded to be just outside the window. It was in that twilight moment where reality and dreams converge to mask their identities. I came to in baby steps. The growling started as my school bus that morphed into the backhoe laying the new sewer line on Hoyne Ave. The scratching was my mother taking the edge of the butter knife to the burned toast.

The others were asleep. The moon's reflection beat against the back wall of the tiny bedroom. I heard it again, a steady guttural sound that was no bus or backhoe. If I crawled to the end of the bed I would be centered on the window. But I didn't dare. I waited to wake up while the sounds continued.

I willed myself to my knees and peered over as far as I could without leaving the protection of my sleeping confines. There was something, a shadow, short and quick. It danced in the vivid moon glow. Then, a gust of wind through the open window had me crashing back against the wall. I fell hard enough to sway the peacock wall hanging above my headboard. No one stirred.

Now it was just the wind. I inched forward. The moon was fading with the night. No shadows, no sounds. The breeze felt nice against the sweat beading upon me. I took hold of the window sill like it was the safety bar of the Silver Flash rollercoaster. The warmth drew me in. I was resting my arms on the sill to revel in the solitude when my shirt collar was snatched in a vicious grip. I was being pulled through the window.

My initial thought in those wild first moments was it was Faid and the others tormenting me again. But I knew Gamal and Adli were asleep across the bedroom, and the snarling coming from my attacker was not human. I flailed my arms uselessly against the side of the house. I must have been screaming or banging the outside walls hard enough because I soon felt hands pulling at my legs. I was stripped out of my shredded pajama top. Like a stone from a slingshot, I plummeted back into the room. Adli and Gamal were lying on top of me. My left shoulder was bleeding from several tears and puncture holes. I was in shock; the pain came later. "What was that?" I managed to spit out.

They offered nothing. I saw the terror on their faces that I was sure was still on mine. Yamma ran in. Then Sue and Johara. Faid and my uncle stood beyond the door. Yamma pulled the boys up. Johara ran to the open window and began screaming out to something. I understood none of her commands but they were forceful. At the same time Yamma was laying into Gamal and Adli. I looked up to Sue. "No," I told her, "they were helping me; tell her they were helping me."

I was brought to the hospital in Ramallah by Abdel where I was given a tetanus shot, a bottle of pain medication, and twelve stitches. Sue came, too. Abdel told the doctor what happened. I had no idea what that was. The pills were good. I was tired and fairly numb by the time we got home. Abdel studied us in the rearview mirror for the entire drive. Not a word was said. Sue slept, and I felt as exposed as I did on the examination table. When we got home we followed Abdel until he left us standing alone in the kitchen while he went to bed.

CHAPTER 6

When it was oppressively warm at night and the others were asleep, I'd sit at that window ledge. I'd try to count the stars but became bleary-eyed there were so many. The sky, it was as endless as the desert. In Chicago I heard night sounds of trucks and sirens. In the summer I heard the neighborhood alive until well into the early morning. Here, only wild animals and insects and the chalky rustling of palm fronds were heard. I would lean against the sill and settle in to imagine the warm winds from a jet airliner taxiing before me as it raced away into an endless sky.

I learned the many moods of the desert from this place. Its many faces. I would learn to love its searing sun and radiant moon. I would come to fear, then respect, its strange creatures. I would recognize its voices of wrath and calm. I would eat its fruits and even its birds. I would witness how all things live and die here, and understand that regardless of the events of my life, it will never change its patterns.

Faid and Gamal tried to scare me with stories of the mountain witches and the Fugara of the Bedouins, the desert dwellers who roamed the village at night. And the beastly Nowar, the homeless gypsies who would grab children from their beds to make them slaves to dance naked in the village streets while people threw scraps of bread for them to eat.

But I knew of the Bedouins from my father. He never mentioned the Fugaras, their mystical shamans. He spoke of the Bedouins' quiet lives as sheepherders and farmers, and their great respect for each other, so I wasn't afraid.

I knew the stories of the mountain witches were untrue, too, because Siidi told them to me. They were legends his Yamma told him and his brother to keep them away from a cave the children would play in, and it worked for years. It still held sway because I could see that even Faid let off a nervous vibe when there was talk of them.

I didn't know what to make of the Nowar. I knew about homeless people and was told by my parents they were just poor people with no family to take care of them, and I heard of a group of gypsies who came into our neighborhood in south Chicago to steal from people by pretending to do home repairs. But I never knew of either group to steal children. Faid and Gamal's track record was such that I figured the Nowar story to be as bald-faced a lie as the mountain witch. But when they talked to me of the wild pariah dogs, I had quite a different reaction.

It was one of those animals that attacked me that night. They roamed the streets of Dayr Ghasana when summer droughts drove them to it. Three summers ago was the worse, so I heard my uncle explain to Siidi with just enough English words and actions to scare or impress me. Domesticated animals were easy prey. Families watched pets taken from their yards, sometimes even their houses, in ravaged bits and pieces. A beggar was torn from his roadside perch when he was unable to escape their mad rush from the hills. There was nothing anyone could do. It was over so quick and there were so many. The townspeople buried the remains of their pets and cattle into landfills. Soldiers were called in to hunt the dogs down.

Only my attacker was not a wild beast, not like the packs that roamed the hills. He belonged to my cousins. They named him, Amir; Prince, in English. He was found in the Red River Valley by Abdel as a pup. Yamma wasn't keen on the idea of having what was essentially a wolf around her family, but it wasn't unheard of. It was felt that such a dog, if found young enough and trained well enough, could be an effective guard dog. As seemed to always happen in the Karim household, it was Yamma who made it happen.

Amir wasn't allowed into the house, but he was Yamma's constant companion until he became wild enough to chase and catch the chickens, and at least one sheep. That was when he became solely a guard dog, chained out back in the day, away from the family and the grazing animals, and released at night outside the fence to keep watch. Now only Yamma could control him.

We had an outhouse. On the first day, Yamma told us in a condensed version, to use the bedpans at night. We didn't understand, and Sue certainly didn't appreciate such a dictate. Yamma opened the door to the howling of what may have been Amir, may have been any of the pariah dogs. We understood that we were not to be out and about at night. "Ghost stories," Sue whispered, and she continued to use the outhouse at all hours as the lesser of the two abominations.

Yamma had simple thoughts on most things. Animals, she said, live within their instincts. People have the capacity to live outside them. The greatness in living is in following the right instincts. It was as much a riddle for me as it was a philosophy of life for her. This, she said only once in passing, as if it she hadn't given it much thought. In time, I learned differently.

There would always be pariah dogs out there. Even when trained they would maintain the instincts that told them to stay far away in the hills until the hills no longer satisfied their needs. I learned to respect that and not fear them for being true to their nature.

To me, the greatest instinct was to stay alive, and to do so meant using whatever means it took. As I grew older, I found it hard to distinguish instinct from ego. For the pariah dogs, it was instinctual to stay in the hills. Only when the need to survive dictated did they come into the village. Ego didn't make them stay when the militia drove them out. The instinct to live was paramount and ego would have been the greater threat.

I hadn't seen Siidi for three days the night he came in after dinner. I was in the kitchen helping Yamma and the girls clean up. They ran to him, Sue included, calling to him in reverence, "El Hajj Mahmud, Ahlan wa Sahlan."

I stayed by the sink rinsing dishes. I did not feel such warmth or reverence to Siidi at the moment. I was sure he told them where he was spending his time. I was sure it was with old friends or family, here or in another town. But he should have told me and Sue. It was crazy of him not to think we'd be scared in this new place. As scared as I was, I had plenty of room for anger, and I let them all know it.

From the corner of my eye I could see Siidi making his way around the women. He was watching me intently. He took my wrist. For such an old man his grip was incredibly tight. "La," he said. He looked back at Yamma and repeated it more harshly. It was Johara who reached me next and took the bowl I was washing from my hand. She pushed me to Siidi as if I was her sacrifice to a god. Siidi guided me from the kitchen into the front room where Abdel and the boys were sitting. The room was cloaked in cigarette smoke. Both my uncle and Faid smoked constantly when in the front room. Neither of my parents smoked so both Sue and I had to suffer wheezing and burning eyes. I didn't fail to notice how Gamal and Adli enjoyed my discomfort.

I was made to sit while Siidi had a heated, one-sided talk with Abdel. Abdel would nod, turn to look at me, then nod more. Gamal and Adli snickered, and Faid shook his head in disgust with the cigarette dangling from his lower lip. I was relieved when Siidi sat down beside me and rubbed my head. "Mama baby," he said. That's when they all laughed. But Siidi raised his hands to stop them, which they did at once. "Nehm," he said, looking down at me and pointing out the window. "Najmah."

They all nodded in agreement. To me that meant little in the way of comfort. My cousins always nodded vigorously whenever Abdel spoke; everyone did likewise for Siidi. I may not have known much Arabic, but I knew enough of fathers to realize not everything they said was worthy of such ready agreement. Many nights I went to bed with a sore backside for the insolent manner in which I responded to my father's commands. So for all I knew, Siidi was instructing them to blindfold me and let me loose in the desert. And for what, I hadn't a clue.

True to form, the kids left the room while Abdel and Siidi turned their backs to me to speak in intense Arabic. The kids scurried around their bedrooms, barking orders to each other. Yamma was gathering up food items from the cardboards. No one told me a thing. "I think you're going on a trip," Sue said.

"Where?"

"I don't know."

"Are you goin'?"

"I don't think so."

"Then I ain't goin'."

"I think you have to; I think it's just the guys."

Yamma pushed me gently towards my bedroom. She pulled a Chicago Bears sweatshirt from my drawer and tucked it under my arm. Her smile was reassuring so I knew that wherever I was being sent, it wasn't life threatening. There was a loud greeting at the back door that had Yamma dashing back to the kitchen.

I followed to see a tall, thin man holding Johara in a bear hug. His hair was long and unkempt, curled over his forehead and the back of his neck. He had a sparse beard on a gaunt face, and deeply recessed eyes.

But they were bright and alive, like Yamma's when she was cooking. And like Yamma, I took to him right away, the way he smiled for everyone he greeted.

Samir El Assad was another cousin, but on my uncle's side. I saw no resemblance in looks or demeanor. He lived in Ramallah. Though he seemed much more mature and worldly than the rest of the family, he was just seventeen, in his last year at The Friends School.

"So you are the two distant ones from Chi-car-go?" He said to Sue and me in English, with only a hint of an accent. Sue stepped in front and shook his hand. "Sureia," she said. "This is my brother, Nasser."

I liked Samir, but as with the others, I didn't much care if he liked me. I felt no compunction in letting him know just how American I was. "I'm Joe," I said. "And she's Sue."

He grabbed my hand. "And I'm Sam," with a handshake and tone that let me knew he understood.

I was overjoyed to meet someone here who spoke English and genuinely seemed to enjoy meeting me. Yamma didn't count, being a mother. Sam came down just to meet us, he explained. He was learning English at school but had little opportunity to use it. "I want to," he searched for the word, "converse, with real Americans about real articles. I am bored with 'the book is on the table, the car is on the street, would you like to eat a pizza pie?'"

Sue's heartier than normal laugh was embarrassing as it carried through the tiny kitchen and obviously into the back rooms from where the boys and Abdel came running.

Something was not right. They all stood behind us and peered around at Sam as if they didn't know him. If Sam noticed it as readily as I did, he didn't let on. He waltzed around me and hugged his uncle who left his own arms dangling worthlessly at his side. He approached the three boys who were at the ready and extended their hands, but Sam made a mockery of this by hugging each of them heartily in turn. And there was little any of them could do to resist for Sam was three inches over Faid, and though thin, he had the reach advantage.

The chatting was one-sided, with Sam leading the way. I saw Faid, Gamal, and Adli, follow their father's lead. Distant, detached, disinterested. I couldn't see how Sam missed it. It was uncomfortable for all of us in the room, like watching a comedian bomb onstage. The only one working at complete ease was Sam, and for the five minutes he spoke, I began to enjoy watching him make my uncle and cousins squirm in their own home.

Yamma came to their rescue. She spoke first to Sam, then to her husband, then back to Sam. Sam was in agreement. Abdel was verbally noncommittal, but all his other signals were crying out his rebuff. Finally it was decided. Sam came over to me. "A camp out," he said. "Haven't done so in years, sounds like great fun, yes?"

I turned to Sue who was still quite infatuated. "Is that where they're taking me?" I asked. "I don't want to go away with them to camp out."

She put her hand on my shoulder but Sam interjected. "No problem; we're not going far. I'll be right with you, yes."

The camp out was suggested by Siidi, Sam explained. He then laughed, saying Siidi thought I was becoming like *Tiflah,* a little girl. That was what Abdel was smirking about and the cousins were laughing at. Kitchen work was woman's work, Sam said. "Then what is men's work?" I asked. Sam smiled. "Whatever it is they want to do."

I couldn't read Sam's take on that, whether he believed it or not. Back home I enjoyed helping my mother prepare dinners: turning on the gas stove, slicing vegetables for the salads or tacos, rolling dough, breaking up spaghetti, boiling rice, anything except the clean up. I didn't much enjoy that part in Yamma's kitchen, either, but it beat hanging with the guys.

I was kept out of the preparation for the camp out, as well. I felt it was intentional so Adli and Gamal could pick out the best equipment and best camping spot. Plus, my standing around made me look lazy and removed. I was neither. I was scared at every turn. Nothing was familiar; no one was encouraging. Even Yamma, for all her compassion, was of little use outside her daily routine. There was nothing she could offer to help a young American boy integrate here. As it was, her extra attention made it worse, fueling jealousy and resentment.

Eventually, Gamal tossed me a flattened pillow and tattered blanket. I followed them all out the back gate, the blanket and pillow under my arm. It was nearing sunset. I heard dogs barking wildly in the hills around us. I thought of the pariah dogs still in the hills, perhaps this night plotting a return to the village. About a quarter of a mile away we passed through the family olive orchard and ascended a steep hill. I trailed behind, waiting for Sam, who vowed to be along soon. Siidi was stepping out quickly for such an old man, as if being pulled along by an unseen rope.

They reached the ridgeline well ahead of me and stood in a row along the crest. The sun was setting just behind it, bathing them in a brilliant orange. They stood transfixed as I approached. It had the eerie look of a sci-fi movie. I arrived winded with sore legs. I bent over to catch my breath and noticed no one was making a sound but me. I saw why when I stood.

A lush green valley unfolded just beyond the cliff wall at our feet. Nestled upon the ridges and in the draws were groves of fig and olive trees that rolled into the forever. The sun blasted a river on the floor beneath us, glorifying it into a vibrant blood-red ribbon. Birds of prey, wide and powerful, glided and swooped well below us. Griffon Vultures, Red and Black Kites, sparrow hawks, and harriers picked clean the valley and rock crevices. It was a trip through the looking glass from the desert world behind us.

Siidi moved along the ridge, slowly this time. Abdel and the others followed several paces behind. I saw this as a part of Siidi's journey home. At some point and time, this was his perspective of the world. Perhaps the vista had changed dramatically over the years; perhaps not at all. I watched him measuring his steps with somber precision. He was back there, back then, with his boyhood friends. I felt a sorrow and a happiness for him. The sorrow was that he had this childhood place to reflect upon, for as beautiful as it was, it wasn't South Chicago. The happiness was for his believing that it was.

Siidi stepped off. I made a sudden yowl of panic for fear he had fallen, or worse, jumped to his death. Gamal, Adli, and Faid turned and laughed, then followed Siidi down the mountainside.

CHAPTER 7

It was a narrow path made of worn rock that crisscrossed the steep descent. It was so neatly packed and the rate so steady that it was hard to believe it wasn't laid out by the Corps of Engineers. It had been the way down the mountain for generations of sheepherders, Siidi being one. This was told to me by Sam who made it to us as we were entering the path.

The group halted abruptly. Siidi disappeared around a dome of rock. No one followed. The looks on the boys' faces was the look I'm sure I had when I thought Siidi had gone over the cliff. "The Ghoulies," Sam whispered to me.

"The what?"

"Ghosts of the cave."

So this was it. The cave Siidi spoke of, the one his mother scared him away from with her tales.

Siidi came back around and bid us all to enter the cave with him. Slack-jawed, my three cousins gave the haven a wide berth as they scurried around it. The fact Siidi had entered it didn't seem to make much of an impression. Perhaps they believed an El Hajj had spiritual protection from such evils. I followed my cousins' lead to add to the myth. As Siidi's mother had used the gruesome legends, so would I. The cave, I understood, was the one place I was sure to be alone.

Johara and Sue were suddenly behind us when we stopped on a grassy plateau midway down the mountainside. Sue had a large basket. "What are you two doing here?" I asked.

"Yamma sent Johara to say the prayers; I came to keep her company and carry the snacks."

Johara stood solemnly over us. All the man and boys moved to the center of the makeshift camp, around the fire Abdel had made, and went to their knees, heads bowed to the ground, arms outstretched. I had seen the posture from my father. It didn't look too awfully comfortable or sensible.

Sam nudged me to follow along. "It would be more harmful for you not to do it," he whispered. He translated quietly to me as Johara recited: "So Glory be to Allah when you enter the evening and when you enter the morning, and for Him alone is all the praise in the heavens and the earth, at the sun's decline and when you enter the noon."

She recited it three times, which made it a long prayer. My left knee was on a tree root and my forehead banged another. If the others had picked the same type of terrain they didn't let on. No one so much as twitched, except Sam as he interpreted to me.

"Great, we will be covered for the night," Sam said to me as he stood. He assisted Siidi up, brushing off the front of his Thobe.

"Covered for what?" I asked.

Sam shrugged. "Anything." He cleared the ground of several stones before spreading his blanket.

"Is there something out here?"

"Oh, snakes and lizards and spiders. Then there are the evil ones."

"No, Adli and Jamal tried to scare me with all that but I know it's not true."

"Good for you, then. Yet there are those who believe. Better check the ground for snake holes."

Sue and Johara were sitting on the ground behind us. Sue jumped to her feet upon hearing Sam's warning. "What kinds of snakes?" she said. "Like, little harmless garden ones?"

"No, mostly deadly ones. Vipers."

"Then what are we doing out here?" I demanded.

"It's good. Men have been doing it here for a long time. And we have the dua to protect us. But you girls must be heading back up."

"Tomorrow we can talk about Chicago," Sue offered eagerly.

"Yes, tomorrow will be good. And you will visit me at school, when you come to Ramallah."

Sam helped me search my area and set up. The sun had nearly set. Shadows made it impossible to see holes, especially ones small enough to house a snake. I watched the others who had chosen their spots before me. They knew the area. I was sure they left me and Sam the dangerous plots of ground. "Not too close to a tree," he said. "Rats and spiders."

"It's too dark to see," I said, close to tears but working feverishly to hold back.

"Saying the dua three times before nightfall will protect us from all things."

"For real?"

He shrugged again. "If you believe."

Abdel and the boys were gathered around Siidi, my Siidi, talking and laughing loudly for my benefit. Sam lighted a cigarette from the camp fire as I made a show of swishing away the smoke from my face. "Sorry, the smoke is bothering you."

"A little."

He laughed. "A lot I can see. Bothers you, too, in the house with Khaal Abu Faid and Faid, yes?"

"I'm not use to it. They don't smoke back home."

He took a long draw on the cigarette and held it as he lay back. I thought he swallowed the smoke to save me the discomfort. But then he let it out in a long, slow stream that he seemed to truly enjoy. "Smoking only works when you do it to relax. Like this," he said. "Problem is men like Khaal Abu Faid, they do it when they are ... confused. No, that's not the word. Stressed, that's it." He turned to look at the group. "And Faid, who smokes to be like his father, something important."

"I don't like him," I said, instantly regretting it for fear I had misread Sam's relationship with him.

"There is much not to like with that boy," Sam said. "But he comes by it honestly. See what his father is wearing?"

It was the white thobe, the same type Siidi was wearing. "Yeah?"

"Abdel Karim works with the Relief and Works Agency as a manager in a food aid station. You know nothing about the agency, but many Palestinians work for it. Some good, some bad. Abdel has the insufferable job of counting and inventorying food sent to us from the United Nations. For that he gets to wear a suit and drive a state car. It is important work but ... what is it? Bourgeoisie, yes?"

"I don't know that word."

"Okay. Ahhh, rich, okay?"

"Okay."

"The thobe is worn with a belt around the middle, and maybe on the arms, for men who work in business all day. It keeps it from running loose." He made a flowing motion with his arms. "But Abdel Karim wears his without such belts, like El-Hajj who is old and with leisure time. Abdel thinks himself such a man of importance and status. But he is not, nor will he ever be. Nor will his sons be."

"Why not?"

"They were not born to it. And it is not possible here to work to it."

Abdel turned to look at us.

"I think he heard you," I said.

"He's knows very little English. But you are right, he was listening. He knows how I think about him."

He sat up. "You know, Joe, you don't need to be hearing these things about Khaal Abu Faid. He is your uncle and respect him for that. He is important in your life for right now."

"But why did you say those things?"

"Because I do not need for him to care for me. Come, your grandfather must tell us a story."

"Why?"

"You are full of questions for a young one."

"I've been yelled at for that before."

"What's 'yelled at?'"

"Made my parents angry, I guess."

"Oh. That's not a problem, making people angry. Not if it is for good reason. So, your grandfather must tell us stories because he has many. Isn't that what you do on your camp outs, yes?"

I never had a camp out before, but I knew Siidi had many good stories. We approached the circle where Sam made a space for the two of us. He reached into the basket and broke off a long piece of bread, a block of goat cheese, and a handful of dates. I was hungry enough for the goat cheese but not the dates.

"Why are we here so late?" I said to Sam, more as an unfiltered thought. "We can't see anything."

In Arabic, he translated my question to the group. Siidi answered. "He says it is more the feel than the view," Sam said. "If he were blind he would know this place."

I was upset at Sam announcing my comment to the group, and I was about to protest his violation of what I saw as a private trust between us when he called across to Siidi. "I asked for him to tell us a tale," he explained to me. "I told him to say it slowly so I could translate for you."

Adli and Jamal chimed in, tugging at the bottom of Siidi's thobe while Abdel slapped at them to mind themselves.

"A childless woman prayed to Allah for a child," Siidi began in his low, hoarse whisper. "Not just any child, a daughter. Not just any daughter, but a beautiful daughter, and sturdy and bright. 'But,' the woman pleaded, 'if I cannot have a daughter, at least give me something. I would take a cooking pot if it pleases Allah.'"

The two boys sprang to their feet. "La, la, la," they were yelling. They knew the story. It was a baby's tale. They wanted a different story, one fitting for the night.

"Tell it to us, then," Siidi instructed.

"The pot is put onto the shelf by her mother to sit until she is of age to be outside," Gamal said.

Adli continued, "She gets tired of being on the shelf and begs her mother to be let down. When she gets down she runs away."

"She doesn't run away," Gamal said.

"Yes, she does."

"No, her mother lets her go to the town where she tricks a rich man into thinking she is a magic pot."

"Quiet now, you two," their father scowled. "This is El Hajj's story."

"No," Siidi said. "Let them tell it now."

So Gamal continued. "The rich man throws money into the pot and the pot takes it home to show off to her mother. The next day, the pot begs to be taken down off the shelf and let out again. Again she goes into the town where a king believes she is magic and throws gold to her. She takes the gold home hoping to impress her mother. On the next day—"

"Let me tell it," Adli pleaded.

"No," Gamal said.

"If Adli knows the story let him tell it," Siidi commanded.

Adli was glowing as he recited. "The third day the magic pot sits in the road. A Bedouin who had seen the pot the other two days believes the pot is not magic but is a fraud, being set out by tricksters to get money. So the Bedouin takes the pot behind a shed and shits in it." Adli covered his mouth and giggled while the others laughed hard to hear young Adli tell the tale so brazenly. I did so myself when Sam translated.

When the mood settled, Siidi asked for the moral of the story. "Ahhh, now comes the moral," Sam whispered to me. "All Arab folktales must have morals."

"For little children to wait until they are ready to venture outside," Adli said.

"And?" asked Siidi.

"Keep your lid on until the stranger presents the gold," Faid said.

Abdel nudged him in the ribs.

"Learn what's right and what's wrong from your elders first," Gamal added.

Siidi nodded in approval. "And do not forget that the magic pot was made to return all the money and gold she had taken. You all tell that story much better than I."

Sam piped up. "I think Faid had the best interpretation of all; and the pot has the right idea about life."

"It is the right thing to steal?" Abdel said.

"No, it's not right to steal, though it is done all the time by men with better sense than a cooking pot. But tunjur, tunjur, tunjur all day inside a house is no way to live a life."

"Oh that is just you talking," Abdel said.

"And the cooking pot is a girl, is it not? Perhaps if it was boy his behavior would not be so criticized. He would be seen as bold and would need some readjusting, but there would be some champion in him. When he comes of age, he will turn out in the world where his only crime will be in getting himself caught. But our little cooking pot, she must be put back upon the shelf to sit until she can come down and tunjur, tunjur, tunjur the rest of her days in her family home."

"It is a story about right and wrong," Abdel said angrily. "That is all."

"It is a story about how bad little girls must be grown into good little mothers," Sam said, smiling, enjoying putting Abdel in such a fit.

I felt the tension between the two. But Siidi was staring down into the valley at this point, and Adli and Gamal were at him to tell a real story. "What's tunjur?" I asked Sam

"It's, how you'd say … rattle, the sound of a pot rolling in a house."

"I think you made uncle angry."

He lowered his head to whisper, though with Abdel's limited English, there was no need. "I can only try." He then looked over at Abdel who lighted a cigarette from the fire. It was his first of the night and I thought on Sam's suggestion that Abdel smoked only while under stress. I'm sure it was Sam's purpose that night, to make Abdel light up many more.

Siidi began to speak. I take it he was telling another tale. Sam reminded him to be slow so he could translate for me. "What difference would it make, "I heard Abdel say to Sam through translation. "You'll just make up your own story as it goes along."

"I will tell the story word-for-word," Sam said. "I only make opinions on the moral."

Abdel flicked his half-devoured cigarette into the fire only to light another.

"A King lived upon a hill in a walled castle," the story began. "So proud was the King of his property that he wished for all his people to see how grand it was. But his most trusted adviser told him not to allow subjects in. 'If your desire is to share all you have, then by all means, let them come in to see. But if you do not wish to share, then keep them out for they will only want more.'

"Of course the King did not wish to share, only to show how great a King he was, for if he were not a great King, would he have been so blessed? The question then was how to show his subjects his greatness?

"Build grand gardens on the hillsides outside the castle walls so that my subjects, and all people, can look up from the valleys, and across all the mountainsides, and from all the pastures, to see how truly great their King is.

"The wise adviser knew this to be an equally bad idea. He also knew that to tell the King so would mean the end of his employment at the palace, as the King was so intent on demonstrating his greatness.

"'Let me handle that, my lord,' the adviser said, 'as I know the best gardener in the kingdom.' And so the adviser was sent out to bring the gardener to the castle for a consult. Only the gardener was no gardener at all, but a sorcerer. 'I see large hedges cut into the shapes of all the animals in your kingdom, your highness,' said the sorcerer, 'to display not only your earthly treasures, but your dominion over all living things.'

"And so it was that the hillside was planted with a great menagerie of giant horses, camels, goats, and donkeys. Then there were the great snakes, moles, rats, shrews, tree frogs, wolves, and reptiles, all laid out among the most gorgeous and bountiful flower gardens the land had ever seen. People from all over stood below in amazement at the size, colors, and scope of the King's magnificence.

"And the King thought, this is good, for he long believed his subjects to be loyal and loving, for high above in his castle, his advisers told him so. 'I wish to go speak with them all,' the King said.

"'There is no need to travel down to see them,' his adviser said, 'it will only lessen you in their eyes for they will see you as one of them, and your highness, it is well known that no one wants to be one of them.'

"Blind to the obvious flaw in this argument—most Kings are blind to the obvious—he chose to believe for it suited his purposes nicely. But the adviser knew the truth, that his subjects deplored their King. He knew this because, unlike the King, he went to the towns and villages in disguise to sit amongst them. You see, the adviser was not in league with the King so much as he was in league against anything and anyone who would threaten his own position of power. And most certainly an uprising from down below would do such a thing."

I looked around at my cousins who were growing restless as Siidi spoke slow for the benefit of me and the story. I, having grown up with such dreary titles as alderman and wards, had much fascination with kings and kingdoms and hung on every turn. Sam translated while on his back, smoking, his eyes closed.

"The adviser settled into a chair at the bazaar. There was talk between several men about destroying the gardens but the adviser interceded. 'I am a close confidante to the King," he told them. 'I have a better plan.'

"The men were quite obviously taken aback by being overheard by a confidante to the King, but one spoke up most belligerently. "Says you. You are a confidante to the King, but how are we to know?'

"Just then, an old man from within the group came around to inspect the adviser. 'I do know this man, and he is indeed a valued adviser to the King,' for the old man had been a cobbler for a time at the castle. The adviser nodded in feigned recognition for there was truly no way he would know a man who worked so far below eye level.

"'Then why is it you come to us?'

"'Because what you see from below I see from within, and I suffer with you for what I must witness.'

"'So what is your plan?' one asked.

"'I can control the guard watch,' which, of course, he couldn't since the foolhardy King employed no guards at the gardens, knowing full well how much he was loved. 'You can come in at night and whisk away the flowers to have them replanted below so the arrogant King must look down to see your grandeur and greatness. Such a sight will drive him mad. But,' he added absolutely, 'you must not disturb any of the animals of the menagerie.' The deal was struck with both parties knowing one thing for sure: the townsfolk would steal the menagerie.

"So on the prescribed night, the townsfolk crept up the hillside with oxen and carts to make quick work of uprooting the great animals. They worked as they never had before to replant the menagerie around the town, in plain view of the castle so on the next morning the King could see.

"The King was both enraged and confused, to which his adviser reminded of his warning, *if you do not wish to share, then keep them out for they will only want more.* 'But I have prepared for this moment,' the adviser continued, 'so be with me on your terrace tonight at midnight, but be forewarned, it will not be pleasant.'

"At the given hour, there were great shrills and screams from below, mingled with horrific growls, and terrifying, terrifying roars not heard since the last great battles."

Now the cousins came awake, leaning across the fire into Siidi's shadow.

"The King and the adviser saw men and women racing through the streets, many climbing the hill to reach the safety of the castle walls.

"What about the children?" Gamal asked.

"Yes, them?" Adli demanded to know.

Siidi took the opportunity to draw them in. He stared at the fire, closed his eyes, and nodded slowly. "Yes, children, even younger than you."

"And what?" Adli begged.

Abdel slapped the ground. "Hush, now."

"It was hard to tell in the low moonlight," Siidi said. "But by the light of the torches being carried and thrown, the king saw the great animals had come to life."

"Jinns," Gamal said, "I knew it."

"Perhaps," Siidi said.

"Jinns?" I whispered at Sam.

Without stirring he said, "Spirits created by Allah. Genies you call them. But these are not jinn."

"What then?"

He raised his head and squinted in the smoke. "It's a make believe story; they are nothing."

I missed the next few lines of the story, entering back into it as morning had broken over the kingdom. "'Now will be a good time for you to leave the castle to visit your subjects,' the adviser told the king. They rode down the hill with a great cavalcade of soldiers. The sight was too gruesome to be described by an old man such as me to ones as young as you, but let it be known that not one man, woman, or child survived. Nor were any found to be dead in a single piece. So complete was the destruction that there were no pools of blood for it had served as wine for the spirits created by the sorcerer. And the great animals of that fine menagerie were nowhere to be seen. Some believe they wander still since the sorcerer was not made present to reverse the spell."

Siidi sat back. I heard the labored breathing of my three cousins, Abdel, too. "Learned here," Siidi said, "be wary of joining forces with those in power for when power is the reward, it will rarely be shared and never given up."

"Oh, and I have one, El Hajj," Sam announced from his prone posture.

"There is only one moral to this," Abdel said, harshly, "and El hajj has spoken it."

"Not so. A man of El Hajj's experiences knows there are many ways in which to see the world."

Siidi nodded.

"Rather than look to those on the mountain top for the things you desire, look to yourself. That way, you are beholding to no one, for you control what you have as rightly as you control what you don't have."

At that, he tossed the last of his cigarette into the fire and rolled onto his side, a most contented and somewhat beguiling grin on his face, while Abdel and Faid both lit another and grimaced into the dark.

CHAPTER 8

I thought I was the first to wake up that next morning on the hillside. I crawled on all fours to the edge. It wasn't far, barely five feet, and I realized I was just that far from rolling to my death during the night. And with the nightmares I had been suffering of late, it was a miracle I hadn't.

It was a cool morning that would soon burn off with the sun. I stayed hunkered down on my belly, my bare arms buried beneath me. Sam walked up the path from the valley. He waved while I stuck my hand out in lazy response. "Sleep well, Joe, my friend?"

"Cold," I mumbled, my chin in the red dirt as I stared down at the valley.

He sat cross-legged beside me. It was a steep climb, but already he had caught his breath. "We should walk down there later," he said, "when the others go back home."

"They won't go down?"

"Nooo. Too old and too lazy."

The sun was above the horizon now so I no longer had to squint to see the valley floor. The rays hit the river below, painting it orange. The dew was burning off the blade of grass grazing the side of my nose. It would be hot, and I chose to be one of the lazy ones not wanting to go down the rest of the mountain. "No, now it's too hot," I said.

"Joe, you cannot use weather as your guide here, if you do, you'll never do a thing."

I sat up and pushed away from the edge. The others were still asleep. "Sam, why do you hate Abdel?"

"Don't you?"

"Yes, I mean, I don't know. They don't treat me very nice, but maybe they will."

"First, it is not hate. And it is not him."

Sam went on to tell me how Palestine came to be. I understood very little of it. The upshot was that while the world spoke of the Palestinian-Israeli relationship; he saw the Palestinian-Jordanian union as more detrimental. Palestine was a socialist state where Palestinians were made wards of Jordan. Jordan did everything for the people of Palestine except give them the opportunity to advance and better themselves. And while there were many men willing to talk of war with Israel; they were careless in their vision that accepted their fate as Jordanians.

Jordan, Sam explained, had become a highly addictive drug. "That will change," he said, "and men like Abdel will need to live like a man, not hide behind a King and fables."

"Is Siidi also like that?" I said, reminding Sam it was Siidi's stories he had attacked.

"Yes. But he cannot change the nation's past or his past. He grew up here when it was all new and no one could know what would become of things. Then he left. I do not know if he ran away because he saw the problems arising or because he was afraid to face them. Now he comes back to do old man things like tell stories he learned as a boy. And give them the same morals he learned back then. And he walks the land he knew so well, like this valley where he pastured sheep as a young man. He sleeps here, on this spot, where he slept then, and tries to pretend it has not changed. So I give him new morals to his stories to let him understand that it has changed, it has all changed. But he doesn't care because he has come home to die."

Siidi? Home to die? I looked over at him to be sure. Under his blanket I couldn't see him breathing and in a matter of moments I saw him as dead. The anger that had subsided overnight came back to me. I was sent here to learn to live a new life with a man who came back to die. If Sam knew such things, certainly my parents did. Sam saw the notion flush my face. "Do not worry. El Hajj will be fine here with you."

"Then why do you say those things? Do you hate Siidi, too?"

It was a question I thought he would deny without hesitation, if only to alleviate the fears of a young boy, but hesitate he did. He was a thoughtful man who valued his truth regardless of his audience. He would sooner chastise a child for letting his dog run loose than console him when it was killed by a car. It was a quality I came to love and hate, and to fear.

"I told you it is not hate; I cannot hate a man for his ignorance. El Hajj, if he saw problems as a young man and ran away from them, then he is not a man of honor in spite of his age. To come home only to live out memories is to give up.

"In his story of the vain king, neither he nor Abdel would have played a part. They would have been one of the many who were satisfied to stare up to the palace in wonderment. They would never have thought to own it or steal a piece of it."

"I don't want Siidi to think of stealing anything," I said.

Sam laughed and rubbed my head. "Of course. In your world you do not need to do such things. And I am sorry for making a boy your age think so much. But you have to know, you must be careful of those here."

"Who?"

"You were attacked by a dog."

"Amir."

"Yes, Amir. It was not an accident."

"I was leaning out the window. He was out there and grabbed me."

"He was out there because Gamal and Adli caught a rabbit and tied it up outside your window."

"No, they pulled me back inside."

"They didn't mean for you to be hurt, only scared."

"Who told you this?"

He shook his head. "You do understand that Amineh is very happy you are here."

"That Yamma?" I said, not recognizing her real name.

"Yes. You and Sue were all she would talk about. So when you arrived you were like a new child here, and you know what a new child does?"

That I did, and I loved it. Being the youngest at home I got the most attention, the bigger birthday gifts, more Christmas presents. Being punished was more often followed by a guilty hug, even from Sue and my brother, David. It was the way I extended my belly, dropped my chin, and pouted. I was irresistible, a male Shirley Temple. Didn't work here.

"That's because Gamal was the youngest. You took that away from him."

"I didn't mean to."

"No need to talk about that further," Sam said. "Young boy games are sometimes more dangerous than young man games when they do not know control. Here is what a boy your age needs to know; see that red river in the valley?"

I looked down and it was indeed dark red. "The sun's reflection," I said.

He shook his head. "Witches."

"There are no witches."

"They kidnap young boys and cook them up here. It is their blood that runs down the mountain, sometimes like a waterfall, that makes the river run red."

"Not for real?"

"Right now, it is as real as it needs to be for you. And like all good Arab tales there is a moral."

"What is it?"

"That, young Joe, I will leave for you to find." He leaned in to at me. "Guess the dua does help."

"I know. I didn't roll off the cliff." I said.

"And your scorpion friend has not stung you."

I looked to where he was nodding, on the back of my right shoulder. There sat a scorpion a half a foot long. I screamed to Sam to push it off. "Now don't go crazy and scare it into stinging you," he said. "You have been lucky or blessed so far, best not to mess up either one."

***

The Friends School of Ramallah was a source of great hope to the Christians in modern Palestine. It should have been as much for me. Its name seemed like a promise. Friends. It was a word I knew. All of us pronounced it the same. Surely it had the same meaning. I was willing to accept what adults said as the truth. Writing it in stone on a building assured it. But my attitude kept me on guard.

The school was started by New England Quakers in the mid-eighteen hundreds. Girls first, boys by the turn of the century. While the girl's school was in Ramallah, I went to the boy's school in El-Bireh, about a mile and a half away. I started in the first grade and for once, felt more at home than my new classmates.

I had already noticed the way girls and women were treated in this world. They ate separately from the men. They ate after them. Yamma, Johara, and Sue sat in separate quarters to talk. If in the same room with the men, they never spoke unless it was an answer to a question from Abdel or Siidi. In the markets Yamma kept veiled under her hajib and to herself. It was creepy to watch, like watching a ghost.

But in first and second grades, boys and girls were put together. While it made them all uncomfortable, it was no big deal for me. While they all sat fidgeting at their desks that first day, it was as comfortable for me as being in Yamma's kitchen.

We traveled an hour by bus from Dayr Ghasana; Sue, Faid, Johara, Gamal, Adli, and me. They all had friends on the bus who sat in the back where the ride was bumpiest. I sat alone in the front. It was hot and dusty. I didn't need to know Arabic to know I was being made the fool; spit balls shot through straws seemed to be a universal weapon.

A month before I left home, my father made a delivery trip to Northwestern University in Evanston. The lush lawns, the treed pathways, the stately buildings that looked more like church cathedrals had me gaping. I ran crazy behind my father who was oblivious to the grandeur, or more probably the novelty was gone for him. He called over his shoulder for me to keep up while I rubber-necked at every step. That such a place was built to teach kids was both breathtaking and shocking in light of the schools I had seen in my neighborhood.

My father explained that students paid a lot of money to attend school at Northwestern, whereas ours were paid for by the taxes. Having no idea what taxes were, I concluded the Taxes had to be a very nice family who used whatever money they had to help poor families.

That visual of the university was my impression of the Friends School upon my arrival, and I knew it was not paid for by a family like the Taxes. Sue and I stared out the window with the same open-mouthed expression I had back at Northwestern. When the bus stopped, Johara grabbed Sue by the hand but pushed me back when I attempted to follow. She shook her head and pointed up the road. I looked back at my cousins and their friends. I understood. This was not to be my school. Mine would be a cinderblock hut with mud floors. It would be surrounded by desert for miles in all directions. I would be ridiculed by my cousins, their friends, and bent old teachers who would poke at my stomach and fat cheeks, speak that crazy Arabic, then laugh at my ignorance. School would be the hell I dreamed it would be.

It was "poor me" once again, but as self-centered as I was becoming, I was happy for Sue. She was in a good place, a nice school, and Johara had taken to her right off. I realized I couldn't stand behind Yamma the whole time. That wasn't cool for a boy in any country. As long as Sue stayed grounded in this place, I'd have her to lean on.

I sat as the bus lunged onward. We were in a city, old but with gracious buildings and thick groves of trees. The road was lined with them, and it was as busy as any in Chicago. I waited for the desert, for a village like Dayr Ghasana where I would go to school. But as far forward as I could see there was no sign of a desert or dust-covered men herding sheep and goats.

We pulled up in front of a stone building wrapped in ivy. My cousins and their friends sprinted past me before the bus came to a stop. This was the campus in El-Bireh and it was more spectacular than that in Ramallah. Brick pathways disappeared into abundant gardens and evergreen bushes. The campus was full of almond, orange, apricot, and of course, olive trees.

I knew from my first day of Kindergarten I wasn't going to be a good student. I had the patience of a housefly at a barbecue and was not fond of being cooped up indoors, even in the worst weather. To this day, sitting in one spot, even to watch the Sox, is wearisome. But this place looked more like a park than a school; more inviting, more like its namesake, friendly. For the short time I was there, it became my emotional oasis. At this place there were adults who cared about me, and more importantly, kids who didn't care one way or the other. Years later, back home in Chicago where my scholastic aptitude was always lacking, I respected what good teachers could do with a stubborn mind.

"Ma'assalama" the bus driver said to me, motioning outside with his head.

I took my backpack and slowly made my way towards the door. Below the steps, Miss Chloe Stewart waited for me. I walked a few steps past her before she called out my name. I stopped but didn't turn. "Nasser Khudayer?" She called again. "From Chicago?"

Miss Stewart was a tall, wide woman with a stern gaze but warm smile. Both got your attention immediately. She was from Australia and had been at the school for ten years by that time. "I go by Joe," I told her.

"Very well then. Come with me."

She moved out quickly for a big woman. I walked slowly a few feet behind her. I had an instinct to run, but there was nowhere to go. I'm sure they weren't, but I had this scratchy feeling that all eyes were on me, the fat new kid, as we walked though the brick walkways of the campus. She brought me into my classroom where all the other children were sitting quietly, feet firmly on the ground, hands folded on the desk. It was a disturbing moment that seemed to go on forever until Miss Stewart turned me towards the class and announced me as "Joe Khudayer from the United States. Say hi to Joe."

The chorus went up. "Hi Joe." Then there were high-pitched giggles. I was made to sit in the second row. I can remember that desk today, brown laminate top and orange chair attached to shiny steel legs. It was brand new and smack between Lambertina and Raha.

Lambertina sat in front of me. She was from the Netherlands. She was shy, smart, and smelled like cherries. She stayed for only six weeks until her father, who worked at the embassy, was recalled back home.

Raha sat behind me. She was from Iran, or Persia as she vehemently proclaimed whenever the subject of nationality came up. She was a tom-boy who hit whenever her sharp tongue failed to persuade. The only English phrase she seemed to have mastered was, "What are you looking at?" She didn't smell half as nice as Lambertina, nor did she smile half as much, but we got along great. The other boys didn't know what to make of her, but she was more like the girls I knew back in South Chicago and that made me feel at home while Lambertina made me feel all sorts of wonderful. For reasons I can't describe to this day, Raha was just about the coolest person I've known besides Sam.

I began to pick up Arabic quickly in spite of my dedication not to. My syntax was weak, but I was good with pronunciation. And, I could string together enough words to get a point across. But I was having difficulty grasping the complexities of religion. It seemed there were many kinds at the Friends School, all practiced openly and without scorn. While I saw some of the older kids going off to perform salaat at noon, I saw others blessing themselves with the sign of the cross before lunch. There were Qurans, there were Christian Bibles, there were Torahs. I even saw a Book of Morman.

Of course I didn't know the Book of Genesis from the Book of Ether, and though I didn't understand the differences amongst the creeds, I did see them. As I continued to grasp the language, I felt something vital was missing. It was a vague notion, like the feeling you forgot to pack something for a trip. It just hung in the air and swirled around me. While others were going through rituals taught them by their parents and churches, rituals I once saw as silly and sometimes bizarre, I wondered about some connection outside myself. It surely wasn't encompassing my every thought; there were far greater fears and frets for a young boy. Yet while they were merely nudging me, they took Sue in a bear hug and had her leaving Dayr Ghasana and Uncle Abdel far behind.

CHAPTER 9

The deepest, darkest secrets of a six year-old boy are the same the world over. The same fears, the same growing pains, the same complexes. Had I understood that, perhaps Adli, Gamal, and myself would have become immediate friends. But as it goes, sharing those secrets is one of the many fears.

Same for young girls who were too old for dolls and too young for love. Because I had no relation with my male cousins, I took an interest, and a pleasure, in watching Sue and Johara's. They were the same age, with some of the same likes and dislikes, and I was amazed that even this far around the world, in a culture so different, Johara was just as goofy as the girls back home. "What is goofy?" she asked when I told her this.

Hard to explain, so I went to her drawer and pulled out the Elvis Presley "Kissin Cousins" poster Sue had smuggled to her from Chicago. I unrolled it and began wailing the high-pitched hysterics I had heard on television. I watched as Johara's face imploded. Her eyes, cheeks, neck, and I swear her temples, were sucked into her skull as if an internal vacuum had been switched on. Madly, she raced at me and grabbed the poster, tearing the top left corner which I was left holding. She shoved the badly mauled poster under her mattress. I had already ceased my sarcastic bellowing but she covered my mouth with her palm as her eyes pleaded with me. I waited for her hand to drop as she waited for someone to barge in. No one did and she relaxed her body, face, and hand.

Johara and Sue made an immediate connection owing to their ages and both being girls. Looking back, though, it could have gone the other way. Both were outgoing; both were intelligent. They were, long before I knew the word, rebels. Not many Arabic girls were sewn from that thread. Sam told me of a girl he met two years earlier in a village not far from Dayr Ghasana. He used the word *met*, but explained he never spoke with her, only made eye contact when they passed each other in the morning. He was working as a printer's apprentice; he figured she was walking to school. The looks were casual but belied something more affecting.

One day, she hurried her pace as they approached and didn't look up at him. The next day, she veered off her path altogether to avoid him. The next day Sam stopped her and gave her his name. The next day, she didn't return. Nor the next. The printer broke it to Sam that the girl's father was an Imam in the village and had his daughter, his only daughter, turned out of the house after hearing of her violations with him. He beat her severely, then left her on the side of the road near the bus stop so she could at least get a ride out of the village. That, he told villagers, was the dignity he left her with. I know this story to be true as I was to witness such cruelty myself.

Johara was forever talking all things western and not always out of earshot of others. Heck, I heard her constantly talking about the Monkees, Clairol hair spray, *Tiger Beat* magazine, and *Beach Blanket Bingo* poster things. No doubt Yamma knew, though she would never snitch, least I didn't want to believe she would. But the boys, they certainly would.

Johara convinced Sue to have things sent from Chicago. Posters and magazines, mostly, some clothes. Of course they weren't mailed to the house, and they weren't sent from our house. Mom was an outsider, religiously and tribally, but never would she consent to letting her daughter be a bad houseguest by unduly influencing a cousin. Sue had her friends send them to her at the The Friends School where it wasn't a cause for suspicion to receive care packages. From there it was rather easy to secret them into the house.

All this until Sue and Sam became an item, or so it seemed to me and from what I could tell, to Johara. I was years away from understanding and enjoying Arab television so this drama suited my needs. Knowing all the actors made it more intriguing.

Being in the same school made it easier for them to see each other even though Sam was three grades ahead. In light of the story Sam told of the village girl, he was as circumspect as he could be, though I saw the little things. He met her on occasion when the bus arrived. He would wait behind an avocado tree down the front walkway. I would see him come forward to meet her as the bus pulled away. He would never touch her, not there. And he made it a point to greet Johara and Faid as graciously as he did Sue. More often, they all walked back to the bus together at the end of the day, but he was always beside Sue while Faid and Johara led. He would incidentally bump her, then take her arm to steady her, or touch her shoulder to emphasize some comment he made. But it was back in Dayr Ghasana where it became most noticeable.

As Johara told it, he rarely came around before Sue and I arrived. Now he was there once a week, at times overnight. It would have been nice having a man around who spoke English and spoke to us, except for the fact Johara also had her eyes on him.

"But he's your cousin," Sue told Johara when the fateful confrontation occurred.

"So?"

"You can't date your cousin."

As it was, she could, cousins with cousins being not so bizarre as in the States. It went back to their tribal living where extended families lived in close proximity. There was even talk about an arranged marriage between Sam and Johara. "They still do that?" Sue asked incredulously. "Make you get married?"

"They don't make us; we get married because we want to."

"The universal we, right?" Sue challenged.

"I don't know what that means," Johara said.

"It means it sounds like there are too many people involved in something only two should be involved in."

"What do you know," Johara said. "You're an American."

Sue and I had this typical brother-sister thing going. I admired her immensely, though never would I confess it to her. We both sensed each other's isolation those first few months. Even with Johara at her side constantly, I saw that she was feeling as alone and abandoned as I was. I guess she saw mine, too, as she took every opportunity to comfort me in ways I used to find overbearing and creepy. She'd sing to me, and recite poems. She brought photo albums with her to show to our cousins, but I never saw her pull them out except to look at with me when we were alone. I'd wake at night sometimes to her touch as she stroked my hair and back. So when the bus pulled up to the school in Ramallah one afternoon for the return to Dayr Ghasana, and Sue did not show up, I was concerned.

I was up front as usual. Johara passed by me coldly and said Sue was being kept after school. Sue would never have been *kept* after school, and if she decided to stay on her own accord, she certainly would have told me herself. I thought it was just Johara's nasty conflict with Sue. When the bus door closed, I went to the back and demanded more information from Johara who only looked at me dumbly and said she didn't know anything.

"How is she getting home?"

Faid came over and pushed me away. I fell into the aisle, smashing my knee against a metal post. He stood over me as I defiantly made it to my feet. "I want to know where my sister is," I screamed.

"I don't know," Johara said.

"You know something or you wouldn't know she was staying after."

Her English was progressing better than my Arabic so I had no way of expressing my anxiety other than with my panicked expression. Faid must have seen it as challenge for he took me by the shoulders and tried to force me to the front. I fought my way back to Johara, all the while screaming, "What do you know, what do you know?"

Ordinarily, Sue's absence would not have caused me such distress. She was far more capable of handling our new lives than I would ever be. She was intellectually wired that way, to accept new situations and find ways to control them. But this place had such strange ways. Sam's story of the village girl beaten and turned out consumed me of late, and I wouldn't put it past Johara and the others to alert the adults that they had a budding romance in their midst.

"Where is Sam then?" I screamed. "Why wasn't Sam with you?"

At the mention of his name Faid stopped pushing and Johara shook her head. "All I know is she was crying and talking to a teacher," Johara said softly.

I wanted to know which teacher. Johara didn't know. Although Faid was not following our conversation, he saw Johara's uneasiness. Rather than seek a translation, he threw me into a seat occupied by other boys who threw me back out. At that ruckus the bus stopped and the driver rose from his seat. I took the opportunity to run from the bus and back to the school.

Sue's last class of the day was theology. I knew this because the week before Sue wrote a note requesting that I be allowed to sit in on it. The Friends School was all about understanding differences. Though it was a concept wasted on a child my age who saw all differences in the light of how strange they made me feel, Sue was taking it all in.

This class had taken two trips down to Jerusalem. She didn't talk to me about them, but I noticed a certain calm about her after the visits. What I knew of the Holy Land could fit into my shoe. The incredible oldness of everything gave me a melancholy I never got over, even as I learned the language and culture. Had I not tuned out the world so readily, I could have seen what was happening. I could have been of some help to my sister. But I suspected nothing of Sue's distress until I found her that day.

In the classroom she was wrapped in the arms of a teacher, her head buried into her chest. The teacher rocked with Sue sobbing rhythmically. I stood at the door, afraid to disturb a moment I knew nothing about. I'd never seen her cry. I had seen her make others cry with her caustic, sharp tongue that pierced some thick hides, my brother's included. Here, not having the words, her intellect was useless. She was defenseless and so now she was crying.

My only thought was that she had fallen and hurt herself. I saw no blood or bandage. I gave the rest of her the once-over, but saw no injury. I was confused and standing in the doorway. The teacher caught sight of me and nodded. I approached cautiously, but kept my distance while she whispered to Sue who slipped from her grasp.

I walked silently behind her back to the school plaza. It was eerie. She was sobbing and shuffling. She never shuffled. It was like watching Siidi stroll the olive groves. I didn't dare ask her why. I was afraid of the answer.

Abdel was waiting for us. I assumed he was there because he received word we needed a ride. I looked from Sue to the car to Abdel. He was not happy. The tension was as thick as the sandstorms I had watched sweep through the desert. Abdel was not a nice man in many ways. He was not a good father or a good husband, and I was to see many examples of this in the years to come, even after I left Palestine. Yet as I look back, I know he was no different than my own father, or myself, when I became a man. I guess it's like Yamma would say when making her pies, "Only so much you can do with an over ripened fruit."

I had learned from Faid that my parents were sending money to Abdel, in addition to the fifty dollars a month stipend they sent to us. The money to Abdel was paying our room, board, and school tuition at The Friend's School. It was as good a motive as any for him insure our safe transport back and forth.

But then our monthly payments ceased. Abdel convinced our father we were spending the money foolishly. Contradicting Abdel's claims wasn't an option for us. We never got to talk to our parents on the phone. Abdel would do that for us, always laughing and joking as if our life with him was a carnival ride. Even Siidi was on his side. We could only communicate back home through letters; letters he would review prior to letting us mail them. He didn't speak a lot of English and probably read less, but he knew the word "money." I once tried to slip it in but he caught it made me rewrite the entire letter. I supposed I could have mailed a letter secretively, but I had become an abnormally paranoid child. Abdel seemed to know all that was going on with us. I was sure he had spies about. Perhaps even that wicked King Hussein. I have no doubt the money began flowing directly to him.

We saw very little of the money from then on, a dollar here and there to keep us from getting too mutinous. Though I loved working in the garden and kitchen with Yamma, there wasn't much I was fond of eating yet, so my money was spent on Chef Boyadee beef ravioli and Nehi grape soda. A small store in Ramallah stocked American food for the tourists and workers who came through. It was no Dominick's, but their inventory suited my needs. Sue saved her money for school trips to Jerusalem. These were things we certainly didn't consider frivolous.

Abdel stood in his black suit by the black Mercedes, both covered with the eternal film of dust. He tried to look so officious, his arms folded, his evening whiskers darkening his scowl. I noticed Sue wouldn't look at him, even when he reached out and took hold of her harshly by the shoulder to turn her around. It was a gesture I would never forget.

On the ride home he was grilling Sue. Something about her trips to Jerusalem was all I could gather. She was all the while shrugging her shoulders, repeating. "la a'lam." Abdel was growing more furious the more he talked, the more she shrugged. I was beginning to hope she would toss him some bit of information to cool him down. I was sitting next to him. I could see the veins on the back of his hands and in his neck and forehead pulsating. He flipped the rearview mirror back and forth, wanting to stare Sue down then not wanting to see her at all. I thought when we got home he'd go after Sue physically. I knew by the way he grabbed her shoulder he wanted to hurt her. But there were too many people at school. Back in the village, there was nobody who could help.

But instead, when we arrived home, he attacked Johara who was standing in front of the house. He grabbed her by her hair and dragged her around back. I waited with Sue in the car. She had stopped sobbing. I think she had gone into an emotional shock. Abdel came back alone within a couple of minutes. Yamma was with him, or I can only guess at how he would have treated Sue, and maybe me. Instead, he calmly came around and opened the door allowing Sue to get out. He ordered her to her room. Yamma took my arm but I shook her off and followed Sue.

I had watched movies where the convicted had gone to the gallows with shoulders slouched, head down, beaten. Good had triumphed; justice was done. I'd go to bed convinced I had just seen a slice of life, and that no matter the evil lurking in my closet, someone was looking out for me. But when I saw Sue with that same defeated stance, I saw real life, and saw it was evil that had prevailed.

She stood condemned before Abdel as he peered down at her bed. He fixed his eyes on it and narrowed them disturbingly. I stood back at the door as I had done earlier at the school, as if doing so could detach me. Johara brushed past my shoulder. She didn't stop or turn to look. She went into her room and shut the door.

With a sudden rage, Abdel grabbed the mattress and threw it at the door towards me. I sidestepped it; Sue never flinched. Abdel stared down at the floor beneath the empty springs as he fell into a trance.

I had seen Sue slip items under her mattress on occasion. Until I saw Abdel pull them out, I had no idea what they were. He reached down and took hold of a small statue. When he held the icon aloft a gasp was let out by Yamma who had come up behind me. It made me jump. Abdel pumped it in the air and then out at Sue who stood morosely silent as if she had just been found guilty of a heinous crime. My conversational

Arabic had become respectable by this time but it was no match for Abdel's fast and furious screams.

It was a small statue. His hand covered the entire thing, and he shook it so fast and violently that I couldn't get a look at it until he hurled it to the floor. It was the Virgin Mary painted in blue and ivory. There was more: a crucifix, a statue of a haloed Christ with outstretched arms, a painting of Jesus as a baby, as a man, with Mary, and at the Last Supper. There was an ivory box with medals and chains. I watched as Abdel tossed Anthony, Michael, Francis, and a host of others across the room. He was outraged, he was incensed, he was hurling Arabic words that made Yamma blush. Then he smacked Sue hard across the face.

I attacked him with a force so furious he fell into the bedsprings, drawing blood from a metal shard. He then beat me with wild punches that landed mostly on the top and sides of my head. My anger outweighed the pain. Up to this point, I truly didn't get it. I thought he was angry at Sue for keeping a messy room. Never had my parents thrown such a wild tirade, but if they had, I would have taken it. They were entitled; Abdel had no such title to us.

Yamma pulled him away. I grabbed Sue and pulled her outside. "We can't," she screamed.

"Let's go," I said as I tugged. She continued to pull back to the house, but with my weight and low center of gravity, I made a formidable anchor.

I knew where to go. I took Sue back to the cave where I vowed to stay until Abdel grew old and died. As we ran, I heard Johara crying and Abdel going after her. Sue tried to pull away, wanting to go back. "He's crazy," I said, "he'll hurt you again."

"We can't be out here," she sobbed.

"Not ... going back," I yelled breathlessly over my shoulder.

"He'll go after Johara."

"So let him. He's her father, he can hit her if he wants. But he can't hit you; he can't hit us."

CHAPTER 10

I was happiest at the cave. It was where I could get dirty and adventurous. I could pretend to be anything, anywhere, with anyone. I would have preferred a friend to enjoy it with: still, it was a great place to just be alone. It was like school, where in the morning all of us would sit quietly with our hands folded. If there was a harsh thought about me I didn't hear it. In those moments I was untouchable.

The stories of the ghoulies were enough to keep other kids away, some adults, too, so entrenched were the legends. I would have thought they'd also keep me away. They were enough to keep me far from Old Lady Tomilson's house at night, especially on Halloween, but I guess I was desperate for a place of my own.

I was just a kid wanting to do kid things, but Sue was growing up fast. To do it here was difficult on her. She was very outgoing and unabashed. She asked questions and expected answers, but here we were learning there were places children just did not go.

Siidi should have been there to tell us. That he wasn't made me as angry at him as I was at my parents. I had a friend back home, Paul Curry, who moved all the way to Cicero two months before I came to Palestine. He was angry at his parents for it, and I was devastated for him to be leaving friends and going so far away. Now here I was; not across the city, but across the world, cultures and languages removed. No one but Paul Curry could possibly understand how mad I was.

It got cold that night in the cave. I don't ever remember being so cold in my life. We heard Yamma calling to us but we didn't answer. I loved her but she was powerless to help us. Sue explained to me what had transpired. She had been secretly collecting Christian artifacts she purchased on her school trips to Jerusalem. Sam helped her. Johara knew, but didn't help. She refused, being a devout Muslim girl and knowing the wrath it would bring down from her father.

I don't believe I ever talked about religion when I was in Chicago. I'm sure I never heard Sue mention it. My father was a devout Muslim so there must have been something unspoken between him and my mother that said, keep your religion on your side of the house and I'll keep mine on mine. Trouble was, they didn't know where to put us kids. So when I watched the crazy daily ritual played out by dad, I had no idea it was considerably more than just a morning cup of coffee.

I was learning Islam from the family and at school, but it was more as a witness. No one pressured me, but I always felt Sue was getting the same treatment even at school. The teachers there were very broadminded. As a matter of practice, criticizing or ridiculing another was more heinous than cheating; even a single incident was grounds for dismissal. Me, I was made fun of because I was fat, shy, American, and couldn't speak a lick of the language, but never because of my religion, which, if asked, I'd have to admit I had none.

It was Sue's nature to be curious and intellectually bold. When she began taking school trips to Jerusalem, she stayed true to this nature, taking in all she could. As we shivered in the blackness, she told me how she would slip way from the group in Jerusalem to the Church of the Holy Sepulchre and purchase her icons. Sam would wait for her and carry the articles back to the house. She described this place to me in terms that made my head spin. It would be decades before I would revisit that night to understand how a concept so ethereal could affect a young girl so passionately.

I heard on this night that this Church of the Holy Sepulchre was built near the Temple Mount where the Dome of the Rock stood. It was built around at the site of Jesus Christ's crucifixion and burial. Golgotha, she called it.

She went on about the Temple Mount and the wars fought so that mosques could be built over churches that were built over temples, and walls where the Jewish people cried and prayed only to be told by the Muslims that it wasn't their wall, but then the Jewish people got the wall back only to have the government tell them they could only pray at certain times. Oh, and the Christians claimed the Temple Mount, too, but they used the site to dump their garbage. The Muslims and Jews didn't like the Christians being there anymore than they liked each other being there, so they allowed the Christians to pray only in Bethlehem at Christmas.

It was like keeping track of all the reality shows on television. It reminded me of that previous winter when my friends and I built a snow fort at the southern end of Lindblom Park. Another group of kids tore it down that night and built their own. So we snuck back the next night, tore theirs down, and built another. That silliness went on for four nights until they ambushed us with the most intense snowball fight I've ever been in. The fight was more fun than building the fort, but I'm happy it didn't go on as long as the Crusades.

Her voice grew soft and her chattering from the cold stopped for the time. Outside was a sea of stars that lit the mouth of the cave like footlights on a stage, while we, the actors, were recessed in the darkness just beyond. In a near breathless tone that was brought on either by the chill of the air or the majesty of the moment, she spoke of the Emperor Hadrian who erected his temple to Aphrodite to obliterate the Christian site. It would be Emperor Constantine, the first Christian ruler of Rome, who built the church over Hadrian's pagan edifice. Caliph Omar, a Muslim, captured Jerusalem, but saved the church as a gesture of goodwill. She talked of Godfrey of Bouillon and Caliph Hakim, and denominations with strange names; Coptics, Ethiopian Orthodox, and Syrian Orthodox.

I'm sure I've messed up the facts as they were related to me back then; I'm also sure I haven't messed them up anymore than the so-called scholars and theologians have. This host of names held wild visions for me. I saw Batman, the Caped Crusader, and his vicious, but colorful, arch enemies doing battle in Gotham. I supposed being huddled in the cave helped foster the imagery.

She couldn't explain it to me, she said, any better than she could explain it to herself, but the church, or the idea of it, drew her in. "It's not going to a museum where you go with questions and come away with answers," she said. "In Jerusalem, you always leave with more questions."

It wasn't faith she had, or a calling, but curiosity at first. The idea that a Roman Emperor such as Constantine, the leader of the very civilization who tortured and crucified Christ, came to glorify him with such a magnificent church intrigued her. An emperor, as she explained it to me, was like a king which further cemented my disdain for them.

The place Sue and I were living, the land of Canaan, held all the promises of a great God. That so many noble civilizations came together here throughout the eons in the name of that God should have led to magnificent things. Great cultures, thriving economies, unquenchable thirst for knowledge and understanding, bountiful harvests, a garden paradise. But something went horribly wrong. There came children who never grew up.

I used to think uncontrolled rage and jealousy were innate properties of a child, and that barring some freak of psychology, say being born an emotionless amoeba; they were traits a child had to pass through on the way to adulthood. Once grown, such characteristics would become part of those embarrassing moments one tried to forget. But I know now they don't go away, and though they are still petty, they don't lose their grip on us easily. Their effects just burn more intensely and their consequences become more dire as we age.

Even now I sit and shudder over the many self-indulgent and irresponsible things I have done, but nothing, not the worst of them, ever came close to war or genocide or whole-scale neglect, corruption, and cold-bloodedness. The mistakes I've made have been born out of pure ignorance, not reckless intellect. When I have been selfish it has been for self. It never took down a civilization. And never, never, in the name of God.

Sue did a great job of explaining in simple terms what had been going on in Palestine. So simple and plain that I wondered why the answers to the violence weren't as clear. So I did what kids do, I asked, "Why don't they just share?"

"Because they think their God doesn't want them to," she said.

"How can they know what he wants; he's not even here?"

"It's written in the Torah, and the Bible, and the Koran."

I pondered that. Three books to explain one God. I read where archeologists in Turkey found carnivore and herbivore fossils from the same cave near the crest of a mountain in the Ararat mountain range, far from where these particular animal bones were usually found. Carbon dating gave every indication they died in the same period, the same way. Most probably by drowning. It gave evidence of a great flood, possibly the great flood of Noah and the Ark. But whatever the reason, these mortal enemies were brought together in a glorious effort to live or die trying. Maybe that's what it will take. It should be life, not a dead history, that dictates what God wants.

I made plans to sneak back to the house but the pariah dogs were howling around us. Sue and I huddled tight. I had no idea of the time. It could have been ten at night or two in the morning. Had I known the constellations, I could have come close to the correct hour, the way the ancient Bedouins did. On a more rudimentary scale of this rudimentary technique, I watched the brightest star in the sky move from left to right. Sue was oblivious to any movement. As cold as it was, she stared out the cave without a twitch. I thought about a story Siidi told us about the Zar ceremony, where the witches would inhabit a young girl's body, then send her into the village to perform dastardly acts such as setting fires and stealing food, cattle, and little kids. I made up the last act, not really understanding all of what Siidi was saying, but knowing where witches were involved children had to be. It was just a wild legend, but I half expected Sue to stand up and walk away wailing in Arabic-witch tongue.

Siidi was gone again. I don't suppose he knew what was happening to us. Partly because he was rarely there, but another part of him that wanted to be ignorant of what we were going through. Up to this point I couldn't say I was much different. I had remained an observer. Not out of reverence, as Siidi had done, and certainly not for the intellectual separation of a scientist or philosopher. Being angry, it satisfied my youthful sense of justice.

I chose to stay out of the game, though for the most part, I had no choice. I was still overweight at this point, woefully shy, and basically the village punching bag. Though no physical blows were yet leveled, I was sure they were to come. I had been pushed, spat upon, and of course, ridiculed, so that punch would either be at me or by me.

"You feeling okay?" I asked Sue.

Without taking her eyes off the entrance she told me she was fine, just cold.

"You don't look cold; you're not even shivering."

"We need to be getting back," she said.

"I want to go home."

"I do too, Joe, but we can't."

"You know Gamal and Adli made Amir attack me that night."

"Stop that, Joe, we have enough real trouble here without you making things up."

"I'm not; Sam told me so. So, you know, you shouldn't be going outside at night to use the outhouse, like Yamma said."

"Worse things inside than outside. And until I'm in traction, I'm not using a damn metal tray to do my business in."

"I can sneak away and call dad," I said.

"It's more than that; you're too young to understand."

"Understand what?" I said, indignant at the insult.

"We're not on a vacation, Joe, we're here to learn."

"I'm learning nuthin' here that I couldn't learn better back at Earle Grammar School."

"Not at school, with Khaal Abu Faid. We're here to learn how to be Muslim."

When I considered the many possible reasons for my parents sending us here, that one never occurred to me. I knew Muslim kids in Chicago who were doing fine without being here. "Why would knowing about Jesus anger Abdel? It doesn't make learning to be a Muslim impossible."

"Being a true believer means renouncing all other Gods," she said.

"What's renouncing?"

"Rejecting, refusing to believe."

"Oh. Do you? I mean … do you refuse to believe in Jesus or are you refusing to believe in the other one?"

"Allah," she said. "The Muslim God is Allah. Don't you even know that yet?"

I had heard Allah mentioned many times, but honestly, I thought it was just a term like *damn it* when you hit your finger with a hammer. *In sa' Allah* I heard all the time. I would nod or smile or sometimes just act dumb because I didn't understand. "It means, 'God willing,'" Sue said.

There were complications here that reached far above my head. Sue's intellect was failing her. She was becoming a victim of it. Too much thinking, not enough anger, is what I thought to be her problem. "This isn't right," I said, "him going off on you like that. What about Johara, she started it, I hope she gets hers."

"Don't say things like that, Joe. You don't understand how important this is to Khaal Abu Faid and his family. It's like when dad does his prayers in the morning, only he doesn't do them all the time or in the prescribed way.

"Like when he gets too drunk the night before?" I said.

"Hush. There are rules here and you follow the rules. That's why I accept what Khaal Abu Faid did to me. In Palestine, Islam is very, very important. Many people perform all their prayers five times a day.

"Abdel doesn't pray five times a day," I said. "But I've heard him curse out Yamma and us that many."

"And he'll tell you he apologized later when we're not around. The point is it's a thing of great pride for him and most Muslims. It's not something you can fight, trust me, Joe. People have tried."

"I can't believe you're letting her get away with that," I said.

"Who?"

"Johara. Did you see how Abdel just ignored all of her things she had stashed under the bed? He only got mad about yours. She told him, y'know."

"No. Maybe. It doesn't matter."

"Well, I know for sure. When you didn't come on the bus she wouldn't tell me what was wrong. Now I know why she didn't. It's Gamal and Adli against me, and now Johara against you. Only Faid is leaving us alone."

She laid down in the sand, her face turned away from me. "No, Joe, you don't know for sure, you really don't know."

CHAPTER 11

We finally fell asleep. I don't know for how long but it was still dark and cold when I awoke. I was wet and ached as I rose from the dirt floor. I walked to the cave entrance to stretch my back and legs while Sue slept. It was quiet but for the wind sweeping up the valley and pushing debris across the worn stone. I shivered as if in a Chicago blizzard. I didn't know the desert could be so cold. I wanted to wake Sue and go back to the house where I'd be safe and warm but I worried for her. Even after her explanation I couldn't understand Abdel's riotous behavior.

I then came to the realization that unless something changed for the better, we'd be at the cave indefinitely. Tonight I was cold; soon I'd be hungry. It would only get worse. Other than Yamma, I didn't see any of them giving a damn we were gone, so no one would look, which now I knew was as bad as it was good.

I left the cave to go back to the house. I knew the way, but damn if I could find it in the dark. It seemed the cold wind altered the hill in a way that made it not only treacherous, but evil. The ghoulies were not real, yet they weighed heavily on me as I ascended. Every twisting bough was a groan from the beyond. Every rustle of leaves at my feet were bony fingers. In the distance I heard packs of pariah dogs, or maybe just the wind as it wormed its way through me.

I made it to the top but didn't know where I was in relation to the house. I saw no lights so I walked along the cliff edge, treating it as a guide. In horror I realized I had paid no mind to my exit point and so now, the trip down could have me bypassing the cave and dumping out into the Red River.

I wrapped my ineffective arms around my waist. "There are no such things as ghoulies," I muttered not-so-softly to myself. Yet there was Abdel and Amir and hateful kids. There was a fall from the rocks into the valley. There was the cold and the hunger. The number of real things I knew to be bad were battered about me by the wind. I was turning to find my way back to the cave when I spotted a dim light that may or may not have been the house.

I came through a field that could have been any field. The wind was not as wild on this flat ground, but what there was made the grasses dance with a rhythm I found unnatural. Coming from Chicago, something as commonplace as a field of grass was anything but.

I stood still and stared into the blackness, spinning three-hundred sixty degrees, trying to understand it as nothing more than a field. There was a waning moon, and, under it, my dance became a frenzy. The night closed in on me, long wispy blades scratching me along my arms and legs. The grasses waving madly convinced me I was amongst evil. I made a frantic dash through them, sure they were there to swallow me.

In that instant it wasn't a disturbed uncle or wild dog that unnerved me. It was everything around, the essentials of childhood that had somehow been turned against me. And as I ran I knew it was impossible to outrun this place, and if I ran into the waiting jaws of Amir, he could just take me.

But there was no Amir on the other edge of the meadow, and no wind, and a light from the kitchen window shined. I stopped short to catch my breath. I recognized the cement outhouse just ahead. Now a blade of light shot into the sky behind me. I knew it as dawn arriving in the valley. It would be nearly an hour before it arrived here when Yamma would rise to begin her day, soon followed by the others off to school.

I stayed hunkered down listening for Amir. Perhaps he was up in the hills, or terrorizing the town. Either worked fine for me. I crept up to the back of the outhouse where I found a neatly folded stack of Afghan blankets. I lifted them and found a hefty picnic basket. It was filled with dates, figs, cheeses, bread, and some canned fruits, along with a large bottle of water. It was meant for us, I knew. I mouthed my thank you to Yamma.

Now there was the challenge of getting it back down to the cave. I guess knowing that, Yamma tied a rope to the basket. As I began to drag I noticed the tidy trail I was leaving behind, distinct enough for anyone to follow. I picked the basket up, maneuvered it forward a few feet, set it down, then began again. That got me all of fifteen feet. My heavy breathing spooked Amir whom I could hear growling behind me. I grabbed hold of the top Afghan as the closest thing I had available to throw. Turning to throw and run, I could see Amir's faint profile straining against the rope that held him back. There was no doubt he was secure; there was no doubt he would have attacked me savagely had he not been.

The trail be damned, I dragged the package through the field to the cliff's edge. It was a glorious sunrise cradled in the lap of the valley. The wind was now a pleasant, warm breeze that dried my sweat-soaked clothes as I made my way up and down the mountain. It took me four trips as I unloaded the basket of all I could manage to carry.

Sue was still asleep. My first trip was with the blankets. I tucked one around her. My last trip was the basket. I reloaded all the food into it then lay down in the sun at the opening of the cave.

I awoke in a pool of my own sweat, the Afghan still wrapped tight up to my neck. Sue was sitting on a rock just inside the coolness of the cave's mouth. She had a lapful of dates and cheese which she ate inattentively. She never asked where they came from or who brought them to us. If she suspected me she didn't let on with a warning, reprimand, or thanks. I could see she was beyond that.

I couldn't spend another night out there. I told Sue this without her fighting for or against it. We waited until nearly two before going back, before Abdel returned from work and the kids from school. This was my strategy; Sue had none. In fact, she hadn't said as many as ten words since falling off to sleep the night before.

I left the Afghans, the basket, and the remaining food at the cave, knowing I would return at some time for some reason. Yamma was tending to the chickens. She greeted us warmly, but not like long-lost children. I figured she noticed the trail of the basket disappearing through the field. Sue spoke for the first time to her. "Is Khaal Abu Faid here?"

"No, he's not here," Yamma said, with a sad smile. "Lunch for you two?"

"La," Sue said. "Joe, you want some lunch?"

I nodded to Yamma who dropped her pail of feed and took my hand. My parents fought often back home. It was disturbing enough when you knew the words that went along with the looks and the gestures. Yamma's sad eyes told me something much worse than last night's episode had transpired.

"Something's wrong with Yamma," I said to Sue.

"She gets very upset when Khaal Abu Faid yells at us."

I shook my head. "No, something else. Like when mom and dad fight."

"Trust me, Joe, it was about last night."

The way she blew it off upset me. "You know, Sue, it's like mom says, it's not always about us. Something is bothering Yamma a lot and it's not you."

After lunch, Yamma and I spread the nets beneath the olive trees. It was harvesting time, something I had forgotten about when I rushed off to the cave. Sam explained to me the importance of the olive is terms of economics and tradition. All I gathered from his talk was that the family made a good deal of money and the trees live to be over five hundred years old.

In a rare display of culinary curiosity, I pulled an olive from a branch to sample it. I spit it out immediately. It was inedible by anyone with taste buds. Yamma laughed. "La, la, la, "she said. She picked an olive off the ground. "It's not ready to eat." It was a phrase she used quite often, mainly in the kitchen when I poked around the food preparations. I think secretly she was learning English to help us along. I had never seen her away from the house or farm except to shop in the town on occasion. And there, she never associated with anyone outside the shops. Such efforts made me love her all the more, and worry about her latest mood.

Abdel didn't come home that night. No one asked why or where he was. He didn't come home that entire week. I saw him next on the first day of the harvest. He spoke to no one but the neighbors who came over to help. While the adults picked and we kids beat the branches with sticks, Abdel stayed to the far side of the field. He stayed home that night as the harvest lasted well into the evening that first day. He was gone the day after, and again, no one asked where or why. Yamma was exhausted and hurting. I couldn't speak to her in the adult words that were needed, even if I knew the language. And from what I saw, no one else tried. But she went through her day and tucked us all into bed each night. I was last and when she said, "have sweet dreams," I could only smile and nod and wish I could. I really wished we both could.

CHAPTER 12

The harvest was a good one from what I could tell. Yamma was able to buy a new refrigerator and school clothes for her children. She bought me a pair of jeans and Sue a long skirt that she never wore.

School was let out for three days and the entire village went farm to farm to help in the harvests. Even Sam, who I learned was not much for physical labor, came to help, and to be with Sue. It was as hard a labor as I have done since. Tedious when inspecting, picking, and sorting the olives; back breaking from retrieving the fallen ones from the nets and when the olive bags got so heavy they pinned us kids to the ground.

But it was easily made into a game. Amazing what boys can do with sticks. Careful not to bruise an olive, it was quite a skill to bang a branch in just the right spot to release as many olives as possible. Gamal was good at it, but Faid had achieved near-legendary status in the town. Being a young man now, he considered it beneath him. He relegated himself to the one-at-a time adult method. He would begrudgingly strike a branch when hounded enough by the little kids, like a hall of famer participating in the old timers' game.

Adli was just two years older than me. He was quiet, like me, and though not as fat, he had little athletic ability. He swung like a girl and destroyed as many olives as he brought down. When the kids ran from tree to tree, he was always dead last, even behind me. He tripped often on what he blamed to be rocks and roots but were more often his own feet. The two of us usually trailed behind the rest, enjoying picking up the olives from the netting where there was no competition to single us out.

I saw him play soccer at school. I never played until Palestine, but it didn't seem too difficult, just a matter of moving the ball up to the other team's net. Playing soccer at recess, he wasn't cocky then. He wasn't swaggering. He looked confused and worried. He couldn't send a pass more than two feet, and if he tried to dribble with anyone in his vicinity, the ball was quickly taken from him.

As cruel as he had been to me, I felt sorry for him for I understood that before I arrived, he had to endure the ridicule that I had taken on. I saw me in him, the way I felt my first days there. Only I would eventually overcome it; he never did. So it made sense to me that whenever Gamal was preoccupied with his friends, Adli took the opportunities to form a bond with me.

One night I saw Adli writing something at the kitchen table. He had that look, like he was trimming a bonsai tree. His tongue was out and his eyebrows were knitted up like stuck caterpillars. I didn't read or write Arabic, but like most kids I was a sponge. Within six months I could speak it well and write it fair.

When we were alone he was usually pretty friendly, but not this night. He pulled the paper away, but not before I saw his name scrawled idiotically across the page in a downward slant. Even if I didn't know the characters, I could see the childish penmanship.

I recalled the class he played soccer with at recess. They were all sizes. Some were obviously older, some younger. They played on a field in the back, away from the others. One girl watched from the sideline in a wheelchair. One boy, maybe twelve years old, walked with a severe limp and his left arm hung uselessly at his side. Actually, Adli may have been the best player out there.

The word I knew for it back then was "retard." I said it along with everyone else to describe anyone we didn't like, or more appropriately, didn't want to like. So it wasn't a word I used for Adli. I just put two and two together to understand he wasn't very smart or athletic and was embarrassed by it. The thing that confounded me was no one at home seemed to notice or give a damn other than Yamma who gave him what precious little time she could. But no one sought outside help. I have no doubt it was the school that saw it and put him in the special class.

I know Abdel was ashamed, and Yamma's function was to raise the family, not worry about a boy's future. I wish I could say I tried to help him and that I defended him when the others were so unmerciful. I think, though, he knew I accepted him for who he was. Sometimes that's all you can do.

He taught me kid-useful Arabic phrases. It started slow, with words kids here had to know, like *kalbouz,* a friendlier way of saying "chubby." And more colorful ones like *wald il qahbaa,* son of a bitch; *anta kalbee,* you are my dog; and my favorite, *Abu l-himmuur,* your father is a donkey.

And through his limited English and my limited Arabic, I learned some things about him. He liked basketball, the Boston Celtics, and dropped names like Cousy, Russell, and Lustocoff. I had no interest so the names meant nothing. He took me to a wooden gate on the far side of the olive grove. The worn path led over a steep rock face, down to a flat site surrounded by large pine trees. I hadn't seen a pine tree here since arriving. I drew a deep breath to inhale the sweet scent.

Adli had nailed a bottomless wicker basket about six feet up one of the trees. He retrieved a soccer ball from behind a stone and tossed it to me. I took a wild shot that sailed into the pine grove. Adli laughed heartily and raced after it. He dribbled it awkwardly on the hard-packed pine straw floor. He muffed several dribbles behind his back and through his legs before landing a sweet lay-up.

We shot around until the time we'd be missed. I was surprised by his lack of competiveness. I figure this was the place he could top someone, especially me, who had never touched a soccer ball, never mind used one to shoot around as a basketball. This was his place, like my cave. Here he could be king; he could be Faid, sultan of the olive stick. But perhaps this was him, the boy who wanted to share and have fun, who understood being different, the outsider who was like any other boy and knew his greatest fears lay not in a cave of myths, but in himself.

I doubt he had brought many others here. I appreciated that he would share it with me, though I had no intentions of returning the favor at the cave, knowing how arbitrary kids my age were when it came to friendship. I didn't have to wait long.

That night, as I crossed the olive grove with a full basket, I heard the others jeering loudly while Amir howled in obvious distress. I thought they were yelling to me but there was no way they could see me coming, not at such a distance and at night. Then I saw Adli just up ahead. I called to him, anticipating he was there waiting for me. But he sprinted back to the house, calling ahead, "yallah, yallah", *come on, come on*. But he wasn't calling to me.

As I got closer to the house I could see Gamal and his friends waving wildly in my direction. Only they weren't waving; they were throwing rocks. Not at me, but at Amir, driving him mad. It so happened that Amir's long rope gave him a wide berth, wide enough that I had to travel a good distance around him to get to the house. It was no easy task with my heavy satchel of olives.

I wasn't getting the game. I didn't understand why Adli met me on the path. I didn't understand why they had chosen this place and time to torment Amir. But as I neared him, I worried that his threadbare rope may not be enough to hold him, not the way he was rearing and kicking like a rodeo bull. So I made my path as wide as possible, nearly out of the olive grove.

Then, just as I came into the clearing, the boys shrieked and I saw them rushing to the outhouse, Amir closing fast. I was now closer to the wild dog than I was to the house. Running either way was not an option. I could only hope Amir would use this opportunity to escape the yard. But when the boys disappeared into the house, he caught another scent. Mine.

He turned when he deciphered the wind direction. At least he made his intentions known by crouching low and bearing his teeth. It gave me time to turn and get a head start. Had I not had that, I'm sure I wouldn't be here today.

I ran through the grove in an absurd belief the olives would throw him off the scent. I got to end of it and even over my own desperate panting I could hear his. Ahead of me was the pine forest of Adli's basketball court. I anticipated the drop off and took a leap of faith into the dark space. I'm sure it wasn't more than a three-foot effort but it felt like an Air Jordan moment. A tree branch appeared out of nowhere, stuck out there just for me. I feared it would crash to the ground with me onboard as soon as I wrapped my arms around it. But it held, and I held.

So involved was I in holding on that I let my legs dangle a moment until I felt Amir take hold of my foot. I was fat, weak, and uncoordinated, but I was scared enough to overcome all that and straddle the branch just out of his reach.

I was sure they'd come for me just as sure I was that Amir would get bored and leave. The kids never came and it took Amir over an hour to tire. I couldn't be sure he was gone; maybe just lying in wait. It took me another thirty minutes to sneak back to the house.

Adli and Gamal were sitting at the table. Adli was snickering. Gamal's snorting laugh was made more ludicrous by his trying to conceal it from Yamma. "Joe, were you outside all this time?" She asked.

"I was picking olives," I said.

"This late?"

I looked down at my two cousins whose giggling stopped, as, I was sure, did their breathing.

"You were lucky. Amir ran off his rope tonight."

With much effort I put my canvas satchel of olives on the counter. Yamma reached over to help. "That's quite a load," she said.

"Yeah. It was really heavy. I spilled it a few times so I had to keep stopping to pick them up."

Gamal, Adli, and I held eye contact for a long moment. If this were a television show, Gamal would nod his thank you. Adli would've winked. I'd give them a knowing grin. The next day we'd walk to school side by side by side. But this was real life. Gamal blew out his cheeks and belly, and Adli burst into laughter. Adults may say childhood goes by in a heartbeat, but kids know there's no end in sight.

CHAPTER 13

Abdel was living back at home, but now he came home from work later than usual. Siidi helped during the olive harvest, or tried to, and injured his back. He spent long hours in bed. The day he could get up and around, he made a trek down the mountain pass, the one he took as a young sheepherder. He was halfway back up when he collapsed. If it wasn't for a sheepherder heading down he may have died there. It was dehydration and a host of old-man ailments that had Siidi back in bed.

I often heard Yamma crying in the kitchen at night. And Sue was slipping badly. Even Sam had had enough and stopped coming around. Johara was trying to make amends. I found her sitting on the edge of Sue's bed reciting Robert Frost poems in a stuttering, staccato voice. Usually that would make Sue laugh, but she lay quietly. I don't think she was even listening.

School had become my haven. I hated weekends and holidays. I spent a lot of time studying in the kitchen. That way I avoided contact with everyone and stayed in Yamma's company.

The only period of school I hated was the one I was most looking forward to in Chicago. Recess. There it would be dodge ball and baseball and card flipping and capture the flag. I sat watching from the steps most days as kids played A*l manyya,* a game of team tag; *elhuj-jarieh,* the chicken and the egg, which is a game of picking up numerous stones simultaneously, and of course, soccer.

One day I guess my Persian friend, Raha, had had enough of my moping and dragged me out to the big field where they were playing soccer. She had been suspended from playing just a week before for getting into a shoving match. Actually, that was what they caught her doing. They missed the knee that clocked the kid's genitalia.

She mostly sat with me during that time. She taught me *Takhteh nard* which is backgammon, and I taught her how to flip baseball cards. It was something I was very good at. I brought fifty of them from back home in hopes of winning more in Palestine, but it wasn't a popular pastime here. I showed her my neatest trick: a very light coat of candle wax, barely perceptible to the eye or touch, on a 1962 Tom Tresh rookie card, which made the card fly like an F-4 Phantom.

On her first day back from suspension she yanked me from the stoop and pulled me into the middle of the dustbowl soccer field. Talk about feeling stripped naked. "Lo'ba," she said to me, but loud enough for the others to hear. The goalie at the far end of the field punted the ball, and more by chance, I'm sure, than design, it pounded me on the head. "Jai'yed, jai'yed," Raha said, patting my head as she ran past me to retrieve the ball that I sent twenty yards out of bounds. The others got a charge from my accidental header; some patted me, others jeered. It was the best play I made all game.

I touched it only one other time, with my hands as it came towards my face. Hysterically, they all began screaming at me. "La, la, la, regl, regl," pointing at their feet. "I know, I know," I began to protest to defend what little honor I had left at that point, but it was to no use as they were off to the other end of the field.

I'd like to say it was great fun being invited to play, enjoying my first shot at camaraderie. The fact was, most times I was running wildly, usually in looping circles, as the dry sand choked me. No one else was having trouble navigating, yet I was constantly arriving too late to make a play, or cutting the wrong angle, or bending over to catch my breath.

There were three kids out to insure I never ventured onto their playing field again. One was on my team, and it was there I was first introduced to the concept of conspiracy. Every time this one kid got the ball, he passed it off to me, even when I was covered or nowhere near him. The other two would then sandwich me, usually one high, one low. Soccer be damned, this was great sport for them.

At one point Raha flew to my rescue, literally, by knocking one of the boys twice her size and nearer to mine, into a chain-linked fence. I was embarrassed, too embarrassed to quit and walk away. But Raha's action pushed me into humiliation.

For sure it wasn't her intention, and if she left the kid sprawled by the fence without a word said, I don't think anyone would have put two and two together. They did when she went over and kicked him in the side, all the while screaming "Mesleh sag bemire," which I learned in Persian means, "may you die like a dog." And when the other two came after her she turned on them with more insults. They pushed her until she fell, until a teacher came over to break it up, while I stood there useless.

Raha was suspended again, as was the boy she was kicking. As poorly as I played, I would have made up for it in spades in her eye and in my own had I so much as spat at the kid. I would have shown honor to myself and Raha. But my actions, or lack of them, had others greeting me with *aarun aleik,* shame on you. That went on for a week until Raha tried to retaliate against another boy for saying it with a string of her own colorful insults. This time I intervened with one I learned from Adli. "Kul khara we moot," I said to the kid. *Eat shit and die.*

Gamal witnessed the incident and back home he presented me with a soccer ball and an invitation to play with him and his friends. They began slowly with dribbling and passing drills, then shooting. They were patient and because of the language barrier, did most by demonstration. I was impressed with the power of Gamal's kick. He would approach the ball at an angle and with one step launch it low and hard against the side of the barn, rattling the entire wall. He had by far the most potent leg, though all of them could send it. I was no good, and though I enjoyed their efforts, I had the uncomfortable feeling they were up to something as sinister as the nasty tricks with Amir.

Next, they directed me towards the barn wall and gently took shots at me. If it was a step or two to either side, I let it pass. Shots directly at me I awkwardly kicked back to them. Gamal stopped the action as he showed me how to crouch, move side-to-side, catch, and discard the ball to the side. He smiled and patted my back.

This was good; this was a connection after all this time. I was smiling as I crouched, slipped left, then right, wrapped the ball in a bear hug, and tossed it away. Off towards the house I saw Adli watching pensively. I couldn't know then if he was angry or wary.

You can leave a frog in an uncovered pot of water on a stove, and the stupid thing will sit there until it boils as long as the temperature is increased gradually. I was that frog, and before I could jump out, there were two, three, up to four balls at once crashing in on me at the same velocity used to rock the barn wall. All the while Gamal was staring me down with what I can only described as a demonic sneer.

But I couldn't leave; I wouldn't leave. I took every shot they gave me: to the head, chest, back, and groin. My forearms and thighs were stinging, and my eyes were swelling. I fought back the tears to stand in that crouch, determined to make every save. They lined themselves up in front of me, at one time four in a row from left to right. Gamal gave the signal and all four balls exploded at me chest high. But I stood my ground, focusing on the one shot by Gamal. It came at my head, but I shielded it with two hands. The force knocked my hands back into my face. One hit my nose, giving me that nauseous feeling of wanting to throw-up. But I had made the save and gave Gamal a sick smile. He met it with that sneer, and I knew this wasn't about him scoring on me; it was about him hurting me.

They gathered the balls to line up the shots again. This time I planned to catch Gamal's and kick it down into the olive grove for him to chase. Moments before Gamal gave the signal, I was shoved viciously to the side. Having my eyes shut tight, I didn't see that it was Adli who now faced the onslaught. He was able to deflect all but one of the shots and that one put him on the ground.

Gamal charged at him, his voice enraged. But Adli got to his feet before Gamal reached him. I had never seen Adli doing anything but laugh and jeer at me while with his brothers. Today he was different. To this day I don't know what was said. I know less of why it was said. But I surmised Adli was taunting Gamal to use him as the barn wall because he was understanding the pain I was going through.

I can't describe the elation I felt at that moment. At such a young age I couldn't articulate such feelings. Rather than run to be my rescuer as Raha had done, Adli ran to join me. I was no longer a pathetic loser, but part of a team of pathetic losers. And that was a damn sight better than where I had come from.

It would seem these two episodes would provide the essentials of encouragement for me. And they did. Recess became bearable as Raha, I, and now several others began flipping baseball cards. She even won my Tom Tresh that she then used to dominate others. At home, I became somewhat of Adli's big brother, even though I was more than two years younger. Homework became a nightly ritual, and a happy one, as I helped him with school work the best I could. And through him I learned to carry out mundane but civil conversations without the use of Arabic curse words and insults. At night he would join me at the window sill in my room.

I had learned a few of the constellations from my brother; Adli learned from Yamma. As I pointed and called them out, Adli translated: "Orion" to "Al Jabbar;" "the little dipper" to "Ad-Dubb Al-A'sghar;" "Cassiopeia" to "dhat Al-Korsi." Then he took over, pointing out Al-Kalb Al-A'kbar, Al-Ghurab, and Al-Hayyah. Not only was I surprised by his knowledge but also by the fact that way out here folks cared enough to look at the stars and give them names.

It was the first realization I had that the things on this side of the world, though called by different names, looked the same as those on the other side. The sounds, the smells, the touches, then perhaps the loves and hates, all of different names, meant precisely the same thing. What I learned to be the only difference was not in *what* was said, or even *how* it was said, but by *who* said it.

As I was finding my way, the winds were blowing cold for others. Sam came to the house, and ignoring both me and Sue upon his arrival, sat with Yamma in the olive grove. I watched from the window but what I saw made me feel sick. Yamma's head was in her hands while Sam spoke. At moments she would throw her head back and wail into the sky. I went to Sue in her room. "Yamma's crying again," I said.

"Why?"

"I dunno. She's outside with Sam."

"Is Khaal Abu Faid with them?"

"No. And don't call him that. It's supposed to be a good thing and he shouldn't be called anything good."

"It's respect, Joe, we need to show him—"

"And don't say that," I screamed. "He hit you; he yells at me, he makes Yamma cry."

"So does Sam, looks like."

"Sam must be telling her things about Abdel."

"I'm going to Ramallah to stay with a friend," she said.

"When?"

"Tomorrow."

"For how long?"

"I don't know, Joe. But you can't come so don't ask."

CHAPTER 14

At times, I believe had I been there alone it would have been easier to bear. While Sue was a source of great strength to me initially, as she fell into despair, I spent many hours a day worrying over her. Over the years I've tried to isolate the moment she lost it. I know it was a combination of events, but it was one harrowing incident that had her questioning not herself, but humanity.

Halloween had gone by without me realizing until a week later. I was upset and shared my feelings with Adli. It was the first time I attempted to share personal issues with my cousin. By this point my Arabic was becoming reasonably good. I had no measure of how good, but I could at least make conversation. But dressing up as a Ghoulie to get candy wasn't easy to explain. It scared the hell out of him, actually.

I was ready for Thanksgiving, though, which came and went without fanfare. Sue explained Thanksgiving was a strictly American holiday which made total sense once I recounted the school plays I saw.

Sam was right about Siidi. He came back to Palestine for the memories. Even at his age he didn't have enough memories to keep him busy forever. He went back to Nicaragua on Thanksgiving Day.

So convinced was he of our being in safe hands and on the path to salvation, he barely said good-bye, and certainly gave us no warning. Yamma explained that his health was failing quickly. I thought that was the point of his trip, to come back here to die, but in the end he chose to die in the place he knew best and where he was known.

I registered a complaint to my parents when I spoke to them a few days after he left. "How come he can go home and we can't?"

"He's an old man," my father said, "he can do what he wants."

He and my mother listened as I ranted about our treatment here. When I at last I took a breather, they came back with what became my standard to my kids. "It can't be all that bad. Give it time," they said. "Every new change takes time."

I had an overactive imagination and Sue was melodramatic, both qualities my parents readily agreed with, is what Abdel told them when he took the phone. It ended with Abdel telling them he and Yamma were taking good care of us and the cousins loved us being there. That said, what could possibly go wrong?

"So what about Christmas?" I asked.

"You won't see that here either," Sue said, matter-of-factly, as if it were no different than missing Halloween or Thanksgiving.

I was near tears. How could they eliminate the only holidays kids could enjoy? "Don't these people have anything?" I asked.

"Ramadan," she said. Then she explained the one month celebration which included starving during daylight hours. "It is a celebration of Allah's revelations to the world through the Koran."

"Us, too?"

"No, only adults and older kids."

"You're older."

"Yeah. I don't know; I don't think so," she mumbled. I could always tell when she was worried or nervous; she never answered the question directly. Instead she would mumble her private thoughts.

"I like our way to celebrate God." I said, "There are lots of presents and food." I was not impressed, nor was I inspired, to learn Ramadan was to begin on January the fourth.

During that night in the cave, when Sue described to me how she came to possess the Christian artifacts that so outraged Abdel, she said she understood Sam's bias towards Islam and hatred of the Jews. "I listened to him with one ear and left the other ear open to hear other voices," she said of their trip through Jerusalem. Being a poet she talked like that on such deep matters.

Now, in her room, this was the one theme that lifted her spirits. "I'm going to get back to Jerusalem to learn more," she said. "I want to go back to learn not what happened, but why. And not like a history lesson. I want to learn from people who truly believe."

"Who's that?"

"I don't know; I'll find someone."

"Yamma believes," I said. "I've heard her praying. Abdel does, too, but he wouldn't be a very good teacher for you."

"I love Yamma like you do. She believes what she is told to believe; it's in her head more than in her heart."

"Is that why Yamma's crying?"

"I don't know why she's crying. But you cannot tell her about this, or anyone. I'm telling you so you won't worry."

"I want to go with you."

"I told you, Joe, you can't."

I was determined not to cry, not after all the other crap I suffered through without giving them the benefit of a tear. But the thought of Sue leaving me had me blubbering. "Don't," Sue chastised with a tone that could have come from my mother. "They'll wonder what's the matter and start asking questions."

I got angry at that. "Why is it *you* who has to get away? What about me? You have Johara; you have friends at school."

Sam came in unannounced. He heard the commotion I was causing but ignored it with a big grin and slap on my shoulder. "How's it go, Joey? That what they call you at school, Joey?'

Most of the kids called me Nasser, knowing I wanted to be called Joe. Except Raha, who would do anything to be contrary. "Joe or Nasser," I said.

"Not at The Friends, in Chi-car-go." He sounded Hispanic when he said the name, 'Chi-car-go,' heavy and loud on the first syllable. I've since heard others say it similarly, and though it never bothered me from Sam, it drives me mad enough now to make the correction.

"No, just Joe," I said. He was disappointed at having me shut him down on his new-found slang.

He took a seat next to me on the bed. "Your sister is still sad."

"Not sad," I said, "mad."

"Oh?"

"I'm not sad and I'm not mad."

"You can certainly be both, or you can be one, but I know from your face you cannot be neither."

"She's running away," I said, hoping it would pinch her, but she just smirked and looked at the back of her hands.

I took it as a sign of emotional exhaustion. I prided myself on being able to infuriate her but she didn't have the energy to do battle. I was surprised to hear Sam say, "I know, but not tomorrow."

"You know?"

"Yes."

"Why not tomorrow?" Sue asked, frantically.

"Things have happened here."

"How come you get to know?" I said.

Sue protested. "I have to go; you know I have to go."

"Please Sue, lower your voice. I have things to tell you, about here, about Amineh and Khaal Abu Faid. Joe, please leave us here. These are not nice things."

"I can hear them," I said.

"Not for young ears."

"I live here, too."

"He can stay," Sue said. "He needs to know whatever it is I need to know."

"Okay, Khaal Abu Faid is leaving Yamma and the family."

I was elated. It was one less heartless male to contend with. Sue seemed genuinely concerned which I found puzzling. "He's already never here," she said. "Where is he going?"

"Far away, I hope," I said.

"Ramallah."

"That's not far away."

"What about Yamma?" Sue asked.

"She is why you cannot leave. She will need you."

"She has Johara."

"This is gonna be good, Sue," I said. "You don't have to leave now. With Abdel gone you don't—"

"I have to leave more," she screamed. "I can't stay here longer."

"It does get worse," Sam said. "Khaal Abu Faid denies Adli to be his son."

We both looked stunned at such a thought. That such a situation was possible was foreign to me. Adli lived here. He ate and slept here. He was as cruel to me in the beginning as his two brothers. "Whose is he then?" I asked.

"He is, of course, Khaal Abu Faid's son. There is no proof to the contrary, yet he denies such a son could come from his lineage."

"Why?" I asked.

"It is hard to understand for you. Just say he is not proud of his son."

"That is totally preposterous," Sue said.

"Excuse me?" Sam asked.

"Majnoon. Crazy. You cannot disown a child because he doesn't measure up to you. And who is Khaal Abu Faid to set the standards anyway?"

"I am sorry, Sue, your words are not familiar to me and you speak them so fast."

I had to agree. Sue was as fired up as I had seen her in weeks and she was not ready to slow down. "If he wants to disown a child he should start with … forget it; it is none of my concern."

"But you must make it your concern," Sam said. "Johara does not have … the word … the will, maybe spirit, to help Amineh through this. And Adli will need to be cared for."

"It's not my responsibility to care for Khaal Abu Faid's family. Yamma must have known the type of man he was when they married; she can handle it."

"No, she did not know him until the day before the wedding."

"One of those, like you and Johara."

Sam laughed. "No, not like that. As you may know, I am different. I will be going to Birzeit University to be a journalist. Then to America, maybe Chi-car-go, yes?"

"Will they get a divorce?" I asked.

"Perhaps. He has another in Ramallah."

"Another son?" Sue said.

Sam laughed again. "Yes, perhaps he does, but I meant another woman."

"Oh, dear, God," Sue said, "does Yamma know this?"

"She told it to me."

I saw Sue turning the situation over in her mind. Yamma didn't deserve this. "It's Yamma who should disown him; it's Yamma who should be demanding a divorce."

"It is not done that way.'

"Even if he cheats on her?"

"What is 'cheat'?"

"To be with another woman."

"Many men have many women. This is not a problem. The problem is for Amineh. She did not agree to a divorce in the contract so it cannot be.

Only Khaal Abu Faid may demand for a divorce. This is not so in America? "

"Not even close, I'm glad to say. But how can you disown a child?" she asked.

"There is no proof that Khaal Abu Faid has, so they both must swear according to the Surah al-Nur before a qadi who is a judge. Here, they both bear witness four times before Allah that they are truthful. Then, a fifth time, accepting the curse of Allah if they are not."

"Then what?" I asked.

"They are separated, and Adli will lose his father's name, taking the last name of his mother, which is very shameful for him, as well."

"Where is the justice in that? Who can know who is lying?" Sue said.

"Allah knows."

"But he's not here to judge."

"Judgment doesn't happen here, only Sharia happens here."

"That is total nonsense."

"Enough," Sam demanded. It made us both jump.

It was obvious to even me that Sue had crossed the line, but that was how she was. Sam's conclusion that it had to be Sue, and not Johara, to help Yamma through this mess was well intentioned, but I saw all kinds of problems. One was playing itself out at the moment. Sue had taken the beating from Abdel for the Christian icons because it was her trespass for which she knew the consequences. But Yamma had made no such blunders. She was dutiful, caring, responsible. She was above all, a wonderful mother, and Sue would not stand for much of what Abdel had to say or do to her.

"I do know some of your American thinking," Sam continued, two octaves lower now. "It is good in a classroom, or on paper, but it should be left there while you are in Palestine. Even Ramallah can tolerate some, but you are in Dayr Ghasana, and talk such as that will not be welcomed. You need to help Amineh with more quiet talk.

"To be a divorced woman is very bad. Amineh will not be able to live without a husband now, and no other man will have her. She will have to leave this house and move back with her family. But before that, you will talk to her and you will find she is not what you think she is."

CHAPTER 15

Sue agreed not to leave Yamma. It made for a settling night on that account. But I lay awake in the dark listening to Adli softly singing. His pitch was high, and being on his back, his voice had a gurgling tone, making him sound like a delighted infant. I knew kids back home who had no father. Brian Monaghan's dad was in prison for selling stolen truck cargo. Timmy Clausen's dad died in an explosion at the Standard Oil refinery. A couple of others had divorced parents, and I don't think Tyler Counts knew who his father was. But I never knew one whose father traded him in like a used car.

It certainly didn't surprise me that Abdel would do such a thing. It made him look slimier than he was, and though I reveled in the knowledge that I had him pegged right from the start, it did my heart and mind no good that Adli was the victim. Like Yamma, he didn't deserve it.

When Sam said Abdel was not proud of Adli, I knew what he was referring to. I was never made aware of the diagnosis; I'm not certain there ever was one. What I saw was a young boy, often as scared as I was, never knowing why he wasn't good enough, struggling hard to be better. At what and for what, I'm not sure he knew.

Yamma would sit with him at the kitchen table when she found the time, which was rare. She was the first one up and the last to bed, she had little energy for what Abdel considered family non-essentials. As with everything she did, she was patient and encouraging with him. I knew the effort that took since he tried my patience after thirty minutes.

I didn't understand the dark depth of Abdel's looks of disgust when walking past us at the table doing homework. I didn't think Adli even noticed, but looking back, I'm sure he did. Every son is attuned to how his father views him until the view becomes so painful he turns away from it one final time.

I sat with Sue on the bus to school the next morning. She stared straight ahead, barely blinking. I stole glances at Adli who was laughing loudly at whatever it was Gamal and his friends were saying. He caught my look a few times and smiled. I wondered, had we not become closer would I have even cared about all I heard last night? As surreal as it was, would I have shrugged my shoulders and shook it off with a "serves him right" attitude? It sounds cold to think I might have, but I was still in survival mode and maybe I enjoyed his company on the unwanted side.

When we arrived at the school in Ramallah, I watched Sue shuffle down the pathway, lagging behind Johara and the others. When Johara stopped for her to catch up, Sue shooed her onward with a wave of her hand. That was the last thing I picked up on as the bus moved on to El-Bireh. I ran to the front of the bus. "Istanna," I called to the driver, "Istanna." I bent over and cupped my hand to my mouth in what I hoped was the universal *I'm going to puke* gesture. The driver got the message and let me off. I ran from the bus back to the school where I saw Sue walking down to the corner. She stopped at Al-Zaybaq coffee shop.

She wasn't going to school and she wasn't getting coffee. The sidewalk was busy with walkers and shopkeepers opening up so she was completely unaware of my furious approach. "You said you were staying for Yamma," I screamed as I took her arm.

To say I scared her near to death would not be an exaggeration. She was furious, I saw that in her face, but it took a few moments to vocalize it. "Let me go," she said, shaking me off like a nasty bug. "What are you doing here, you brat?"

"I saw you," I said. "I saw you sneaking away."

"I wasn't sneaking. And you're supposed to be at school."

"So are you." I wanted to accuse her of running out on Yamma but I had no words in mind, only all sorts of righteous indignation for her self-serving actions. While I spent my night worried for Yamma and Adli, she spent hers concocting her escape plan. Sam came up behind her. "Now you're gonna get it," I said.

"Get what?"

"He coming with us?" Sam asked.

"No!"

"She promised she was going to stay; she promised," I said.

"Stop yelling, will you," Sue said. "I'm not leaving here, just leaving school, just for the day."

"To where?"

"Never you mind."

"Then I'm not leaving."

"You'll leave right now and go back—"

"If I do, I'm going to the office to tell them you left."

I had her exasperated. She moaned her grief. "Better let him come," Sam said. "He's not going back to school and we don't have much time."

He bribed me with an ice cream at Rukab's. The thing was, I wasn't sure I wanted to go, having no idea where it was I was going. But the battle having been won, I wasn't letting go of the victory. We followed Sam to his car, a 1960 Volvo Amazon, parked behind the coffee shop, and headed south along highway 60. Sam lit up a cigarette, forcing Sue and I to roll down our windows. Sam laughed. "Better desert dirt than my smoke, yes?" he said.

It was exciting driving someplace new, though all around me was unspectacular. There was only our highway with narrow left and right spurs that rolled into the valleys. The landscape was browns and tans, mostly. Even the greens were faded, as if soaked in hot water and bleach. As we drove into a valley covered with stone terraces, I saw a large city rising ahead. Knowing Sue, it had to be Jerusalem.

"It will be fine for you to speak with Amineh about our talk," Sam said to Sue. "I told her I discussed it with you."

"I don't know that I will," Sue said. "It's not my issue."

"It's so funny to me for Khaal Abu Faid to be shameful of Adli," Sam said. "That's because it may be from his lineage that Adli is so deficient."

"You're related to him, too" Sue said.

"Yes, but I can tell you I have no such deficiencies. You know, your uncle would not approve of these trips of yours to Jerusalem."

"Yes, he's shown me that."

"But I do. I believe you should learn all you can about this place, and take back to Chi-car-go new ideas and new beliefs about us. If you are not allowed to do these things, you will spread falsehoods about Palestinians, that we are not tolerant."

"Can you put out the cigarette?" she said.

"I do this when I drive. Smoke. It helps me enjoy the feeling of freedom."

"I'm getting nauseous."

"Ah, a new word for me."

"Sick. I'm going to throw up."

Sam obliged. "Things will change," he said. "The way America and the world sees us will change. Nothing stays as it is. It happens always. It's why there is history. Look after the World War. Your enemies of Germany, Japan, and Italy are now your allies, yes? You are trading partners; America has military there, and ambassadors. There are treaties for business cooperation and to fight with each other. Soon it will be so in Korea. And in Southeast Asia when the fighting is done there. To deal with Palestine believing it always will be a state of Jordan is stupidity. To deal with Israel as if it will always have a hold on this land is also stupidity."

"I don't know about all that," Sue said.

"Yes, many Americans do not. Not knowing about things outside your country is dangerous."

"That's why we elect people, to do that for us."

"That is also dangerous."

Sue's interest in Jerusalem had nothing to do with politics. For Sam to speak to her in such terms, he may as well be speaking Arabic to me. Whether her interests transcended his or not was a matter of interpretation. She was as true to her passions as he was to his. Both looking at the same vista, both saw different things. Both had their own analysis of the city and what it stood for.

"Last time, Sue, we came to *Bab al-Nasr,* the Gate of Victory. I thought you and Joe would like to see *Bab Mihrab Daud,* the Gate of the Prayer. We also call it *Bab el-Khalil,* Gate of the Friend."

I couldn't see any gate. All I saw were gigantic sand-colored stones that matched the desert we drove through. The tops of the walls had the cut-outs I saw on the plastic forts in the Sears catalog, where archers would kneel to shoot arrows down on invading armies. It was exciting to think that right here where we sat in our car a force of racing chariots may have been slaughtered from the tops of these very walls. "I don't see any gate," I said.

"It's tucked into the wall over there; it's a hidden gate made that way by Suleiman the Magnificent to slow invaders."

This was just getting too cool.

"I understand naming the gates in different languages," Sue said, "but why so many names in the same language?"

"In Palestine, because our history means many things to us, it's useful to use many names so that the importance will not be lost. The west will know it as Jaffa Gate for the road leading down to the city. It is called *Gate of the Friend,* for Abraham. Because he is buried in Hebron, so it is also called the Hebron Gate. *The Gate of the Prayer* is for King David who Islam sees as a great prophet and a great king, nearly as great as Suleiman the Magnificent."

"Makes it confusing," I said.

"Not if you are willing to learn, Joe."

Sam couldn't take us back to Ramallah, having things to do in the city in the afternoon. He gave us a tour that Sue found fascinating and I found tiresome. The stories of sieges were exciting, but after listening to centuries of change made by men with unpronounceable names in dates with only three numbers, I lost interest. Sue's questions never stopped, and unless Sam was improvising, he was a very learned man.

I'm glad I came to see Sue so animated. She hadn't been in weeks. And I caught Sam and her exchanging glances and occasionally touching hands. He brought us to the bus terminal where the bus would take us back to Ramallah before school ended. As we got out of the car he said, "I need to tell you, Khaal Abu Faid is taking you both out of The Friend's School at the end of Ramadan."

It was the most devastating thing to happen to Sue and me since we arrived. "Do you know why?" Sue asked.

"I do. It is too expensive and he is having to use some of his own money. This I learned from my father."

"So we don't go to school?" I said, not necessarily a bad thing for me.

"You'll go the village school in Dayr Ghasana."

"Is it a good school?" Sue asked.

Sam lowered his head. "No, it will not be good for you."

Sue sat miserable on the bus. I didn't comprehend Sam's ominous warning about the new school like she did. We sat beside each other in the front seat not saying a word. Our first stop was Beit Hanina in East Jerusalem. No one got off except the driver; it didn't look like many people got on or got off there.

The driver went inside the terminal and kept us waiting. A young man hopped on. He had long hair and a shaggy mustache. His jeans were loose and greasy and had a tear in the knee. But I knew he wasn't a bum. His face had the same impassioned expression as Sam's. A European college student, maybe, or even an American one, like I saw at Northwestern. He smiled at me and Sue, who didn't notice, her head being down most of the ride. "Aina almataar?" he said to us.

I nudged Sue and the man repeated himself.

"Ahh … Ana mish fahma," she said.

"What does he want?" I asked.

"I don't know."

"Nemal HaTe'ūfa?" he said.

Sue gave him a tight-lipped smile and shrugged her shoulders. He sat beside her and rested his hand on her shoulder. "Ilaa ayna tazhab?" he asked.

"I don't know," Sue said. "I am an American visitor."

"Ahhh, American." He leaned in close to her. "New York City."

"No, Chicago."

He shrugged. "I go to Montreal. In Canada, from Lod. Law samaht, ayna ajedo al matar? "

"What's he saying now?"

"I don't know," she said. "Something about an airport."

The boy was quite animated and getting louder knowing she was American. Sue was getting embarrassed by the attention she was drawing. I could tell she was hoping he'd leave but he began peppering her with what I assumed were places in Canada he wanted to see, and the names of rock and roll bands, and songs. He proudly bastardized a few lines from the Rolling Stones, *I Can't Get No Satisfaction*. Sue nodded and grinned uncomfortably.

I had seen the driver exit the terminal just as the kid hopped on the bus. I didn't see him again until he led two other men on board. In a rush they grabbed the kid by his arms and tore him from the seat, knocking Sue to the floor. The driver picked her up, but rather than seat her, he led her off the bus behind the terrified boy.

"Shoo malak?" Sue said. *What's wrong?*

I watched from the seat, too stunned to respond in any other manner. The kid was struggling for all he was worth to free himself, pulling and kicking. He was thin but wiry, giving the men all they could handle. At one point he broke free and would have made his escape had he not tripped over Sue and the bus driver. When the men recovered him, they were making sure there would be no more close calls.

I was focused on Sue who was, herself, trying to pull free. I had collected myself enough to jump into action when I heard the splat of a large pumpkin on cement. Only it wasn't a pumpkin.

Sue stopped her struggling long enough to respond to the sickening sights and sounds with the rest of us on the bus. Even the driver pulled back in horror. The kid was now face down on the street, a pool of blood spreading rapidly around his head. There were now four men over him, knees flexed, steel pipes raised above their heads, a barbershop quartet of vengeance, ready to strike again if the need existed. There was no need.

CHAPTER 16

We sat in the police station where they tried to talk to us. We didn't understand enough to respond. Even if we did, both of us were still too shocked to give any rationale answers. The police didn't try very hard to soothe us. Finally, an older man came in to speak with us. He had the look of a Bedouin, wrinkled and leathery like the ass-end of a hippo. Sue was still shaking uncontrollably but when he reached and took hold of her hand, she stopped immediately.

He introduced himself slowly, in fine English, as Kareem Saeed ibn Beni-Hasan. "Kareem ," he said, "is fine for you. It's all right. They sent for me to speak to you. You are Americans?"

Sue nodded.

"I see. You don't know what this is about, do you?"

"No," she said. "How is that boy?"

"I don't know. I came into town only now when they called for me."

"Sure. There is no one else here who can speak English? No one else here who can tell us why that had to happen? They had to wait for you while we sat here and got interrogated?"

Even now I cringe when I think of Sue's tone and attitude. We were in no position to create a stir. Even back in Dayr Ghasana when Adbel smacked her, she stood there stoically without a word in her defense. She picked a helluva time to become a child of the sixties.

I saw Kareem as a fine, decent man. But he could have been as my sister believed, a plant by the police to get us to say things they could use against us. He nodded in understanding of her anger and her lack of deference. "What you did was talk to a boy who was not your relation. The charge is that the conversation was of a sexual nature."

"That's crazy," she said.

"And you know this because?"

Sue looked stunned. The fact was, she didn't know what he had said to her. "Because why would he?" She protested. "Why would *I*? I never saw him before."

"I know," he said.

"Why would they suspect that then?"

Kareem shrugged. "It's hard to know."

"And you mean to tell me, you really don't know any more than this? Sue asked, slightly less accusatory but highly agitated now knowing the charges levied against her.

"I went to college in Boston a long time back," he said. "Then I became a visiting professor at George Washington University. I was arrested for participating in the Bonus Army March on Washington. Have you been taught that in American History?"

Sue shook her head.

"Strange. It was a big deal at the time. Anyway, for that I was deported. For my protest I was deemed an undesirable back there *and* here. I use the education I received in foreign relations to teach English to Palestinians. For that reason, and that reason only, I was asked to be here."

"Is what they think happened serious? I mean, will I get into trouble?"

I knew the answer, having heard the story from Sam. With Sam, others had seen him and the girl trading glances. Gossip soon took over. The bus driver must have seen the boy smiling at Sue, and touch her shoulder. That was all it took. Of all this I kept my mouth shut, hoping Kareem would discard Sam's story as urban legend. "It's possible," he said. "Such acts are haraam. Forbidden. 'If he had stabbed you in the head with a piece of iron, it would be better for him than touching a woman whom it is not permissible for him to touch.' So proclaims the prophet Muhammad, peace be upon him."

"I didn't touch him," Sue protested.

"Did he touch you?"

"No."

"Yes he did," I said.

Kareem asked me where and how. "On the shoulder, like this." I demonstrated on Sue.

"For how long a time?"

"I don't know. That's when they came and took him off the bus."

He asked Sue to explain exactly what happened. She gave him an abbreviated version, not mentioning the kid's planned trip to Montreal or his rendition of the Stones. And ignoring my version, she neglected to add the touching episode. "And who is your relation I can contact here for you?" he asked. Sue began sobbing.

"You can't call anyone," I said.

"Yes, I see. But you know, someone must come and speak for you or they won't let you go." He waited until Sue composed herself. "We have come as far from Sharia Law as America has come from the Common Laws of England. What happened to you did not come from the police. I can explain that you speak little Arabic and did not know what the boy was saying, but that is all I can do for you. Trust it, though. Regardless of what you may have heard, there are laws of justice here that are upheld."

He left us alone in the room. We never saw him again. The police brought us manakeesh and the two grape Nehis I asked for. They were polite, or so it seemed, but offered us no information about when or if we were leaving. It took nearly two hours before we were released to Abdel.

We all three sat while listening to the police commander who sounded to be lecturing us. Abdel nodded and ground his teeth while Sue and I sat there too exhausted to care anymore. As we were leaving, the commander, a tall, creepy looking man with a thick mustache, bushy eyebrows, and hairy nose and ears, bent down over Sue and said in perfect English. "You should know better."

"But I didn't do anything," she barked. "And I don't know what he said."

"So you say."

"What happened to him?"

"You don't know him?"

"No. I don't know him."

"Then why should you care?"

"I don't need to know him to care."

The two were eye-to-eye, him staring down hard; her staring up with equal resolve. Again, her attitude scared me, but I was in awe in light of the odds against her.

"So perhaps you do know him," the commander said.

Sue felt herself being led into a trap and kept silent. Abdel had no idea what was being said, but he didn't like the tone of the conversation. His eyes darted between the two speakers, his teeth still grinding. The teeth grinding more at Sue than the commander.

"You should just worry about yourself," the commander said as he stood. "If you are to stay here, you must learn our ways."

I now understood the role Kareem played. I liked him. I wanted to trust him. I *needed* to trust him. He was a more with-it Siidi. I felt a great comfort with him there; his English, his pleasant smile, his apparent benevolence. Had he talked to me alone I would have filled him on the voids in Sue's story. But Sue challenged him at the outset, challenging his motives.

She was right, and I had nearly blown it. The line recited from the Koran went over my head. With the commander's appearance I now saw it as the good cop, bad cop routine. I don't whether we escaped a prison sentence, a public stoning, or just a stern lecture, but I was thankful for Sue's fortitude in the face of what she knew to be an injustice. And I'm sure those actions and words from a woman so young flummoxed the men in charge.

Abdel was not as impressed as I was. He ranted all the way home. Not understanding a word did nothing to diminish their impact. As usual, Sue ignored him, which as usual, infuriated him more. Finally she looked up. "I thought you left?" she said deadpan.

He looked at her quizzically, trying to read her for the meaning. "Eskoot," he said in disgust. *Shut-up*.

Sue ran from the car as soon as we got home. The car shook, Abdel slammed the door so hard. I wandered in behind them. I was content to stay in the kitchen where Yamma was preparing jameed for the lamb dish called mansaf. She didn't want to know, and I didn't want to talk about it.

Johara came in asking why we weren't on the bus. I stuttered out some excuse when we heard a crack, like a whip snapping against the air. It was followed by three more in quick succession, then by Sue screeching a rare, but all-American, "fuck you."

We all ran into her back bedroom, Yamma in the lead, having bulled her way through us. Sue was backed into a corner. Faid was sitting on her bed. Abdel, the source of the cracking whip, was at arm's length from her, his thick leather belt at the ready to snap again. There was a red welt on the left side of Sue's face. Blood was beading on her right forearm from a defensive blow. But she didn't crouch or cower. Her arms were dropped daringly at her side even as Abdel raised the belt.

Yamma charged into the room, bounding clumsily, but with determination. She screamed, "Batal, batal." *Stop, stop,* as she charged. Abdel paid her no attention, though he should have.

He stepped in to strike Sue once again. Yamma collided with him like we did when playing football, with none of the finesse but all the brute force she could muster. He was sent hard against the wall, Yamma holding onto the belt. She held it long and tight enough to allow Abdel to whip her around him. The small of her back landed on the closet doorknob and she went down in a lumpy pile.

"Bitch," he called her. "You are not to become involved with this."

Through her pain she told him. "You left this house and family; you have no rights here. You are the one who will not become involved. You are like a dog to us and are to be treated as one."

That set Abdel off once again. He approached Yamma with the intent of striking her with his foot but with so many witnesses, he withdrew his leg. "Shlok'keh," he called her as he bolted from the room. *Slut.*

In the midst of this action, I watched Sue run from the room and out the back door. She went quickly through the field towards the ridge. Yamma tried to stand. She grabbed at the bed covers that let go under her weight. Faid was still on the side of the bed. He hadn't moved except to dodge Yamma's initial assault on his father. Now Yamma reached for his leg to anchor herself in an attempt to rise. Abruptly, he pulled his leg from her grasp and stood while Yamma tumbled back to the floor.

Of all the appalling sights I witnessed during my three years in Palestine, that's the one I cannot shake. If there were great changes forthcoming, as Sam had predicted, they wouldn't be starting with Faid for in that moment of rejection, he made his alliance not only with his father, but with centuries of dreadful tradition. While he was witness to the same familial tragedies that we were, and had watched as Yamma dedicated herself to her home and her children without a thought of self, he chose the easy path, the one laid out for him generations ago. It was a choice that was not only absurd, but one which would doom the family and me.

Johara and I struggled with Yamma. She was hurt enough to see a doctor, perhaps for a stay in the hospital, but there was no money for that. And by now the word had made it across to the village that Abdel had accused her of adultery. No doubt Abdel would now be telling them he had been attacked without provocation by his jealous whore of a wife. There would be no sympathy for her out there today.

I went to kitchen to get some uncooked lamb, dates, and flatbread to bring down to the cave where I knew Sue would be. I wrapped it all in a towel. I was halfway across the field when Adli called out to me, "Where you going, Joe?"

"The cave," I said, knowing it insured he wouldn't follow.

"La, la, la, Joe, you do not go down there."

I kept walking.

"It's not safe for you. I know. I know these things, Joe."

I could feel him staring as I marched madly away.

"Okay for you Joe, I will pray to Allah for you that you will be safe. Insh' allah, nothing will happen to you. You will be fine there, okay, Joe?"

I waved him good-bye without turning around. I'm glad he was staying back to pray to Allah for me. I saw his prayers as just more superstition that would keep him away, like the witches, jinns, and ghoulies.

Sue was sitting on a stone at the mouth of the cave. Her face was serene, with the pensive look of one overlooking a red river in a green valley, not at all the look of one just having witnessed a merciless beating only to be beaten herself in return.

I set the blanket beside her like an offering. She didn't seem to notice the blanket or me. To start small talk, I picked on Adli. "He told me it was bad to come to the cave," I said from behind her. "What a chicken. He's praying to Allah to keep me safe. I knew for sure he wouldn't come, just by telling him this was where I was going. Abdel left, you know."

"You know people have lived in caves for centuries," she said. "Not just Neanderthals. Whole societies and cultures."

"Yeah, it's cool," I said.

"There's a cave in China with over a hundred rooms. And the Anasazi tribe in Colorado lived in a one with a hundred and fifty rooms.

Italy has one people lived in until just about ten years ago when the government kicked them out."

"How come?"

"They said it wasn't civilized. Bet people lived in this one a long time ago."

"It's small."

"Not really. Can only be in one spot at a time, Joe."

I enjoyed the topic and the thought that I could possibly be sleeping in an ancient bedroom, but Sue was speaking as if in a trance. I wouldn't have been surprised, though very freaked out, to hear her tell me it was her cave back a thousand years ago. "You like being in the cave, Sue?"

She turned to me. "Yes, Joe. I like it a lot. It's a good place for me to be right now. I'm glad you showed it to me."

"Are you afraid of the witches?"

"I'm not afraid of anything anymore."

CHAPTER 17

I have no idea what happen to the boy who was bludgeoned on the street that day. If it was big news, no one told us. And who were we to ask? After so many years I became as nonchalant about it as the authorities were at the time. We never even found out his name.

It wasn't that we didn't care. Sue cared so much she dared to question them on it. I believe Sue saw herself in his situation. Here was a young man on his own adventure to what? Meet others? Teach? Learn? Discover himself? He makes a wrong turn at a wrong time in a wrong place. I think Sue was finding herself in that same wrong place. The thing is, I no longer claim to know who was right.

I'm not defending what was done that day, just that I see it now for what it was. As Americans, we know better, we have one moral compass to guide us. We're humane, and understanding, and just, and the fact of life is, so were those goons and those police. It was a piece to their puzzle they were putting together. It wasn't right or wrong, it was simply the picture they had before them. And it's not about me choosing sides. Basketball has sides. Soccer has sides. A house has sides. A side implies there are rules to adhere to, or a structure you can measure and touch.

***

The blankets I stashed at the cave were now soaked and mildewed. The fire helped warm us until it started to rain. I told Sue Abdel had been run from the house by Yamma, that I was sure he wouldn't be there to hurt her. She said she knew. "I feel dirty, Joe, do I look dirty?"

It was dark; I couldn't tell. "No, you're not dirty. We can go back to the house now."

"No," she said. "I don't want to. Joe, I'm dirty, can you get me a pot of water so I can clean myself."

"You're not dirty."

"And thirsty. Get me some water in a bucket and then you go back to the house to sleep."

I wasn't sleeping at the house without her. I wouldn't leave her alone. We were all we had. The incident on the bus was our bonding moment, cemented by Abdel disowning Adli and abandoning us and the family. What we had heard and seen was unthinkable to us up to that moment in our lives. It was as hurtful as it was shameful, and while I was focused on the hurt, it was the shame that was affecting Sue.

"I'll get water," I said, "but I'm not leaving you here to sleep alone."

"Yamma will need you."

"She has Johara and the others. You have nobody."

I was able to get to the big Lister bag hung in the tree by the outhouse. It was used for hand washing, the occasional sponge bath, and drinking. It had a taste of mildew, like you'd expect of water from a canvas bag. But Sue wanted it to clean up. If she was thirsty enough, she wouldn't mind the canvas aftertaste.

I had to empty half of it to get out of the tree and another third so I could drag it behind me. It was a struggle of love to get it through the field, over the rocks, down the trail to the cave. I learned to respect the hell out of canvas that day, the invincible fabric, and often swore if my kids came home with tears in their pants I would make their clothes out of the stuff.

I had Sue help me lift it onto a nearby tree branch. She picked a tree near a stone whose branch wasn't as thick as the one I had chosen. "I want to be able to sit down while I wash up," she said. I didn't object. I was sure it would be just for the night.

"You go back up there now," she said, directly.

"I'm not leaving."

"That was the deal."

"What was? That I do what you want and then I do what your say. Not much of a deal for me," I said.

"Joe, you know how you said you love coming down here to be alone?"

"Yeah."

"Well, I know this is your place, but I'd like to have a place like that. A place where I can be by myself."

"Like here?"

"Yeah, Joe, a place like here."

It was a hard position to attack since I was gave her the ammunition. "You gonna be fine?" I said.

"Insh' allah."

I worried about Sue. It was very cold as the sun set on the ridge. With all the talk and dragging I hadn't notice until I was walking back to the house. Perhaps I was having premonitions. Perhaps it was just getting colder. She had damp blankets. It was still drizzling. I wasn't sure she even knew how to build a fire. I was making excuses to go back to her.

There was edgy talk going on in the living room when I arrived. It was Johara, Adli, and Gamal talking non-stop and with great passion to Sam who nodded patiently at each of them. His back was to me. He turned when Gamal screamed at me, "Shem et Duat Miboon," *Go to hell, faggot.* Adli laughed.

"Joe, where have you been all this time of excitement?" Sam asked.

"Out."

He patted the seat next to him. "Sit."

I did.

"Amineh is sleeping well," he said. "I have a friend who will come tomorrow to check her." He said to the others. "For no money, he will come to check her. She did a pretty amazing thing, yes?" He said, redirecting to me.

"I guess."

He laughed. "You guess, Joe? It was amazing what she did. There are sides of her you'll never know because there are sides of her she'll never know. And if she did, she would never tell a soul. Where is Sue?"

I looked around the room as if searching for a lost marble. "I'm not sure."

"Ah-huh. Do you know that large mural painted on the wall in the lobby at the The Friends School?"

I did. You couldn't miss it. It was a twenty foot long, floor to ceiling, mural in the administrative building at the Ramallah campus where Sue and the older kids attended school.

"Amineh painted it," he said.

"Yamma did? When?" I looked at the others who seemed to already know or not care.

"When she was a student there. It is considered too good to paint over. It is the view at the place we slept outside with El Hajj."

"The river in the painting isn't red."

"The entire scene is different from what you or I see. It was the way she saw it. It's what makes it hers. See, she is more than you think she is. This is why in the end it will be a good thing that Khaal Abu Faid has left."

He was speaking to me in partial English. The partial Arabic were things he wanted the others to hear. Johara spoke out in protest. "She is now useless in her own home. She will be run from the village. She will have to go to her father's house to live, and take us with her."

Her family lived in Beit Jala, a predominantly Christian town on the west side of Bethlehem, across the Hebron Road. There were Muslims, a small minority. Her father was a stone mason who now drove a cab because his hands became too arthritic. From Yamma's accounts it wasn't a bad place to be, but I knew where Johara was coming from. It wasn't home.

"You let Amineh do what she must," Sam said. "If you don't, you are no better than your father. She will take care of you as she has always done."

"Faid will take care of us," Gamal piped in.

"Faid will take care of us," Adli parroted.

I caught Johara glancing at Sam with a discouraged look. Sam, ever the optimist said, "We will all take care of each other."

"Who is this 'we,'" Johara wanted to know. "You will be going to the University. What time will you have for us?"

Sam was to attend Birzeit University, five miles north of Ramallah, majoring in journalism. It wasn't much further away than he was now but his free time would be limited. He was forever talking about the power of journalism, how a strong voice on paper can reach thousands, millions, and move them to action. It was from him I first heard the name Thomas Paine and of his noble piece, *Common Sense*. Sam spoke critically to us of Benjamin Franklin, a man I only knew for flying kites and wearing knickers. "A man of his influence," he said, "was shameful for wasting his skills writing a magazine of silly sayings, puzzles, and weather forecasts.

Sam stood to hug Johara. "Always I'll have time," he said.

"Well, we don't need your time," Gamal said.

"We don't need your time," Adli added.

"Don't you think Sue will be cold at the cave?" Sam said.

"I'm taking her a blanket," I said.

"Let me do it."

"No, it's okay."

"I'd like you to stay here, Joe. I'd like to see Sue alone." His voice took on an authoritarian tone that had me both worried and compliant.

I was afraid to see Yamma. Afraid to see her in her bed, and in pain. I wasn't prepared to witness her this way. It gave me a disconcerting feeling just to see her sitting down to rest. So I sat in the kitchen as the night came on. It was depressingly dark and still. Though the rain had stopped, the clouds took their time moving on. The final sounds of the goats and chickens faded away. Amir barked his annoyance at not being released to patrol the grounds.

Gamal came in looking for food. The kitchen was as Yamma had left it, chunks of jameed, dates, olives, and hummus left on the counter. And the two slices of lamb I had left behind. Gamal mumbled his annoyance as he took half a pan of Knafeh from the refrigerator. He dug a few spoonfuls out with a wooden ladle and ate them where he stood. He ignored me up to that point, an attitude I hoped would continue.

"Jabaan," he said, turning on me from the counter. "You are a coward. You are Yamma's favorite, but you couldn't even protect her."

"I am not a coward," I protested. "Your father did this, and Faid sat and watched." Although I didn't respect Abdel or Faid, I was not in the habit yet of insulting people, especially adults, but Gamal had been riding me hard. If he was going to lay blame, he could at least put it on the right people.

"You couldn't even protect your sister," he said. "I would have; I would have tried. I wouldn't have been a coward."

I had been working on a relationship with Adli, especially after finding him to be slow. But I long ago gave up on having one with Gamal. I envied him on many levels. He was the most athletic boy I had ever watched. I marveled at his abilities with a soccer ball, running, climbing a tree, throwing rocks, wrestling. He was easily the best amongst the boys in his class. Like all kids that age who were, he knew it and used it to his advantage. And the worst thing you could do with a kid like that was to let him know you thought so.

I developed contempt for him that was well founded. It was my first fit of lingering hate for another human being. He was a leader in that others followed him, not only Adli. He was a leader in the way Abdel was. He was loud. He was obnoxious. He was arrogant. He was pushy. With so few friends around I was forced to sit and watch things happen around me.

I noticed that it was not Faid, the oldest and most obvious, who took after the father. It was Gamal, the youngest. In many ways Faid was more like Adli. He was quiet, chillingly so. And detached. He was a brooder. He sat by himself on the bus. I saw him come and go from the house alone.

Sam, with his swagger and easy smile, with his challenging attitude and respectful disrespect, with his empathy and compassion, was a man I would follow. His qualities were so obvious it was difficult for me at that age to understand why Gamal and Faid were not learning from him. Now I see the reason as very simple. It is the reason most men of authority don't emulate good leadership. They simply can't.

"Said bousak," I said. *Shut your mouth.*

He grinned wickedly as he approached, the way boys do when they are ready to kick your ass and know they can do it. I stood to accept his challenge. There are stories your parents and after-school specials tell you about the bullied boy who stands his ground, to be rewarded when the bully, so overwhelmed by this act of bravery and in an act of unnatural maturity, nods an honorable truce. In the universe I lived in, that doesn't happen. The beatings continue until the bully becomes bored or someone moves. I knew I had one choice, to pound him as soon as he was within reach.

He came in cocky, as in everything he did. He was expecting me to accept whatever pounding he was to give. I balled the fist at my side while discreetly readying my feet. I picked out a point on his left jaw where I was to land my haymaker. But that opportunity never came.

CHAPTER 18

I don't remember taking the step into Gamal, but when Sam's violent entry into the back door interrupted us, he and I were chest-to-chest. Sam was carrying a sleeping Sue in his arms. I thought she was sleeping until I saw her arms flopped as if made of soggy bread. Then the streaming blood that landed with sickening plops on the floor. Sam stood before us, breathing hard, unable to speak, seemingly without a clue as to what to do with her. He then turned sharply and kicked Sue's bedroom door open. Johara came racing from Yamma's room. "Johara, call for a doctor."

"I don't know any."

"Find one. Quickly. Call the hospital if you must. Gamal, boil water. Very, very hot, in a very clean pot. Joe, cut up a cushion into small squares. Just the cushion, no upholstery. And tape; we need tape."

There were too many instructions coming at machine gun speed to just ignore and insert a demand for an explanation, so none of us did. We all scattered while Sam disappeared into the bedroom. I grabbed a knife from the kitchen and a cushion from the parlor. Yamma was calling from her bedroom. "Shuu fii?" *What's wrong?* I heard her struggling to get out of bed. Johara screaming into her, "Nothing's wrong, Yamma, back into bed." Yamma begging us all to help her so she can help us. And a deathly silence from Sue's bedroom.

Adli came running in to tell me, "She's dead. I saw her, she's dead."

I stopped ripping at the cushion long enough to stare a hole through him. "She is not or we wouldn't be doing all this."

"Her hands are all blood and she's not awake."

I was unnerved but trusted in Sam. I heard Johara on the phone to whom I prayed was the doctor. I hurried with my task and ran the cushions into the bedroom. Sam met me at the door to take them greedily from my hands. He was sweating hard and had not yet caught his breath. I was sure Adli was wrong, that Sue was not dead, but she was in bad shape. That much I gathered from the usually cool and calm Sam.

I followed him inside, noting the trail of blood on the floor. Sue's arms, waist, and thighs were soaked with it, as was the bed. It was impossible for me to tell where the wound was, but it didn't appear to be her head. Her face was gray and anything but peaceful. "What happened to her?"

Sam didn't answer as he unwrapped strips of cloth from her arms. "Where's the water? Get Gamal. Get me water. Hot water. Now."

I ran back to the kitchen where Gamal had dutifully filled a bucket. He was struggling to haul it across the kitchen. Adli helped by shuffling beside his brother, his hands cupped uselessly underneath. "We have to hurry," I said.

"I know; I am," Gamal muttered under the weight of the load.

Sam met us again and grabbed the bucket with one hand. We soaked each piece of cushion and applied them to Sue's wrist, strapping them down tightly with strips he made from Sue's sheets. As the blood washed away, I saw wide, jagged gashes. Sliced wrists were not part of my world. The concept of attacking oneself was inconceivable to me, and so my obvious conclusion was a wild animal, or worse, ghoulies.

"Was she attacked by dogs?" I asked.

"No."

"What then?"

"She wasn't attacked by anything."

"Something happened."

"Later, Joe."

"She cut her wrist, with a big, old knife, I bet," Adli said.

I gaped at him, horrified, then back to Sam. "Where's the doctor?" he said, much more relaxed for my benefit, I'm sure.

I was hoping more than ever Adli was playing the fool. "Why would she do that?" I asked, wanting there to be a sensible explanation to this mad scene before me.

"I saw a man with his throat cut," Adli said. "In the village. He wasn't dead; just making funny sounds. He died later, though."

He wasn't trying to be tactless and cruel. He had no idea that he was. He wanted to be part of this. He cut no cushions, gathered no water, notified no doctors. So he was telling me a story we could share.

Johara came to announce she had summoned a doctor. Yamma was behind her. She was doubled over in obvious pain, making it just so far to collapse on edge of Sue's bed in grief and horror. She held tight to both of Sue's wrists, adding pressure to the makeshift bandages as she prayed.

"La hawla wala quwata illah billah." *There is no strength or power except for Allah's.* "Asta Ghfir ullah, Asta Ghfir ullah, Asta Ghfir ullah." *I ask for Allah's forgiveness.*

At the time I couldn't understand the prayers that moved Yamma deeply as she rocked gently over Sue. Later Sam explained for me. "Amineh forever blamed herself for that night, for what happened to Sue," he said. "She prayed for Allah's forgiveness many times each day." I never asked him why she thought that, for at the time he told me, I was immersed in guilt trips of my own.

We were banished to other rooms when the doctor arrived. Johara sat with Yamma in her bedroom. Gamal went to his bedroom. Of course, Abdel was not at home, probably in Ramallah. And I had no clue where Faid was wasting his time. I chose the kitchen, having new found doubts about the safety of the cave. Adli was intent on keeping me company. "I told you not to go to the cave, Joe. Bad things happen at the cave."

"How do you know? You never go to the cave."

"I hear things."

I was irritated and scared. The two people I had come to rely on were lying in bed, their bodies more debilitated than my spirit. "You hear stupid things because you are …." I wish now I could say I regrouped into my right mind before I blurted it out. I wished I had the sense to anticipate how badly it would hurt him. The truth is, maybe I knew exactly how badly it would. "Stupid." And I said it with such conviction there would never be the chance of taking it back.

Adli had heard it before, for years, from his friends, from his family, though I was sure never from Yamma, and I'm sure he never expected to hear it from me. He looked about to cry. That's when I let him have it. "You do no thinking for yourself. You do no talking for yourself. Everything you say comes from Gamal, and his things are stupid, too."

He slid off his chair like a worm being washed down with a hose. "I would," he said, "if people let me."

I felt no remorse. It was that haymaker to Gamals's face I didn't get to throw. It was peaceful with him out of the room. Soon, though, I was suffocating. My emotions hung like a wet, wool blanket. There was nowhere to go, and no one to go to. I was angry at them all. At my parents for this ill-conceived adventure that was having none of the positive effect they promised; at Siidi for being old and tired and sick, and incapable of staying with us a day past his memories; at Abdel for his greed and ego, and raising kids who were no better; at Yamma for trying too hard and failing in the end, and at Sue for leaving me to write the ending.

I fell asleep at the table, awakened by the doctor in the hallway talking to Sam. I saw Sam point to Yamma's door. The doctor nodded, knocked, and entered at Johara's greeting.

"She okay?" I asked.

"Insha' Allah, she will be okay. On the outside, she will be okay."

"Is Adli right? Did she cut her wrists?" I asked.

"Yes. Only her veins, not her artery, which would have been much worse."

"She wanted to?"

"I would have to say, yes, Joe. Though do not ask me why."

I didn't know what that meant. Whether he didn't know, or didn't want to say. We were both exhausted and he looked to be as lost and confused as I was. For someone who had so many answers, and spoke them so elegantly, I now saw him as just a young boy, much like my brother, David, who couldn't answer the big ones, the ones that counted, and went mute when the world didn't cooperate.

"Was she in the cave?" I asked, recalling how she made mention of herself living in one.

"She was outside. From my distance she looked to be asleep. I thought, how strange she would fall asleep sitting upright on a rock. Then I saw she was propped up with her hands in a canvas bag filled with water."

"Why was she sitting like that?" I asked.

"Now, Joe, you really don't need to know these things."

"I need to know."

"Warm water makes the veins swell so the blood will flow better,"

I was in horror to know she had pulled me unwittingly into her plan. I had not only provided her water, I had done so in a canvas Lister bag, designed to keep water warm by absorbing the sun's rays.

"Do you have a sister, Sam?" I asked, not to break the tension, but because I wanted to know.

"An older sister."

"Does she live here?"

"No. With her husband in Tehran."

"Do you get to see her?"

His face twisted. "No, Joe, we do not see her."

"Why?"

"Why do you ask these questions?"

"Because I almost didn't get to see my sister again. I wouldn't have liked that."

"I suppose not. And I suppose you think I would not, but truly, she made a most unfortunate decision to leave with a man not of our faith."

"He isn't Muslim?"

"He is, but Shia."

"Oh." It was a word I hadn't heard before. I tried to place it amongst the many insults hurled at me from my cousins and their friends. "That bad?" I asked.

His concrete expression broke. "Joe, I know that when I was your age, I believed that the grown-ups who told me I was too young to understand were wrong. But the truth is they weren't always wrong. You are like me. If I tell you the reason, you will say it's crazy. And I will tell you there is a deep history. You'll say that it's in the past. I will tell you some pasts cannot be let go. You'll say we should let go of all pasts that hurt. And so it will go on. But I will tell you, her decision was not a good one and so we cannot see her, and that Joe, is that."

The doctor came out of Yamma's room. He pulled Sam to the corner where they had a quick conversation.

"Well, Amineh will be in bed for a time," Sam said. "She is badly bruised in the ... how do you say this thing?" He reached around to touch my back.

"Spine?"

He nodded. "So all will be okay, yes?"

No. Nothing would be okay. Not here, not anywhere. Not for me.

***

The worse times of my life in Chicago were Sunday mornings in winter. I tried to sleep in as long as the others, but it seemed I was the first one awake no matter how long I delayed it. You'd think I'd love having the run of the place. Most young boys would. But dark sky, gray smoke from the B and G factory, bare trees, crusted mud, frosted windows, chilled floors, sights, sounds, and smells of cold and death kept me cuddled under my blanket beside the radiator in the corner of the kitchen. I was in fear of its inescapability, of being trapped forever in desolation. It was usually for no more than thirty minutes, but it seemed to me like weeks.

At the first signs of movement from anyone, I would rush to watch them shuffle into the bathroom. If they went into the toilet, I'd slump against the wall outside to wait. I'd stand behind them in the mirror to watch them brush their teeth or hair. I'd wait outside their room while they got dressed. Anything to avoid another cold, winter moment alone.

That was how the next days felt, every moment a Sunday morning in winter. The bedroom window sill was my kitchen radiator, but there was no movement in this house to make me run from it. I'd sit in contempt while the boys busied themselves in the room behind me. There were comments made that now I could translate. I didn't give a damn what they were. I had no passion to respond. I'd sit and watch them walk to the bus stop and drive off. Only then did I get up.

I didn't go to school that week. I could no easier bear the long days away than I could the long days at home. No one tried to make me do otherwise. Johara stayed home too, to take care of Yamma. She made note of my truancy once or twice, but she was in no position to direct me to do anything as I had pinned the blame for Sue's suicide attempt firmly upon her.

Sue slept a lot. I sat with her in the room most of the day and night, leaving only to get my dinner and go to bed. Johara came in often to check on us. She asked if I needed anything. I never said yes.

"I called your parents and told them what happened to Sue," she told me. "I wasn't sure if anyone had."

"What did you tell them?"

"The truth."

"That because of you she tried to kill herself?"

"I had nothing at all to do with that," she said.

"You told Abdel about the things she bought in Jerusalem."

By not denying it straight off, she made her admission. Then she offered her mitigation. "I had to. He made me."

"She was always nice to you. She told you all about America, whenever you wanted to talk about it. She bought you all those things, and snuck them in for you."

"She was very good to me. I didn't want to get her into trouble."

"But you did."

"My father found the posters."

"So?"

"He made me tell him where I got them."

"He knew; where else could you have gotten them? You didn't have tell about those things Sue had."

"You don't understand, Joe."

I snapped, much like I did at Adli. "Everyone says that," I screamed. "Everyone says that, but guess what? Siidi's gone home. Abdel left the house. Sue tried to kill herself. You snitched her out to save yourself. And I'm still here. I'm still asking questions to find out why, and nobody has the guts to tell me. All they say is, 'you don't understand.' Well, it's you all who don't understand, 'cause if you did, you wouldn't be doing these stupid things. "

Johara looked about to cry. "He hit your sister; he hit Yamma, you think he treats me any better? I don't know what to say to you, Joe. I heard you say many times to Sue that you should not have come here. Perhaps had you not, many of these things would not have happened."

She may have been my first crush, but things weren't the same after that conversation. To have her lay blame on Sue and me for the problems that had bubbled on the surface of her family for years was, to me, unforgivable. We were the victims, of that I have never wavered. To this day, when friends and family come to visit with me for a length of time, I make them my priority so that certain memories never befall them.

Johara never apologized, for as firmly as I believed I was a victim, she felt in her heart she was. And in truth, we both were, but, of course, as victims we could never admit such things.

CHAPTER 19

Sue must have been awake for my tirade. Awake and with enough awareness to wait until Johara finished hers to make herself known. "She's scared, Joe, don't mind what she says."

Between my despair at my plight and my happiness in hearing her speak, I could do nothing but collapse on the corner of her bed to weep. Sue let me. Either that or she fell back to sleep. I felt horrible for making a bad situation worse. But I had spoken my mind. I truly was upset at Sue for what she had done. I saw her as no less a coward than Siidi and Abdel. And my joy in hearing her voice was a selfish one. It meant there was a sliver of hope that this place perhaps wasn't a death trap.

"I'm sorry," she whispered.

I stared down at her, expecting more, but what more could she say? She was sorry she tried? Sorry it didn't work? Sorry I was made to witness? Either way, did she expect me to accept what I didn't recognize as an apology but rather an excuse?

She was sent home on the morning of Christmas Eve, brought to the airport by Abdel. He came to the house like a taxi cab driver, scooped up her bags, and had her follow him out to the car. Yamma and Johara were at the door to greet her. They took her in a bear hug. "La hawla wa la quwata illa billah," Yamma said. *There is no power and no strength, save in Allah.* I heard Johara crying. She walked her to the car, holding her hand the entire way.

When they got to the Mercedes, Sue turned and gestured for me to come to her. I approached slowly. Abdel, unfocused in the background, fidgeted impatiently. Sue threw her arms around my shoulders. "Tomorrow is Christmas," she said. "It's the first Christmas we won't have together. And you'll be alone. I put a present under your mattress. Wear it, Joe. No matter what anyone says, just wear it."

Christmas would be like any other day to me so I didn't care to be reminded of its emptiness. My parents sent a few gifts. They arrived before they knew Sue would be heading home. Sue left a few back for Johara. She told me where they were so I could give them to her

Christmas morning. "They don't celebrate Christmas," I said. "They're just a gifts," Sue said. "They're not for Christmas."

She walked me to the side. "I'll tell them all when I get home. I'll tell them what's been happening and how you feel about being here. They'll send for you, too."

I never knew the plan for us. I knew of no time table, whether tomorrow, the next day, or the next week, month, or year. Would it take a sliced wrist to get me out? But I trusted in Sue's plan. I had to. That would be worth waking up for, to hear Yamma call me into the kitchen, telling me to get packed. Even that one last trip with Abdel would be worth it. I smiled trustingly as she was driven away.

I told myself I would take Christmas as any other day; that I would go through it as the other kids here did. After all, there was no snow, no decorations, no tree, no singing, no *Mister Magoo Christmas Carol*, no *Babes in Toyland*, no Andy Williams. And it was on a Wednesday. I didn't even get to stay home from school. That night, Christmas Eve, I was at my lowest. I even said a prayer of sorts, though it was more of a rambling bitch session on why this was happening to me.

I came home to a familiar smell. Turkey. And the gifts my mother sent, hidden by Yamma when they arrived, were beneath a small fir in the front yard. She and Johara even sang a barely recognizable chorus of *Jingle Bells.* They all sat to watch me excitedly open the gifts. I ravaged the wrapping paper, tossing it aside without a thought. But the Frosty the Snowman, reindeer, and of course, Santa Claus illustrations intrigue them all, even Faid who sat back smoking, pretending not to care.

Besides the ration of clean socks and underwear, they sent me an Etch A Sketch, the Game of Life, and a Slinky. Of course, mother wrote that Santa brought them to Chicago early, asking that she send them along.

They were a big hit, especially the Etch A Sketch. Without stairs, the Slinky was rather lame, but Adli perfected bouncing it from palm-to-palm. I remembered the gifts Sue left for Johara. I ran to my room and brought them out. Johara was taken aback as I put them on the table in front to her. She looked to Yamma who motioned for her to open them: a fringed suede vest, a print of the Roy Lichtenstein drawing, *Drowning Girl*, and a troll doll with pink hair. The vest was long on her but looked very nice. They passed the troll around while we waited. Gamal and Adli ran the tiny comb through its hair. "What does it do?" Johara asked. "It's for luck," I told her. Faid call it skaheef. *Silly*.

"What does this say?" Johara asked, pointing to the voice cloud above the drowning girl. I looked over her shoulder at the girl in the swirling water. Fortunately they were small words I was able to read. "I don't care. I'd rather sink than call Brad for help."

She nodded. "What is a Brad?"

"It's a boy's name."

"Yes, I see," she said.

The gifts, the song, the dinner put on by Yamma were for my benefit, and I truly appreciated her efforts. Had Abdel been there, the moment wouldn't have happened. And I could see Faid nervously smoking, his jaws working, his forehead knotting, trying to decide how far this should go.

That night, I remembered Sue's gift for me. It was in a small unwrapped box under the mattress as she had promised. I took it over to the window sill where the waning moon gave sufficient light for me to see it and read the note packed inside. As I suspected, it was a silver medal on a chain. The depiction was of a man on horseback, a lance in his hand which he prodded at a large lizard. "This is St George," Sue wrote in her note. "He slayed a dragon who had eaten many animals and people. That made him known as, 'St George the Dragon Slayer.' He is a hero to both Christians and Muslims."

I had no idea what that meant, a hero to the Christians and the Muslims. And I was sure she threw the dragon part in there to convince me to wear it. But I didn't need to have Abdel strip searching me or rifling my things like he did to her. I tucked it into the back pocket of the dress slacks my mother packed but I never wore.

Adli brought the Slinky to school the next morning, and the next few. I had made the mistake of telling him how it walked the stairs. This he couldn't wait to try on the school bus steps. Oblivious to the driver's rebukes, he kept on with it until Faid had had enough and on the third day grabbed it away from him and twisted it out of its designed coil. He heaved it out the bus window where it caught on the front bumper of the car behind us. They all ignored Adli's cries while they congregated at the back window to watch the sparks fly while it dragged along the concrete roadway.

I witnessed, once again, Adli's vulnerability, and Faid's rising power. He was starting small to experiment, testing his reach. I had no doubt he noticed his affect on Adli as clearly as I did. I know he enjoyed it as much as I loathed it.

He had no one to answer to at home. He was beyond Yamma's control. He was a man, heading off to college soon, or perhaps a job. There would come a time when I would be his next victim. I didn't have to wait long.

CHAPTER 20

The minaret of Dayr Ghasana was the tallest and grandest building in the village. That said, it wasn't very tall or grand. It was thin enough that I imagined the staircase going up to be as narrow and rickety as those fire escapes of the old Chicago apartment buildings. But it had the classic onion dome that's kept it a captivating fixture in my mind all these years. The mosque it was connected to was easily the oldest building in the village. It wasn't in the center of town. That was reserved for the local police headquarters.

In the beginning, the lyrical strains of the muezzin calling adhan from atop the tower was as chilling as it was mesmerizing. When I learned adhan was the call to prayer, five times every day, I had visions of the Eloi from the movie *The Time Machine* being summoned by the air raid siren to feed the cannibalistic Morlocks. In that I didn't participate in prayer, the call became white noise to me within a few weeks.

Ramadan began right after the new year in 1965. It was a rude awakening into the strict discipline that was the Muslim religion, and I once again attuned myself to the muezzin's calls. Though still a mystery to me, I find myself greatly admiring the glorious manner in which they treat their God. I know of no American Christian who would willingly surrender the basic needs of life for thirty days for anyone, let alone something as ethereal as a God-figure.

As a child, I was not obligated to partake in the fasting, but I was affected by it nonetheless. It's how I know that frustrated and angry are universal emotions, and the cruelty they produce is common to all people, of all races, of all denominations. For Yamma, fasting all day made her too weak to care for us, and Faid took it as the perfect opportunity to assume control.

After the routine with the Slinky, a move Faid said he had to make to stop Adli's unholy obsession, he threw Johara's troll into the fire pit. I told Johara that girls would affix the troll to their bathroom mirrors or headboards. Some to their pocketbooks or book bags. She chose her book bag where it drew much attention, positive and negative.

Faid had no poker face. He had a face that telegraphed his big moves as he feverishly worked himself into his next mad frenzy. I saw it that morning, extending into the ride home. His eyes burned into Johara and her troll the entire ride. I could have warned her but, what would it have done? Only delay the inevitable. Besides, getting involved further in this family's battles was not in my plans.

At home he went straight to the fire pit to stoke it while Johara and the rest us went to the kitchen. In five minutes he was ripping the troll from the bag. Johara left the bag on the kitchen counter as she always did. No one was there to mind it, though I put myself in a strategic position to see what Faid was up to. He made the effort to alert everyone by shouting, "Na'uzhu-bi-Allah." *We Seek refuge in Allah.* "Tawkkalna-'ala-Allah." *Our trust is in Allah.*

Johara chased him outside. The troll was well into the flames before she arrived. "You had no right," she screamed.

"Leave luck to the heathens; you have Allah."

"It was a gift."

"It is an insult to all of us. It is an insult to Allah."

"It's just in fun."

"This is not in fun. Your clothes are not in fun. The silly paintings and toys are not in fun. Beg Allah for forgiveness."

"You beg," she said. "You are the one in shame before Allah."

She spit on the fire and was turning when Faid grabbed her arm. As she straightened up to him, he hit her hard across the face. I was at the kitchen door and heard it. I turned around for other witnesses, but there were none. Johara shook herself free and ran to the house, past me, and into her room. I ducked back inside before Faid spotted me. It was to be this way until I left Palestine.

By puberty, adherence to Ramadan is expected. Not only the fasting, but the spiritual cleansing, the enlightenment, the humility, patience, charity, and benevolence. In essence, deep introspective change. Things of this world are to be put aside. Devotion to the ways of Allah is the only path, and all thoughts are turned to him. Food and other earthly delights such as sex and socializing are confined to nighttime hours.

At my age I was exempt, as was Gamal. Adli could have been, being mentally handicapped, but Faid tried to force them into observance in spite of Yamma's protests. Faid talked it over with Abdel who agreed it was time for Gamal. As for Adli, he was Yamma's child, Yamma's concern.

"Why not Adli," Gamal complained. "He's older than me."

"It is not your place to question," Faid ordered, his voice booming as I had never heard it before.

He gave me a pass, probably for the same reason one was provided to Adli. I had already decided I would fight him on it, much like I was ready to fight Gamal. And I was prepared. Before Abdel convinced my parents to send our monthly allowance directly to him so we would not be wasting it on "the foolishness" as he called it, Sue and I managed to stack up a good number of cans of Chef Boyardee ravioli, Nehi, Moon Pies, and Sunkist tuna fish. It would be a month of feasts for Adli and me.

Noticeably absent since Sue's tragedy was Sam.

In a month that should have cast me into further desolation, I actually found my way, and without the fasting and reflection. It was the month Adli and I became very close friends. We ruled the day while the others conserved their energies. By the second week, they had no time for anything but their own survival. It was great watching Gamal waste away. And though he ate like a king at night, he was exhausted the next day at school, sleeping on the bus and in class

We played basketball daily. We fished at the Red River. January was unseasonably warm so there were a few days we could strip down and swim. He taught me how to catch birds using an ingenious trap. "What do we do with it now?" I asked when we caught one. He cut the string with a pen knife so it could fly off.

He wanted to torment Amir with stones but I refused. Though the dog had attacked me on more than one occasion, he was one of the few things here I felt no animosity towards.

Adli had me teach him *The Game of Life* I received for Christmas. Of course I had to read him all the cards and make the life decisions for him, but he loved spinning the dial, which I let him do for both our turns. I had brought a yo-yo with me from home. I had it stashed in my suitcase. I found him swinging it around the room, and of course, he promptly struck me in the jaw with it when I approached. Try as I might, I couldn't get him to learn even the basic throw down. He was content to swing it full circle, and usually without warning.

It was all just little kid fun. He was forever with a smile. I was relaxed. He had no ego that would otherwise spoil the day, and I was a patient teacher and eager student. He never spoke of his father's leaving. I mistook that for his not understanding, but he understood all too well. "I'm different," he said when we were walking back up the valley from the Red River.

"I know."

We were carrying our shoes around our necks, attached by the shoelaces, and our shirts in our hand as we trudged upward. Adli was being tested while I practically ran up. I was used to the trek, at least half of it, by virtue of my frequent trips back and forth to the cave. He hadn't been on the hillside since our camp session with Siidi. "No. I'm different … really … different," he panted.

I stopped to let him catch up, believing it was his motive for saying something so random. I was proud of my conditioning without realizing that's what it was. To push the point, I started walking as soon as he caught up. "That's what Yamma says, that I'm different."

"Then I guess you are," I said.

"Know why?"

"Yeah, 'cause Yamma says so?"

"Know why she says so?"

I stopped. The old adage about walking and chewing gum at the same time fit him well. He sat on a rock. "Allah wants me to be," he said.

"For real?"

"Na'am. Most kids are smart; only a few are like me. So we're special. And Yamma will always take care of me."

"How can she do that?"

"I'll live with her. She says now that Ab is gone I can."

"But you're younger than her; she'll die before you."

This was a shocking revelation to him. "La, la, la," he said vehemently, shaking his head. "She won't do that on me, she needs to take care of me."

"It's okay, Adli, you can take care of yourself."

"If I take care of myself, then I can't be special."

"Yes you can still be special even—"

But he wanted no part of this. He had been freed from the chains put upon him by Abdel and so many others. Yamma provided him with this comforting identity. He was now a fortunate son, and I was sending him back. "I am special. I am special. Allah made me special." He repeated as if his personal dua.

I walked beside him the rest of the way. He stopped just in sight of the cave, refusing to go further. I always had to wait for him as he went on his wide berth off the trail to bypass it. It would have me waiting ten, sometimes fifteen minutes. To show my disdain I would wait inside the cave, coming out only when I heard him calling to me from up the mountain. This day, I had had enough. The only evil done in this cave came from my sister, not witches, not ghoulies. I was the only one who needed to be terrified of this place, no one else, and I was aggravated with Adli for thinking he could share that right with me. "Keep walking," I commanded.

"La." Like an infant refusing peas.

I pulled him roughly by his shoulders, knowing it was the only method to work on him. He pulled back violently. "No, no, Joe, stop."

"I've been in there," I said, not giving in, "I've slept there. There are no ghoulies." I led him all the way to the mouth of the cave, to the point we could feel the cold wind blowing out at us. I let go. He stood frozen in place beside me. "It's okay. We'll stand here awhile, but you are not going to be scared of this place anymore."

Though terror was still in his eyes, he looked trustingly to me. I let him stand there to take it all in. "I feel her," he said.

"It's just wind," I said. "It comes from the back of the cave. There's a tunnel that goes all the way into the mountain; I think wind comes out of it."

"She's cold."

"It's not a girl; it's not a person. Just wind, like out here."

Then a low growl came from inside and Adli retreated back to the cover of a thin tree. I admit it freaked me when I first heard it. But I picked it out as coming from the small tunnel in the back. I checked it out and that's what it was. When too much air was sent through, it made a low growl, sometimes a high screech. I explained this to Adli as best I could, using hand gestures and silly sounds that had him laughing. I inched him in slowly from there.

I believe it was the proudest moment of his life as he stood in the middle of that cave, the cold air and low moans swirling around him like so many bad memories. It was a nervous smile that parted his lips but a smile nonetheless. "You can tell Gamal, and you can tell Faid, that you've been in here." I said.

"Na'am, I was in here," he said dreamily. "Now can we get out?"

I kept him there until the sun set on the cave opening as a way of increasing his confidence. Though we were both famished, his combination of fear and excitement, together with my big-brother complex, had our hunger as a secondary state.

We were late getting home, and it was Yamma's standing order, we all ate together. Yamma was perturbed, but no less gracious, as she had always been with me. She even took the moment to listen to Adli's cave tale and nodded favorably at him as he spoke. To everyone who came to the table, Adli crowed about his feat, never seeing, as I did, the rage in the eyes of Faid and Gamal. "Who cares about you in the cave," Gamal said. "You made us wait."

We ate a large meal which was greedily consumed by all of us. It was hilarious to watch Yamma attack it with all the manners and finesse of a pariah dog.

"You're jealous now of me," Adli said, "just as Joe said you would be, right Joe?"

I busied myself with dishing out the falafel. I wanted no part of this discussion which was destined to end badly.

"That's a baby thing; I am not jealous," Gamal said.

"Adli, you are not to speak at our table, especially during this time, but not at any time," Faid ordered.

"Yes I can."

Faid pumped his fist in the air. "I say no. I say no voice from you will be heard while I eat at my table."

"It's the family table, Faid," Yamma said quietly. "Now, eat, all of us."

"He is not family," Faid yelled across to Yamma, "And I say he will not speak."

"I am so family. It's you, you're not family."

I watched Yamma intently for her reaction of which she had none, or so it seemed. She was hoping it was going away but I knew better. I knew Faid. Pitiless. And I knew Adli. Stubborn.

"I commanded you not to speak."

At that, Adli began singing a nonsense song. "Ada deenoo safala kateenoo safala kateekato. Eelek beelek boom eelek beelek boom."

Yamma's attempts to stifle him aroused his chorus all the louder. She glanced over at Faid who was waiting for her to fail so he could pounce. "Fettah," she said, holding a piece of the fried bread to his mouth. "You like fettah. Eat before it gets cold."

He pushed it away and continued, staring defiantly at Faid, then coyly at me as he sang. "I broke the stick, I found worms in it. Hey stone-cutter, hey carpenter, Bring the tools and the saw, And meet me near the front door of the house."

"Try the fattoush," she said. "You helped, remember? You picked the vegetables with me, remember?"

It was sad to see Yamma struggling so before her eldest son. It remains one of those moments I regret not having the power to stop. I could have told Adli to be quiet. He would have listened to me. I could have taken him from the table, destroying the opportunity Faid had to say what he said next.

"Ibn haram," he shouted. *Bastard child.* We all stopped but for different reasons. Me, to see how badly Yamma would hurt. Johara and Gamal, waiting for an explanation. Adli, in his ignorance. And Yamma, in grief of this final betrayal.

"Who?" Johara asked.

Faid looked to Yamma, and in that instant I prayed for an epiphany to seize him. But it did not. "You can tell them," he said, jutting his chin at Yamma. "It's your story."

"There is no story, Faid, you have been told wrong."

"I know what I've been told."

"I know you do. And in your years you have been told many wrong things. This, I am glad to tell you, is one of them. Now, all of us will eat."

I was astonished at how quickly she regained her composure. She seemed relieved the issue was out, literally, on the table where she could address it in her causal way.

"But who?" Johara asked again.

"I said it was not true, Johara. Lies are never to be passed over our food during this season. So let it be."

But Faid would not.

"Father swore it was true; he told me so."

"And so I swear it is not. I leave it up to you who you will believe, Faid. But remember, just because you believe does not make it true."

Yamma went back to eating, the fork against the plate being the only sound in the room. Adli began again. "I broke the stick, I found worms in it. Hey stone-cutter …"

Faid pointed. His finger shook as he spoke. "You. You ibn haram will remain quiet or you will be eating with the dogs."

Johara stared at Yamma in horror. "What does he mean, Yamma? What does Faid mean by this?"

It was only Yamma who remembered the real victim in this. She rose slowly, gathering her plate, utensils, and glass, and bid Adli to do same. Johara started in again, but Yamma silenced her with a look. She led Adli outside where it was dark and cold but where there were no questions. She could be his Yamma for a few moments more, before the lies came and forever destroyed the two of them. They could look at stars, listen to dogs howling, sing silly songs. I knew later he took her down to the cave, all by himself, to the place he gave up his childish fears.

Though I was aware of the troubles brewing here, I couldn't appreciate what Yamma had done in that moment, not until now. There are truths and there are other truths, like beauty, they lie with the beholder. Yamma took her truth outside that night to share it one last time with her son, for she knew on this night, it would be lost forever.

CHAPTER 21

"Sharmuta," I heard Gamal say. Then a crack and Johara cursing him out. Before I headed off to bed, I knocked on Johara's bedroom door. "Come in."

I pushed the door and stood there sheepishly at the entrance, not wanting to enter. "I heard Gamal saying something to you tonight. Then you slapped him. What did he say?"

"He called Yamma a whore."

"Oh," I said, relieved it wasn't about me for once. "What's that?"

"Not a very nice thing, Joe."

I turned to leave but stopped, needing to know. "Do you miss Sue?"

"Yes. Do you?"

"Ah huh."

"Joe, I know you're angry at me for what I did, but you must believe me, I never meant for her to be hurt. Never. We were like sisters so very much. I loved her."

She had been sitting cross-legged on the bed but now she dared to stand and come to me. "We have so much sadness in this house, so much anger and hurt. It wasn't always so. But more anger, more hurt, will only do us more harm. Joe, you need to be above that for all our sake."

She hugged me while I stood there limp-armed. I had no intention of making friends with her. I just wanted to know if she missed Sue. That was all.

***

Sam had given us the warning of being pulled from the Friend's School. I didn't hear another word about it until near the end of Ramadan. Myself, Johara, and the two boys would be going to the school in the village while Faid would finish his last year at The Friends. I was disappointed, while Johara was furious. The boys didn't much care either way. The reason given: it was too expensive, which no doubt it was. I also suspect that my monthly stipend paid for Faid's last year because from that moment on, I saw barely a penny of it.

I heard the heated argument between Faid and Johara over it. The upshot was she was never going to use such a fine education, Adli wasn't worth it, and Gamal would be there alone. Yamma had an opinion, but no leverage, since she didn't hold the purse strings.

I didn't fight it. I knew I'd be leaving any day now. Any day Yamma would come to me, bury me in her huge hug, and teary-eyed tell me I was going home. Abdel would arrive. Unlike with Sue, he wouldn't load my bags. He would sit in his car while I did it myself. I wouldn't care. I'd carry two at a time and sprint to the car. I'd listen to Adbel snort and snarl all the way to the airport, all the while smiling and thinking to myself, *Hell to you, old man. I'm going home; you have to stay here for the rest of your miserable life.*

That last day at school my Persian friend, Raha, handed me a paper bag. I looked at her quizzically. "Open it," she said. Wrapped and rubber-banded into seventeen unequal packs were my baseball cards. Throughout the school year, with the five cards I loaned her, she was able to win every one of mine. I hated her for a time. I wouldn't even talk to her. She made it worse by striking a 1963 Al Kaline batting pose nearly every time she saw me.

Now, here they were, neatly wrapped. "I put them together by teams," she said. "See, you have more of Pittsburgh Pirates than any other. And look." She unwrapped the Yankees and fanned through to the waxed Tommy Tresh.

"They're yours," I said. "You won them fair and square."

"It was for fun. And they'd be no use to me back home. But in America, you can be champion again. Maybe someday I will come to America and win them back."

Then in front of everyone emptying the school, she gave me a hug and a kiss on my cheek, one that seemed to linger until I was no longer in shock, but in my own piece of heaven.

By this time, Adli was experiencing relentless condemnation from nearly everyone he knew. The worst part was he didn't understand why. When he came back to the house after showing Yamma the cave, he said, "Joe, what's that that Faid called me? Ibn haram? What is that?"

"That you are not your father's son."

He laughed. "That's silly, of course I am Ab's son." That satisfied him as he went on drawing interminable lines on the Etch A Sketch. "Can I have it?"

"Have what?" I said.

"The square writer."

"It's an Etch A Sketch. No."

"Oh. Why do you have it?"

"It was a present."

"From who?"

"Santa Claus."

"Oh. Who's that?"

"He's the man who brings presents at Christmas."

"He didn't bring me one."

"That's because you don't believe in Christmas."

"Oh. If I believed would I get a present?"

"I don't know, maybe."

He pursed his lower lip in thought. "Okay, Joe, I believe."

Had the illegitimacy issue stayed in the family, it might have been bearable for him. But when Gamal and his friends, and then people in the village he didn't even know began to comment, he came to believe it may be true. "Why wouldn't I be his son?" He'd ask me. "Whose would I be then?"

Of course, I knew only what Sam had told Sue and me, and I knew nothing of the sexual element involved, so I told him it was a mistake people were making. "You know what?" he said. "There are a lot of people making it."

The first days at the new school were shocking. The building, the teachers, the students, the rules. From the house we could walk about a mile along the road, but slightly shorter if we took the path through the desert. Everyone took the path but the girls. To do otherwise was to be doomed to the most heinous ridicule known to boyhood. But the path was narrow and littered with stones and ruts. And dusty. My shoes wouldn't last long. I carried a torn piece of bed linen to use as a handkerchief to blow grime out my nose after the back and forth trip.

By now I had a good handle on the language. Common words and terms I learned at home. Out here, I was called nearly every offensive thing they knew. If Adli couldn't translate, I would use Johara. But I kept most of this to myself. Playing the dumb American kid had its benefits.

I took to walking with Adli a good bit behind the group to avoid their taunts at me and to protect him from hearing himself called a bastard. I vowed to be with him as often as I could. During the first month we walked to school before sunrise. Gamal and his friends would kick stones into our path, which caused us to stumble on occasion, but they were more of an irritant. This day the gang slowed to allow us to catch up. I watched as each of them bent down to collect a stone. I waited for them to drop them in a pile designed to trip us but they never did.

"Go ahead of us," Gamal said.

"Why?" I asked.

"Your turn."

Adli was already walking ahead when one pulled a rock from his pocket and rolled it in his palm. I suspected a rock fight was to ensue, but I was sure they were all meant for me. Surely Gamal wouldn't allow them to stone his own brother. Then again, he no longer saw Adli as his brother. Gamal told them to spread out and take aim. The one nearest me stepped a few feet to my right to line Adli up.

My brother, David, said many things to me, but only rarely did he take the time to teach me anything. I got into it with a kid at the park. I came away with a split lip. "Here's the rule," David said, "the only rule in fighting: you don't lose. Got it?" I nodded vigorously.

"No, you don't got it, Joe. You don't got it because you just got your butt kicked. Know why?"

I shrugged.

"Because you didn't throw the first punch. If you know there's gonna be a fight, why wait for it to start without you? Why? 'Cause you don't, that's why. Pick your spot, step in, and throw your punch. You do it right, the fight is over then and there."

I tried it once or twice back home, always with my haymaker. It worked swell, no need to think it wouldn't here. Maybe better since the kid I drew a bead on not only had no idea he was my target; he was preoccupied. I knew Adli would get hit, nothing I could do about it. But I would let them know on whose side I stood, and this poor bastard would carry the scar.

I didn't wait for the final order. I stepped hard into the kid whose face scrounged into an agonizing mess of wrinkles before my hand even connected. He went down quickly as every rock but his flew. I was still watching my handiwork when I heard Adli howl.

Adli was bent over, holding his head. At this point, though, all eyes were on me. I stood firm with my fists balled and arms in a boxing pose. No longer having an element of surprise, I had to rely on pure bravado. Adli was crying. The kid I hit was recovering, coming slowly and clumsily to his feet. "What'd you do that for?" Gamal demanded.

"You won't throw rocks at anyone again," I said, surprised at my moxie.

"Or what?"

All except Gamal seemed skittish to take me on, his boldness coming from his familiarity with me. I may have lost the element of surprise, but I now had the opportunity to reinvent myself. It was now or never. I had no choice but to take him on. I readjusted my stance for no other reason than to display my intentions to attack. He did the same, much to my chagrin. The odds were not good. There were three and a half of them at the moment. I heard Adli still bawling. I looked. He wasn't hurt, not really, just the shock of having rocks thrown at him for no reason.

It struck me. Nothing could be worse for me than having Gamal kick my ass right here in front of everyone, and after I provoked it. Suddenly, I felt very much in a life and death struggle. Then he made a disastrous tactical move.

He stepped hard into me, expecting to make this a one punch fight. I was facing him square without a chance to move. Something inside him made him leave my face and vitals alone. Instead, he gave me a hard chest shove. My feet didn't budge, not an inch, not a wave of my upper body. A look of disbelief crossed his face. He came at me again. I knew this one would be a punch to my face so my hands were at the ready. But he came at my chest again with the same result.

Now there was panic in his eyes. He was quick. He was nimble. He could have out-boxed me up and down that desert trail, sniping me with quick jabs from every direction. But it was no longer about the fight. He had failed to move me and that was the only battle he was focusing on. "So fat," he said. But his tone wasn't so terrorizing, his friends didn't laugh so heartily, and I didn't bow away in humiliation, for it was this fat that had beaten him.

"You're too fat to move," he said. "Much too fat." His laughter was weak. It weakened more when he realized his friends had not joined in.

I ignored the comments. "No more rocks," I said. "No more tripping or pushing either of us." I turned slowly in a circle. "None of you." I left them to join up with Adli. I was John Wayne and nothing would be the same again.

CHAPTER 22

I never knew how much I could hate a school until I was forced into the village school in Dayr Ghasana. I have since seen the insides of prisons and this was close. There was no quarter given to me. I was expected to know the language, the culture, and the religion as well as any of them. There was no Raha to play with me, no sweet-smelling Lambertina, no lush grounds, no smiling teachers. No one was allowed to call me Joe, only Nasser, my Arabic name. And they were unmerciful to Adli who was forced into a regular class and was punished for calling me by my American name.

I even missed the bus ride to Ramallah, the hour long drive I had once dreaded. I spent those two hours, riding back and forth, gripped in the tightest anxiety hold I've ever experienced as I focused on nothing but the noise and laughter in the back of the bus, convinced it was directed at me. Every movement in my peripheral vision had me convulsing, knowing for sure it was one of them coming after me. And it wasn't paranoia for oftentimes they were.

But as time wore on, tormenting me lost its novelty, at least on the bus, and I began to lose myself in the landscape. The bumpy ride was no longer jarring. I enjoyed its ruggedness. I enjoyed being the unknown stranger coming out of the desolate outreaches of the territory. I fancied myself Clint Eastwood as The Man With No Name in *A Fistful of Dollars,* riding into San Miguel to deceive and eventually steal a load of gold from two feuding families, only in the end, to do the righteous thing by staying to fight for a cause.

I liked sitting in class with Lambertina and Raha, neither of whom spoke English well enough to converse with me but whose glances and eyes told me, "yeah, like you, we're just visitors here doing the best we can." I enjoyed Miss Stewart, my teacher, whose Australian accent and casual ways took me to another place away from here. And the bus driver who greeted me each morning with Ahlan sadiqi, *Hey, friend,* and with Assalamu Alaikom, *peace be upon you,* at the end of each day.

At home, Adli and I continued our bizarre relationship. Even though it had become old for everyone else, he would poke my stomach and push his out, his favorite joke, when Gamal was nearby. He would laugh uproariously. When he finished he would grab my hand and lead me to his basketball court.

At night, while I was still outside finishing up gardening or husbandry chores for Yamma, he would rile up Amir, the only real fear I had not overcome, and never would. Even though Amir had been put on a thicker rope, nearly impossible to break, I would tremble uncontrollably, unable to proceed. It wasn't Adli who would rescue me. He'd lose interest and go inside. So I had to wait for Amir to lose interest and lay back down in the corner. At times, that would take an hour as I sat shivering in the olive grove. Then, without a thought about what he had done, Adli would sit with me at the sill to trace the constellations when the lights went out for bedtime.

He didn't make the connection of his actions. To him it was all good fun. If it was funny once, it was funny every time. If it made Gamal and Faid laugh once, then it would make them laugh again. There was no differentiation between laughing with and laughing at. In his mind, it was innocent. I tried to explain how it made me feel. "It's like when they call you stupid," I said.

"But I am stupid," he would say.

To him there was but one truth: that which others asserted. He couldn't comprehend having his own point of view, his own truth. Whether the cause was his mental incapacity or the neglectful way he was treated, I was never to know.

I now had a reputation at the village school as news of my stand-off with Gamal made the rounds. Fear didn't make me more popular, just ignored on a different level. But the way I saw it, fear was a better reason for isolation than ridicule.

And it gave Adli a standing of sorts, too. He was still himself, simple and a bastard, but no one dared call him on it. Not when I was around, anyway. I was never sure what reached him. After the rock-throwing incident he didn't thank me. But he put his arm over my shoulder as we walked to school. And back home, when Gamal pranked me, and not out of kinship, Adli joined him. They barred the outhouse door on me, a gag that happened frequently to the point I'd leave it open, not caring if Johara or even Yamma happened by. They'd write Khaneeth—*faggot;*

bous tize—*kiss my ass;* and bashokh aleek—*I piss on you*—on my Etch-A-Sketch and leave it on my bed. I knew Adli was involved in those because although he couldn't spell or control both dials simultaneously to draw diagonally, he would go into hysterics each time I read it.

Gamal knew enough to annoy but not provoke me. I was glad for that. I alone recognized that had he chose to box me, the results would have been very different. Soccer was a different matter. He would outmaneuver me easily but once in a while, by my design, he found himself at my side where I would check him aggressively off the ball. It was my way of reminding him.

I hadn't seen Sam since he brought Sue back from the cave. I found it strange and insensitive. The day I did see him at the house, talking to Yamma in kitchen, I ignored him. He was leaning forward with the deep, furrowed look of a judge. He glanced to his side at me as I scurried past. Ten minutes later he was gone without stepping in to see me.

Yamma was still at the table, another troubled look upon her face. It seemed Sam only brought problems with him and left worries behind. Faid had taken charge of the household in a more miserable way than Abdel ever did. Abdel had cemented his son's power by providing him with the household money to dole out as he saw fit, or as Abdel dictated. It left Yamma in a foul mood. Being admonished by her son on what to cook, where to shop, how to dress her children was wearing her down.

Her crossness carried outside her dealings with Faid. She rarely smiled, even at me. Her sweet songs were gone. Her home cooked meals had slowed so that I was forced to dig into my stash of Chef Boyardee. I knew instinctively the topic of Sam's visit had everything to do with it.

One night I sat across from her, dragging the chair hard across the floor. She didn't look up. "Sam said something to upset you again, huh?"

She nodded.

"Abdel Karim coming back?"

She looked up. "You want him to, Joe?"

"No way," I said. Her smile at that was lonesome. As much terror as he had caused, there were surely moments she treasured.

"Yamma, do you think he left because of me?"

"No, of course not. You know his reason."

"Yeah, but why now, why when I came?"

"Well, I should have said you know the reason he gave us. His real reasons were different, and Joe, they are not things to concern you."

"Johara says he sees a woman in Ramallah. Is he tired of living here?"

"Yes, I suppose he is. But if a man tires of one thing, he can tire of anything. Even youth and beauty. But I'm happy you're here; you've been a great help to us, especially Adli, and I see him getting better all the time."

"Do you miss him? Abdel Karim?"

"Like the desert misses rain. It manages just fine without it, and too much of it causes floods, but a little bit is nice. Yes, he's coming back. But he will not stay."

"Why?"

"Because I won't let him."

I caught her looking at my knuckles so I balled up my hands and hid them beneath the table. "You go now, practice salat and study."

She knew. Rapping knuckles; it was the school's way of instilling Islam, and parents had little say. Salat was not taken lightly even with my American heritage and at my tender age. I was expected to learn along with everyone else. My hands were rapped with a ruler for every Raka'ah I messed up. That was a lot since I could speak and understand the language well enough to communicate, but the words didn't roll off my tongue in a natural way, making my pronunciation terrible.

It shook me so much on those first days I couldn't concentrate on the proper body or hand positions during salat. I tried to follow along with the others but it was a very confusing game of *Simon Says.* I was whacked for that, too.

It hurt like nothing I had ever felt, but I refused to cry which pissed the teachers off more. The punishment became a challenge to them, as if making a six-year old cry should be a worthy goal.

On the upside, it added to my rep as a hardcore rebel. As I saw that developing, learning the pillars of Islam became less important to me. After all, I would be leaving soon. And it was better to bear the wrath of teachers for a few hours a day than that of my cousins and classmates for crying like a baby.

On Saturdays I was expected to take over the farm chores for Yamma. I did so without protest. She not only deserved it but I enjoyed caring for the goats and chickens. We would start as soon as Yamma removed Amir and tied him up in the back. Since Faid's reign, however, it was just me and Johara. Adli would help if he woke up in such a mood.

I saw Abdel's Mercedes in the drive when I came from the barn with the bag of feed. The engine was running. The sun reflected off the windshield but I could see he wasn't behind the wheel. I saw a flash of a bracelet or watch from the passenger side. I set the feed down and shaded my eyes. A young woman waved at me. I thought, Sue, and moved quickly to the car. The window rolled down as I approached. It wasn't Sue and the silly smile I wore to greet her dropped from my face like wax lips.

She was young and striking with a ruby mouth and steely-black eyes. Her hair had a fashion model sheen. It flowed like a silk dress. Her smile was radiant and grew brighter when she said, "You have to be Joe from Chicago."

"Ah-huh."

"I've heard all about you. I'm Zaynah." She reached her delicate hand part way out the window. I was able to grasp only the ends of three fingers. It felt as if I was shaking hands with an infant.

Abdel came out of the house with Yamma on his heels. She stopped dead in her tracks when she saw Zaynah. It hit me; this was Abdel's new girlfriend from Ramallah. As taken as I was with her beauty, at that moment it was seeing Yamma in her heartache that captured my attention. Her lips quivered before she covered them with the back of her hand. She moved a few steps closer, perhaps to pull me away, maybe out of her habit of being a gracious hostess. But she stopped and withdrew to the safety of the doorway.

I thought the endless hours of lonely toil was the worst that could befall a woman like her. Now I saw her as a person who suffered the agony of betrayal as deeply as I did. Abdel, though, was reveling in it. He had Zaynah step out of the car to talk to me even though we had already met. He had her stand there is full view of Yamma. His prize. Proof to himself of his virility. I was as humiliated as Yamma, being made a player in this obscene spectacle.

"Get in," Abdel said.

I looked at Yamma who stood forlornly at the door, her hands fidgeting at her waist. She nodded her approval. I sat in the backseat to await further instructions.

We drove in silence toward Ramallah. Zaynah glanced out the window then over at Abdel, waiting for him to speak. "Tell him where we are going," he said, in Arabic.

"He wants me to tell you where we are going," she said. I thought it a wise move on my part not to let on I understood him just fine.

"We're going to the Amari Camp. He wants to show it to you and what he does for them."

"Why?"

"Just something he wants to show you."

I thought it was a boy's camp, like the one at Jackson Park where my brother spent several summers. Swimming, hiking, camp outs. I'd like that. Just not with Abdel.

"I am speaking for him because he speaks very little English." Zaynah said. "I spent a time at the University of Chicago. That's where I learned my English."

I never did believe that. I think Abdel knew the language better than he let on. Everyone there seemed to know English, at least as much as I knew Arabic. Surely a man who dressed in a suit and drove a black Mercedes did. His motive at such ignorance was unlike mine: I liked to eavesdrop; he needed to display his superiority in not having to converse with me or Sue.

Amari Camp was just south of Ramallah. It was thick with cement buildings. From the entrance I thought it was just one large one, but as we drove through I saw alleyways that were barely a Chicago-sidewalk wide. Most people were sitting outside, cooking in huge metal pots. They stared at us as we drove slowly through.

Abdel spoke continuously as he drove. Zaynah translated. "They pay no money to live here, and they get all this. They get their food and water from the agency your uncle works for."

We drove to an open area used as a playground. The swings and slide were rusted but they were being used by children my age. Clouds of dust kicked up as they dragged their feet and dropped from the slide. It reminded me of that first day we drove through the dust storm on the way from the airport. The kids watched us through the clouds.

Like in Ramallah, there were shopkeepers on the sides of the road. I saw some wrapped foods but couldn't make out what they were. "Do they work for that agency?" I asked, pointing.

"No, those people own shops and sell things."

"I thought everything was free?"

"The things they need to live. Extra things they buy themselves."

The roads were mostly dirt, like in Dayr Ghasana. Any cement road was cracked and crumbling. The walls had graffiti paintings on them, very much like buildings in Chicago. But it was all very different here, the look, the feel. The squat, tightly packed buildings had me gasping for air. It was crowded and no one seemed to have a place to go. Those seated looked bored; those moving seemed to be wandering.

Ramallah bustled with comings and goings. Everyone was doing something, even though I had no clue what it could be. There was purpose on their faces. Even their smiles, nods, and waves belied a need to move on. All that was missing here, just a few blocks away.

"There are two schools," Zaynah said. "All paid for so all the children get a proper education."

The schools were nice. Surrounded by pine, tamarisk, and carob trees, planted flower beds, and clean concrete drives. There were two soccer fields and a running track. Abdel turned back to me and spoke. "He said, 'wouldn't you like to go to these schools?'" Zaynah translated.

I nodded. Anything was better than where I was currently going. But Abdel had no intentions of sending me here; I knew that right away.

We drove down side streets with more cramped cement houses, more outdoor shops, more dust, more graffiti, more empty stares. We never got out of the car. I found that strange.

"What your uncle does is to make sure this camp and many others have enough food to eat."

"Do these people live here all the time?" I asked.

"Of course."

"Why do they call them camps then? Camps are just for overnight."

"Not this one," she said. "As a matter of fact, some people have been allowed to stay here since it opened fifteen years ago. And they'll be able to stay here for a long time from now."

They brought me back to the house and let me off without coming inside. Abdel said nothing, but through Zaynah told me I had learned many good things about Palestinians and how they take care of each other as part of Mohammad's teachings. May peace be upon him.

There was no one home. I had never been at the house alone. I walked it room to room. It seemed no bigger than the cement buildings I'd just seen. It was the land around it that made it feel so big to me. And Yamma, who moved from inside to outside as if there were no walls between the two.

I was exhausted and fell asleep on my bed, just an hour or so. I was awakened by Faid violently shaking me. He was cursing me out with words I couldn't quite grasp for he was speaking so quickly and loudly. When I was fully focused, I thought he was just flexing his muscles again. When I saw the look of horror on Johara's face when she came in, I knew it was more than that.

"What's he saying?" I asked her. "Why's he yelling at me?"

Johara took hold of Faid's arms that were still flailing madly above me as I lay on my side. She stepped in front of him and asked me, "Did you let Amir off his leash?"

CHAPTER 23

I vehemently denied it to Johara which didn't settle well with Faid who was on me again. Johara maneuvered him out of the room. She sat calmly on the edge of my bed, the way Sue would do when she was about to get very serious. "I need you to tell me the truth," she said.

"Why? What happened?"

"If you did, better to tell me than to have Faid find out himself."

"No. I didn't. I wasn't even home."

"You were home before us, Joe."

"But I was asleep."

"The entire time?"

"Kinda. I looked for Yamma but she wasn't here, no one was here."

"Where was Amir when you got home?"

"Tied up." I gave her a not-sure look. She picked up on it and gave it back to me. "He's always tied up."

"He wasn't when we came home."

"Where was he?"

"Joe, he got into the pen with the goats and killed two of them. And a rooster."

"Maybe it wasn't him, maybe another—"

"He's gone, Joe. Amir is gone so we know it was him."

"Well I didn't do it. I'm afraid of him, you know that."

She pursed her lips while letting me lay there in the unnerving silence. "All right. Yes, I know that. And if you say you didn't do it I believe you."

"I didn't."

She smiled as if she believed me and left the room. I looked out the bedroom window where I could see the barn and a little of the pasture where the goats were corralled. I didn't see anything that resembled the slaughter she described.

I lay there listening for another thirty minutes. I heard the rattling of pots in the kitchen, and Johara speaking with the two younger boys. Every tenth or so statement was a cursing from Faid. What I didn't hear was Yamma. I finally managed the courage to join them. There was a sickening moment of silence which Johara rescued me from by having me set the table for dinner.

"La," Faid bellowed so loudly I fumbled with the stack of plates she handed me. He grabbed the plates from my hand and slammed them on the counter. "You will eat what the dog left."

"Faid," Johara said, "don't be ridiculous."

"You be silent, Johara. It is my decision."

"If Yamma was here you—"

"Yamma is not here. He let Amir escape—"

"I did not," I protested more heatedly than I did in the bedroom. I had to, my dinner was at stake and I was famished. I don't know if it was by error or design, but Abdel neglected to stop anywhere for us to eat, though we passed through food stands all day.

Faid moved towards me. I saw his father in the crazy furrows of his forehead, but something else, too, in his eyes. It was a rage that looked to be taking control of him, as if those eyes were pulling him along, commanding him to reach out and grab me by the throat. He tried, but Johara must have seen it, too, for she threw her arm between us. He failed to get a solid hold before I was able to draw away. He chased me from the house.

"There are goats and a rooster for you to eat," he shouted. Gamal, and of course, Adli, were behind him laughing. Their heads were poking around Faid because the fun in watching a beat-down isn't complete until you see the wretched look upon the face of the victim.

"You go take those animals away and bury them before the dogs come down from the hills to tear them and you to pieces." The door slammed, and I could hear the fight Johara started but wouldn't win.

For edification, I had to see what the fuss was about. The rooster lay stripped and torn by the shed door. I pictured him protecting the hens which he ferociously did whenever I approached. Behind the shed a goat carcass was pulled half-way through the barbed-wire fencing. Its head was dangling by mere threads of tendons and skin, and still dripping blood. I didn't see the second goat until I made my way to the cave. Amir had managed to get that one to the backyard where he made a meal of it. There was no way I was going to move those animals. I'd let them sit and rot, stink up the whole place, make them all sick to their stomachs every time they breathed.

I had to admit, the thought of Amir bringing his friends back in the night to feast had me petrified. I'd be at the cave where I'd be safe from them, but I let myself revel in the thought the pack would break through the flimsy front door and drag Faid and Gamal into the hills. I even had myself hearing them screeching my name for help. Then I had to reconcile the fact that Johara and Adli would most probably be dragged off as well, and I couldn't stand the sound of them begging for my help.

I peered into Yamma's bedroom window from the back of the house. It was remarkable that she was not preparing the meal or coming to my rescue. The room was empty. I could still hear Johara pleading my case, Faid attempting to deride her but Johara giving him no room to speak. I stood there a long while until the sun disappeared behind me. I wasn't waiting for an invite back in necessarily, just for someone to throw a square of Knafeh out the window. Finally the threat of wild dogs arriving sent me down to the cave where I spent a miserably cold and hungry night.

Sleep was not really the objective, nor an option. I was hungry and I had no food. It was cold and I had no blankets. It was only by luck I had my jacket on, being thrown out of the house before I had chance to take it off. I curled myself into a tight ball on a patch of sand in the rear of the cave. Besides an attempt to stay somewhat warm, my motive was to stay hidden from any dogs that may wander down. I had my first real nightmare that night.

I had plenty of bad dreams but not nightmares, which I classify as having people metamorphosing into bizarre creatures. This one had Faid sneaking into my bedroom, staring at me from the doorway with those crazy eyes that flashed brilliant yellow-green. In the shadows I heard him let out a low growl. He was joined by a chorus of long, lonely howls. He approached my bed slowly, shrinking, seeming to melt into the floor until he was gone. Yet I could hear him still moving somewhere below in the dark. I dared to lean out of my bed when he snapped upright as an olive-brown snake. He sat coiled before me but made no effort to strike. Each time I moved he would rattle but gave no other hint of his intentions. I pleaded with him to tell me what he wanted but of course he couldn't. He was a snake.

I awoke the next morning with cramps and couldn't bear to stay balled up in the cave any longer. It was dawn. I made my way up the hill, listening along the way for sounds of the dogs. Only birds. The goat carcass was gone from the back yard. So, too, were the other goat and the rooster. It was too clean, so I supposed Faid and the boys removed them. Someone had put a plate out back for me. Whatever they placed on it was just a memory.

I don't know if my next move was an act of desperation, a protest, or an adventure. Adli had taught me how he caught birds, only to set them free. Catching them was not the real challenge, not compared to releasing them. They put up valiant fights with beak and claws. But Adli never stopped in his efforts to do so, even when beads of blood were drawn. But I was starving to the point of hallucinating; I had no intentions of setting anything free.

The trap was a simple device, a heavy string pulled through a hole in the top of a stake. The stake was two feet long and pounded into the ground near a nesting site. One end of the string had a slip knot; fastened to the other was a large rock. A fabricated perch was fitted tightly into the middle of slip knot and tucked snugly against the stake. It became the noose. Just below the perch, chicken feed was scattered. When the bird landed on the perch, it fell away, releasing the rock and tightening the noose around whatever part of the bird was caught inside, usually its legs.

I set my stake under a grove of trees behind the makeshift basketball court and scattered the chicken feed I grabbed as I past the coop. This was where Adli pointed out nesting Myna birds. I went back to the ridge above the court where I could lay down to watch the comings and goings at the house. I had no idea of the time. They could be off to school in a minute or an hour. I settled in to wait, dozing off as the sun began to warm the rocks I was resting on.

What started as chatter from a dream woke me. It transformed into a set of shrieks from the woods behind me. I raced to the trap to find a Myna bird swinging upside down by one leg. It looked to be the size of an eagle as it spun and flailed its wings. I don't know if it saw me approaching or had any concept of its predicament. It was obviously an extraordinary position to find itself in, one it couldn't possibly have instincts for. All it could think to do was scream and thrash about in hopes that this danger would pass.

For sure it wasn't going to let me take it easily. To attempt manhandling the bird would mean a struggle; I was in no mood for a struggle. I found a thick pine branch and used the bird as a piñata. It took three blows to do the job, a fourth to be sure.

I had not a clue what to do from there. Feathers would need to go as a first step. But what do I do with the head, the legs, the innards? The birds I ate had them already removed. Someone had to do it. I supposed that someone was now me.

It didn't look near as large with its feathers plucked, hardly enough to make the slaughter worthwhile. I tried pulling the head off but it only stretched. Finally, I twisted it like a bottle cap and it popped off in my hand. Removing the legs was an easy, though sickening, task. By that point it was no bigger than a normal-sized chicken breast.

I had no matches. Yamma kept a box inside the chicken coop for building small fires in the pit during the winter. I went back to the ridge. The old Peugeot Faid was driving was now gone. I went down to the coop for the matches then tried get inside the house. It was locked. I wanted to smash a window. Not to get inside but to fight against them for turning me out. Instead I returned to the bird, impaled him on a stick, and roasted him over the fire.

I ate him in small bites, spitting out any gristle that may have been intestinal. I reset the trap, realizing I would need to catch a flock to make a dent in my hunger. I caught only two more before Johara came home from school. By the third bird I had perfected stripping the meat from the fragile bones while avoiding what I perceived to be his organs. Stupid birds. You'd think they'd be watching me from above.

Faid was still going to The Friends School and his arrivals home were varied, but Adli and Gamal were usually about a half hour behind Johara, being let out of school later. I took this slice of time to get into the house to see where Yamma was and get myself some decent food and water. I hoped Johara was still on my side.

She rushed out to meet me when she saw me coming from the olive grove. From her look I must have been a fright. "You have a cut," she said, staring at my face.

"I don't think so," I said,

She rubbed my cheek with her finger and showed me a swatch of blood. It was from the bird. "Yeah, maybe a little one," I said, preferring not to share the ghastly details of how I spent my day. "Where's Yamma?"

"She is away visiting family."

"She didn't tell me that," I said.

"It's just for a few days. We drove her to Salfit. You look a mess. You must be hungry."

"A drink. I need something to drink."

She guided me inside as if I was infirm. I watched greedily as she poured out a large glass of apple juice. She scooped out a bowl of Mjaddara, rice and lentils. "No knafeh left?" I asked.

"I put the last piece out back for you last night. Didn't you get it?"

I shook my head.

She caught me looking out the window into the driveway while I ate. "Faid is working after school; he won't be home for awhile."

"I don't care about him."

"What he did was just horrible. Yamma will be told."

I no longer had faith in Yamma's ability to protect me. At times I thought she wasn't even trying. I wanted to know but didn't ask why she left so suddenly. I believed she was running away, afraid not only of Abdel but of Faid. How long before she was afraid of even Gamal?

"You can stay in the house tonight," she said.

"Did he say I could?"

"It'll be okay."

Gamal came busting in, Adli on his heels. They were breathless and laughing. Adli greeted me with a hug while Gamal ignored me as was usual. "Faid threw you out of the house," Adli said laughing.

"Yeah."

"Because you let Amir kill our goats and rooster."

I pushed him. It was the first time and last time. "I didn't let him go," I said. "So stop saying it." Adli was set to cry. I didn't care. My mind was close to being convinced this was a grand conspiracy. Perhaps even Yamma was involved.

"That's enough for both of you," Johara said. "I'm tired of all this fighting. We're falling apart when we need to fight to stay together."

I ran to my room and pulled my blanket from my bed. Johara chased me down. "Where are you going?"

"I'm not staying here. Everyone blames me and nobody will leave me alone until they believe me."

"I believe you, Joe."

"You don't matter. You can't make the rest of them leave me alone. And when Faid comes home he'll yell at me some more and kick me out anyway."

"I won't let him."

"You can't stop him. No one can."

That night while sleeping in the cave, I staggered to the entrance, violently ill from half-cooked birds. I leaned over the cliff and vomited into the great valley below. The echoes of my suffering came back around to me. As I listened to my own agony, I thought back on Sue. Her pain was buried deep inside, but I doubt it equaled mine at the moment, and like her, I wished like hell I was dead.

CHAPTER 24

Yamma was home by the next morning and all was made right. She kept everyone home from school, to include Faid, and sent Adli out to find me. "Joe,' he hollered from the mouth of the cave, "Joe, you in here?" He crept inside. I heard him kicking up rocks, his breathing unsteady. He was scared but at least he was in. He was less than three feet from where I was curled under the blanket. It was a tailored-made opportunity to make him shit his pants, but I couldn't do it.

Adli not only became my friend but one to himself. When I first met him he was Gamal's shadow, mimicking all he did. He was also his puppet. When Sue left, I fell in desperate need of someone to grab hold of. I didn't choose Adli. I didn't choose anyone. And he didn't choose me. Fate, not good intentions, put us together. And I wish I could say, even all these years later, that it was like Yamma said, that I was good for Adli and he became so much better because of me. I would have been pleased to serve such a purpose. But I saw none of that. There wasn't a selfless nerve in me back then. My life was becoming as instinctual as Amir's. I saw things, all things, in terms of how they affected me.

By teaching me, Adli found a usefulness. By learning from me, he found an awareness. And he conquered many fears in those years, the cave being his first and biggest. I didn't want to be the one to take him a step backward because his usefulness, awareness, and courage coincided with my own. To shake his so easily would only confirm my own vulnerability.

"I'm right here, Adli."

"Where?"

"Under your feet."

"Yamma wants you to come home."

"She's home now?" I asked.

"Yeah. So come back home."

I gathered my blanket which was heavy and damp. Adli took hold of one end as we hiked up. "You were gone for a week, Joe."

"Just two days."

"You slept here?"

"Yeah."

"And you weren't even scared, were you?"

"No."

"Yeah, we could hear the dogs out here. We thought they may find you. I told them you were probably in the cave. I, Faid, and Gamal dragged the dead stuff back into the woods over there." He pointed nearer to the cave then I liked. "It was horrible. The goat's leg fell off in my hands. And all his hair."

"They knew I was in the cave?"

"I told them you probably were."

"But you threw the dead animals near here, anyway?"

"No, over there." He pointed again.

"But that's close."

"Yeah. Sure is. Did you hear the dogs?"

"I think I did.

"Johara gave me a piece of knafeh to give you. I put it on a plate outside. Know what, though?"

"What?"

"I took a bite." He clasped his hand over his mouth and laughed as if he had shared an indecent joke with me.

"I think the dogs got it," I said.

"Didn't you eat anything?"

I told him about the Myna birds, how I killed them while they swung helplessly in the noose; how I poked the stick through their anus and out their neck, and roasted them. He didn't freak. His eyes grew wide as if I was reading to him from a Green Lantern comic book. He wanted to do it; he begged me to show him. "Show you what?" I said. "You're the one who showed me how to catch them, that's the hard part."

"Yeah, but you can kill them?"

It hit me. He released birds not because he wanted to, but because he thought it was the only thing he could do. He was enraptured by this new option. He made me repeat the sequence of events, slowly. He was insistent enough to make me take him up to the pine grove where we set up the trap. "Now we can wait," he said.

"I wanna go home and eat," I said.

"We can eat the birds."

"No, I got sick from eating them."

"How sick?"

"Real sick."

"Did you throw up?"

"Yeah. A lot."

"Oh. I don't like throwing up," he said. "But I like eating birds."

"It's different than chicken, you know."

I convinced him to let me eat at home and check the trap later. He was concerned the bird would die before we got back, denying him the joy of batting the thing senseless with a tree branch. This schizophrenic shift reminded me just how easy it was for his brothers to manipulate him.

Yamma greeted me warmly without overdoing it. She tapped my behind and shooed me to my room to get cleaned up. Adli worked her unsuccessfully for permission to catch and prepare his own dinner.

A car door slammed in the drive. I watched Abdel from my bedroom window as he stood by the Mercedes with his hands on his hips, surveying the farm. I doubt he even noticed Amir or the goats missing. Sam, our trip wire, told us he would be by soon to tell Yamma it was time to leave the property, to head back to her parents in shame and disgrace.

He turned to stare at the house, now his house. I ducked back inside my room, certain he saw me. But he hadn't, for, as always, he was preoccupied with what was outside, not inside.

And what if he had? What would I care? What could he do? I was to be gone along with Yamma and the kids. Out of his sight and mind. I laughed, wondering if he realized as I went so would go his extra money.

Johara was calling to Yamma, telling her he was here. Yamma planned the strategy a while ago which was for all of us to sit tight and stay away from him. If he called we were not to answer, no matter how loud he ranted and raged. Faid was not to be brought into the loop. She gave us no reason nor did she explain her part in the plan.

It worked for me. Gamal voiced his disagreement, and of course, told Faid. I sensed this was to be the great battle within the family but Yamma dismissed Faid's harangue, not with a curt lecture, but with an indifferent look. As it was, Faid was not home when Abdel arrived and Gamal was in the room with me.

"What are you looking at?" he asked as I watched.

"Abdel is here."

Gamal started from the room but I blocked his way. "Move," he said.

"Yamma said not to go see him."

It infuriated him when I referred to her as "Yamma," but he never voiced it. He was too old for a tirade over something so childish, yet still childish enough to feel me a threat to the sacred relationship. His brow furrowed as his eyes blackened. He worked his jaws so I nearly heard his teeth grind. Where it used to panic me, I now found it beneficial in adding to my power base.

"He's my father." Gamal said as he tried to move me, again working to my strength.

He had learned a little about leverage since our last encountered as he flexed his knees and pushed me at waist level. I wobbled but stood my ground. "Get out," he said.

So impressed was I with Yamma's stare down of Faid earlier that I did the same to Gamal, standing mute and cocking my head stupidly like a dog trying to make sense of his voice commands. Of course, like last time, he could have cold cocked me, but either he didn't think of it or he didn't have the balls to elevate it to that level. In any event, we would have stayed there the rest of the night had we not heard Abdel getting into it with Yamma through the bedroom window.

Abdel sounded so furious at that moment that Gamal preferred the confines of the house. We both rushed to the bedroom window to check it out from a safe distance. Yamma was standing at the doorway, her arms loosely folded at her waist. I had to focus to understand what Abdel was saying for the more unflustered Yamma stood, the more heated his speech. He was telling her because of her disgrace, it was time for her to leave and go back home to her parents. Infidelity was haraam, *forbidden*, and so as the hadith proclaimed, she was to be banished from her family and her home. "You have no way to survive here," he said.

"Why? Because I don't have you?" It was a question with a pointed tip she jabbed deep into him. He didn't like it.

"You have nothing."

She looked around casually. "Looks to me as if I have it all."

"Listen to me, you—"

"No, you listen. This house was bought with money my father gave to us as a wedding gift. The furniture was paid for with the mahr you provided me, and other pieces were passed down by my family. As were the dishes. And most of the other things you never appreciated. All given to us so that we would have a home to raise our family. Now you are gone, but my family is not."

"You defiled your family, have they no honor?"

"How far do you plan on taking this lie, Abdel?"

"It's your lie," he said.

"We both swore our truths to Allah, Abdel. But there can be only one truth. I know what it is, and you know. Surely Allah knows. It's you with no honor."

Then he said something that made me, and I'm sure Gamal, blush. "I will do this; I will take you to bed this last time to demonstrate that I may be willing to take you back. Perhaps during this iddah. But right after we do, you must leave."

"I am not accepting ruju from you, Abdel. This is final from me."

"You have no job," Abdel screamed. "You cannot support this house, this farm."

"I do fine with the harvest. And I will work in the village."

"Ha, like hell you will. No one will have you. They all know what you have done."

"You over-estimate your reputation; you always have. I have secured a job."

"Where?"

"It serves me no purpose to share that with you."

"You're lying."

She shrugged her indifference to his accusation, another dagger into his ego. "If I am, come back to claim the house and farm as your own because I will have abandoned it."

Faid drove into the driveway. Abdel grabbed him from the car and walked him to the backyard. His back was to us so his words were muffled. But his arms flailed and it took no imagination to figure out the theme of their conversation. When I turned to look for Yamma she was gone. I heard her in the kitchen, of all things, singing her songs.

Gamal ran from the room and into the yard to join his father and brother. I took company in the kitchen with Johara and Yamma. I don't know where Adli was. Another car arrived, kicking up stones as it skidded to a halt. I knew it was Sam.

I expected a lukewarm greeting from him. No reason he should, just a distance I felt. But he spotted me a big grin when he came in. "Hey, Joey. How's it hangin'?" He'd been working hard on his American slang and used it proudly, if not very appropriately.

"He doesn't look very happy," he said to Yamma, glancing out the back window

"He's not," Yamma said.

"He having you leave right away?"

"I'm not going anywhere. I'm staying right here; we all are."

Sam cocked his head to her. "That so?"

"I have done nothing wrong and refuse to act and be treated as if I have. My children will not be punished for what he's done."

"Amineh I am happy for you, but what about his accusations of you? It's in the hadith that in such a situation he can compel you—"

"I know the hadith. These are lies," Yamma shouted.

"But the people of Dayr Ghasana believe him."

"Then let the people believe him. If they do they're no friends of mine and they can keep to themselves."

Sam took the hint. We all did, and so all kept quiet until Adli came busting through on his way out the side door. "I think we caught one," he said. "Let's go."

"I haven't eaten yet," I said.

"We'll eat the bird."

"You will do no such thing," said Yamma. "You eat a normal meal."

She dished Mutabbal into bowls for all of us. It was an eggplant dish I had come to enjoy before I knew it was eggplant.

"I was told Khaal Abu Faid took you to work," Sam said. "Which camp did he show you?"

"Al Amari."

"Ah, yes. Schools, health clinic, cinderblock huts, a food distribution center, electricity, a—what is it called—a verification from the United

Nations Relief and Works Agency. Tell me, Joe, did he take you into one of the houses?"

"No."

"Babies sleep in cardboard boxes. Inside there are no walls so if they want privacy, they hang newspapers. Floors are dirt, or hard cement. You go into the schools?"

"We drove past them."

"What if I was to tell you Al Amari is possibly the best camp in the West Bank."

"It is?"

"What if I was to ask you if you would like to be in a place where everything was given to you?"

"I'd like that a lot."

"You would have to because there would be no chance of leaving. There would be over fifty students in your classroom. If your family was small, about five of you, you would live in a one-room hut. More than that, you get two rooms. You would eat whatever it was Khaal Abu Faid and his group brought to you. You couldn't cook it yourself, though. Families have no kitchens."

"Where can they cook?"

"There is a center stove where a baker cooks but you have to pay him. Food is bought for you by other countries, mostly America. There is usually enough to go around but that is all. No extra. Amari has a water supply, but many camps do not. Water is trucked in so it goes like food, sufficient but no extra.

"It is very hot in the summer, very cold in the winter. Your father would be fortunate to have a job. Most times it would be temporary. For the better jobs he has to go to Israel. The worse part, you would most likely raise your family in the camp, and your children will raise theirs."

"I'd just move."

"That's the point," he said, "you can't. You see, Palestinians do not own land. The land is occupied by Israel and we are like visitors. No … guests here. But it is more than just having a few belongings. You are never free. Joe, have you ever fed pigeons at the park?"

"A few times."

"And they flock as if they'd been waiting their whole lives for you. When you leave, they flock to another. When there are no others around, they sit and wait. That's what those people in the camps are; they're pigeons, forever depending on handouts from the rest of the world."

"Abdel told me they were taken care of."

Sam's face burned with a fire that flared his nostrils and brought out thick veins in his neck. This was the first conversation where I heard Sam's deep passion for the people. Prior, his words were instructional, like a tour guide. "These are not zoo animals to be taken care of," he said. "People are never to become so tame that they dare not venture outside the bars put before them. Do you not understand that even at your age?"

He caught his breath, then smiled. Putting his hands on my shoulders he continued, "You are very young and being taken care of is the only world you know. As a child, that's the only world you should know. But it's a world to grow out of, not to grow into. For Palestinians, this is the world being created for us. People are born, live, and die in camps like Al Amari. They have children there. The parents do not leave; the children do not leave. They grow to be old men and women, but do not grow to be real people. It's the world men like Khaal Abu Faid maintain. So now you see, that is why I dislike what he does."

"Sam, be kind and truthful," Yamma said. "Work done by Khaal Abu Faid and the agency is a good thing. Many would die of thirst, disease, or starvation were if not for them."

"That is what you believe, Amineh. But look at what you have just done. You made a powerful decision, an unheard of decision. It may work for you or it may not. But no matter, right? It was made and that is the important thing." He turned to me. "There is an English word I learned that so fits Palestinians. Displaced. Do you know the word, Joe?"

I shrugged.

"To be removed from one's usual or proper place. But there is another meaning, one far more dangerous to people in places like Amari. It takes place in the mind, when one tries to change a dangerous situation into a safer one. They do this to protect themselves, yet it is most often a false place they go."

"How do they make it change?" I asked.

"It doesn't really change; they only think it does. They then get happy, thinking they're in a good place when they are really in the same bad place. So they never try to leave. You were shown that place to convince you it wasn't evil."

"It's evil?"

"The minds that live there without fighting are evil in a way that has nothing to do with ghosts. Or perhaps it does. Perhaps that's what lives there now. Only ghosts."

Adli got up and ran to the door. "C'mon, Joe, I know there's a bird in the trap; I just know it."

He sprinted as I walked. I wasn't anxious to trap another bird. I quickly lost my initial sense of accomplishment, the feeling of dominance. It wasn't the stomach ache that dissuaded me. I saw it as me swinging in the noose, awaiting my fate, praying it was the benevolent boy who had ensnared me not the hungry one. This time it would be neither, but I know I wouldn't be able to stop Adli from killing it.

Adli was screaming wildly. "We got one. Joe, we got a bird."

To hear him so excited you'd think it was his first. I took my time getting there. I found him at his basketball court where he was searching the ground for a stick. "Help me find one, Joe, a good one. I got one."

It was more like a log. It took him two hands to wrap it up and some effort to lay it over his shoulder. There'd be little left to cook if he managed to hit it. I followed him over to the trap and saw an exhausted white dove flapping in vain.

Adli was raising the branch when I called out for him to stop. He looked at me quizzically. "You can't kill a dove," I said.

"Why?"

"You have no reason to."

"I do so."

"No you don't. Let it go."

"I will not. I'm going to hit it and kill it and eat it."

"You can't. Do you know the story of the captive dove," I said.

"No."

I gave him the condensed version, and told him about *Ikwhan al-Safa*t, Brethren of Purity. "See, Adli, like when I was getting hit hard with soccer balls by Gamal and his friends."

"I pushed you away," he said.

"Yeah. You got hit so I wouldn't."

"And when you got in that fight with Gamal and the boys when they threw rocks at me," he said.

"Yeah. Like that."

Together we untied the dove. It lay there, near dead from exhaustion. We stood back while it struggled. Finally it set its feet. It took us in, bobbing its head, cooing as it strutted about of the ground. "Look," Adli said, laughing, "It's cursing at us." We watched it fly off then got into a game of basketball.

It was a good day, the best day I had had in Palestine. I had seen two of my favorite people take a good turn in their lives. I knew it was only a matter of time until it was my chance.

CHAPTER 25

Back home in Chicago we had a Black Forest cuckoo clock in the hallway. It was an antique my father's mother sent us. It was originally in the living room, but my mother complained she couldn't hear it from the bedroom while my father complained it cuckooed every time a critical scene came on the television. So it was moved to the middle of the house.

We had it since I was an infant so there was no novelty in it. No one seemed to notice it except when it ran down. Each half hour the Bavarian girl came out the door to ring the bell as an ompha band played *Happy Wanderer*. And not a minute later someone would ask for the time.

It had an eight-day movement that mom rewound every two weeks after much consternation in the household. It was a bone of contention between my parents and David and Sue, once they became old enough to yank the pinecones to rewind it. Like the trash basket that doesn't get emptied until it's overflowing, and the clothes in the hamper that don't get washed until they reek, our cuckoo clock was another test of our family's mettle. The smart thing would have been to get rid of it, but I never heard anyone suggest such a thing. I suppose every family has a cuckoo clock, and conflict is just as vital as harmony to a family's survival.

Amir had come back to the farm. He was that thing that had to be taken care of. And like the clock, that thing that was disregarded. He was ignored by everyone except Yamma, other than as a tool used by the boys to torment me. When he chose to torment on his own, it was decided he was a thing to be destroyed.

Faid racked a shotgun behind me. I recoiled as he spun me around by my shoulder. I had never heard one shot or being loaded. I had never even seen one. He held it at port arms and thrust it into my chest.

"Amir scares you," Faid said.

I nodded. I was still in shock while cradling the piece of hardware as if he was a squealing baby about to drop from my arms. It grew heavier the longer I held it, physically and emotionally.

"You need to kill what you fear," he said. "Understand?"

Hell no, I was six-years old. "I don't want to kill Amir."

"Then he beats you. You stay afraid and he wins."

"I'm only afraid when he attacks me; when Gamal and his friends make him attack me."

"Then you must kill him."

"Gamal?"

"No. Amir."

I saw this as a ploy to be rid of Amir and humiliate me, to show his brothers my weaknesses, whether it be my inability or refusal to shoot. "I can't lift this," I complained, making a melodramatic show of it, knowing for sure he would see the folly of his plan.

"That is why I brought you this." He pulled a revolver from the back of his waistband. It didn't occur to me until years later how perilous it was to have such an arsenal handy to Faid and Abdel. "The shotgun will be for me in case you miss."

Yamma raced from the house. She took the shotgun from my hand and masterfully unloaded it. She turned to Faid. "Who are you to decide?" she demanded. "You're like your father; you think your word is the final one. You look at things your way. You don't consider other people or other things."

"Amir is a wild animal, you said so yourself."

"And an animal, wild or not, cannot have its own thoughts?"

"Animals have instincts, not thoughts, and Amir's instincts are to kill. It killed our goats and rooster when Joe let him loose."

"It wasn't Joe. It was me. I was bringing him around the house and kept him off the rope because no one was home. When I left, I forgot about him."

Faid only glanced at me, avoiding my I-told-you-so look. "It doesn't matter who," he said. "Amir has tasted blood and needs to be destroyed."

"What he has tasted is freedom. He needs to be set free."

"He will keep coming back."

"He will go where he needs to live or die. But we will not decide for him."

We all kept our distance while Amir surveyed his old grounds. He sniffed the fence where he left the one goat. Then over to the chicken coop where he slaughtered the rooster. Looking for the remains, perhaps.

Or like an old soldier, exploring past battlefields. Was he ashamed? Was he back to gloat or make amends? Yamma could have corralled him but she let him investigate. He pawed at his old rope then glared up at us as if to let us know that he remembered all too well. Finally he turned and ran into the hills. "He made his decision," she said.

"Yes, and now he'll be back to kill again."

"As it should be. That is his nature, so we do what we must to protect our property."

"I was doing that," Faid protested.

"We can do it without killing."

We watched like parents sending a son off to war, Amir disappearing over the ridge to a world that didn't know him as "Amir," that didn't know him at all. A world he only ran through in dreams, where food came to him from a mystical hand, not from Yamma or corralled neatly for his convenience. There was no need for our intervention after all. I never saw him again. As Yamma said, he either lived out his days on some remote mountaintop, or died at the jaws of his own kind.

***

By this time Yamma had seized control of the household. She had secured a job in town working for a man and his wife who made candles and rolled cigars. She came home at night reeking of tobacco, but she enjoyed being out there. I wish I could report the villagers had taken her side and there were dozens of them reaching out to support her. But it was just the one. I heard even their business fell off dramatically on account of them taking in a shlicke, *a slut*. I'm not sure I believed that. Being a small businessman myself now, I don't know how or why they would have kept her on if that was the case. Then again, they may have been much like Yamma, willing to take on a good fight.

It didn't mean Gamal and Faid were held in check. Quite the opposite, they had more time to annoy me and Adli, who by this time had grown very close to me. Within time Faid grew weary of the nonsense games. He moved off to college at the University of Jordan. There was no fanfare. Abdel came one day, picked him up, and he was gone. I rarely saw him after that.

Gamal and his friends remained a pain-in-my-ass but it was subtle, they being much too afraid to confront me by this point. As Yamma had gained control at home, so, too, had I at school. I fought regularly until there were no more takers. I fought with the teachers until they realized their beatings had no effect on me. The turning point came when a ruler splintered as it impacted my knuckles. The story went through the teachers' lounge like lice. It became part of my legend.

I was waiting. Biding my time until mom and dad came to my rescue. It was imminent. Sue had been home for months. She told them of our plight, my plight. I was in distress. I was in danger. Hell, these people made her slit her wrists. God only knew what drastic actions I would be forced to soon take.

But that letter never came. Neither did the life-saving phone call. It was Sue who called to tell me. It was a terrible connection, with her voice fading and cracking. "Joe, I talked to Mom and Dad."

"Why did it take you so long?"

"Be quiet, you need to listen. This is not up to Mom, okay?" she said. "She didn't want us to go in the first place."

"So why were we sent here?"

"It was Dad."

"Oh. Okay."

"Yeah, so Mom didn't make the decision."

"Yeah. But how come—"

"So she can't make the decision to bring you home. And Dad doesn't want you coming home yet."

"So when?"

"When you graduate."

"I did that two weeks ago."

"High school, Joe."

"That can't be," I screamed. "No way. They told you that?"

"They fight about it all the time. Mom wants you home. She misses you, she really does. But Dad says this is best for you. He hates Chicago for us to grow up in. He's very afraid. He even has a curfew for David and me. But he trusts in Khaal Abu Faid; he wants him to teach you about Allah's great love."

"I hate it here, Sue, and you promised. You promised you'd make them take me back."

"I really tried, Joe, but he talks to Khaal Abu Faid, who's convinced him he will insure you learn the Muslim ways even though he is no longer at the house."

"They can't do this."

"Joe, calm down, listen to me. You must not let him. Faid and Khaal Abu Faid are not about Allah."

"I know. Faid is gone but—"

"Yamma loves you. Yamma is the one to learn from."

"She's gone working most of the time. And Gamal fights with me."

"So you must be like the dragon slayer."

"What?"

"Like Saint George, Joe. You must be strong like he was."

"They hate me here."

"I told them everything," she said, near tears herself now as I could hear her voice cracking, "but Dad says he's lost one daughter to disease, one to an accident, and a son to the streets. He wants us to know Islam so we will be spared."

"Does he know about why you cut yourself?"

She didn't answer and I thought the connection had broken. "Does he, Sue? Didn't you tell him?"

"I told them all I could," she said, defeat in her voice.

"But does he know Abdel steals the money sent here for me? He—"

"It doesn't matter, Joe, he's not listening to us. Another thing, Joe. I heard Dad arguing with Khaal Abu Faid on the phone. He wants you going somewhere."

"Who does?"

"Dad. He wants you to—"

Her voice crackled then died. "Where? Where he is going to send me now?"

I heard what Sue said about the why's of my new existence, but all the while, my mind was racing. What I heard and what I comprehended were on two vastly different planes. It registered as Dad and Mom didn't want me around anymore. What evil could I have done to make them do such a thing to me? I thought back on the weeks leading up to my departure: my messy room, losing the keys to the car, breaking the corner streetlight, stuffing twelve toads into a milk bottle.

I know this, a child needs a safe place to go, to be loved, protected, and valued. And for every instance a child is not afforded this, humanity sinks a little lower. And so my young life became a day-to-day thing which I hated and dreaded and cursed. No religion was going to reach me now. I made that my mission. If this Islam was the thing to save me, I was determined to fight it as I did Gamal and his friends and my teachers. If this Islam wanted to join the axis of evil against me, so be it. By defeating it I will be defeating my father and mother, as well. And Sue, whom I was sure didn't try hard enough. I was tough enough by this time to take them all on. And I was devastated. In that moment I knew another thing a child should never know: what it was that could drive a person to suicide.

***

I began walking home from school alone. Adli would wait, but I'd push him along without me. I had also taken up smoking. Not a lot, as I hadn't mastered the inhale-exhale yet which made me nauseous, but it was enough to add to my reputation. There were several packs left behind by Faid. I did it on the backside of a hill behind the school.

There was a cottage I passed by each trip. It was good distance away and I couldn't make it out as ramshackle-abandoned or ramshackle-inhabited. It sat precariously on a craggy ridge where further along there was a row of boulders twice its height. The silhouette fascinated me. I imagined a giant child playfully rolling the boulders down to crush it.

On one of my late afternoon sojourns home I came across an old man digging twenty feet off the trail. I stopped to watch. He wore a seedy dark thobe and kufeya. Here was dry desert. There were no trees or bushes to uproot or plant. I saw no trash he may have been burying. The ground was unforgiving, but whatever it was he was burying or unearthing had to be important for the broiling sun did not slow him from his hard labor.

He made decent progress in the time I'd been watching as he worked the spade in and pulled out two or three loads of sand before having to bend his brittle back to dislodge stones the size of my head.

As was my custom, my self-indulgent treat, I nursed a can of grape Nehi on my way along the trail. When at last he stopped to take a break, he turned to me. "Salam alaikum."

I nodded. "Walaikum assalam."

I held the can out to him. He nodded and smiled, toothless, like many of the old desert people I had seen. He drank it greedily and handed it back empty. "Shukran," he said. I nodded my "you're welcome."

"What are you digging?"

"A hole."

"Oh. Do you live near here?"

He pointed to the cottage on the hill.

I suppose I could have offered him some help but, at seven years old, physical labor of that sort did not inspire me. Besides, he seemed genuinely happy to be working so hard. "You want, I can help carry something down for you," I said. I really just wanted an up close look at the cottage and imagine further it getting bowled over.

"No need, young son."

"Okay. Awfully hot," I said.

He looked at the sky as if he hadn't noticed. "Good day," he said. "Always a good day." I saw his knees were bleeding. So were most of his knuckles. Like with the blazing heat, he didn't appear to notice.

I was happy to share my beloved grape Nehi with the man but couldn't bear the thought of traveling the rest of the way empty handed. So although these two purchases ate up nearly a half of the weekly allowance Abdel gave me, on this day it was worth it. I went back to the school shop and purchased another can.

A dust storm blew up as I left the building. Like Midwest tornadoes, many came in from nowhere. Most folks who lived here all their lives knew when they were firing up, but to me they sprang up like summer sun showers, and while some blew through just as quickly, others lasted for hours or even days. I wasn't at the point where I could effortlessly endure them like many of the Bedouins I had seen out here. And unlike a January blizzard, they weren't kid friendly. You couldn't make sand balls. You couldn't sled in them. They didn't melt away by a fire. They hurt. They were blinding. And they stuck with you for days: in your hair, your ears, your nose, your shoes, your bed.

I hid my head under arm and behind my very lightweight jacket. I walked backwards. I duck-walked, thinking that perhaps like a fart smell the effects would be lessened the lower I went. I glanced up on occasion to see if the storm was coming to an end but it wasn't like looking for rain clouds. Sand clouds were as endless as the desert that spawned them.

Nearly thirty minutes longer than the trip normally took I arrived back at the hole which was minus the old man. It was half filled in by the blowing sand. I jumped down and crouched hoping the storm would soon pass. The bottom was rather soft and unsteady. As I adjusted my footing I saw a white cloth beneath me. I brushed the sand away and was startled, no terrified, at what I saw. It was the old man, on his back, arms folded over his chest, eyes closed as if placed there by others. He didn't yell when I stepped on him. He didn't even move. I was sure he was dead and I scurried out like a dog from a bathtub.

The wind was still howling and the sand whipped but it was now the last thing on my mind. "Hey," I yelled. "Get up." I don't know what I called him. Old man, or mister, or just you, but I was pleading and begging for him to rid me of my horror. But he didn't twitch.

I raced wildly through the storm to get back home. Yamma was in the kitchen. "What are you doing in such a storm?" She asked.

I pointed but couldn't get the words past the sand down my throat. She turned to look out the window. "No," I stuttered, "back there, the trail."

She was cleaning her hands, readying herself to follow me back to the old man and the hole when she did something that confused and infuriated me. As I became more animated with the story, she relaxed and sat at the table. She let me go through the story, asking a few questions. "What was he wearing as he dug?" What was he wearing in the hole?" Questions that had me thinking she didn't believe me.

She took my hands. "Joe," said, matter-of-factly. "What the man was digging was a grave, his grave."

"No, I told you, he fell in and got buried."

"That's why he dressed in a white thobe. It's why he picked this time when the haboob was coming in."

I looked dumbfounded at her.

"It's how some desert people prepare to die when they know it's time."

"Did a doctor tell him it was time to die?"

"He just knew"

"But what if he was wrong?"

"I'm sure he knew."

"What about his family? Shouldn't we tell his family?"

"They'll find him and finish the burial if it's necessary."

Her attitude shocked me. She dismissed the old man as she had dismissed Amir. Back in Chicago there'd be cops and ambulances racing to the scene. I had seen it on television shows. And for a funeral there'd be a church and a coffin and crying friends and family. The thought of me being sent out to dig my own grave petrified me. Worse, I knew it would be Abdel making me do it.

"For some, dying is done as simply and as independently as living," she said. "When their time has come, you will rarely hear the old or sick reflecting upon death. That is for the poets; the dying are much too preoccupied with doing it."

CHAPTER 26

I spent many summer afternoons after that first year swimming in the Red River alone or with Adli. It flowed strong and I wasn't much of a swimmer. But there were pools in the river bends where the water slowed and warmed. We'd ride the current from pool to pool. The river was narrow in most places but where it did widen, Adli would allow himself to drift into serious water where I was forced to retrieve him. It didn't make me a better swimmer, but I did become a more confident one.

When he wasn't with me I would float on my back. Everything was a haunting echo with my ears bobbing just below, then above, the surface. Common sounds like birds and the rushing waters and the wind through the trees took on spiritual qualities, precisely the sounds I wanted to be hearing down here. New voices that spoke only to me and needed no response.

It was a lonely summer. At times it delighted me while at other moments, when I reflected not only on my past but on my future, it was misery. Sam was away in Europe. Johara had a job in Ramallah. And Yamma spent much of the day in the village. With Faid in Jordan, it left Adli and Gamal who were often away with Gamal's friends. I supposed it was why Yamma made her plan.

The plan was to have me live a few weeks with other relatives. It was the move Sue had tried to tell me about on the phone. Yamma was waiting for me at the house when I came up from the river. With her were my father's mother and his brother.

They were sitting in the living room. Yamma stood to take me to them. She was nervous. I felt her hands shaking as she guided me slowly to them. My grandmother was frail. It was an effort for her to lean forward to take my hands from Yamma, even with her son's help. Tears welled up in her eyes; Yamma's, too. She spoke no English, Yamma told me, but learned enough to make me comfortable.

At that moment I didn't get the connection. I thought they were friends come over to visit Yamma; a nice old lady with cold hands and lips that quivered even when she wasn't speaking, and her quiet middle-aged driver. That made no sense though. No one came to visit Yamma anymore.

Yamma introduced them by their first names, Nadirah, and my uncle, Hatim. Nadirah had no teeth. It was frightful the way her lips curled around her gums. Walt Disney sure got it right with his witch in *Snow White*. Her eyes were snake-like slits with pockets of sagging skin. I swear, she smelled like a camel.

And Nadirah? How was I expected to bond with a strange old lady who didn't even have the decency to have a pet name for me to call her? So trained was I to address my elders with deference that I didn't realize men who shaved and women who wore high heels even had first names. It wasn't until Abdel that I could muster sufficient contempt to understand how despicable some could be.

"How do you do, Joe?" Nadirah said slowly as if coming out of a ten-year coma. She hadn't let go of my hands. It had been nearly a minute and they still hadn't warmed. Instinctively, I felt something in that, and my instinct was the one thing that had become highly developed while I was in Palestine. I had that up-chuck taste in my mouth and my smile reflected it. Uncle Hatim noted my resistance and nudged me with his hip, insinuating I had an obligation here.

I looked up at him only to realize I was glaring. It was then I understood my relationship to his man. This was my father. It was his nudge, his look, his quiet disregard for me. I shook free of Nadirah's hands and backed away. Hatim bent over to intimidate me. Yamma stopped my retreat with her outstretched hand. I was trapped.

"I have a bag packed for you," Yamma was saying from behind.

"Go, hug her," Hatim whispered.

"Joe, it is so fine to have you," Nadirah over-annunciated.

You people, I wanted to scream, *you people leave me alone. I don't want to be with you. I want to go home. If you won't send me home then I want to be left alone.*

Hatim knew my intentions and was readying himself to snatch me before I made my escape. I saw my father's intolerance in his strained brow, dark eyes, and tense jaw. If I had any notions about quality time with them, Hatim was enough to dissuade me. He would tell me lies just to get me to go away with Nadirah, away to a new village, a new house, a new school. Perhaps a gaggle of new cousins. But the end, the end would not be new.

I bolted from the room. I ran out the kitchen door, across the olive grove, and into the pine forest. I spied down from the basketball court. No one came out to look for me, which made me both relieved and angered.

I made my way around the outer perimeter of the farm over to the cave. I had never taken this roundabout route before. The forest was thick and the ridgeline I traversed was steep and rocky. It took nearly an hour. I was exhausted and parched. My ankles were swollen from rolling them. My hands were cut and sliced from grabbing tree limbs, rocky ledges, and Thorny Broom as I worked my way along the hillside.

I collapsed at the mouth of the cave to make use of the evening breeze that blew up from the valley. I knew that no matter how hard I fought, I'd have no control of my life here. I cried hard, knowing I couldn't run forever. I would be brought back to them or surrender myself. At one point I conjured Sue bleeding on the rocks. I fell asleep before I could play it out further.

In bed, I awoke in stages, often repeating each stage several times before full consciousness. But at the cave I slept in short spurts, and awoke quickly, fully alert, like an animal of prey whose survival depended on it.

I was awakened by my nightmare of Abdel turning from a mad dog into a snake by a loud, relentless hissing. I was in my usual posture, curled tightly on my right side. My eyes shot open to see a rust-colored Palestinian viper coiled not three feet away. His head bobbed continually to within a foot and a half of my face. From my prone viewpoint, that was too damn close for me.

Wild dogs and snakes. Those were the two creatures of the night my cousins tormented me with. The dogs I knew intimately. This was the first live snake I had seen. I recognized it as a viper from pictures on the school walls, the ones that warned against getting too close to them.

In Chicago the older kids would catch garter snakes and chase us around with them. The kids were more horrifying than the snakes, which actually looked cute, except for the forked tongue. The viper, thick and scaly, was every bit that image of the dreaded diamondback rattler Roy Rogers had to dispose of at least once an episode.

I knew enough not to move. It went on for hours, so it seemed. It looked content to stand its ground, as if I was in his space. I was holding my head off the cave floor at a crazy angle so I could watch it.

The blood began to pool in my hand, my shoulder went numb, and my neck was cramping. I freaked. I guess I was hoping it would miss. But this snake had no such defects. I hadn't made my first twitch when it struck true on the top of my left shoulder. The shock sent me reeling to the back of the cave.

I was now seeing and hearing snakes everywhere. My arm was on fire. I dared to look and saw the vampire-like bites and smears of blood. Rushing from the cave didn't occur to me. I passed out and awoke in those hazy stages. The sun was beating down on me. I was sweating while shivering from chills. No, not the sun, it was a bright light hanging above me. And I was covered in cool white sheets. I heard chatter in the hall. And laughter. I was in a hospital. I was alone. My senses were clearing. My throat was terribly parched. I yelled for anyone but don't believe I made a sound.

In my mounting frustration and feverish state, I must have called out in an ungodly tone because a very cross nurse came in and shushed me harshly. "Water," I begged.

She pointed to a blue plastic bottle on the table. I had an IV in my right arm. I reached for the bottle with my left but it fell back uselessly. Fear was waking me quickly now, but as shocking as it was to wake up in a hospital, I was too busy craving the water to worry about it. "Please," I said pitifully, holding my arm across my chest.

She returned and poured me a cup. I drank it greedily, then called her back for a refill. At that she smiled as she waited while I took in three mores cups. Water and time cleared my mind. "Why am I here?"

"You were bitten by a viper."

Yes, at the cave. I remembered. But I was alone there. "Who brought me here?"

She shrugged. "I was off duty then. You need to eat; can you eat some food now?"

I wasn't very hungry, a bit nauseous, really. I shook my head.

"But you need to. You haven't eaten in three days."

This wasn't true. I had breakfast just before running to the cave. I told the nurse and she laughed. "I'm sure you did but that was three days ago."

She left me alone with those notions. Was it true? Three days ago? There was no calendar in the room to check. No matter, I didn't know the date anyway. She brought in a bowl of sliced peaches and sat me up. "I can't," I said. "I can't move my arm."

"Try," she said, tucking a cloth napkin under my chin. "It's from the bite. You have to exercise it."

It was swollen and numb. It felt as if I was lifting a leg; someone else's leg. I watched the spoon go up and down with no sensation that it was under my control. The napkin was soaked with juice when I finished, but the feeling was returning to my arm.

"He must have been a big one," she said. "It injected a lot of venom."

I didn't remember any of that, only standing in the blackness at the back of the cave. I felt myself nodding off again. I fought it, afraid it would be another three days before I awoke.

When I did come to Yamma and Johara were standing above me. "Did I fall asleep for another three days?" I asked anxiously.

Yamma laughed. "No. We've been waiting to see you."

"A viper bit me."

"Yes."

"It left a lot of poison."

"Allah was with you."

Johara was teary-eyed. She hadn't spoken and averted my gaze.

"Can I go home now?"

Home. I said it quite naturally but with mixed emotions. This was home for now, yet to say it out loud led me to issues I wanted to stay clear off. Issues such as acceptance and understanding and appreciation. Yamma picked up on it. I know it delighted her, though she let it pass with only a smile. As for Allah as my savior, I was willing to accept it as a thing Yamma truly believed. "How did I get here?" I asked.

"Hatim drove you," Yamma said.

She noticed my quizzical look. "Your uncle. Your father's brother. Remember, he came to the house with your grandmother, Nadirah."

Johara spoke for the first time. "He drove you to the hospital, but it's not how you got out of the cave."

"How did I?"

"Adli brought you out."

"He carried you up the hill to the house," Yamma added.

I poked my head up. "Where is he?"

"He's in the waiting room," Johara said. "He's nervous to see you."

"Why?"

Yamma looked to Johara. "I'll go get him," Yamma said. "He will tell you himself."

Johara and I sat in elevator-type silence for a long minute. Used to be she filled in dead time peppering me with those questions about America. I adored that undivided attention, my childish descriptions of TV shows and cartoons captivating her as thoroughly as Sue's singing of *With God on Our Side.*

"I was so scared for you, Joe, we all were. We did not think you were …" she looked away again. "You used to like me, Joe. Very much." She gave me a coy smile. "I was like a rose to you."

Yes, she truly was.

"But you found my thorns," she said, "my fear of my father; my fear of ending up like Yamma. I guess if I truly was afraid I would do something to make a change. Perhaps someday I will. If I can, I may be that rose again."

I was about to respond when Yamma came back in, Adli slouched behind her at the door. It was good timing because I really didn't know what to say to Johara. In time, she would indeed be that rose and I would understand about thorns, but in my current state I wasn't forgiving.

"Come on in, Adli," Yamma said. "It's all right."

He did, slowly and reluctantly. Coming off the heels of Johara's discourse, I thought somewhere lost in my immediate memory was an insulting word or action I had done to him. And I was perturbed Yamma would parade him in here for an apology for a thing I could not yet recall.

"Hi, Joe," he said so softly I only got the greeting by reading his lips.

"You found me in the cave?"

He nodded.

"He's thinks you'll be mad at him," Yamma said.

"Why would I be?"

"Go on, tell him."

"I went to find you," he said, his voice shaking. "I called but you didn't answer. But I knew you were in there. I walked inside, all the way to the back. I was really scared but I did it; I went inside." He announced that part proudly. "I found you lying there, but, I couldn't wake you so I pulled you out."

"Go on," Yamma implored.

"Okay. When we were at the front of the cave I saw a snake. He was big and hissing. I ... I couldn't get you by it so I ... I killed it with a big rock."

By now I could only nod. I was growing tired again, effects of the antibiotics rather than the company.

"Is that okay? That I killed it?"

"Of course," I said. "Why wouldn't it be?"

He smiled. "You don't like me when I kill things, Joe, so I thought it would make you angry at me."

I was too tired to explain it to him. I'm not sure he would have understood if I had. The last thing I saw before I fell back to sleep was the three of them smiling. I was alive. They were happy. It was almost all good.

CHAPTER 27

The first genuine smile I remember having about Palestine when I returned home to Chicago was when Mister Lussier, our fifth grade music teacher at Earle Grammar School, had us open our music books to page twenty-three. "This is a song about the Israelites escape from Egypt when they entered Jericho in Syria. Joshua led them in a great battle against the Syrians and—"

I interrupted with, "Canaanites," and Mister Lussier peered around the kids in the front rows at me.

"Excuse me, son, did you have something to say?"

"It was the Canaanites in Jericho, not Syrians. And Jericho is in Palestine's West Bank, not Syria."

"I see. And do you know the song?"

"No."

"Then I suggest you sit quietly and pay attention to the more important parts of this lesson."

It was absurd to me even then that one would consider a song about Jericho in a fifth grade music book more important than its history, but I was proud I knew it, even if it did put me on the teacher's shit list the rest of that year.

***

I was released from the hospital in five days. There was another week at home to recuperate. Yamma had never unpacked my suitcase. I was still going with Nadirah and Hatim.

Nadirah spent several nights at the house where she would sit with me in my bedroom. She'd read me books, tell me family stories, and practice English, mainly by reciting nursery rhymes from memory she thought I still enjoyed, and always, always, she butchered it with made-up lines. It made them more entertaining than the originals.

Little Miss Muffit, sat on her two tits, eating her cud today, along came a spider who drank all her cider and so Miss Muffit was gay.

She loved candles, day or night. She was never without one. She'd light a small one and set it in front of her. The eeriest vision I've ever known was her mouth and hooked nose illuminated at night by that tiny flame whenever she raised the candle up to blow it out. It had me nervous that it would be the only source of lighting where I was going.

Though she was sedentary and oftentimes very quiet, I grew to enjoy her company. Unlike the silence that deepened the void when I sat with Abdel and my cousins, the space between Nadirah and me was alive. It was scary to watch her lose her gaze in the flame. Her lips parted slightly; her eyes never blinked. In time, I was doing the same. Like moths, our thoughts collected there.

She lived in Ariha where she raised my father and his two brothers. "Ariha," Yamma said. "You may know it as Jericho. You know Jericho, right?"

I shook my head, but I must have known of it. I'm sure my dad mentioned Jericho and my uncles but I couldn't recall. It was her wish, Yamma said, to finally meet her grandchildren from America. It was never possible before as Abdel wouldn't allow it. As Yamma explained it to me, every time my father brought it up, Abdel would tell him Jericho had bad influences, and although Nadirah was very nice, his brother, Hatim, had connections to bad people. That, I could believe.

Yamma had no idea who Hatim was hooked up with, if anyone. It was Yamma's belief Abdel came up with the story to keep me in Dayr Ghasana. He was afraid I would stay with Nadirah and lose the support money my father sent.

But Nadirah was as insistent as a mother could be. She kept in contact with my father and with Yamma daily when Abdel left the house. She chastised my father. "You may think what you want about your brother's friends, but how dare you suspect he would put your son in danger? How dare you suspect I would allow it?"

She cried endlessly and prayed to Allah every waking minute I was in the hospital. "I wish I could have met Sureia," she said the first night I came home. "It is such a shame what happened to her." She sat back in her chair and gazed at me, her eyes full of tears. "But Allah kept you safe for me, Joe."

As soon as I was well, I drove with Nadirah and Hatim to Jericho. Before I left, I asked Yamma if I would ever see her again. She laughed. "Of course."

"When?"

She assured me I would be back before the start of school.

"For second grade?" I asked, so paranoid of betrayal and abandonment.

"Yes, Joe, you will be home at the end of this summer. You will like Jericho. There is a lot to see and do. You will learn much, if you open your mind, and be loved much, if you open your heart. Both will depend on you."

The drive was long and quiet as Nadirah slept and Hatim had nothing to say. I had time to think. Abdel was upset to lose me and the money I brought him. Yamma was *not* upset to lose me and the love I gave her. I took both personally until I broke it down.

I remembered what Yamma said about wild things and people, that animals will live within their instincts while Allah gave people the capacity to choose. The greatness in living, she said, is in the choosing.

It was her choice to devote herself to all of us, though I'm sure there were moments she thought of a different path. I never saw that, nor had she ever hinted, but she had once painted a mural so beautiful and revered it remains on display today. To The Friends School it is a work of art; perhaps to her it is a battleground, a reminder she once had choices. Therein was the rub. What were her instincts, what were her choices, and had she chosen well?

Abdel, on the other hand, lived well within his instincts. There were no battles raging inside him. He hadn't passed down any great works of art. He left behind no talents, no skills, to give others. All he had done he had done for self, like Amir, like a wild creature. When his future needed redefining, he did it with someone new. His past was a throwaway.

Who was I, then, to deny what Yamma had planned for me? She had proven her love through actions that put her words beyond reproach. If she said Jericho was to be a great experience, so it would be. If she said Nadirah would treat me well, she held her to high standards.

Jericho is the oldest continually inhabited city on earth. It is also the lowest inhabited point on earth. It is also near the Dead Sea. Those three facts told to me by Hatim upon our arrival made for a pretty cool start.

As quiet as Hatim had been in Dayr Ghasana and on the ride down, he made up for it once we got to Jericho. He loved Jericho, this I could tell, and though I never warmed to him, I appreciated his enthusiasm. He'd have made a great history teacher or tour guide, the kind that even if you cared nothing for old things, he'd have you hooked by his passion.

The adults in Palestine were strange that way. Unlike back home where there was always talk about a new movie, a new toy, a new store being built, a new season for the White Sox, Bears, and Black Hawks, here there was always talk of the past. Unless you were in school, at a museum, or visiting grandparents, no one talked about the old days in Chicago, there just being so much new going on.

"Hatim, quiet now," Nadirah told him. She took my hand. "He must be tired and very hungry."

"The tree. What boy wouldn't want to see the tree?" he said.

"Do you really want to see an old tree?" she asked.

I shook my head eagerly. I couldn't help myself. It wasn't *a* tree, it was *the* tree.

Unlike Yamma and my cousins who lived on the outskirts of a village, Nadirah's house was in the center of town. It wasn't a Chicago, but I had been in Palestine for nearly one-seventh of my life so Ramallah was becoming my new big-city standard. Hatim stepped out and bid me to follow.

We walked down a back alley and out to a busy main street. As in Ramallah, maneuvering through them as either a car or pedestrian was more haphazard than by design. Fortunately, in Ramallah I had the convenience of riding a bus that dropped me off and picked me up in the school lot. What was going on elsewhere was of no concern to me.

What I thought was a very dicey location, about twenty feet from an intersection, Hatim stepped off with a scant look left or right. Horns blared that startled me but never fazed him. Actually, horns here more squeaked than blared, and they squeaked constantly, often for no apparent reason. I was to stay in Jericho long enough to learn how to move with similar verve.

We made it across the street and I could focus on looking for the tree. There were trees everywhere, mostly palms. I saw nothing that stood out. We walked for several blocks. I was by now twenty feet behind him. At last he stopped at a bend in the sidewalk with several others. It was the wrought iron and mortar fencing I first noticed. He was staring through it.

I felt the coolness of the shade that covered us. Above were the umbrella branches of a sycamore tree. Hatim pointed at its trunk. "Climb," he said.

"That it?"

"Yes, yes. Climb."

It was a great climbing tree with low, long branches that spread fifteen feet from the center in all directions. There were several kids already in it. People were taking photos. Others stood around pointing. I heard English being spoken by many of the onlookers. I was good at tree climbing. The hard part was finding hand and toe holds in the immense trunk to heave myself up to a low-hanging branch. From there it was like walking a diving board with enough low branches that I could reach the top easily.

I tight-rope walked to the end of the branch. Hatim was waiting for me down below with a huge smile. "Scared?"

"No."

He nodded. "Like your father. No fears."

"My father climbed this tree?"

"Many times. We all did."

I sat on the end of the branch. Kids would come out halfway and hop, shaking it. I had a good grip and, like Hatim said, no fear. The idea of my father climbing this tree, climbing any tree, intrigued me. "Did he make it to the top?"

"Oh, yes." He pointed to a branch two above mine. "He jumped from that one."

"Wow."

"Yes. Broke his ankle. Majnoon."

Hatim allowed me to explore for a while before calling me down, telling me there'd be plenty of time to climb. This time he walked beside me with his arm on my shoulder. "We spent the best days of our young lives in that tree," he said. "Your father was older than me. And much bigger. Like you. He was my protector. One day I threw a rotten apple at a boy on his bicycle. He chased me up the tree. He didn't know your father was up there. When the boy grabbed me your father threw him out."

"Threw him out of the tree?"

"Nobody messed with him. Nobody. Then your father brought me home and beat me for making him have to do such a stupid thing."

"Hatim?"

"Yes."

"Why were all those people taking pictures of us climbing it?"

He tapped my head and laughed.

"No, not of you. The tree is famous from the days of the prophet Jesus."

It didn't surprise me that Jericho should have yet another old thing to boast about.

"It is called the Zacchaeus Tree. Zacchaeus was a tax collector in Jericho, a very wealthy, powerful, and hated man. Because he was short, he had to climb the tree to see the prophet who was on his way to Jerusalem. Jesus saw him and invited himself to Zacchaeus's house for dinner. So impressed was Zacchaeus by the prophet that he repented and became a good and generous man."

To me, it seemed the greatness of the tree was in being able to climb it. But I nodded, knowing the story was obviously a sense of great pride to both Hatim and Jericho, as well as to others who had come to point and get pictures.

I liked Hatim for this, but I never saw him after that day. No one spoke about him except to say he was strange, having never married, and always being away. If they ever cared about him at all it was a long time ago. Perhaps he bored them with his antics, though I found they made him more intriguing. If he had bad friends, as Abdel had claimed, no one spoke of them. When I got back to Chicago and mentioned the day at the tree to my father he only grunted.

Though I grew distant as I aged, it upset me that my families in America and Palestine disintegrated as they had. I was young and never knew all that had passed, or not passed, between them, much as my children will never fully understand the dynamics of my childhood. Something inside us that makes us want to know it is also that thing that makes us keep it hidden.

I do know that after all these years I love closing my eyes to see my father climbing and jumping from trees, fighting with neighbors and brothers, and dodging wild traffic. In those moments I know all I need to know about him.

CHAPTER 28

Nadirah lived in back of a store front she owned and rented out to a small fruit market. The store was once used by my grandfather. He died before I was born, and according to Nadirah, he was the best potter in Jericho, perhaps the entire West Bank. I had nothing by which to gauge her assertion, but the bowls she kept were noticeably better than the ones Yamma used.

It was a small house with two levels. There were three bedrooms upstairs while downstairs was a kitchen, sitting room, mud room, and tiny backroom now used as her bedroom since she could no longer climb the stairs. I slept in the room my father shared with Hatim. There were knife carvings in the beams I couldn't make out. I wished for Hatim to come back so I could ask about them and my father.

The first two weeks I ambled about the house and downtown Jericho. Nadirah and I became comfortable enough with each other that we didn't have to talk all the time. I loved that Yamma took time to teach me the language, farm chores, the culture, and a bit of Islam, but Nadirah didn't seem to take my visit as a learning experience. If I wanted to know something she was gracious with an answer without rolling it into another topic. Even prayers didn't appear to be a big part of her day.

She kept a small library of Arabic children's books. Somewhere she came across several old Golden Books for me to read; *The Poky Little Puppy, Little LuLu and her Magic Tricks, Animals of Farmer Jones, The Little Red Hen*. And so she was happiest rocking in the sitting room while her candle burned and I read, the only sounds being the squeaking of the rocker and my mumblings as I sounded out the words.

Prior to my arrival, the owners of the fruit market did her errands and provided her fruit as partial payment for the shop. She allowed me to take over the errand runs, which I enjoyed. Running the streets of downtown Jericho was a nice break from working the farm. It wasn't like in Chicago where my mother would shop for two weeks at a time. I ran errands every day. Nadirah was used to cooking small portions for only herself. She rarely had extra food lying around. She had me buy treats for myself. My favorites were *Timriyyeh,* pudding wrapped in fried dough, and *ka'kaban,* candied apples.

I was feeling grown up. Back in Dayr Ghasana many of the chores I did were superficial ones that often Yamma had to re-do. But Nadirah needed me. I knew the renters of her shop felt running her errands was inconvenient. They would leave the packages on the doorstep without telling her and would forget things. But I could run her errands any time. I got to know many of the shop owners. I learned the back alley shortcuts.

But more than that, Nadirah was lonely. She was married for 48 years. She lived in the same house where she raised my father and two other sons. The house was full of ceramics and photographs of her young family. She answered my questions about my father, but offered nothing on her own. Maybe she had forgotten, or maybe talking memories bothered her.

The third week she gave me an extra long list of things to pick up. It would take me at least four trips. "Are you having company?" I asked.

"Yes, we are having company, lots of company," she said. "My son is coming to visit."

"Hatim," I said excitingly.

"Not Hatim. Ramiz."

I now knew enough about uncles to suspect there'd be cousins in tow, especially with her announcement there'd be lots of company. They were there when I arrived back from my third run. They came in a green and white Volkswagen Microbus. I could hear kids' voices upstairs, loud and already obnoxious. I wanted to do what the renters did, drop the groceries and run, but like the cave, I knew I couldn't stay gone forever.

I entered softly like a thief, hoping for a mystical invisibility. Uncle Ramiz spotted me first. He was an elf of a man, short and round, with a high-pitched laugh that was not manly, but which he used with reckless abandon. He didn't pinch my cheeks, pat my belly, or rub the top of my head. In fact, he didn't get out of his chair. Instead, he patted his thigh and said I was his brother come back to live as a child again. At this he laughed. "Is that not the truth, Yamma?" He said to Nadirah.

"He is himself," she said, "young Nasser Khudayer from Chicago who is called Joe."

His wife was as quiet as he was loud, and as tiny as some of the girls at school. She wore neither the burqa or an hajib, but rather a simple long linen skirt and white blouse. There was an unstylish red kerchief tied loosely on her head. She smiled as she gave me a gentle hug. "Sureia," she said.

I was excited. "That's my sister's name."

"Yes."

"Boys, come down to meet your cousin," Ramiz yelled.

I held my breath, expecting another awkward and testy introduction. The four nearly tripped themselves racing down the steep, narrow staircase. They ran to me. Two little ones gave me a hug around my waist. The middle one, seven-year old Bahir, I was to learn, braced my shoulders. But it was the oldest one who stood silently in the back who disturbed me. I held his gaze. He gave a tight-lipped smile and nodded. I waited in my paranoia for a telltale sign of his real intentions. He smiled down at his animated brothers who bounced around me.

They came across as old friends, as if we had left off somewhere. "Joe, Joe," the little ones chanted, "take us to the tree."

"Let him sit and eat," Ramiz said.

Their oldest brother wrapped them up, one under each arm, and pulled them away. He came back and introduced himself as Tariq. He was ten years old, but tall for his age. I pegged him for twelve or thirteen, especially after he spoke. He had a rich, deep voice, full of authority. I surmised he developed it being the oldest of four boys. "They don't remember going to the Zacchaeus Tree," he said, "I told them they were there last time they came, but that was two years ago." He pointed to them. "Twins, Hana and Khahil. They're only four."

"Not only," one of them said. Hana, I think. I never did get them straight.

"Bahir is your age. Seven, right?"

I nodded.

His mother and father sat quietly watching as he spoke and made the introductions. I felt as if I was participating in a family ritual, a rite of passage for Tariq. Any minute I thought Ramiz would stand and critique his performance or give a standing ovation. But he said nothing as Nadirah announced she would be making lunch. Sureria stood to help.

She shooed her three youngest outside as Tariq sat down beside his father.

"The tree," the twins chanted.

I spoke up feebly, feeling every bit intimidated by Tariq's confident air and the outgoing nature of his brothers. "I can take them." It came out more of a question than a statement.

The three adults looked at each other. "I'd like to see it again, too," Tariq said. "If Joe doesn't mind me coming along."

The word "diplomatic" hadn't yet become part of my vocabulary, but I recognized it as what he was being. And it made me feel good that he had the sensibility toward not only me, but his brothers.

It was an enlightening moment. There *was* a way to make everyone happy. It meant accepting the fact Ramiz, Sureia, and Nadirah thought me too young to bring the little ones on my own. It meant Tariq discreetly interceding. And it meant me being willing to meet in the middle.

Tariq let me lead the way while staying tactfully by my side, and between the streets and his brothers. "It's nice of you to take your free time to bring us," he said. "Nadirah told us how many errands you've been running for her lately."

I stopped in mid-step, forcing the twins to run up my heels. "I forgot to get the flour."

"Is it near here?" Tariq asked.

I looked around. Having gone a different way to get to the tree I was disoriented. "I'm, I'm not sure," I said fretfully.

"No problem," he said. "we'll backtrack from the house when we return."

That was a perfect opportunity for him to pounce, but he didn't. It was his age, I determined. No, Gamal was just a year younger and Faid seven years older. Age didn't deter them.

The four boys were to stay for two weeks while Ramiz and Sureia went back home to their home in Rafat. Tariq was a great help to Nadirah. Not only with the boys but doing repairs such as electrical and plumbing. He even stopped a three-year old problem leak that had been coming through the roof in a corner of the kitchen. It hadn't rained in weeks so to test it he filled a five gallon pail of water that I helped him lug up. We dumped it directly over the patch job. No leak. Ingenious.

It was the best two weeks I had in Palestine. They showed me genuine concern and interest. And it wasn't all about my being American. I had the impression they were happy and proud to live in Palestine. No boasting, no dispersions, no judgments. We laid things out in order to know each other. They didn't jeer when I told them I found the Koran a bore, and I didn't scoff when they said they didn't like rock and roll. It was nice.

We did everything together. When there were problems on where to go or what to do, we sat down and talked about it, even the twins. During those times Tariq sat quietly like his father. He weighed in; he had his opinions and his own ideas, but they weren't as important as making his brothers happy.

I told them of the cave, playing basketball, walking to school in the desert, The Friends School, and swimming in the Red River. I didn't explain the legend of the witches who turned it that color with the blood of young boys for fear it would frighten Hana and Khahil. Tariq asked a lot about the Friends School. He wanted to go there, but with three brothers behind him, it wasn't affordable now.

I told them of Lindblom Park back in Chicago and my neighborhood hangouts. Strange, it had only been a year but I was already forgetting much of the detail. In time, I'd forget nearly everything about back home.

They had a pond behind their house in Rafat that was only full in early spring. In summer, before it became dry as the desert, they played mud soccer. I pictured a Chicago pond frozen in winter, a gaggle of kids playing hockey. They had no cave but their father had built them a tree fort where they sometimes slept at night. We made plans for next summer when they would come swim in the Red River and I would sleep in their tree fort.

On the next to their last day, Nadirah arranged for the fruit shop owners to take us to Quruntul Mountain in lieu of a week's rent. The best part for us was the cable car ride and staring over sheer rocky ledges into the valley. But I was lonesome for Sue who would have appreciated it as the mountain where Jesus fasted and was tempted by the devil.

That night, Nadirah fell asleep in her rocker. Tariq and I read by her candle as the others slept upstairs. Nadirah was the soundest sleeper I knew. Every night I had to gently wake her and walk her to bed. So I had no concerns talking about her as she slept. "Is Nadirah Muslim?" I asked.

"Yes. Why?"

"I never hear her reciting salat."

"Does that bother you?"

"I just thought all grown-ups did."

"Not all. Like in America, I'm sure. But she prays silently and away from you. She told my mother she does not want you to be anything but a boy while you are here. No school, no Islam, no work. I do the same because she asked me to."

"But I do work; I run her errands."

"Is that work for you?"

I shook my head.

"I understand there were problems back in Dayr Ghasana for you and your sister."

"It's better."

"That's good." He looked at Nadirah whose chin was resting on her chest. "My father comes to see her every week. It's a hard drive to this place and it makes him miss work sometimes, but she has no one else. She likes having us boys around. It would drive me crazy if I was her age."

"How come Hatim doesn't visit" I asked

"My father doesn't talk about it."

Tariq was smart. And he was obedient. But unlike me, he seemed to be a boy who didn't much care if mysteries went unsolved. I saw that a problem in being too good a son is that too many things are left uncontested. Perhaps what went on in the lives of his uncles was of no interest to him. Me? I wanted badly to know if Abdel was full of shit. "You father work near here?" I asked.

"He travels. He works for the same agency Khaal Abu Faid works for: The United Nations Relief and Works Agency. He works for them so when I grow up, I won't have too."

"Why not?"

"Because they will not be needed, not in Palestine, anyway."

"It's going away? What about the people in the camps? Who will—"

"There will be no more camps. People will live outside them where they belong."

It was Sam I was listening to, his thoughts, his concerns. I thought Tariq was much too young to be involved with Sam's views. As Sam had said to me, he should be listening to silly fables. Only unlike Sam, when Tariq spoke such sobering words, there was no hate in his eyes. There was a calmness about him.

"I have a friend in Dayr Ghasana who says the same thing."

"A lot of us see it."

"He's much older than you. He says people in the camps are like pigeons who need the agency to feed them or they will die."

"That's true, but not for long."

"What's going to happen?"

"Palestine is going to be free. The West Bank and Gaza will be like states in the United States. They will be their own government but working with the Israeli government. The West Bank will have what you call a governor. And I will be governor."

I knew governors better than I did kings. My father had a *Re-elect Otto Kerner* poster in our front yard for months. He got very drunk with neighbors the night he won. "You mean, like soon?" I said, not wanting to make it seem like a silly idea.

"No. It will take a long time. But I'm going to go Birzeit University when I am ready to study—"

"That's where my friend Sam is going," I said so loudly Tariq jumped.

"It's good we have people who believe in our future. It's good they go to learn to do great things in the right way. Some people don't believe it will happen peacefully. My father says those people don't believe because they want war. They see it as the only way to make change. So I choose not to believe in them because I don't want to see my brothers and friends fighting. It will happen, and we'll be free. This you will see."

Yes, same thing Sam had said to Sue and me on our ride to Jerusalem: "It will happen, you will see." Yet, though the words were similar, I heard two vastly different messages coming from Sam and Tariq.

We awoke Nadirah. I walked her into her bedroom where she lay down on her bed while I placed her candle on her bedside table. "Joe," she whispered.

"Yeah?"

"Lay down with me."

I stayed on top of the covers. She put her arm around me and pulled me in close. There was the warmth I came to know from my grandmother. I wondered why she never came to Chicago as Siidi had. Why my father never spoke of her, or his brothers, or Jericho. In the morning I'd invite her to go to Chicago to see my father and Sue. Though I couldn't be there, I would be like Tariq, making things happen in spite of themselves.

I drifted off, mesmerized by the shadows made by the small flame on the wall before me. An occasional car and her shallow breathing was all the sound. I awoke to a chill. It was early morning. The flame was out. No cars were driving past. Nadirah's shallow breathing had stopped. She was gone.

CHAPTER 29

Childhood in Palestine was fleeting. For some, it was nonexistent. Parents didn't tell their children there was no boogeyman. They didn't tell them not to be afraid of the dark. You didn't hear phrases such as "there's nothing in the night that isn't there in the day."

Schools ran air raid drills regularly. They weren't taken lightly by anyone, not like the quarterly fire drills in American schools. Village homes maintained family-size foxholes that were constantly re-dug and cleaned out. And in cities like Ramallah, for fear of bombs, siblings didn't ride the same bus together. Better to lose just one, the reasoning went.

War wasn't a movie. It wasn't just for text books or a history lesson. You saw it on the faces of adults and in their eyes. Like a small child anticipating the popping of the Jack-in-the-box, they stared out at the world with an uneasiness. Ramiz was the first person I met who had what I knew as a Chicago-easiness. He, and of course, Adli, who didn't know better. Even Yamma and Sam lived as if every movement had to be considered, every breath measured. Nothing was random. Nothing was inconsequential. Like Siidi's stories rife with morals, there was a lesson to be taught and learned or doom ensued. I was convinced it wasn't just the dry desert air and scorching sun that gave them faces of leather.

My first year it gave me an odd sensation that I don't figure a child born here would pick up on. Of course in time, the sensation left me, as well. It was a sensation of being adrift with no one in charge of a world where little mattered. Efforts, great and small, served only one purpose, to survive the next day.

There was a Twilight Zone episode I watched just before coming here. A man and woman were alone in a town that was made of fake trees and houses. Cars didn't work. Neither did phones. A large shadow would drift over them, forcing them to run in terror. I freaked at the ending when they were scooped up in the hand of a young girl no more than five. Her father, from a race of giants, had gone to earth and brought humans home for his daughter's playscape.

These two adults, whom I would look to to keep me safe, were helpless in the hands of a child. They would forever be bent to her will, doing what she commanded, when she commanded. It turned upside down the world of order I knew. So it seemed in Palestine, as I waited for a giant shadow to eclipse my sun, and a careless hand to snatch me away.

It was April of 1966. Sam came down to tell us. He was shaken and in tears. Israel had attacked. My God, I thought, what kind of man could this Israel be to make Sam become so undone?

It was Yamma who asked the significant question "Where?"

"Rafat. They attacked Rafat."

Yamma gasped and cupped her hand to her mouth. "Why? What's there for them?"

"There was no reason," Sam said. "There's never a reason."

I knew the town but wasn't sure from where. It had to hold some deep connection or Sam and Yamma wouldn't have been so affected.

"Are they all right, Insha' Allah?" Yamma asked.

Sam shook his head. "No, Amineh, the attack took place in the early morning. Their house was one of the ones that got hit. Unfortunately, they were all at home."

Yamma began to moan and sob. Johara grabbed hold of her and wrapped her up. I was sure now it was a close friend or distant relative whom I would now never meet. Yamma held her hand out to me and bid me to come to her. She dried her eyes. "I'm sorry for you to hear this, Joe. Such a fine young family, such good people."

"Who?" I asked.

"Your cousins. The ones you were with in Ariha last summer."

"You mean Tariq, Bahir, and the twins?"

"I'm afraid so," she said, as she settled back into a sob that would last the night.

It was the most surreal moment of my time in Palestine. The death of the old man in the desert was disturbing, but I had no relationship with him. So, too, was Nadirah's, but she was old. It was nature taking its course. But these were four young boys, two younger than me. We had made plans for the next summer. Tariq already had plans for his future.

Years later, they are the barometer by which I measure families, the ones I've met and the one I wanted to create. They were verses of Eugene Field poems. This was certainly not part of the natural flow of things I wanted to know and accept. As Yamma said, what could they have done to Israel?

I didn't cry. They were dead, I understood that, but I couldn't grasp the brutality of their situation. Death, to me, was still gentle, a thing one drifted into. Even my favorite westerns had them bloodless and in slow motion, and good guys always, always had their moment to say something for the ages.

We all let it sit there for a long moment. Yamma, I'm sure, was remembering while I was contemplating an empty summer without them. I really wanted to see their tree fort which I now envisioned in splinters. And I wanted them to come with me to the cave to create a new generation of Palestinian kids not afraid of witches and ghoulies. It was Sam who broke us from our own brands of sorrow. "This will be one of many this year," he said. "Palestine cannot sit back and wait."

"Sam," Johara said, looking up at him woefully as she held Yamma.

"But you see, this is what they want, for us to grieve ourselves into complacency."

"Not now, Sam."

"*Now* is the only time we have."

Yamma pushed free from Johara and slowly stood. "You," she said to Sam, "you and those like you, here and in Israel, why must you forget about life to embrace death? Insha' Allah, we all dwell on the life we are given rather than the death we create."

"They were family, Amineh," Sam said.

"Yes, they were family. I have heard that from so many as the reason to make war. So if killing family is the cause to fight, what will be the cause to stop? All those who die are family to someone on either side. So always men like you will have a reason."

Sam tried to continue his piece. "You have no concept—"

But Yamma put up her hand. "If you choose this time not to mourn, please take it outside."

Though I'm sure it became a rallying cry for Sam as deep and resounding as "Remember the Alamo," we never spoke of it again at the house. I cannot recall where I was the day President Kennedy was shot, but unlike most men, I can pinpoint that day my childhood ended.

***

As the months passed, the fears, mysteries, beauties, and wonders of the country were lost to me. It became too easy to walk into a brilliant desert sunset without a moment spent to reflect. I rarely heard the pariah dogs in the hills. I cursed sandstorms without fascination. I stomped scorpions underfoot, not out of fear of them but because I could. I became so adept at whacking olives from tree branches that I no longer did it except at harvest time. I didn't sit with Yamma much in the kitchen; she was rarely there. When she was, she had no time to waste talking with me. I guess those moments grew tiresome for her, like my nights of watching the sky and tracing constellations from my window sill.

The language was mine now. I could converse, curse, and gesture as well as the natives. My skin turned olive. My hair grew out and curled in ringlets on my forehead, cheeks, and neck. I grew thin and taller than most my age. And I grew distant and difficult to most everyone save Adli.

It was a daily ritual for us to traipse into the valley, being sure to stop in the cave on the way down. Adli would make me stand in the precise location he did that day I brought him in. "I know you are afraid, Joe," he'd say, mimicking me but in a most sincere way, "but there is nothing to be afraid of. Now you can go back and tell Gamal you came back to the cave."

First off, I didn't give a damn what Gamal thought of me. Second, I was never afraid to go back to the cave. And lastly, his problem was with a fairy tale while my problem was with a very real snake. But I didn't say any of this to him. Instead, after his third intervention on my behalf, I thanked and told him I was okay now.

As oblivious as I was to the natural world around me, I watched as Yamma wore herself out working in the village and tending to daily chores. I wasn't much of a help. Neither were Gamal or Adli. Johara, though, was carrying the weight for all of us. There was a time she spoke of a future similar to Sue's. College, travel, perhaps work in America. I saw, now, how women here became tools.

The transformation was disturbing, a thing suited for dark, stormy nights. But I saw it in the earliest light of our morning walks to school, and the sunny afternoon return trips. On warm evenings when her face should have been its most radiant, it was now a sad shade of gray. I knew in time her shoulders would bow, her eyelids would sag, and she would shuffle. I didn't want to be here for that. Already her voice confirmed the weariness of her drudgery. The conversations that once revolved around what she wanted to do now turned on what she had to do.

While we played and Faid learned and Abdel lived, Yamma and Johara toiled for survival. They would wear out long before the dishes they washed and the implements they used. While they worked fertilizer through the soil so that a good harvest would ensue, their own nutrients wasted away. Like their tools, they were insufficient in and of themselves. Their value lay in how well they performed and for how long. Sadder still, as living things, they knew well the waste of it all.

I didn't devolve into a monument to gloom. I hadn't lost all my sense of fun and adventure. Adli and I never tired of drifting on the river. No matter the weather, we'd strip down and plop our bodies in. I never was able to teach him how to swim, but he did learn to float without his usual incessant chatter. Sometimes I had to look up to be sure he hadn't drifted out into a deep pool. Oftentimes he did, and I had to nonchalantly swim out to retrieve him.

And while we teased around on his homemade basketball court, I became a very serious soccer player. Unwittingly, Gamal had made me a tenacious goalie. I could throw a saved ball as far as many of them could punt it. I was awkward and slow left to right, but made up for it by maniacal frontal attacks that scared the ball carrier long before he had a chance to shoot. Adli was always my fullback. Actually, more like sweeper, even when put up on midfield. He didn't understand the positions, or even that there were positions. He was there to be with me, to protect me. My wing man.

By summer there was war talk. Real talk. It wasn't just coming from grim old men and young revolutionaries like Sam. It was as likely to come from mothers and daughters. It was coming and everyone knew it.

I understood by now that Israel was a neighboring country. I understood little else except that I couldn't help but despise them. Not only for what they did to Tariq and his family, but from the horrendous stories I heard from others who swore they were there, or knew people who were, when Israeli soldiers stripped young girls naked and beat and raped them in the street. They beheaded children and smashed babies upon rocks. The things they did were more vile than any witch stories I heard, so they had to be true, for why would anyone make up a story where humans were worse than witches?

There was much bravado. Kids fashioning tree limbs into spears and thicker branches into clubs. Adli was working on a plan to surround the house with man-size bird traps using knafeh as bait. Our soccer games would suddenly break out into a war game like a sequence from a Broadway musical as players transformed into attacking soldiers. The ball would be scooped up and lobbed into their midst, sending them sprawling from the imaginary explosion.

I had never seen war. All I knew was it took six wonderful people out of my life. But it meant other things to other people. It was adventure, excitement, drama, news. The talk of it, all positive from what I heard, emboldened the speakers and magnified the imagery. When Sam came around on the few occasions, his accounts mesmerized Gamal and Adli.

Suddenly a nation of poor, forgotten people in a land the west reflected upon only at Christmas was relevant again. People around the world were witnessing sights far removed from holiday greeting cards. Tanks were driving through Jesus' birthplace, mines exploding in his hometown, attacks on fishing boats in the sea he walked upon, night raids in the city of his crucifixion.

As that summer closed out, we hadn't heard from or seen Abdel. It was pleasant enough for me, but the others, Adli mainly, spoke often of him. He wanted to go to Ramallah. He wanted to see his father. To be nice, I kept my mouth shut. Yamma was dignified, never berating Abdel in front of his children, though hardly enthused at the prospect of them visiting him.

The weekend before we returned to school Faid came home from Jordan. He stood aloof in the doorway as Yamma greeted him with all the affection afforded a returning son. For his part he stood motionless and let her hold him. His arms raised up slowly, as if he didn't know quite what to do with them. He rested them upon her upper back and lightly patted her. I had the impression he felt the need to respond in kind to her, to wrap her up tightly, but something, a force, stopped him.

He could stay the night, he said, before heading to Ramallah to see his father. As expected, Gamal and Adli begged to go along. Faid shook his head, and with a tone as unpleasant as ever said, "I'm going back to school from there; I'm not returning home."

Yamma and Johara prepared his favorite dinner, Musakhan. And Yamma sang. I felt so bad for her as her song was wasted on Faid. He had been a year at school and hadn't changed his attitude a bit, toward any of us. He and I didn't speak, and he barely looked at me. In his defense, I made myself scarce most of the night except for the actual meal.

"Have you talked to your father much?" Yamma asked.

He nodded, his mouth full of chicken.

"How is he then?"

Faid swallowed. "Fine, fine. Have you spoken with him?"

"La."

His eyes shifted to Johara. "You?"

Johara shook her head.

Casually, just before taking another bite, he told us all. "So you don't know. He and Zaynah are having a baby."

CHAPTER 30

Johara dropped her fork. Gamal said, "The truth?" Adli asked, "truth about what?" I looked at Yamma. She didn't flinch. She kept eating, though I caught a glimpse of a tear forming in the corner of her eye. Now, as I understand better the emotions involved, having withstood all three, I wonder if her tears were for love, jealousy, or loneliness.

The rest of the meal centered on Faid's smug silence. It was only the clanking of utensils on porcelain, a sound I usually found annoying but now a welcome break from the isolation Faid manufactured. Even Adli knew something was amiss and kept his mouth shut.

After, Yamma continued the ritual by clearing the table for all of us. "We'll finish this," Johara said. Yamma turned and hurried from the kitchen without saying a word.

Johara turned on Faid. "How could you?"

"What?"

"Don't you dare play stupid. Why did you come here?"

"To see you, to see my family."

"You said one thing of substance all night, and that thing caused us nothing but pain."

"I said you will have a new brother or sister. Yamma didn't seem to mind; is another child a bad thing for you? "

"Again with the stupid talk. Do you know how badly such news affects a woman? How it affects your own mother? Of course she wasn't happy with the news, but you gave her no options but to be gracious."

"I thought my family had a right to know," he said, still with the *what me* look on his self-satisfied face. "At least I came to tell you. Would you rather it come from someone else, or not even knowing until he was ten-years old?"

"There is a time, place, and way for everything, Faid. Another life is a blessed thing, yes, but not here, not tonight."

He turned to Gamal, his safe port in the storm. "Tell me, Gamal, are you happy with the news?"

Johara wouldn't let him answer. "A son would have waited until later, after dinner, when Yamma had a place of her own to react. As it was, you gave her no choice but accept it. No, Faid, what you did was calculated to be cold and heartless. And to be brutally honest, I would have been fine not knowing of the child until it was ten-years old."

Faid left without a good bye to his mother. No one tried to stop him. Even Gamal was stunned by his gall and tactlessness. We cleaned up as if trying to avoid disturbing a dying person, and in fact, that was what Yamma had become. I stuck my head in her bedroom to say good night. She was laying on Abdel's side of the bed, under the covers but still much awake.

"Good night, Yamma," I whispered from the doorway.

She stuck her hand out to the side for me to take. I drew near and held it. She squeezed and swung it playfully as if skipping with me somewhere.

"We cleaned up the kitchen," I said, "so you don't have to go in to clean."

She squeezed my hand long and hard, transferring so much discontent to me. I agreed with Johara, that Faid had a mission here tonight to sink any chance for Yamma to have her family back, and not even her symbolic gesture to keep Abdel's place warm for him mattered.

"That's nice of you, Joe."

"Yeah, well, Johara did most of it."

"Of that I am sure," she said. Then, mostly to herself she said, "No woman wants to get old, but I hate that Johara has no say in how it is to happen to her."

***

The talk of war grew. So, too, did Yamma's phone calls with my parents. I heard only Yamma's side until I got on the phone. We spoke of mundane things, daily rituals that bored me. Our conversations left out the talk of war to protect me, but really, it was a commonplace topic to kids in Palestine. I got the impression my parents didn't see it as dire a situation. I found out why when Sam came to see us.

With Sue gone, Sam turned his attention to Johara. He was the only bright spot in her otherwise dull days. They took long walks and drives. She was still young, just sixteen, and he was twenty, but there were no worries on Yamma's part. "They're gone a long time," Adli would say. Yamma would laugh. "That boy has a lot to say."

And she was glad, for she respected Sam for his intellect and his concern for the family. She was sure their talks were about his travels to Europe, his studies, and his hopes for a future as a journalist. Yamma liked this courting. She would have welcomed him as a son-in-law. He was unlike men of her day with his open-mind and sense of fairness.

But often Johara came home more distressed than impressed. When she came inside with Sam in tow, their conversation would stop cold if anyone was nearby. A bloated pause would follow them until someone, usually Sam, deflated it by bringing in an innocuous topic.

One night I heard her come into the kitchen from the side door while I was reading in the parlor. She was alone. "Sam, not staying?" Yamma asked.

"No. Thankfully," Johara said.

Craving a little drama that didn't involve me directly or indirectly, I crept up to the wall separating the kitchen to listen.

"Tired of him?"

"It's always about war," Johara said. "I try to talk about school and his trip to Europe, but he won't stay on it. Do you know what he did in Europe? He met with revolutionaries in Germany."

"Why does he tell you all this?" Yamma asked.

"I don't know. Impress me with his importance, warn me. But something else, too. Ab has been talking to Joe's father in America."

"How does Sam know this?"

"He wouldn't say except to tell me they have been watching him."

"Who? Johara, who is watching your father?" Her voice went up two octaves as fear crept in.

"We, that's all he kept saying. Some group. And they say Ab is telling Joe's father there will be no war, that Jordan is negotiating with Israel to keep peace. But Sam says it's not so."

"Perhaps your father is right. He has contacts in Jordan."

"Sam tells stories that regardless of what Israel and Jordan do there will be war."

"When?"

"He doesn't say when."

"So that's it," Yamma said. "It's not imminent."

"Don't you see? Ab doesn't want any talk of war that takes Joe away. He wants him to stay here to keep getting money sent from America; money you never see."

"That's ridiculous, to think your own father would be so careless with a boy's life."

"Yamma, are you serious? You know how careless—"

"Now that's enough, Johara. And your father is sending me some of the money, for myself and for Joe."

"So little. We don't even know how much is sent from America. And you use none of it; you put it all aside for Joe."

"That's how it should be. Now, Johara, do you like Sam?"

That is when I stretched out on my stomach to peek around the corner at them. They had clasped their hands across the table. I felt as if I was cheating at hide and seek, but I, too, wanted to know what she felt for Sam. "I don't know anymore," she said, so softly that I was glad I closed the distance enough to hear. "So much has changed. He has changed with all the talk of war. And I wonder ... I wonder what really happened down at the cave with Sureia."

"Do not imply he did anything to harm her," Yamma said, lifting her hands from Johara's for only a moment.

"La, la, la, not that he hurt her physically. It's not that. Just ..."

Yamma leaned into her from across the table. I could see she was squeezing her hands as she had done mine, urging her to continue.

"He offered nothing directly," Johara continued. "Nothing as proof, that is, but when I asked—"

"But, Johara, why would you even ask such a thing?"

"I needed to know, Yamma." Johara was beginning to weep. "Sureia liked him very much, and he liked her. They were together many times. Joe left her at the cave and she was fine. You remember that night, how Sam insisted he go down to get her alone?"

"I thought he was being considerate."

"Yes, of course. I only asked him why he thought she'd do something like that."

Yamma and I both waited silently for more.

"He said he didn't know, but he did, I could tell. He at least suspected something."

"What did he say to—"

"He said it was probably a very personal matter. He said it, you know, in a very guilty way. I cannot explain it well, but I am sure Ab told you things that made you suspect things he was doing just by the way he said them."

Yamma nodded.

"Then he told me not to ask too many questions of too many people. Like he was protecting someone, maybe me, maybe himself."

I don't think Yamma was paying attention at this point. Her head was bowed and she had folded her hands in her lap. Johara continued. "Did he tell her he loved her? Or maybe that he didn't love her. Did he, I don't know, have relations with her? Yamma, he gave me a very bad feeling about it."

"Let it go, then," Yamma said. "Sureia is safe at home. Sam is just an idealistic man, like your father used to be. Trust me, that is not a bad thing."

Something tugged at my pant leg. I thought I had caught it on a piece of furniture until the tugging became persistent. I turned to see Adli's hand poking in and out like a cat's playful paw. I waited to see his face then snapped my heel into it. He let out a yelp that gave me away. "I haven't been spied on since the boys were three," Johara called out, only half mad.

I jumped, literally, to my defense. "I wasn't spying; Adli was pulling at me."

"Oh, I thought you were Adli," Johara said.

"How long you been there?" Yamma wanted to know.

I muttered, "Not too long."

Adli dashed around the corner. "He heard you talking about how Sam always talks about the war and Ab was calling America and Johara thinks he wants Joe's money and Sam likes Sureia better than he likes her."

"Did not."

"Did too because I was right behind you and I heard."

His callous disregard for self respect killed me. I stood there naked in his barrage of shameless truths. Yamma held out her arms to us which Adli ran to before I could respond. Not that I would have. I had grown beyond that. Adli, though, never would and Yamma wouldn't have it any other way. "Lots of changes," Yamma said, "lots of changes."

"I want to see Zaynah and Ab and the new baby," he said, his head nestled on Yamma's chest.

I thought Adli was on the same page as the rest of us concerning Faid's visit. But he didn't grasp the nuances of Abdel having a child with another woman. I was not of the age where I understood it all myself.

"Why?" Johara asked.

"It's Ab's new baby and my new brother. Ab is my father."

Johara and Yamma smirked at each other. I think he added that last part, about Abdel being his father, for self-confirmation more than as a reason to see him. "Well, I won't tell you no," Yamma said.

"But Yamma—" Johara started to say until Yamma held up a hand.

"Asta' ghfir-ullah, Asta' ghfir-ullah, Asta'ghfir-ullah," she said as she dipped her head in rhythm to the syllables. "I ask the forgiveness of Allah many times over these past months, but how much can he give without my giving back? What Adli asks for is not unpardonable. Denying it to him is." She slid Adli off her lap. "I will set it up for you to see them when the baby is born," she said.

"But I want to see them all now. I can help."

"I think you should wait until the baby is born."

"When is that?"

"In a few months, I am sure." Which, as I knew, would keep him hounding us all every stinkin' day.

CHAPTER 31

I amazed myself with the insight I had developed from my paranoia. Paranoia sharpened my senses. I was Super kid when it came to recognizing the negative vibes of adults. It wasn't only knowing what ticked them off; any four-year learned that through osmosis. No, I foresaw adult motives meant for adults. I recognized days, weeks, in advance the techniques they would use to hurt, punish, and otherwise destroy others. I knew, long before anyone, that Abdel would never allow Adli to see him or his baby, and I knew Yamma would resort to any desperate means necessary to not let Adli know it. As the months passed with Adli pestering with a nonstop annoyance similar to, "are we there yet," Yamma did her damnedest to delay the inevitable while I kept my mouth shut.

It was a wet April in 1967, wetter than usual I was told. And raw. We were as anxious to get rid of the rain as Chicagoans were to get rid of the snow. One day, in frustration to do something spring-like, Adli and I took the trail down to the Red River. It was too cold to swim but just being along the shore was good enough for us. The rain had been torrential hours earlier. It was ripe for mudslides.

It started as fun as we would slide, hit a stone, catch ourselves, then go on for more. But as our enthusiasm increased, so did our speed. We hit the mud-rich bottom third and with no ledges to brake us, it was a free fall. I ran it like a surfer. It was great. I took a tumble but came back up in my crouch. Mud soccer must have been a rush for Tariq and his brothers.

As I came to the end of my run, I had a decision to make: come in with the smoothness of a taxiing airliner, or with a spectacular crash. I chose the latter. I hooped and hollered as I landed, and was covered with mud and a smile when I bounced up.

I expected to see Adli waiting for me at the bottom, or close on my tail. I spotted him about a hundred feet up the slimed slope. He was wrapped around a scrub oak, his legs kicking at the mud in search of an anchor point. "Let go," I yelled.

"I can't," he said hysterically.

"Sure you can; it's easier than holding on."

"No."

It didn't occur to me he was afraid. How could he be; how could anyone be? It was a wild, aggressive, foolhardy ride. It was the dare without the devil. The mud and tufts of tall grass turned the ground into a messy, wet featherbed. A fall here would do little worse than cover us further in mud. And better, no one to tell us no. Hell, we could even dip ourselves into the chilly but cleansing Red River if our fear of Yamma's wrath got the best of us. "Slide down on your back," I challenged.

He wrapped himself tighter, bending the poor tree for all it was worth. "Hurry, I'm cold standing here."

"Come get me, Joe, come get me."

He was scared to death. It was a Slip and Slide. It was sledding a hill. It was a feet-up-on-your-bike handlebars glide. He could ski it, roll it, superman it, butt-slide it, or become a legend with a move of his own. But there he lay, squirming like a bug specimen pinned to a display board.

Now I had already determined that climbing up the muddy mess was not going to be easy. Hauling him up with me was going to be impossible. Through a series of sidestepping, herringbone walks and crawls on all fours, I made it up to his spot. All the while Adli hurried me, critiquing my techniques with bone-headed advice. By the time I reached him I was exhausted and more than a little miffed, and I had no clue as to how to maneuver him back up with me.

He didn't help except to offer more advice. "Carry me on your back," he directed, like that was going to happen. Then, "pull me up." "How will I do that?" "Take my hand and start walking."

I thought pushing him made more sense but he dug his heels in mule-like. "I need to see you, Joe. I'm afraid when I can't see you."

And so that was it. Having to rely on himself was his terror. An unbridled ride down a slope was not freedom to him. It was an ambiguity of life he wanted no part of. Slow and steady was his way, but it was not the way I wanted for him. And so I stepped aside, literally, and let him tumble down the hill, free of restraint.

I don't know why I had chosen that moment to impose myself on him. Maybe I was fed up with protecting him. I lost count of how many fights I had on his account. How many otherwise nice kids I threatened. I couldn't calculate because I didn't know how many kids avoided me or hated me because of the reputation I had to develop for his sake. I was just irritated and tired enough to let him free fall for a few moments.

He didn't scream on the way down, least I didn't hear him from my perch at the scrub oak. I was straddling it between my legs, peering around the naked branches. He lay there at the bottom without moving. I was worried for just a moment before his knees went up and he rolled to his side. Even then he didn't scream. I think it was shock.

I slid casually down on my back, hitting the occasional clump of grass that sent me reeling. I exaggerated my enthusiasm as I descended. I hoped it would be contagious. It wasn't. "You pushed me," he said.

"I did not."

"Yes you did, Joe."

"How could I push you? I was behind you. If I pushed you, you would have gone up the hill."

"I'm all muddy."

"You were all muddy before. Wasn't it great?"

"I'm cold. I'm going home."

"Now you can climb back up there." I said it as a challenge.

He walked away from me along the base of the hill. The faster I moved to catch up the quicker his pace. The mud was caking to our skin and clothes. I thought he was going to the river to clean up but he began walking inland. "Where you going?" I called up to him. He ignored me.

He climbed a very steep section of the hill. It was muddy but clustered with trees for us to grab hold of. Adli bounded up like a mountain goat, leaving me further behind as I rested every four or five trees. It was his anger that gave him his energy. He never turned around as he disappeared over the crest.

I reached the peak and found we were just behind his basketball court. I guessed that he had run down to the house to complain to Yamma so she'd give me that look of disappointment usually reserved for one of the others. I wasn't looking forward to being one of the ones who let her down. But I knew he'd loosen up, and she'd forgive me. It *was* exciting; he just wasn't ready to admit it. And Yamma would see what I did was just in fun.

There was a Blue Volvo I had never seen before in the driveway. I thought perhaps it was Sam's. He drove several different cars, none of them his. That was good; Yamma would never lay into me in front of company, and by the time he left, I'd have talked Adli out of his anger.

I burst into the kitchen laughing to disarm any animosity Adli had started. What I saw wasn't amusing. It was rather creepy at first glance. Abdel was at the table. Adli's face was buried in his chest. He was sobbing. Brick-hard mud had dropped to the floor around them. Abdel was obviously out of his element. His hands hovered above Adli's back as if the mud was dog excrement. He was looking around the room at no one and nothing in particular. When his eyes landed on me they quickly moved on.

Yamma was there. So, too, was Johara. Sitting in the corner was a young woman holding an infant. She wasn't Abdel's new wife, Zaynah. Adli held his head up to look at me. All I could think was he must have painted quite a scene of horror to have them all in such gloom.

As uncomfortable as I was having Abdel in the room, Adli was instantly consoled being in his arms. He didn't see it as I did, the noodle-armed hug of a father who didn't know how to show love. Or, more accurately, a father who didn't want to.

Abdel stood, sliding Adli from his chest. He walked to the woman in the corner. He took the sleeping baby from her arms. It was tiny, barely visible in the flannel blanket. The woman, who had made no eye contact with anyone from what I saw, bowed her head as if to fall asleep herself.

Abdel walked the baby over to Yamma. I knew at this point this was his new baby, but why was he here? And without his wife. It wasn't to gloat, I knew that much. I had seen Abdel gloat and this definitely was not how he did it. He stood in the middle of the room surrounded on all four sides. His silence, eerie and unnatural, let me know that I was not the problem here. Something else; something bigger.

"Johara," Yamma said softly, "go into the other room with Joe and Adli."

Johara gave her a disappointed look but under the circumstances, whatever they were, led us both away. I was glad for it on a number of levels. I didn't like Abdel and hated being in his presence. And rather than relying on my intuition, which had failed me completely up to this point, I could ask Johara what was going on. This was the first thing I did when we were out of the kitchen.

Johara shushed me as she listened through walls so thin you could hear a person drinking water through them. Adli was on the chair across the room. He was still sobbing softly, picking mud from his clothes until Johara grabbed his arm as a signal to stop. He pulled away from her, thus beginning another round of poor-me.

"Why is he here? And who is that woman with the baby?" I asked in a whisper.

"His new wife died," she said.

I was sickened. I met her only that one day. As sad as I was for Yamma that Abdel left her, I liked Zaynah very much. At my tender years I didn't delve into the concept of a younger woman versus an older one. I didn't know of such motives. Abdel was mean and cruel. He was heartless. He had no compassion. Those were the reasons he left Yamma and his family. As much as I despised him for those reasons, I found myself understanding his grief.

"That woman is Zaynah's sister," Johara said, her head still cocked towards the wall, waiting for a break in the silence. "Her family was caring for Bara'ah, that's the baby's name."

"He came here to tell us?" I asked.

She shook her head. "I don't think so. He didn't tell us when the baby was born; I doubt we'd know now had his wife not died."

"Maybe he came—"

She held up her hand as she leaned closer to the wall. I could hear them, too, so drew alongside her. It was Abdel. A different, softer Abdel. He was telling Yamma he was sorry. "Must want something," Johara mumbled.

"The child needs a mother," he said. "You know I cannot be a good father, never mind a good enough mother."

I felt a nudge behind me. Adli was off the couch and listening in, as well.

"Zaynah's family has offered but—"

His abrupt ending left the room silent again. At last Yamma spoke. "I'm sorry for your loss, and for Bara'ah's loss. Losing her mother so she could have life will be an incredible burden for her to carry. Insha' Allah, she will be fine. And you will be fine."

"No," Abdel said. "I cannot bear the thought of the child living life as a Yateemah, or having to grow up in a camp."

"Ahhh, but you can bear to leave your sons and daughter. And you can bear to defend life for others as refugees."

"Please stop it, Amineh. This is not easy for me."

"Then say what you mean to say."

"There is no better mother than you. I knew it even then, when I left, so what I am saying is not in contradiction to my actions. No child is in better care than with you."

"Nooo," Johara whispered ghostlike.

"I won't bother you for the house any longer. It's yours. I will give to you all the money sent from America so you will no longer have to work. And a monthly payment we can talk about. It is not about the money for me, it is about—"

"It is not about the money for me either. Abdel," Yamma said. "But really, I do believe that is precisely your concern. A child to care for will cost you much. Much time, much love, as well as much money, three things you never gave away easily."

"I swear to Allah it is for the child. I want her to be cared for by a most loving mother."

"Oh, stop that, Abdel. I am not a swooning little girl."

"If I am lying, then why wouldn't I give the child to Zaynah's family? They have cared for her thus far."

"There is a reason for that, I'm sure," Yamma said. "A reason I don't care to dwell on because I will take Bara'ah,"

At that Johara pushed through Adli and me to rush to the kitchen. We were on her tail. "How can you?" she demanded of Yamma. She turned to her father. "How dare you."

Zaynah's sister sunk lower in the chair. She focused on the emptiness of her lap. In the midst of the drama, I felt her pain. This was not a place she wanted to be. She had lost her sister, was losing her niece.

Perhaps Abdel was telling the truth, that he was refusing to allow Zaynah's family to raise the baby. Maybe it was Yamma whose instincts were correct, they didn't want her. I couldn't help thinking the child was a prop for one or the other, another pawn no one was paying much attention to, thinking it was just an episode she would never know happened. But none of us would forget what was going on here at this moment. How could we? It was life changing for all of us.

"It is the right thing to do," Yamma said.

"For who?" Johara demanded.

"For the only one who matters; for Bara' ah."

"It needs to be a family decision."

"It doesn't matter. Regardless of what you say, I will take her. Ab is right. She should not live as a yateemah or as a refugee, not if there is someone who can prevent it. And she shouldn't go home with him; he cannot even bring himself to say her name. Insha'Allah, she will be fine. Allah has chosen us to be sure of that."

CHAPTER 32

At the end of the school year of 1967, Sam came down to visit. He was off from college and had no plans to travel for the summer. He began to explain why, that too much was happening in the country, but his intuition was as keen as mine and it told him it was best not to pursue the topic.

It was taking us all a while to adjust to having Bara' ah around. She was a crying, eating, pooping, peeing machine. She was born in March, a mere month before coming to us. Yamma and Johara were around the clock with her. It was good that school was over as it was a schedule Johara would have had a hard time maintaining. I became a third caretaker. I learned how to cradle her in my arms to walk her. I took some night shifts. I got good enough where I could hold her with one arm and bottle feed with the other. I was spared having to change her.

When it was warm enough, I took her outside. Since I couldn't sing, I soothed her by pointing out the constellations. I took great pride in thinking she was actually paying attention. I swore to Yamma she was pointing at them with her fat outstretched fingers. "Maybe she wanted to pull one down to give you," Yamma said. I liked that, too.

As expected, Adli and Gamal were no help. It was me all over again. They were jealous of the extra attention given to the baby, especially Adli. I saw Gamal turning into Faid and his father, aloof and disconnected.

Yamma did her best but she wore out easily. I didn't see her being able to dedicate herself to Bara'ah as she did her own kids. I wondered if she could, would she have chosen differently? She enjoyed her work in the village. She didn't have to wait to hear our stories; she came home with some of her own. She met people and got to know their stories. She was very social, an easy speaker and great listener, owing to all her years of having nothing much to do but listen. But if she felt she made a bad decision, we never heard it from her. Again, we knew nothing of her regrets.

Johara teased Sam to hold the baby at dinner that night. "Even Joe can hold and feed her," she said.

"Good for Joe."

"You still think holding and feeding babies is woman's work."

"I never thought that."

It was good to have him here. When he wasn't being intense about politics, he was light and social. He had the knack of putting people at ease. At the end of dinner, when Gamal made his exit, we all stayed and talked, even Adli. Sam had stories of his childhood for us, and of college for Yamma and Johara. Like a good rock concert, he arranged the topics well to keep everyone entertained.

He classified himself as a juvenile delinquent. He skipped school to drink and smoke. The stories disturbed Yamma, but by the end of them she was laughing heartily with the rest of us.

He had a Christian in his neighborhood whose uncle worked in Jordan and routinely brought home bottles of Arak which Sam described as very strong alcohol that tasted of licorice. As a matter of fact, that was how the boy described it to Sam, liquid licorice. "And boy did I love licorice," Sam said with a wicked grin.

The kid wasn't really a friend, Sam explained, but being Christian and 15 years old—a year older and wiser than Sam—he enjoyed tempting his young Muslim neighbor. He told Sam he could only get tablespoons here and there, leaving Sam wanting more. "Really, it was like getting addicted," Sam said. "I mean, the stuff was really good. I hadn't really had enough to get drunk, but it was thick and sweet, licorice honey is how I remembered it. So I practically begged him for an entire glassful.

"Well, he brought it in a small plastic cup. I should have known something was up when he said he couldn't stay around, but thinking back, I'm sure he did. He worked so hard to set me up I know he wouldn't miss a moment of it. It didn't take long. I downed it like apple juice and it hit me before I threw the cup away.

"Of course I don't remember a thing, but somehow I made it home. That was another thing. The kid had me meet him a good half a mile from my house. The good boy in him didn't want me too far from home. The evil in him wanted me far enough to put on a show getting back. I learned afterwards that every Christian I passed knew I was drunk, while the Muslims thought I was possessed by a jinn.

"My parents didn't know drunk from jinn, either. When I vomited they took me to the hospital where the doctor was Christian. I convinced him, no, begged him, not to tell my parents I was drinking alcohol. So to this day my parents believe in jinn possession and bring my episode up as proof positive."

"What was it like, being drunk?" Johara asked

"Johara," Yamma said, "it's a funny story that I'm not sure is entirely true. But leave it alone."

"I can help her there, Amineh," Sam said. "Licorice was my favorite candy growing up, but to this day I cannot smell it without getting sick."

"My brother David is only sixteen and he smokes cigarettes," I said. "He buys whole packs."

"Yes, but has he ever smoked an Argila?" Sam said.

"Sam, you didn't?" Yamma said in a voice so shocked I thought Argila had to be not only a nasty habit but an illegal one, as well.

"Yes, I did," he said proudly. "I smoked from a hubbly-bubbly."

Adli and I broke out laughing. It sounded like a toy from Mattel.

"I did. My friend's father owned a coffee shop that had one." He looked at us. "What it is is a device filled with water where you suck through a tube to smoke tobacco."

"Sounds horrible," Johara said.

"It was, really. I've since done it at the University and it's not bad. I think the kid set it up wrong because we all got sick every time we did it."

"You got sick and you still did it?" Yamma said.

"We were just kids. Who was going to be the first to quit?" he said.

"Majnoon," she said with a laugh and a wave of her hand.

That was why he came: to tell us stories such as those. To make us laugh with each other and forget our problems for just a moment. Of our last three visitors that included Faid and Abdel, he alone came to bring us something besides misery.

Yet he was the one forever wanting to talk about the plight of Palestine, and so I knew he wanted to tell us of the bombings and attacks that were escalating in Jerusalem; of Egypt and Syria moving armies along its borders; of the Egyptian blockade of the Straits of Tiran; and of our great King Hussein of Jordan who had signed a pact to fight against the dreaded state of Israel.

But he didn't. On that night I saw compassion that came out in a most unique way. So subtlety no one noticed what he was doing. It was the way I wanted to remember him. Yet nagging in the back of my mind all that night was what Johara had suggested, that somehow he was to blame for Sue's attempted suicide. I couldn't allow myself to believe it. It would be *Invasion of the Body Snatchers* where, unbeknownst to me, all my closest allies had fallen asleep and been replaced by their evil pod replicas.

He stayed late, past eleven o'clock. He was concerned for how we were faring. "Has Khaal Abu Faid come by to see you or Bara'ah?" Sam asked.

"No, he has not," Yamma said dryly.

It was an obligatory question he had to ask. I don't think it was meant to offend or open any wounds. With it done, he moved on. "Amineh, you disappoint me."

"Now how have I done that?"

"All this time and your children have not heard the story of your school mural."

Yamma commented on how it would be a bad olive harvest this year. "I haven't taken the time to tend to the trees as I should and the trees know when they're being ignored."

"So do I," Sam said.

"Oh, Sam, why are you digging up the past?"

"I told you of my accomplishments in the field of drinking and smoking. You can at least tell us about your accomplishments in the arts."

"It was a long time ago."

"So was the Sistine Chapel, but people still come to see and hear about it."

"Did you see the Sistine Chapel last summer?" Yamma asked.

"I did, and you are avoiding the subject."

But she wasn't, not really. She was anxious to talk about art, just not her own. I could tell by how she fidgeted and looked away when she was the topic of conversation, but refocused intensely when Sam mentioned the chapel.

She did the same when I complimented her dinners, which I often did. She was chipper with conversation about my day at school and hers at home and the farm and the animals, but I could see her discomfort when the subject turned to her good works. While Sam's voice escalated to match his passion when he spoke of his politics, as did Abdel's when he spoke of his work at the refugee camps, Yamma's faded away. It was a humility forced upon her, and I truly believe she found it sinful to be anything but ordinary.

Sam looked at us. "Didn't I say she would not be the one to tell you? Amineh, you're making me look like a liar. It's time to confess. It was you who drew on the big wall in the school lobby, now, wasn't it?"

"Oh, really."

"Just tell us yes or no and we'll let it go."

"Yes," she said softly.

And we let it go. I wished I hadn't, for her sake and mine. I wish I'd asked when she drew it, why she did it. Was it an art project or just something she wanted to do? Were there others? Why did they decide to keep it there so long? Who decided? Did she win an award? How did she learn to paint? It was beautiful, and one of the things from that place and time I enjoy seeing when I close my eyes.

Just before Sam headed back to Ramallah, Adli approached Yamma with more than a whine and whimper. He had a serious plan which he stated directly. "Sam will take me up to see Ab now, and he will bring me home tomorrow."

It was a topic I knew was to come up sometime during the night. I give him credit for waiting until everyone was full of charitable thoughts and too tired to fight him.

"He will, will he?" Yamma said

"Yes."

I don't think that's a good idea," Yamma said.

"You said I could go."

Yamma stole a glance at Sam and sighed. Not only did she say it, but she swore it to Allah. That wasn't something to take lightly. She thought Adli would forget, I'm sure, or she wouldn't have brought Allah into it.

"I can take him," Sam said. That wasn't where Yamma was going with her sigh.

"You are not staying there alone," Yamma said. "And if you father is not home—"

"Gamal can come with me," Adli said as he sprinted from the room to get Gamal.

"Why did you offer?" Yamma asked sharply. "I have been trying to keep him from going all year."

"Precisely why I did. He'll never stop asking. That's just the way he is. I'm here, I can get him there."

"He thinks his father needs him now that Zaynah and Bara'ah are gone. He doesn't understand his father will never accept him. That hurt him terribly, and I can't bear for that to happen again."

"You could be wrong," Sam said, "he could have changed his heart."

"Then he would be back here with us. Johara what do you think?"

"I'm glad he is not back here."

"I mean about Adli and Gamal going to see him."

"I don't like it. Gamal is growing to not like Adli."

"That's not so, they're brothers," Yamma said.

"That's not what Ab is saying and so it's not what Faid and Gamal are saying."

This was an obvious shock to Yamma, that her son could be abandoned so readily by his brothers on the say-so of her husband. Hadn't she explained this all to Faid and Gamal? Didn't they realize this was his ruse to leave the family for another life? Were they so obtuse? Were they so much like their father?

I knew the answer to be yes. I had always known. But while my heart was filled with hate that saw Faid and Gamal only as evil, Yamma's was filled with love and saw none of that. As she wept softly for her boys, I felt shame for knowing the truth. It should have been me who was deceived. I was young; I was new. I had no business being jaded, just as she had no business being deserted.

CHAPTER 33

June 5, 1967. It doesn't have the power and prestige of July 4th, December 7th, or 9/11, but it is an unforgettable day for those of us who lived through it. The day culminated a long, seemingly disconnected chain of events that mapped the destiny for so many people.

Adli came back to us in the kitchen distraught and without Gamal. He slumped at the table. He didn't notice Yamma's mood, being into his own. Yamma recovered sufficiently to ask him what was wrong. "Gamal won't come."

"I see. Did he say why?"

"He has plans with his friends. He says he doesn't feel like going on a long drive."

Yamma looked relieved but at the same time disturbed. In my heart I knew what she wanted. She wanted her family back. She wanted her sons together. She wanted Adli healthy and whole. I shouldn't have done what I did next. It forced her to make a decision that was against her better judgment. "I'll go with him," I said.

Adli jumped up and hugged me as if my volunteering made it so. In the end, it did, with Yamma thanking me and Sam with the caveat that it wouldn't be done until she spoke with Abdel in the morning to make sure it was fine with him and he would be around. Sam told me to get myself and Adli packed for a two-night stay.

Packing the car the next morning, Sam confided in me that Yamma's suspicions were founded; Abdel would never agree to having Adli stay over. Me, neither, for that matter. "So I told Amineh it would be best for me to bring you there and talk to your uncle," he said. "If he still denies you, I'll bring you home, but I doubt he will with me there."

I understood Abdel not wanting to see Adli, and even though I didn't really want to ever see Abdel again, I took offense to his not wanting to see me.

"I guess the best answer to that, Joe, is that he is who he is. He has a simple mind that grasps few things well."

"I don't get that," I said.

"Have you ever had a fight?"

"A lot."

"Have you ever started one but didn't want to admit it because you thought it would be a sign of weakness?"

"I guess so."

"Men do it, too. Your uncle in particular is a man I know who cannot right a wrong with his words or actions. To him, his first response, no matter how flawed, must be the final one."

I still didn't get it, not the particulars as they applied to me. "You do not like your uncle, right?" he said.

"No, I don't like him."

"So why go? Why not let Adli go alone?"

The real reason sounded silly in my head, and those thoughts always sound sillier when said aloud. So I fudged around it. "I don't know, keep him company, I guess." But Sam knew. He knew the cocky kid in me who saw himself as Adli's protector from the usual suspects: school bullies, Gamal, thoughtlessness, and insensitivity.

That night Adli couldn't sleep. Neither could I, but we had different reasons. He climbed into the twin bed with me. "I'm glad you're coming with me instead of Gamal," he whispered.

"Me, too," I said.

"Ab will be happy, too. He likes you. I can tell these things. Even though he never talked much to you, I can tell, so don't worry. Like me. He didn't talk much to me either, but of course he loves me."

I heard his deep sigh of contentment that I didn't want to disturb, but I had to ask him. "Adli?"

"Yeah, Joe?"

"Do you remember why Ab left the house?"

"Of course. He had another baby he had to take care of."

I fell asleep amused, yet uneasy that he could forget so readily such a cruel act done to him. I felt it was a merciless trick of nature. I've since known people whose minds do these things when a tragedy strikes. I no longer see it as a cruel. I see it as one of the blessings given to very good people who never should have had such a cruelty befall them in the first place.

***

We left after breakfast. Johara cooked, Yamma served, while Gamal and the baby slept. Adli was very talkative on the drive to Ramallah. For once I think Sam was out-talked. It didn't take us as long to get there as it did on the bus. Sam was a psycho driver and knew short cuts. That and I think he was anxious to get Adli out of the car. We drove a half hour past the Friends School to the west side of town. "A storm is coming," Adli said. "I can hear thunder."

I would have let it go had I not seen the distress on Sam's face. The thunder was to our south. At one point he stopped the car and stared out. "al Quds," he muttered. Jerusalem. He hurried onward, faster and more furious than the roads and traffic allowed. The world around us took on a frantic pace. As fast as Sam was driving, others were passing him. Cars were stopped at the strangest places. Men were milling about in the middle of the street, pointing and gesturing wildly. "What's going on?" I asked.

"Big storm, looks like," Adli said.

"I'm not sure," Sam said.

We arrived at Abdel's house on the outskirts of the city. It was smaller than the house in Dayr Ghasana. No land except the plot it sat on and just enough for a drive and walk way. He had neighbors so close he could hear snoring at night and belching in the morning. "What if he's at work?" I said.

Sam ignored my concern. He told us to go up and tell Abdel we were there; he would be back in a while. That was not the plan, and I was about to tell him that when he screamed at us to get out now. I had seen him excited; I had seen him passionate; I had seen him scared, but his rage was new to me. I scrambled from the car with Adli. Sam sped off.

Unlike the city, this part of town was either deserted or still asleep. Adli ran to the door and tried to open it without knocking. "It's stuck," he said.

"Knock first," I said.

He did, then tried the doorknob again without waiting for an answer.

"You have to give him time to get to the door," I said.

He ignored me as he continued to fiddle with the doorknob. I could tell by the way the knob barely moved that it was locked. "Why would he lock the door?" he said. "No one can get in."

I was wary of staying around the house. I was sure Abdel was not at home and I had visions of him coming back to find us here. Without Sam to run interference it wouldn't be pretty. But Adli had no such misgivings. He walked around the house checking the windows and the back door. I stood on the side of the roadway.

He came back with a most dejected look. "He doesn't even have chickens or goats," he said.

"It's too small for them, and he lives in the city," I said.

"There are two fig trees out back but the figs are brown and shriveled. They tasted horrible."

"You ate one?"

"Yeah."

"That's disgusting, Adli. Don't go eating fruits you know are bad."

"We can help Ab to grow them."

"I don't think he cares about the figs, Adli , or he wouldn't have let them go bad."

"He has no help here, you know," he said, jumping to his father's defense. "He has no wife or children to help him now." His eyes darkened as he snorted heavy like a race horse. I saw his fists clench at his side.

"I know, Adli. If he wants, we can help."

We sat waiting on the front steps. The thunder was sporadic in the distance where I saw no dark clouds. Dogs were barking in the nearby yards. People came out to stare in the direction of the thunder but none of them stayed long. Two hours past, and I was getting nervous and mentioned to Adli that we should start walking into town. I didn't think we'd run into Sam there but we'd be closer to civilization and that made me feel safer.

"Sam's coming back," he said.

"I don't know about that. Maybe he had something else to do."

"How about Ab?"

I saw a way to get Adli into line with me. "Maybe he's in Ramallah," I said.

"Think so?"

"Yeah."

We walked the direction Sam drove in from. It was past noon. There was no storm coming. With all the talk of war, I knew it had started. I also knew, having driven from Ramallah to Jerusalem before, it wasn't far off. I was scared. I thought back to the bombing that killed Tariq and his family. This was what they were hearing before their house was hit, only louder and closer. It had to be terrifying knowing nothing you could say or do would keep the next bomb, or the next, off your house. No amount of love or pride, confidence or respect would redirect a mindless missile in flight. All Ramiz and Sureia had taught, all Tariq, Bahir, Hana, and Khahil had learned, was useless under these skies.

We hadn't gone the length of a soccer field when a car stopped beside us. "Where are you boys going?" He was an older man with salt and pepper hair and beard. He was dressed in a white button-down shirt, his sleeves rolled to mid forearm. They were thick and dark with hair. His hands had newly obtained grease on them. He was leaning out the window, looking over us at the direction of the bombing.

"To Ramallah," Adli said. "To find my father."

"You from here?"

"No, Dayr Ghasana," he said.

The man gave us an alarmed look. "Long way from home. And on a day like this. Well, you cannot go there, not now. Better get in."

I wasn't sure it was a good idea but it was better than heading off to nowhere with Adli. I opened the back door to get in as Adli protested. "You said Ab would be in Ramallah."

"I said, maybe. Adli, we cannot go walking alone. That's not thunder, they're bombs."

"Bombing where?" He asked as he pushed in beside me.

"Jerusalem, from what Sam said."

"So who's doing the bombs?"

"I don't know. The Israelis, I think."

"No," the man said. "They would not be bombing the Holy City. This morning they attacked Egypt. But this cannot be Egypt's counterattack. Too far. Jordan. Must be Jordan has involved themselves, though I think it's a mistake."

He spoke as if we knew what he was saying. His tone was grim. He took us back to his house which was just past Abdel's. "Go inside," he told us. "I'll be back."

We were left alone again but at least we were inside. We sat in the front room until we heard a commotion at the side of the house. He was back with a very young woman, who he ushered inside. She was there to care for us until the bombing was over. I explained that Adli's father lived down the road and that we were waiting for him. I didn't mention Sam as it was my belief he had gone off to join the fight and would not be returning for us. I brought her outside to point out his house. "Yes," she said, "I know of him a little. He has that sweet wife. I haven't seen her lately."

"She's dead," Adli said.

"Oh?" She was taken aback by Adli's frankness. "I didn't know. I'm sorry for the loss of your mother."

"She wasn't my mother," he said, "Yamma's my mother."

Recognizing Adli's condition, she turned to me. "He drives a black Mercedes?"

I nodded.

"I haven't seen it there for a few days. Does he know you're here?"

Before I could answer, the man came back and emphatically told us we were to stay with her, his daughter, until the bombing stopped. She walked us next door to her house. She was very kind to us for the few hours we were with her.

Throughout the night she spoke to us in comforting tones, never discussing the bombings or Abdel's absence. Her father was a professor at the University. If she mentioned what he taught, I wasn't paying attention. Her husband was a student there, or maybe a professor, as well. She filled us in on all those types of details. They were Christians who lived all their lives in Ramallah. They hoped to move to Spain. She wanted children.

Her comments rolled over me like the rumblings outside. They were lullabies and her soft voice rocked me to sleep. Adli stood at the window, the curtains parted as he stared down the street, waiting for his father. I imagined the bombs were thunder, moving into the distant mountains. I smelled the fragrant rains they left behind and felt the hot, thick air. I fell asleep to those sensations so as not to be haunted by the screams I knew accompanied each pounding of the earth. I needed at that moment to trust in the power of nature over the power of man.

CHAPTER 34

It was an earsplitting whistle, a teapot pressed against my head, that awoke me. Adli was beside me. He didn't stir. It was the bombs. I woke him and he slowly came to, as if it was another lazy summer morning on the farm. "Adli, hear them, the bombs?"

"Who?"

"No. Bombs. We gotta get out of here." Though out there seemed a crazier place to be than in here.

Other than the one I awoke to, no other bombs sounded close, so maybe it was part of the dream that lulled me to sleep and the coming of morning magnified the explosions. Then the girl came through the front door with a lunatic urgency. "It is getting too dangerous to stay here," she said. "We must go."

"Where?" I asked.

She looked out the window and shook her head. "I don't know where."

"Is my father home yet," Adli said.

She picked up on his fears. "No, but that's a good thing. It means he heard the explosions and stayed in his safe place. You'll see him very soon, as soon as the shelling stops we'll go to him." He looked to me for confirmation. This girl wasn't much older than Johara. How did she know what was going to happen to us? Better yet, how to save us? She looked more confused than Adli.

"Is your father coming back?" I asked.

She didn't answer. She was looking out the window again, waiting for him, waiting for anyone. "Is he?"

"Huh? My father? No, he's not going to be able to. Neither can my husband. No buses are coming into Ramallah. But I spoke to him, my father, and he said there are buses leaving from downtown."

That didn't comfort me. It was a long way back to the Friends School which was the downtown I knew. And she didn't inspire confidence as a guide. I realized when it came to random bombing, most people were as lost and scared as children, knowing that skill played as much a part in survival as it did in roulette.

"Quickly, let's go now," she said as she hustle us outside. There were other neighbors forming a convoy. The ones that had cars had them filled with stuff. Just the driver and lots of stuff. Those old and strong enough to walk walked. We were to walk with men and woman as old as Siidi and Nadirah. I stuck it in my memory, if I was around for the destruction of the world, I'd leave every scrap of stuff I had behind, and tie people to the hood and roof of my car to get them out.

The bombing was more sporadic but closer than it had been the night before. The more we walked, the more used to it I became. Every miss was proof enough to me that the next would miss, as well. Having no experience, I felt comfort in applying my own brand of the law of averages.

It seemed like six hours but was more like two. It felt like twenty miles but was more like four. Thing was, it was long and far. We outdistanced the elderly who had to rest often. I felt dishonor in leaving them. I turned continuously as we walked away. I wanted them to be up and following, yet something inside me enjoyed watching them become lesser figures, mere dots on a stone, until like *The Incredible Shrinking Man,* they existed no more.

We were joined by many others. At first we smiled and acknowledged each other with "sabah el kheer." The adults would discuss the events. As the miles mounted, the discussions became briefer and the greetings became nods. Then, like the elderly left behind, responses ceased all together.

It was the Israelis this time; that much was sure to the people traveling with us. Last night it was King Hussein attacking Jerusalem. The king didn't seem so bad to me upon hearing this. He was coming to our rescue and soon he'd be riding into Ramallah to battle the Israelis in the streets. I spent the last mile watching for this.

My main worry was getting out alive. Our guide, Ranya I learned was her name, had at least kept us moving with the crowd. I worried about Adli. I wasn't sure he could make it. But other than initial gripes and complaints, he did better than most and never had us waiting up for him.

I heard the energy of the city up ahead. There were angry shouts and angry horns. It seemed the entire city was set on moving out. A few men and women sat along the sidewalks. They sipped coffee and casually observed the commotion. These people did not look worried or ready to move. I wondered what they either knew or didn't know.

By now we were too exhausted and disinterested to join the mob scene. Buses came and went with people shoving to get on. We watched it as if in the back row of a movie theater. This was when Adli began to lose it. I sat on a grassy path while he moved among the crowd, getting jostled by people who would normally not be so rude. He was looking for Abdel. I knew he wouldn't find him. He was no doubt safely miles away.

A commotion was brewing at the center of town where the buses were loading. A bus driver was surrounded by hundreds of angry people. Ranya snapped her head up like a dog sniffing out a slab of steak. She grabbed my hand. "Come with me." She rounded up Adli and pulled us through the crowd to the driver. Either the moment gave her a burst of unnatural strength or she had been holding it in reserve. She separated that crowd like a rock star body guard.

This was the last bus out of Ramallah. Others would come back for as long as they could, the driver explained patiently. "We will get everyone out."

"Children on this one," Ranya insisted. She pulled us towards the closed doors without waiting for his concurrence.

"Yes, yes, the driver said. "Only children."

He opened the doors while Ranya squeezed us through before the surge she knew was to come. We took the front seat. It was a bizarre scene. The bus shook. Disheveled kids were pushed up the steps. Parents forced others through the windows. Men tried wrenching off the rear emergency door.

I watched Ranya move quickly out of the crowd below. Once away from the swarm she drifted backwards, waving up to us. I waved back. She stood on a knoll, silhouetted above this frenzy. Her hands were folded solemnly at her waist. Like so many others I had known and met, I never saw her after that. She was the one I wished I had. I once saw her standing lost as a child at her window. Somewhere along the road march she grew up.

I pray she survived. I hope she had her children. I believe she saw Adli and me as a test of the kind of mother she would be. Would she battle authority for her children? Would she risk her life for them? I hope she knew she did well that day. I said as much with my wave as we drove out of Ramallah.

***

It wasn't all children on the bus. Men, young men, snuck on. They didn't even have the decency to pretend to be escorting a sick or injured child. The one across from us sat leaning forward, his hands folded between his open knees. He stared ahead out the window. He had the stillness of a frog on the bank of a pond trying his damndest not be seen. Some old men, too, who tried a little too hard to appear infirm. Some slept. Some looked out the window or anywhere a kid's face wasn't. Others wore a look of feigned confusion, as if unaware how they got on board. In addition to scared kids, there was a lot of shame on that bus.

Adli began to cry. I was sure it was to show solidarity with the dozens of others who were in hysterics. It drove me crazy to listen to it; I can imagine the bus driver cursing himself for allowing Ranya to talk him into a bus load of potential orphans. "We'll be fine," I said to myself as much as to Adli.

The Israelis picked that moment to drop a bomb seemingly on the hood of the bus. It was the most horrifying sound imaginable. Not only the decibels, which were proof enough of its power, but the notion it was meant for us. I was sure that back at the square an Israeli spy had called to his artillery unit who locked in on us for the purpose of wiping out the entire busload in view of the people who picked this as our safe haven.

Adli was lifted out of the seat. I heard his high-pitched screech but it was from the man next to us. It went dark for me for a moment. I wasn't sure if I had actually blacked out or just refused to open my eyes. The bus, which had dramatically veered off the road, was now back on course and at a high rate of speed. I found perverted humor in driving frantically away from our near-miss only to possibly meet head on with the next one up the road.

Adli had a big welt on his head which, ironically through shock, calmed him down. It wasn't bleeding, just turning rapidly purple. But there *was* blood. I checked first to make sure it wasn't mine. I turned to the young girl behind me, no more than five, with her front teeth shattered and her mouth a mass of red ribbon. Blood puddled through her cupped hand. Splatters of it were on the windows beside us and on the back of my seat. She stared at me with eyes like black dinner plates. They were pleading with me to tell her she was fine. I looked away to the back of the bus, to kids picking themselves off the floorboard, holding heads, arms, legs, crying, moaning.

I was being pulled from the side. It was Adli, yelling something in my ear. It came out as garbled noise, mixing incoherently with the distress sounds around me. He was shaking me feverishly, demanding my undivided attention. "What, Adli, what?"

"Where are we going?"

"I don't know, out of Ramallah,"

He jumped across my lap and pressed his face against the window. The danger was past but the driver continued our mad ride. The recklessness added a disquieting dimension to the scene. The faster he drove, the more unsettled we became. Our minds were in synch with his lead foot. With no adults worth owning the term on board, we were all out of control with everything about us moving fast and furious.

Adli shuffled up to the driver. Through the noise I couldn't make out the conversation but saw the driver motioning with his hand for him to go back to his seat. Adli refused as he grasped the back of the driver's chair to keep from toppling over. The road ahead was fairly clear and straight, yet the bus swerved sharply left and right. We were decades before smart bombs but this driver saw them coming from every direction. I was wanting him to just stay on course and in control. It was his driving and not the dumb bombs that were worrying me.

I saw Adli's face go ashen. He stood frozen. Stumbling back to me, he told me we were going the wrong way.

"What do you mean, the wrong way?"

"We're going away from Yamma."

"How do you know that? He tell you that?"

"We're heading to Bir Zayt."

I looked out my window. I knew Bir Zayt; we both did. It was where Sam went to the University. Only I didn't know this route. Because of the attack the driver must have felt it best to stay off main roads that were now primary targets. "That's good," I said. "It's the direction we want to go."

"No. No, Joe, it's not. It's going away from home."

"Adli, that's where Sam goes to school, remember."

"Yes, and that's away from our house. It's taking us away."

I saw how his mind was working this. When we used to drive through Bir Zayt on our way to Ramallah, were drove away from Dayr Ghasana. So driving to it now meant we were driving away from home. Only, I knew it was north of Ramallah, as was Dayr Ghasana. I began to explain but he was far too frantic at this point. "Calm down," I said. "Wait. You'll see."

But he wouldn't. He couldn't. The further we drove the more lost I watched him become. "We have to get off," he said. He wasn't looking at me. His eyes were mesmerized on the front windshield. He began a gentle rock meant to relax himself, but he grew more agitated. Finally, he bolted from the seat and down the exit steps. He pounded on the door. "Open up, open up. Besora'a." *Hurry.*

I ran to retrieve him but he locked himself onto the landing. The driver screamed at us to get back to our seats. He saw how futile our attempts were to control Adli, and so stopped the bus ruthlessly, beginning another round of sprawled passengers. The door opened and Adli ran through as if he were trapped miner gasping for fresh air. "You, too?" The driver demanded.

Adli was racing back down the road. "No," I said.

The door crashed closed and the bus hurdled onward. I slipped back into the seat. He was a crazy kid, a lunatic, I was convincing myself. Someone would find him and see it for themselves. He knew where he lived, if not how to get back. They would care for him until they could get him home. I'd be waiting for him and give him hell for busting out like that. But he'd forget soon and I'd forgive; it's how we were.

I ran up to the driver. "Qif," I said. *Stop*. He motioned me back to my seat. I stole Adli's tantrum tactic, running down the steps and pounding on the door until the bus stopped and it opened.

Adli was far from me by now. Out here the bombing was louder. It was close, too. I could feel the ground shake with each explosion. I ran calling for him. I wanted to stop and sit, just to let the world settle down for a few minutes. I was outside the city in farm country. I moved off the side of the road to rest against an oak tree.

The people were going about their farm chores, only occasionally stopping to listen to the turmoil happening just a few miles south. It was encouraging to see but totally incongruous to what I had just been through. Theirs was the reality I wanted to believe, though I was sure it was to change very soon.

I was overcome with a need to sleep. But my chances of catching up to Adli were already slim. I'd seen him move when he was angry and afraid, when he had the one-track mind of an Olympic marathon runner. I was sure he'd be on the main road so I moved out in a slow jog. I was stopped by an old man tending to three goats in his front yard. "You with that young boy?" he asked.

I nodded.

The man pointed to a ravine that ran parallel to the road. "I passed him down there. Better hurry, he was running like the devil was on his tail." I ran off as his voice trailed behind me. "Soldiers moving up, be careful."

I didn't know what soldiers he was talking about, King Hussein's or Israelis. It was a thin worry at the moment; I had to get to Adli. Going home without him was really not an option. I couldn't face Yamma. Gaining a baby girl and losing a son in three months wasn't what she needed.

CHAPTER 35

The ravine, though fairly straight, was what a ravine should be. It widened and narrowed, dipped and climbed, and held run-off water that included drainage from open sewers. Here, it was about six feet deep. I ran beside it. I knew Adli would see it as a great shelter from the horrific bombings. He'd probably be running down inside. I sprinted along calling his name. I saw him up ahead, as I figured, following its contours and soaking wet.

"Get out of there, Adli," I said as I approached.

"No."

"You're wet."

"It's safe down here."

"It's okay now. Listen, no more bombs."

There was a convenient lull that started about two minutes ago. I had no idea how long or if it would last, just as long as it gave me enough time to get Adli out of the sewer. He stopped moving to listen. He gave me a narrowed-eyed stare as if to ask if I was playing a trick, as if I was one of them. "Why didn't you get off with me?" He asked as he climbed up the bank.

"You should have stayed on."

"It was going the wrong way. You're supposed to stay with me; it's what you told Yamma you would do."

"Not when you do something … it doesn't matter now. I'm here with you and the bus is gone."

"Come on," he demanded, still convinced his decision was right. "We go this way."

I said nothing about soldiers coming. I hoped we would hear the bombing soon and he would realize we were moving into them. But it could be too late by then; they could rain on us by the time he figured it out for himself. It was one thing to let him catch a bird for a meal, to let him drift a while in the deep part of the river, to take all the time he needed to get used to the cave, but this was different, this could kill us both. I couldn't take time to be nice or understanding.

I had no experience in being responsible for anyone but myself. I had no mentor in my father, Siidi, Abdel, or even Sam. Yamma was the closest, but for childish things like eating and bathing and sleeping and caring for the animals and picking olives. I understand that's how it's learned, with those little things. This was not a little thing. This was a decision that wouldn't result in being hungry or dirty or tired. Things were out there that could kill us, something I had to make Adli understand now. I had to make him understand that I was right, and if it meant beating it into him, I was ready to do that, too.

I ran up and spun him around. "No, Adli, that is the way into the bombs. Yamma is that way." I pointed north. "I am not sure exactly where because you made us get off the bus. But we need to turn around and follow the road."

He started to argue. I stopped him with my palm in his face. "You made a mistake, Adli."

Being scared to death, he was not taking my commands well. His jaw tensed. His feet shuffled as they dug in. I didn't dare turn to walk away, expecting he'd follow because there was good chance he wouldn't. As luck had it, a series of explosions went off. We both winced and staggered from the shock. "See," I said.

He listened for more. "They're getting closer to us," he said. "We got to hurry home." He turned and ran back into the ravine.

I let out a banshee scream. "No, *they* are not getting closer. *We* are. We are getting closer to them. There are soldiers coming up that ravine with guns. They want to kill us, all of us. That's why they're here. They're looking for us."

I laid it on as thick as I could. I had to create another cave for him to fear. More jinns, more ghoulies, more witches. "For real?" he asked.

"Yes. For real. And that water down there is from toilets, like at The Friends School, so you need to get out."

He climbed up. "I'm hungry," he said.

"Me, too. But there's no time."

Adli took an apricot from his pocket. "Where'd you get that?" I asked.

"There's a grove of them back there."

He pulled it apart with his hands and gave me half. We walked back up alongside the ravine. Adli smelled disgusting but I kept it to myself. There was no sense terrifying him with another doomsday report. We came to the grove of a dozen trees, pruned and shaped. It was clearly being cared for by the owners of the house not one hundred feet away. There was a vegetable garden, too. "These are not wild apricots," I said. We can't take them."

Adli suggested we walk up to the door to ask.

"No," I said. "Better not." My rationale was simple; we were going to take them regardless. Asking and being denied made us thieves. Not asking just kept us ignorant. "We need to leave this place before the bombs start again. We'll rest somewhere until it gets dark."

"But the soldiers," Adli said.

I saw a forest on a hill which I perceived to be a safe distance away. "There," I said pointing. "It's a good place to hide and we can see them coming." It was a story that worked for both of us.

The combination of hunger, fatigue, and the hot sun put us to sleep almost immediately. I had no watch and never was sure of the time throughout those days. Being young and always hungry, I couldn't rely on my stomach to tell me. And wherever we were, it was a Christian village with no minaret to call people to prayer. Now it was fairly dark and getting darker, so I knew it was past eight.

I awoke to the echoes of distant cracking and a steady stream of low growls. The stiff breeze blowing across the desert always brought with it quirky noises. I was used to them. They were usually nothing more than the whistling through grasses and scrub bushes, and the clicking of branches against each other. Some were eerie; the call of hawks, boars, and wild dogs.

I woke Adli. As usual, he was slow to respond. "We home yet?"

"Come on, we can get the apricots now."

My stomach was empty, but I remained patient because we needed the extra time for darkness to set in. "What's that noise?" Adli asked.

"I'm not sure, doesn't sound right, does it?"

As we cleared the forest and descended the hill, we saw a string of lights in the center of town. "Trucks," I said.

"Lots of them."

I wasn't alarmed. I hoped for more buses transferring people out of this village. The thought made me pick up the pace. From the blackness I saw firefly-type flashes followed by the crack of whips. We were still a hundred yards or so away, moving up and down the desert draws and ridges. Adli was falling behind, which in the end was a good thing, giving me time to comprehend what we were dashing into.

It was the screams that filled in the blanks for me. The village was under siege, and though I had no idea what the effective range of their guns were, I was confident I was within it. I turned to hold back Adli. Breathlessly, he solved the puzzle as well. "Those are guns. They're shooting them."

I pulled him into the ravine, down into the nasty water. "I told you we were going the wrong way," he scolded. "What are we going to do?

No way was the right way. We were right in the middle of a war between Israel and King Hussein. One side was shooting at another which was shooting back. If the sides had uniforms it was of no use to me. I had no idea what to look for.

Adli began to crawl on all fours down the creek. "Get back here," I said.

He ignored me. I duck walked down to get him. He let out a horrid scream. When I got to him he was sitting back on his haunches. He was pointing to the middle of the ravine. There was blood on his hands. "You're bleeding," I said.

He shook his head vigorously. "He's dead; that man, he's dead. His neck is gone."

I crossed in front of him to find a man, no older than Sam or Faid, lying still on his side. Adli was right. I dared not touch him. His head was thrown back at a grotesque angle as if someone had tried to twist it off. A hole had been torn out of his neck. Bleeding seemed to have stopped, but there was enough scarlet freshness to indicate it wasn't long ago. Like Adli, I sat in shock. With all the shooting, it shouldn't have surprised me to see more. But it did.

Four more we stumbled across in the ravine. Funny thing about death when it's all around you. You take note, assess it fast, and move on. That first one was a novelty. We didn't enjoy it but there was a fascination, like seeing a birth. We stopped short upon seeing the second. We dodged around the third, hopped over the fourth, and stepped on the fifth.

We were crawling north through the ravine as it hit me. This wasn't a newly formed graveyard. No one threw these bodies down here. A battle had been fought here, and very recently. We had to get out. If this was a battle position for the dead behind us, it was possibly one for soldiers up ahead.

Up to this point, we had done well considering the surreal horrors we were in. Adli was far from home on so many levels. I had seen and done things I couldn't have fantasized in my wildest Army war games. We kept our heads down and voices low. We scrutinized our movements. Our senses of sight, smell, and hearing were at their peak. I swear I could smell the dead bodies minutes before seeing them. Yet Adli was one dead body, one bomb explosion, one tracer round from madness. Saying the wrong thing in the wrong way would be devastating to the both of us.

I stopped and waited for him to catch up. "We can move out of the ravine now," I said.

"Why?"

Adli rarely questioned me when I spoke in such absolutes but he had turned to survival mode.

"Listen." I paused for effect. "No shooting. We've gone past it."

"No. It's safer here," he said.

"Look at all the dead bodies."

"But they're dead; the shooting has passed here."

"No, Adli, this is where they fight."

He hesitated as if trying to read the situation for himself. Finally he made his way towards the walls. I followed suit when I knew he was in agreement.

The sides were fairly steep. Adli moved down the ravine to where a thick root protruded midway up. He used it as an assist. I had no such aids where I was. The handful of clay I grabbed onto broke away, sending me backwards in the stream.

I laughed it off out loud as a way to relieve our tensions. I figured Adli would get a good laugh out of staring down at me in the mud. There were three, maybe four, sharp popping sounds above me. I scurried onto all fours and gazed up as Adli was thrown violently back into the ditch. He lay there motionless in the mud.

Voices above me. I froze. Silhouetted by the starlight were three soldiers in fatigues and red berets. Two had rifles pointed into the hole. "Just a boy?" One said.

"No, no," another said. "I saw him. I saw him jump out. It was a soldier." He turned to a third man who stood solid with his arms folded. His rifle was slung across his waist. He was shorter than the others but much thicker. "You saw, right, sir. That was a soldier I shot."

The other jumped down. I spread myself out like the mud and dug deep into it. "Shit, he's just a kid, a boy no older than mine."

I waited to see him pull Adli up by his collar, to hear Adli call out for me or Yamma. But the soldier poked at him with the muzzle of his rifle and Adli didn't move.

The shooter went to his knees, sobbing. "Dear God, no." What did I do, dear God, what did I do?"

Up to this point the shorter soldier addressed as "sir" hadn't spoken. He hadn't moved since arriving. "Settle down, soldier."

The shooter was staring up at him. "I should have waited. I should have—"

"On your feet," sir screamed. He reached down and with one tug practically lifted the man. The other soldier crawled up using the same root handle Adli had. He shook his head.

"Take him back," sir said. "I want him on the march. Don't let him sit; don't give him to the medics."

"Yes, sir."

The shooter leaned on his escort when they left, sobbing heavily. Both held each other in a shoulder embrace. "Stand on your own two feet," sir ordered. "The only soldiers being carried out of here are the dead ones."

Sir didn't leave. I heard his deep sigh. He took off his beret and held it before him, his head bowed. He was wearing a watch or a bracelet because I heard the metallic tapping against his rifle. He kicked clumps of dirt into the ditch with the toe of his boot. "I see you there, boy" he called down to me. "Take him home. Take him home to his family. Tell them this is no future. This is no future for anyone."

CHAPTER 36

I saw my first dead body when I was five. He was very old, and I knew him only as the old man who sat with his window open while stroking his cat. And like pigeons, we'd flock to him when his window went up and he threw handfuls of penny candy onto the sidewalk to us.

No one really knew him, least of all my mother, who cried when he died. My father told her as much. "I'm going because he died alone and I don't want him buried alone," my mother said.

"Fat lot of good company will do him now," my father said.

She dressed up in a black dress, black gloves, and a hat with a fishnet veil. She looked truly beautiful in her grief. I met her in the kitchen in my gray blazer and bowtie. "You want to go?" she asked. I nodded. "You sure? No place to run off and play."

We walked. The funeral home was only a few blocks away. I'm sure she wondered why I was going as much as I wondered why she was. Yes, he gave me candy. Yes, he lived alone. Was that enough to compel us, or was dad right, "fat lot of good we'll do him now."

A few neighbors did come. It was all very hushed, as if they were whispering bad things behind someone's back. I followed her up to the casket. She stopped me. "You don't have to look at him," she said, but she didn't try to stop me. I tried not to gape as we knelt before the casket. I couldn't help myself. There was nothing peaceful about him. This was not him. This was a store front mannequin, gray and waxen. Though there was no life in his face I knew it was there, wrapped within a clay model.

How could his body stop functioning? It was here, lying down the same way it does when he sleeps. I saw no bullet wounds and everything seemed to be in its place. I had this vision that dead bodies evaporate or somehow disintegrate. I had no concept of the body as merely a conveyance for much greater things.

***

The soldiers were gone. Outside the hole were sounds of cars and trucks and cries. Gun shots off in one direction, explosions in the other. I stayed low in the mud, preferring the cold and wet as better conditions than were waiting for me outside.

I dared to stretch my neck out like a timid turtle, staring over at Adli. We were at eye level. He had done a great job of playing possum. He even held his cool at the end of a rifle and fooled a trained soldier. He could get up now.

"Get up, Adli," I called out. "They're gone, you can get up." It made me feel good to talk to him, at least for the moments the words were coming out, because I knew when I was finished he would respond. He would always respond to me. He would ignore Yamma and Johara at times out of anger. He would ignore Gamal out of spite. But never would he ignore me.

"Hey, you listening? Get up now I said. Get up." Twice more I pleaded with him, more moments of comfort for me. My neck was burning from holding it at such an angle. The least he could do was twitch.

The inevitable caught up with me and I came to my feet. Adli was dead. We were sleeping under trees high on a hill where we were safe. Now he's dead. We ran down together and talked as we crawled. He looked at me trustingly when I told him to get out of the ravine. Now he's dead.

Like the old man throwing candies and patting his cat, his body was now lifeless. He wasn't old. He wasn't sick. He wasn't a soldier. But he's dead just as if he had been any one of those things. I was afraid to see how dead he was, but I had to know. I had to bear witness for the others I'd have to tell. I wasn't ready for the sight and never have I forgotten it.

His back was to me as I knelt beside him. His legs were awkwardly askew and his left arm thrown over his head, but for that, he could have been asleep. I saw just a spattering of blood on his left hand. It covered his fingers so if I wasn't sure before, I knew now he had to be gone. He couldn't stand for anything sticky to be on him, and if he couldn't lick it off, he was scrubbing it off.

I took hold of his fingers and let his hand drop. It exposed a gaping hole in his head. Mixed within the blood were chunks the texture of cottage cheese. I supposed that I was seeing his shattered brain. Lying in the mix like a dangling grape was his eye. Two pieces of his hair-covered skull were resting at my knee.

I turned violently sick. I shuffled backwards, falling on my ass, and though I had been famished, the repugnant sight managed to churn up whatever was left inside me. I had now seen a person dead of old age and one die with her arms wrapped around me. I had watched a man prepare his own grave. I heard the third hand account of the slaughter of a good family. And now this, the brutal slaying of my best friend.

I sobbed quietly, but deeply, the kind that caused uncontrollable hiccups, interrupted by an occasional dry but violent heave. I was alone and so far from home. I knew in my right mind I couldn't carry Adli back, but I wasn't in my right mind. I regained some composure and climbed to my feet. I felt old and useless. The sounds around me that were strange just moments ago I was now accustomed to. Adli was heavy with wet and deadness. Instinctively I kept my arms below his shoulders, as if I could kill him further by touching his head.

I had him rested on my bent knee then heard a revolting plop of his separating head falling to the ground. I didn't look at the ground or at him. I threw him over my shoulder, feet to the front, and staggered to the ravine wall. After looking up hopelessly, I spun in confusion like a character from a video game under an inexperienced hand. I determined to walk the length of the ravine until I found an egress.

We got about a dozen steps when I realized it was an impossible task. To leave him in an open sewer was ghastly, but to drag him above where he could be picked apart by pariah dogs or wild pigs was surely worse. Still, perhaps like the old man in the desert, people would come by to give him a burial. I decided he would be found. The ravine was covered with bodies. In the morning families would come out to retrieve them. They would find an unknown boy and treat him with dignity. I had to believe that, it was all I had.

I climbed out and headed back up the hill where we had slept. I needed to find a road north, but not the one through the village. The Israelis were on that one. Being dark, I could pick out no other road from the hilltop. I decided to move parallel to the main road that ran straight as far as I could see. It would get me a few miles closer to Dayr Ghasana before the heat of the day came.

I'd like to think it was the rough terrain that had me clumsy and falling. But it was no harder than the route I took to school daily, and the starlight, typical of the summer desert sky, was sufficient to light the way. I stumbled onward, thirsty, hungry, and broken. It must have been three hours before I lay down to rest in a pine grove where the wind was locked out and I knew the ground would be soft. There were no lights now. And no war noises. There were only the desert sounds I was used to and enjoyed, only not out here among them.

It was morning and the war had followed me. The first disturbing thing was that I had no dreams. Thousands would follow in the nights ahead, but that first night I slept soundly, as if none of this ever happened. Even sleeping in a pine grove where Adli and I nurtured that friendship on a makeshift basketball court, I didn't wake up expecting to find him there. I was immediately in focus, knowing I was on my own.

A convoy of trucks and jeeps was passing through. All I knew of Israelis I learned the night before: they wore red berets and shot at anyone. I rolled onto my stomach to wait for them to pass. The convoy was long and moving quickly. They were either just finishing up a battle or going to start another. I wondered if I'd meet up with them in Dayr Ghasana. The fear they'd kill Yamma, Johara, and Gamal struck more nausea into me. On a very selfish note, I couldn't bear to witness such a scene again.

I jumped onto the road when they passed. I was following them home. Whether they were going there or not was of no real consequence to me. They meant civilization, as evil as theirs was. Behind me I was sure they had left destruction and death. There was little doubt they'd leave more of it ahead of me. But it was better than nothingness. And I prayed to Allah to let me find some decent life in their wake. Like with Adli's burial, I had to believe that, it was all I had.

I came across more apricot trees, and broke down in tears for the salvation and last memory of Adli they gave me. The soldiers had stopped here. I could tell by the discarded halves and wholes. It my act of defiance I left the easy pickings on the ground and climbed the trees for my own.

I was in a tree about twenty feet off the road when I heard the on-coming roar of machines. I could see several plumes of rising black smoke. Within seconds, the tree was shaking. I could see them now, an army of rattling, clanging, heaving steel monsters descending upon Palestine, created by a mad Israeli scientist to put an end to the reign of the evil King Hussein whose time had come.

But the mad scientist and the evil King were not scurrying like rats through open sewers while dodging the dead. They were not scrounging for over ripened fruits or hiding in trees. They were not in fear for their family and friends, for the war was being fought far from their homes.

I hastily climbed as high as the thin branches would allow and took cover behind a mass of leaves as the monsters drew near. The noise was close to cracking the earth and my skull open. My ears were threatening to bleed. I needed to cover them, stick leaves into them, anything, but I had to hold the branches for all I was worth so as not to be thrown from the tree which I was sure was shaking loose from the ground.

I had a small window from my perch in which to view their passing. Tanks. A herd of the great beasts moving unrestrained not twenty feet from me. Each had a commander who stood in the top hatch. They were nearly at my height. The shaking actually parted the branches that were my cover and I feared being spotted. But the commanders were far too busy making a game of grabbing for pieces of fruit as they raced by to look for boys to shoot down from trees.

They passed for an eternity. I buried my head into the branches. Now my teeth and jaw were sore. My head felt like a piñata, being pelted mercilessly by relentless streams of sound. At last they faded. The last one passed through and they were fast becoming another heinous memory.

I jumped down but waited behind the tree to be sure there were no follow-on units like the puny figure from *The Fractured Fairy Tales* cartoons who swept up after the parade in the opening credits. My head still vibrated and my ears pounded. Slowly the world turned back to normal with sounds meant to be here.

I wondered how the birds responded, if they sang gaily throughout the rampage, or did they have songs of distress and pain. I never gave it much thought to that point. To me, birds were either silent or singing in joy. For them to have sounds of doubt and despair seemed incongruous to what they were meant to be. But then, those didn't seem to be sounds children should be able to make, either.

The road was now strewn with hundreds of downed apricots and branches, newly flattened and broken. It infuriated me. These trees had been pruned and cultivated by someone, an owner who like Yamma brought them to the market to sell. The harvest was meant to buy clothes for his children, food for his animals and family, maybe a small appliance or two. I was looking at the loss of a pair of new boots, winter coats, and perhaps a new toaster. I began to sob. Sobbing was becoming a natural state for me now. I sobbed for dead soldiers, for Adli, for Yamma, and now for damn apricots.

I found a bed sheet that had been torn up by the tanks. I trimmed it down to satchel size and loaded it with fruit. I followed the tank tracks the rest of the day. At times I lost them on concrete roads. They split forces at forks in the road and I had to choose. But knowing they probably joined up again, I didn't think it would matter in the end.

Nothing would. If I marched myself over the end of the earth and fell into an oblivion, it wouldn't mean as much to me as those fallen apricots. Throughout the day I kept the vision of them. Once so nurtured and cared for, so full of promise for themselves and others, now useless. Everything now was so useless that I began sobbing again.

CHAPTER 37

Though I saw no physical destruction as I walked, there was evidence of war all around. People of the towns stared out at me as if I were the ghost of past battles come to haunt them. Those empty stares followed me down their roads, yet dared not speak to such an apparition. I wanted to ask them where I was, if I was going to Dayr Ghasana, but their faces wanted no part of me.

Everywhere was a void that couldn't be denied. If a stranger came into town with no clue of what had taken place over the last two days, he'd still know something was not right here. That is the lasting effect of war, that while buildings and land are broken, and people die, the survivors are the ones who take full brunt of the destruction. They are the ones left un-whole to bear witness.

Around midday it was brutally hot. I finished off the apricots that were boiling in the sheet. I sat beneath a tree in the middle of nowhere. I had just left a town and was entering a stretch of land that promised me little. A rusted pick-up slowed as it approached. There were two older boys in the bed, both wearing black keffiyahs that I would have killed for. The driver rolled down the window. "You've been on this road a while," he said.

I nodded half heartedly.

"I passed you once over an hour ago," he said. "You're not from here."

I was expecting an order from him and his boys to get off his road. But his expression was not like the others I saw. And his boys sat hunched like overheated dogs with no energy to be interested in me.

"No, I'm not," I mumbled through cracked lips. Forming the words was awkward, being the first I had spoken since begging Adli to live again.

He nodded. The sun off his half-rolled window reflected into my face while the desert floor emitted lulling waves of heat. I was well dehydrated at this point which caused him and his words to float before me.

"Where?" he asked

"Huh? Dayr … Dayr Ghasana."

"Up there? Son, you have at least twelve kilometers to go; that is if we get you on the right road. Stay on this road, and you'll double that."

That was far too many words for me to digest in my condition, which I had no clue I was in until we started the conversation. My dazed look was enough for him to step out and walk me to the back of the truck. "We'll take you there. But first, you come home with us. I'm sorry, but you'll have to sit in the back with my sons. They have water to share. I have my last rooster in the cab with me, and I can't afford to lose him from the heat."

I remember his push and his sons pull to get me into the truck bed. I remember them holding up a sheepskin qerba for me to drink from. I remember them draping a water-soaked towel over my head which lay there until I awoke in a strange but wonderfully comfortable bed. "Insha' Allah you are still with us," a woman said. "Sa'ood and the boys came to you at the right moment."

"Is Yamma here?" I asked.

"No, not your Yamma. I will bring you food."

She came back with a plate of mish salad, saj bread, and more water. My head wasn't ready for hot peppers so I pulled them out and laid them on the side. She left me alone to eat. I ate savagely and was still famished but fell asleep before I could beg for more. I awoke in a sweat to a dark and still room.

I dreamed something horrible, yet it wouldn't come to me. It was enough to keep me awake the rest of the night. I heard heavy breathing on either side of me. On my left it came from one of the boy's in a bed. On my right, a boy on the floor. For sure, come morning I would not be a favorite to the one on the right.

I went to the window. I dared not open it for fear it would make a racket. I bent my neck to see as much of the sky as possible. I could see the bottom four stars of Al Mazan. "See," I heard Adli whispering in my ear as he pointed to trace each star, "up, down, up, up." It was how Yamma taught him. I commanded myself not to cry. I sat there tracing the four stars until they faded, then went back to bed. I was up with the sun and waited in the kitchen for the others.

I was fed a generous breakfast. "Sukran," I said to the women, and my appreciation was sincere. "You think you're ready to go?" her husband asked.

"Yes, sir."

"Well, then, let me get my keys."

We drove out of town without speaking. That was fine by me if we drove the whole way without him asking questions. I didn't want to dwell on what happened to Adli, but I needed to plan how I would break it to Yamma. I needed to envision her reaction. "Rahmah" is the word she taught me when helping me learn the Quran. It meant, among other things, compassion. It was, she explained, the most important theme in Islam. It was time to truly understand that, for no one would need compassion more than she at the moment I told her her son was dead.

"So, Adli, what are you doing so far from home?"

It broke me from my spell. I don't recall giving him a name, least of all Adli's. It must have been what I muttered from my heat and thirst induced stupor. "Visiting relatives," I said.

"Alone?"

"Yes," I said, probably too quickly. "I was dropped off, then the bombing happened."

"They left you?"

"No, they drove me to the buses in town but I missed the last one out."

He pursed his lips and looked at me. "Yes, I see."

To break the theme of his interrogation I asked, "Do you think the army went to Dayr Ghasana?"

"Hard to say." He chuckled. "They didn't confide in me."

"Oh. Why? I mean, why are the Israelis bombing and ... killing people?"

"It goes back a long way," he said. "But now? Why now? It started with them and Egypt. Then Jordan came in."

"The king," I added.

He nodded. "Yes, the king. Now from what I hear it is Syria in the north which is why they are moving through here."

Syria. A name I had never heard before. I thought back to Yamma. She will no doubt be home when we arrive. She will see me before I reach her door. Even if she can't hear the truck, which she surely will with the door and windows open in such heat, she will see me for I know she is looking out anxiously every minute. Alarm will set in right away. Where is Adli? She'll greet me lovingly, whole-heartedly, unconditionally, but all the while worrying. Finally she will ask.

This is where I fail to serve her. I'll try not to break down. She'll need me to explain it all. Not in detail, but enough so she'll understand. I will not be good at holding her. I know how loved, how safe, I feel in her arms, and I doubt I'll ever be able to display it so generously with just a touch.

But more. The ultimate abandonment, as the Israeli soldier said, *the only soldiers carried out of here are the dead ones.* Even they carry their dead. Was I worse than the Israelis? I abandoned Adli in life and then again in death. And then another failure to Yamma, I didn't even know where her son was. "What towns did I walk through?" I asked in a panicked.

"I'm not sure," my driver said.

"Yesterday," I was struggling for landmarks he might know. "There were a lot of apricot trees on the road. And a hill with a grove of pine trees. And a deep ravine that ran next to the road."

He chuckled again. "Lots of those things out there. You came from Ramallah; did you follow the army?"

"Yes."

"Well, a lot of towns you passed through. Why? Did something happen there?"

"I just need to know."

"Fine. There is Jiffna, Jalazun, Nitsanei." He went on to name more which made it of no help to me. I sobbed again and the man reached over and patted my leg. Yes, that was as much as I could do for Yamma.

We got there in thirty minutes. I was grateful. It would have taken me the entire day to walk it if I didn't get lost, which I'm sure I would have. There were two jeeps in the driveway. The man looked hard at me. "Israelis," he said. "Sure this is your house?"

I nodded. I'm not sure what he was thinking. That I, a nine-year old kid, had sought him out to turn him over to the Israelis? Or that I was a young spy or sympathizer? I looked around for the obvious signs of war I had come to know: road craters, blown out buildings, destroyed fruit trees, dead bodies. I was relieved slightly to see none of it. "Why are they at Yamma's house?" I asked.

He leaned across me and opened the door. "Don't know. But you leave now, if you say you're home." I don't think he believed me, but he had to know I was much too young to understand the things going on around me. To be fair, he probably didn't understand it all that well himself. No one did.

He left in a hurry without looking back. I felt sorry for the way it played out after all the kindness he and his family showed me. But I couldn't dwell on it. Yamma was in trouble, maybe because of me. So beside the news I had about Adli, Yamma and the others were dealing with a house full of the people who killed him.

I was wrong that she would be waiting at the door for me. She was sitting quietly and red-eyed at the table, Johara behind her rubbing her shoulders. Gamal was sitting in the corner. There were four uniformed soldiers standing around them. I focused in on their red berets the way an abused dog would on a fireplace poker.

By the mournful atmosphere, it was my initial thought that the soldiers had identified Adli and traced him here. That thought soon vanished. Yamma's hands closed over her face and she screamed my name as she broke from the chair. She engulfed me and proclaimed her gratitude. "Allah has brought you home safely to us." She pulled back and kissed my cheeks as she gave thanks. "Subhan'allah, Subhan'allah," she repeated until she let go.

"Where is Adli? He is outside still?"

I looked to the soldiers, of all people, for comfort. They offered nothing. I turned to Johara and Gamal who awaited my answer. I turned violently ill again. Seeing their faces, alive and waiting for good news, was more ghastly than that of Adli's in death. I wanted to run. Part of me wished I never found my way back. This was not something I should have to be doing. *They did it,* I wanted to point and yell at the soldiers. *Ask them. Ask them what happened to your son, your brother.* "He didn't come home," I said.

"What do you mean, Joe? Where is he?"

"He cannot come home anymore, Yamma. I tried to bring him but he was too heavy, Yamma, I tried. I'm so sorry." I couldn't bring myself to say it, that Adli was dead. I was hysterical. I was apologizing, cursing, crying.

Yamma grabbed my shoulders and squeezed tightly. "It's okay," she kept saying. I fought to pull away. What was she saying, 'it's okay.' Hell it was okay. Bombs were exploding; people shot at us. Woman were dead, old men, young kids, dogs, goats, Adli, all dead. There were dead bodies and parts of dead bodies lying on the street and in the fields. Building were crushed and on fire.

When I broke free I stared her down. "They killed him," I screamed. I pointed to the soldiers. "They did it. Do you not understand? The men you have here in your kitchen killed Adli?"

Yamma nearly fainted, or perhaps she did. One of the soldiers reached out to steady her. That was enough to set me off. I don't know if it was in defense of Yamma or being so close to the enemy that lit a fuse in me. I tore at the soldier's hands letting loose with a tirade of curse words I would never have considered using in the presence of Yamma until that moment. "Kanith, let her go," I cursed as I pulled. "Arie Fique. In'al yomak. Khara Alayk."

Two of the other soldiers moved to stop me but a tall, thin man put his arm out to hold them back. Then Johara came up and took Yamma back to her chair. Yamma and Johara rocked and wailed in prayer. I heard a faint sobbing. It was Gamal, alone in his corner with his knees drawn up to his face. And that was all the sound; that and my heavy panting.

I had my cry. In the years to come, I would have many more. At that moment I knew enough of rahmah to allow for Yamma, Johara, and Gamal to digest what had happened to devastate their world. But my panting churned into a hatred. It wasn't respectable to show it now, but I couldn't hide it from the soldiers who stood there like death waiting for a respite in the mourning to continue whatever destructive mission they were on.

CHAPTER 38

The tallest soldier, the one who stopped the others when I was pulling Yamma away, seemed to be in charge. He was thin and gangly but built solid. I pegged him as a sweeper. That was how I sized men and boys up upon seeing them, putting them in soccer positions. I was rarely wrong.

Most were midfielders; players whose purpose was to move the ball up the field on offense and slow it down on defense. They usually didn't get themselves involved in glory at either end. Those like Faid and Gamal, they were forwards, setting themselves up to be the celebrated goal scorers. I even classified Yamma, the defenseman. I would have made her a goalie except that she worked tirelessly with no name recognition.

This man was unique in his quiet, composed style. While the other three soldiers stared at us with restless, wandering eyes in expectation of an ambush, he stayed focused on the time and place. As the sweeper, he was constantly analyzing the field, his mind two steps ahead of his opponent. His body was as graceful as his mind. Never over committing, never out of position. And never giving away his next move to his opponent.

He spoke to me in a language that was very familiar, yet the only words I recognized were my name and "Chicago." He must have seen the confusion in my face for he squatted before me and repeated himself, slower this time. "Hello, Nasser Khudayer from Chicago. My name is Cham Pfalzer. I am a captain in the Israeli Army and we are here to get you home now."

It was English. Said slowly enough I grasped his meaning, yet I was still confused. I turned to Yamma. "What does he mean, Yamma? I am home."

Yamma grabbed my hands. I saw in her eyes I was her focus now. "Yes, Joe, this is always home for you. But it's not safe here anymore. These men are going to get you back home to America."

I now wanted to be back there as much as I had once wanted to be in Dayr Ghasana. Three years, a third of my life, I had been here. I had gone through so much with this family. Much more than I had back in Chicago; fights, divorces, deaths, now war. And I earned my right to be here. I battled hard to find my way and make my place. And I had won. All the growing I had done to this point in my young life I had done here, and Yamma, Adli, Johara, and even, or maybe particularly, Gamal, Faid, and Abdel were large parts of that.

Yamma looked up at Captain Pfalzer and told him that although I was American, I had been three years in Palestine and would understand better if we spoke in Arabic. "Ana Afham," he said. "La moshkelah," *No problem.*

"I don't want to go," I said to Yamma, then to the Captain. "And I can't. Not after what happened to Adli."

"And you believe you can replace my Adli?" she said. She didn't mean it to be as cutting as it sounded. Or perhaps she did. The truth was it was precisely what I had in my childish mind. I couldn't save him but I did save myself. *See Yamma, I'm here for you. I made it home to make everything all right.*

"You asked me, Joe, if I understood that my son was dead. I understand. But you understand this." She took a deep breath. "It's not your fault. It's war, Joe. They are fighting war now, and killing happens."

It was Yamma being strong for me again. She pulled me into her chest and I went willingly. "I don't like war," I muttered.

"Then you've learned more than most, and Insha' Allah, you'll remember this day always."

Captain Pfalzer motioned for his men to wait outside. We all wept softly for so many reasons. All the memories of my days there, from the first until now, all seemed to be linked by tears. I wanted to recall those that made me smile, and laugh, but the kitchen was so small, there was no room. And though we cried for Adli's death, each one of us kept a vigil for some reminder that he was still among us.

"I have packed your things," Yamma said. "You mustn't delay. The soldiers have to get you to the airport in Tel Aviv, a long drive from here."

"They're Israelis, Yamma. They're the enemy."

"Not today, Joe. Today they are your Mala' ikah."

It seemed to be such craziness at the time, but Yamma insisted on me being bathed and in clean clothes for the trip. She filled the tub in the backyard from the Lister bag, and laid out a set of clothes my mother sent at the beginning of the school year but I had never worn. "Why do I need to wear them, Yamma?"

"Because you're traveling a great distance and will be seeing your parents. And you will be coming from my house." It was the pride of a woman with so little left. She fussed about to get me ready. I let her without another question. I was her diversion. That night, when I was gone, she would have time to grieve, a moment she wanted to delay as long as she could.

I was in the jeep and on my way within an hour of getting home. I didn't get time to tell them all that needed to be said. Even now, over forty-five years later, there are things. They come to me randomly any time of the day, sparked by a sight, a sound, a smell, a voice. I've woken up in hot sweats. They've pulled me from intense moments where nothing should have interfered. Some I dwell on for days while others are fleeting. I recognize it now as the biggest challenge in my life, to live day-to-day having never had the opportunity to grieve over Adli. It would be twelve years until I heard news that his body had been recovered.

I sat in the front. Captain Pfalzer sat in back while a surly soldier drove. The other jeep stayed cautiously behind. I supposed they feared I would jump out. As we drove south on the nearly deserted highway towards Ramallah, the thought crossed my mind. How was I to know where I was being taken? How was Yamma to know the intentions of these soldiers? Surely good men would not have killed a boy. Yes, the shooter displayed a fair amount of remorse, but his pleas were to his God for forgiveness, not to Adli, not to Yamma. And the other, he said his prayer for who-knows-what, then commanded me to get Adli home with a warning to stop fighting. I was as paranoid as the driver who drove me home that morning. Both of us had good reason.

The canvas top was up but without sides, it was loud, windy, and dusty. The soldiers wore sunglasses while I squinted and tried to shield my eyes. The captain tapped my shoulder and handed me his pair. They floated on my face but I was happy for the respite from the glare.

I noticed the soldiers' wary looks were not about me but about what lie ahead. Their weapons, which rested in their laps, were immediately moved into a shooting posture when we passed vehicles or groups of men on the sides of the road. We were an easy target with just two vehicles and four men. I could see they wanted to be anywhere else besides driving with me on these unfriendly roads.

Every bombed-out building I saw reminded me of Tariq and his family. It wasn't a matter of *if* someone had died, but how many, how young, and how horribly. When at last in Ramallah, even I felt a relief. I saw enough of war to know that everyone was vulnerable.

The city was now full of Israeli vehicles: jeeps, trucks, and tanks. Most citizens of the city walked about freely, but a group of about fifty were seated along a cordoned off section of the street guarded by armed soldiers. Our two-jeep convoy separated once inside the city confines. The captain made a gesture for the driver to stay with me as he went inside a storefront.

"You're a very fortunate boy," the driver said sternly. "But for the Captain taking this risk, you wouldn't be leaving this God-forsaken place."

I smiled and nodded, not liking him but not wanting to piss off a man with an attitude and a loaded rifle.

"He volunteered to get you," he continued, like a father convinced that the quantity of what he said increased its quality. "I volunteered to drive him. The others were ordered. I came because I respect that man. I'm telling you this because he never will, and you'll return safely to America thinking you were saved by the Palestinians where in truth, it was Captain Pfalzer."

I nodded once again and quickly broke his vengeful stare by looking into the crowd of men huddled on the street. They were a mostly young, bedraggled crew with scruffy beards and dead tired eyes. They leaned amongst themselves and either tried hard to doze off or stay awake, it was hard to tell. Some stared back for something to do. There, at the end, I saw Sam.

I jumped from the jeep, the driver calling me to get my ass back. Sam was in a daze. Even when I called to him he seemed bewildered. "Sam, it's me, Joe." It took all his effort to focus up at me. I saw that he was chained to the men on either side of him. I asked him why.

"Yes, young Joe from Chi-car-go. Do you have food, Joe? Do you have any food?" Like his dark eyes, his voice was lifeless. It came out of him dispossessed of any emotion. Such an emptiness coming from him was sad enough, but what I wanted to know was why he left us in Ramallah and didn't return. To this he simply nodded and asked me again for food. "I have no food, Sam. Adli is dead."

This resonated with him. For a moment his eyes responded by pulling his head down as if by heavy tears. "That is so bad," he said. "Amineh must be told. And Johara."

"They know. I was there and I told them. He was shot through the head, Sam. You left us and we had to run from the war. That was how he was shot." For some reason burdening him with this news did not weigh heavy on me. Actually, I took delight in it. He was chained, hungry, and now grieving. It seemed fair enough to me.

The driver caught up to me. "Back to the jeep with you," he ordered. "Before you get me into trouble with the captain." He took me by a handful of collar and pulled me along. I turned to see Sam, now on his knees as he leaned up to see me off. He looked to me like a begging dog.

Captain Pfalzer was waiting for us. He called the driver to the hood where a map was laid out. I was told to take a seat. They spoke in whispers. I made out the driver saying, "You sure, sir?" and, "I'd rather you not." Captain Pfalzer mentioned Syria and Jordan bombing the areas. Then he said, "Tel Aviv will be safe if we get there in time." Captain Pfalzer folded the map as the driver saluted and walked off.

I had been listening in on a strategy session with me as the mission. Soon, I would once again be sent a million miles away to a place and life I didn't know. With Captain Pfalzer at the wheel, we drove past the shackled men. Sam was watching and flagged down the jeep from his kneeling position. "I know this boy," he said to the captain.

The captain looked at me but I offered no spark of recognition or acknowledgment.

"What is it you want?" The captain asked.

"Where are you taking him?"

"I believe you have your own issues to worry about."

We drove on. I didn't look back. I wanted that vision of him begging like a dog to be the last one I had of him.

CHAPTER 39

We were going to the Tel Aviv airport. It was the only airport where flights were still leaving. He didn't tell me why, but I knew enough about the geography to know the other major airport was in Jerusalem where the bombing started.

"I guess I owe you an explanation as to what's going on," Captain Pfalzer said.

I was looking straight ahead as if my head was locked down tight. I had no intentions of trying to unscrew it.

"Three years," he said, "That's a long time to be away from home. Anyway, the United States Embassy, that's where the American Ambassador works. Do you know of the embassy?"

I had no intentions of unsealing my frozen lips either. All childish, to be sure, but it was the only weapon I had.

"They're the people who talk to us about American interests, and right now, you are one of their biggest."

Too cool not to give at least a hint of a response. "I am?"

"Sure are. The ambassador himself is involved." He let that part sink in before offering his condolences for Adli. "I have two children. How old are you?"

"Nine."

"They're younger. Still, you're too young to have gone through such a thing. I think I am as well."

All along the road were reminders of the war in progress. The freshly smoldering craters in the fields, in citrus groves, and in gardens told me that somewhere miles away men were throwing shells down range indiscriminately. Captain Pfalzer kept his calm demeanor, his vigilance, and his rifle all close at hand.

At times we had to skirt around craters in the roadway and several destroyed trucks, both civilian and military. He drove the gauntlet as nonchalantly as avoiding a scurrying squirrel. He whistled a good bit of the time. At first I thought it was for my comfort, but, now, more for his own. Up ahead I could hear rapid barrages of rifle and machine guns. We were driving into a major firefight.

With no back roads for us to divert onto, he pulled to the side. Not more than two hundred meters up the road an Israeli unit was skirmishing. It was killing him to be sitting back with me. Seeing it from his side, I felt his anxiety. Up there were soldiers he possibly knew. He stood in front of the Jeep with his hands on his hips. In his mind, he was directing the battle. He didn't like what he was seeing.

"Wait here," he said. Then more harshly, as if recalling a time when his own children disobeyed him with catastrophic results, "You hear what I'm telling you, stay put right here in this Jeep." He punched the hood with his forefinger for added emphasis.

The fighting was frightful to listen to. Single, slow gunfire, followed by rapid bursts from machine guns. Then silence. Throughout there were wails of pain and dying. Unintelligible shouts and commands. Women were screaming and children were crying. There was no guarantee he would live through this; he could be dead now.

I waited as told for what seemed to be an hour before following the route he took, reasoning that if he made it, it was safe. And if I came across his dead body, I could beat it back to the Jeep and take my first road test under real fire.

It was a small village of no more than ten, single-story buildings which looked to be only a few years more durable than tents. Nothing nearby but desert and scrawny trees. How or why soldiers would meet here to fight was incomprehensible to me. I lay down behind the back wheel of a pick-up truck. I was on the same side of the street as the Israelis. There were five of them clustered to my front, a hand-grenade throw from oblivion. Suddenly they dispersed, two the left, three to the right. They looked back, I thought at me, but it was Captain Pfalzer on a roof top. He was directing them, and apparently another force to his right.

The Israelis had ceased firing. Across the road I saw a ragtag group of men, kids really, racing around chaotically. They fired hasty rounds that did nothing more than let the Israelis know their location. Captain Pfalzer maneuvered the soldiers into position. I realized that when the shooting began again, I would be in the middle of it. My conclusion was too late.

The Israelis open up with a murderous volley of machine gun fire. I practically dug a hole behind that tire, shaving my fingers and knuckles to near bone. I was breathing dirt but it was better than watching. Through it, I heard a woman's maniacal scream. I watched as a young mother raced into the street in an effort to seize a young child, no more than four, who had dashed into the murderous crossfire.

I imagined the child had broken free and fled at the sound of the shooting. Having no idea why, he was running, perhaps to a candy store or bakery he knew, somewhere he felt safe. Maybe, like me, he saw a man's head explode. Maybe it was his father's. Or his sister's.

This was a tiny, insignificant place, filled with people whose significance was only to one another. Arguments over the cost of bread or a chicken were the only battles fought here. Such massive destruction to them was fire and brimstone, so who couldn't understand a child's irrational dash into death?

To my shock, the shooting didn't let up on either side. A young man raced forward. I heard him hysterically crying the woman's name, "Huma," through the small breaks in the gunfire. He reached her and the three fell in a heap on the ground. Still, the battle raged.

"Rahim'ahullah," I found myself praying as I buried my face, wanting to witness no more. "Rahim'ahullah." *Allah have mercy.*

When I lifted my head to catch a breath, I dared to look. From the corner of my eye I saw Captain Pfalzer sprinting into the gauntlet. As he made it to the middle of the street, the Israelis lifted their fire, but not so the fighters across the way. In a moment, there were four bodies gathered in the middle of the battlefield. None moved, and then, all shooting ceased.

I didn't breathe until I heard the child crying. I didn't pull my chin from the hole I had dug until I saw Captain Pfalzer help the man and woman off the ground. He held the child in his arms as the man and woman embraced. I came to my feet and watched as the Israeli soldiers stood by uselessly.

The scene defied wartime logic. There was no battlefield manual for this. A battle had been stopped, not by ending lives, but by saving them. There was no surrender, no eradication. No one was routed. No one waved a white flag. Yet, for me, I saw complete victory. And the best part, it was for both sides.

I went back to the Jeep and waited for his return. I heard nothing from within the village. I took that as a good sign. The absence of gunfire during this war was like the nights without Abdel at home; it wasn't ordinary, but it sure was nice. Fifteen minutes later and the Captain came jogging back. I waited for him to tell me the story, but all he said as he started the Jeep was, "Sorry for making you sit out here. Thirsty?"

I was. My mouth was coated with desert dust. I guess in the heat of the battle, pun intended, I didn't pay it any attention. He pulled his canteen off his hip and grabbed my chin with his long fingers. Yeah, he had kids, the way he twisted my face left, then right, inspecting the parts a kid usually missed during a face washing.

"Hmm," he said. "Didn't remember you wearing all that dirt when you came on board. And wouldn't Yamma be upset that you got those new pants a mess?"

"The shooting … I got scared and hid under the Jeep."

He smiled. It lit his face so he looked to be different person. "That was smart," he said. "You know, I've taught my own children to do the same thing."

He drove slowly through the town. Israeli soldiers were unloading weapons as the army they were fighting stood by watching. They were townspeople, old as Abdel and young as me. Whereas the Israelis were dressed in matching brown khakis and berets, their enemy could have just come in from an olive harvest. Their weapons looked ancient. The soldiers, the real ones, looked confused on how to unload them.

"Will they be chained up, too?" I asked, "Like the prisoners back in Ramallah?"

"No," he said. "They're not prisoners."

"But you captured them."

He looked at me as if he hadn't realized it. "Joe, you're too much of a veteran of this war already. I'm glad we're getting you home. But them," he nodded at the circle of men, "this *is* their home. The soldiers were a small detachment on a scouting mission. They rolled up and the town thought they were being attacked. We would never attack with such a small force. But what did they know? They hear stories, so they respond as any of us would."

"Did any of them get killed?"

He nodded.

When we got the end of the town he sped up. "What's happening to them now?"

"The soldiers will unload the weapons and stack them out in the desert. They'll put the ammunition in another place. That's so the soldiers won't be shot at as they drive away."

"Why don't they just take the guns away from them?"

"They're not military guns; they're hunting guns. These people need them out here."

"Maybe they'll use them later to shoot at other soldiers," I said.

"Maybe. Then they *will* be killed."

I nodded, appreciating the savage wisdom. I knew the disarmament was his idea; he knew the plan too well. "At least they didn't die this time," I said.

"No, but Joe, I'm a soldier and this is war, if I had to kill them, I would have. And more people will die here today, many more. Men like me will be killing them. If you like me or hate me, if you think me a good man or not, the truth is I will kill or be killed. Leave all that behind but take this home with you, it's like your Yamma said, if you learn to truly hate war, you've learned more than most."

I had seen a lot of fighting in these last days. And I did hate it. Maybe he was right. Good or bad, the instinct to survive had taken over. Like the marauding pariah dogs, something happened in the mountains that drove them into the streets to kill. I was at a loss as to who would drive them back. Maybe no one. Maybe the killing would never stop until no one was left to kill.

We didn't speak again until Tel Aviv. I waited for him to tell me of his actions in the battle but he never did. I found rahmah, *compassion*, in a time and place that I thought had forgotten the word. After days of fighting, I saw firsthand a peace accord. So how could he neglect to instill some hope in all this mess for me?

I had seen it. For once, there was a moment in war I wanted to bear witness to. Somehow that instinct to survive gave way to the instinct to sacrifice. Could there be such an instinct, I wondered? If not instinct, then what? Would a pariah dog throw itself into harm's way for a stranger?

Yes, many will kill and be killed today, but won't many be saved? Why wouldn't he share with me the possibility? Surely there was more to this man, and to the Palestinian man and woman who offered themselves.

He wasn't a small talker. As a father he probably knew how to converse with me, but as a soldier, he had his mind on the road and his head on a swivel. I could have brought it up. We had plenty of time for discussion. But I wasn't feeling generous toward Israeli soldiers. And I wasn't about to credit him with an act of kindness any more than I would Abdel for letting me eat at his table.

He filled me with the dead and dying theme for a reason; like any bully, the facade had to be maintained. I would go back to Chicago telling the world not to mess with the Israelis. They were killers. Child killers, that's how bad they were. Their compassion is deceptive and comes with a price.

The area around Tel Aviv was filled with machinegun-manned roadblocks. We were stopped at one outside the airport. The Captain handed the gate guard a folded piece of paper. The guard took it inside a sandbagged bunker and made a phone call. "Your cousin, the one who was killed, what was his name?"

"Adli El-Karim."

"And where was he shot?"

"In the head."

"I mean what town?"

"I don't know. We got off a bus heading to Bir Zayt. I don't know where. We just walked."

I immediately regretted answering his questions. I felt as if I had taken that dreaded piece of candy from a stranger, but I felt as if I'd been holding my breath for the last ten miles. I needed to talk about anything with anyone.

The gate guard returned the paper to the captain and waved us through. We drove directly onto the runway where a TWA jet was sitting. "Give this to the attendant on board," he said handing me the paper. I crawled out and took my suitcase from the back.

"Here." He held a US twenty dollar bill out to me. I hadn't seen American money in over two years. "You'll need it. You'll land in New York first so don't get off unless the attendant tells you to."

He stayed until I was up the ramp stairs and in the doorway. I turned to see him smile and wave. For a moment which I forced myself to quickly erase, I felt as if we were father and son, destined to see each other again.

The stewardesses were expecting me. They treated me as unique and special, like a pet llama. I sat in first class with a ginger ale. People around me were paying for their drinks. No one asked me for money, but if I was a freeloader, I at least didn't want to look like one. I dug into my front pocket for the twenty dollar bill Captain Pfalzer had given me. It came out with a necklace I didn't know I had. It was the Saint George medal Sue had given to me on Christmas, the one I put in a pair of dress slacks I knew I'd never wear. Yamma must have found it when she was going through my clothes. Being three years ago, those pants would no longer fit the taller, leaner me. Yamma tossed the pants but salvaged the medal.

I held it in my palm. "Be strong like Saint George," she told me when she called that day to tell me I'd been abandoned in Palestine by my father. A hero dragon slayer, she called him. I didn't feel like a hero and I certainly had slayed no dragons. I put it around my neck and wondered if it wasn't just as silly a superstition as the hamsa, and maybe too little, too late.

I was once again on a plane taking me to a place I didn't know. I was sick. I couldn't escape the churning guilt that was ripping up my heart and mind. The guilt inside me was like a child predator. It found me a hospitable host. I was young; I was alone; and, I was afraid. It was burrowing itself in for a long stay.

CHAPTER 40

I don't know what the note said that I gave to the stewardess, but it got me all the way to my house in Chicago without me having to give one direction, which was great because I didn't know any. The cab dropped me off and I never did have to break the twenty.

The house looked empty at three in the afternoon. The lawn was overgrown in some spots, bare as the desert in others. I remembered it as always being green and neatly manicured. It was the way my father kept it, like his hair and beard, except for the green part. Damn I was scared. And this was being majnoon, *crazy*. I lived here once, many years ago. It was home. But it didn't feel like coming home. I felt a new set of anxieties from a new set of disasters.

It felt strange even having to knock, being so used to just pushing through the screen door of Yamma's kitchen. Sue answered. She nearly fainted with a huge smile on her face. She hugged me and cried. "Joe, you've gotten so tall and lost so much weight. You look grown up."

I was just a few inches shorter than her now. As we held onto each other, her more tightly than me, I stared at the room over her shoulder. The details came back of watching television here, sitting at the kitchen table drinking lemonade and eating Hostess cupcakes with my friends, and cold Sunday mornings huddled against the radiator in the kitchen corner. But it wasn't home again.

Who was this person holding me and sobbing? She was the one who tried to kill herself, then left me there, the one I needed to get me back home years ago but who, instead, called to tell me I was being left behind. I was home now only because of the war, so maybe it was the Israelis I should be hugging.

I pushed away gently, and the first place I looked was not at her face but at her wrists. Her scars had healed. She caught me staring but made no attempt to cover them, nor did she speak of it.

"We didn't know you'd be home so soon," she said. "I'm glad you are but really, we had no clue."

On the plane I had heard a lot of English but I conversed very little, so although the words were coming back to me, their meanings and the syntax were not. I didn't want to let on to Sue. Pride, I guess, and maybe the fear I'd be labeled here like Adli.

"Where is everyone," I stuttered in broken English.

She looked at me queerly for just a moment. "They're visiting David."

"Oh. He doesn't live here?"

"You okay, Joe? You need something to eat or drink?"

I nodded and took my suitcase as she led me into the kitchen. "We don't have the food you're used to," she said, "but we have the food you use to be used to. Some leftover macaroni and cheese, mom's original recipe. Want that?"

"Na'am. I mean, yes."

She put a ladle full into a tin tray and pre-heated the oven. This was the type of moment microwaves were invented for. Two minutes from refrigerator to mouth. No time for chit-chat, and no room with your mouth burning from scalding cheese. Now we had this unfilled space to fill in with lots of questions.

But we sat silently. We both feared the questions as much as we did the answers. I could have started by reeling off the recent events that took place, but they would have led back to those questions neither of us was ready for. "I'm a senior this year," she said. "And you'll be starting fourth grade, back at Earle Grammar."

I nodded.

"There's a new family in where the Culpeppers used to live. You know, down near Gray's Laundromat. That's gone, by the way."

"I know that house."

"Yes, a boy your age lives there now. Maybe a year younger, or older, I'm not sure. Looks kinda young."

Wasn't that oven heated up yet? This was foolishness but somehow I couldn't get past it. Having not seen each other in three years we should have been all about hugs and smiles and nonstop questions. The guilt from Palestine had followed me across the sea and met up with my anger for this place. I don't know explosives, but if those two emotions were ingredients of one, the bomb in me would take out a small country. As usual, it was Sue who dared break the ice. "How's Yamma?"

She said it softly, as if she didn't care if I heard it or not. I almost didn't. It was a general question that could have been answered with a single word or a master's thesis. It could lead us to a civil conversation or a bare-knuckle brawl. It could be filled with laughter or tears. But the real answer was I had no idea.

I left her as I had Adli, lying in a ditch. Only Adli was in no pain, while Yamma was deep in it. "Okay, I guess."

She nodded. "Was she sad to see you go?"

"Did Sam do something to you at the cave that night?"

"What?"

She said it with the most quizzical look on her face. But she knew what I meant.

"Who told you such a thing?"

It wasn't even a question I had in me. I had lots of them, but that was never one. It was just an overheard conversation between Yamma and Johara. But now I hated Sam for what he had done to me and Adli, and perhaps, I wanted a reason to hate him more.

"Something I heard, that maybe ...."

She put the macaroni and cheese in the oven. She worked slow enough to be in the process of forgetting the question, hoping I would follow her lead. But then she took a seat across from me and put her hands, palms open, on the table, inviting me to take hold. I wasn't ready for that yet.

"I'm sorry, Joe, for what happened there. More for you than for myself. I promised I would get you home. I didn't. But you must believe me, I did try."

She wanted a reaction from me that would help her through this, but I wasn't giving her one. I was not the boy she went over there with. I was hard as nails on the outside, a worked over callous that had seen more than I could ever tell over a warmed up casserole.

"What I told you on the phone was the truth."

"Yeah, but it wasn't what you were supposed to tell me," I said.

"I know, but I really did talk to mom and dad. What you had over there was far better than what I had over here."

"I doubt that." My anger was bringing my English back. But there were thoughts and emotions only Arabic words could express so most of my responses were mere fragments of how I was really feeling.

"What I am going to tell you, you must never mention to Mom or Dad, or anyone."

She waited for my promise which I only shrugged.

"That's not good enough, Joe. I mean it; you cannot mention it in this house. Ever."

"Okay. Aidouka. I mean, I promise."

"The answer to your question is no. Unless you mean did Sam save my life."

"So you really did try to kill yourself?"

She bowed her head and nodded. "I'm not proud of myself for that."

"Because of Abdel, his beating you."

"Is that what everyone believes, everyone back in Dayr Ghasana?"

"I don't know what anyone thinks. No one talked about it."

"Okay. Okay, Joe, and this is what is never to be mentioned. "Do you know the word, rape?"

"Ightisab. Yes, I know it."

"Okay. Faid ... he raped me."

I looked at her as if she was on a movie screen. As if I could leave to get a bag of popcorn to detach myself, then come back when the scene was over.

"Did you understand what I just said, Joe?"

I pictured Faid. His dumb stare, his moody talk and lonesome ways. I tried to put things together, but many of the memories I lost when I learned of the dastardly plan to leave me there. I was stunned. I was confused. "When? I mean—"

"It was the first week we were there. The fifth night. It wasn't rape then, just, he came into my room while I was asleep."

"I don't want to hear," I screamed and eagerly grabbed her hands.

"I know. I won't talk about details. I don't want to hear them either. That night I pretended to be asleep and he started touching me, but only on top of the covers."

"Did you tell anybody?"

"No, not then. I was confused about what he was up to and I didn't want to upset anyone. But a couple of weeks later he ... well, he did more and I told Yamma."

"She didn't do anything?"

"She did. She talked to Khaal Abu Faid but he didn't believe it. He never did believe it. Still, I thought it would stop, since they both knew."

"But it didn't?"

"For about a month. One night he did more to me."

"What about Johara, wasn't she there, didn't she know?"

"She was never home at the time. You remember, she spent many nights at her friends. But I'm sure she at least suspected. She saw my mood changes and asked me about some of the bruises I had."

"He hit you?"

"No Joe, that wasn't how I got the bruises."

The casserole was smoking. "Damn," Sue said, jumping up to salvage it. She had to scrape most of the cheese off. It didn't matter; I wasn't hungry anymore. "Did you tell Yamma that time?"

"I did. But she was helpless to do anything, especially without proof."

"Then you should have given it to her," I said. "You should have shown her the bruises."

"Bruises I couldn't prove came from him?" She shook her head. "I do know she brought it up to Khaal Abu Faid several times. It was the reason he got so angry at me the day he tore through my bed."

"Not about the stuff from Jerusalem?"

"A little for that, I'm sure, but that was more of an excuse. That was the day you found me crying with my teacher, do you remember?"

I did, the day Abdel came to pick us up and hit her the first time.

"I made the mistake of telling her about the attacks. She thought she was doing me a favor calling Khaal to tell him. I knew then I had to keep my mouth shut until Faid either stopped or got caught, but the only person who ever witnessed it was Adli."

"Adli knew? He should have told me; you should have told me."

"I wasn't going to get you involved; you couldn't have stopped it, either. And I'm not sure how much Adli even understood. Faid jumped all over him when he walked in the room one night. He ran out as shaken as I was. I don't know what it was Faid was saying to him; I'm sure it was threatening. All I remember is the way he looked at me. His mouth wide open, his eyes staring into me."

"Were you ... naked?"

"No, no he never got me naked. I was under the sheets. As scared as Adli was of Faid, he was furious, too. Remember the night Amir attacked him?"

I did. It was a wild scene. It was more like a mauling. Yamma was in bed asleep but when she heard Adli screaming she raced out like a lady on fire. The rest of us were well behind but I could see her frantically searching for where the screams were coming from. To me it sounded as if the dog was tearing apart a cat, the screams were so high pitched.

But it was Adli in the vegetable garden. I give him credit, he was giving Amir all he could handle, cracking him over the head with his fist, kicking him in the ribs, while Amir leapt around him, tearing at his arms and legs. Yamma grabbed a broom and flailed away. Eventually Amir let loose and disappeared into the olive grove. I remember now, it was just Yamma, Abdel, Gamal, Johara, and me. Faid and Sue weren't there.

Sue continued. "When Adli came home from the hospital the next day, all bandaged, he said to me, 'Ana saaweeto ashaanek.'"

"I did it for you," I translated.

"Yes, he did it for me. He tried to get Amir into the house, to attack Faid. Pretty crazy knowing how uncontrollable Amir was. I really believe that was another reason Khaal disowned him. It was all about protecting his first born son.

"I told Sam. I told him everything in Jerusalem that day. Being in the Holy City, it just seemed natural for me to confide in someone I trusted."

I was more than a little miffed that it wasn't me she came to, but I had to remember, I was only six.

"Did he believe you?"

"Of course he believed me, why wouldn't he?"

Because he's scum, was what I wanted to say but that wasn't the Sam she knew. "What did he say?"

"He was at a loss. He knew I would never convince anyone without proof, and even then .... Anyway, then that boy was pulled from the bus and beaten. And Khaal brought us home and followed me into my room."

"And slapped you," I said.

"I didn't care about that. It's what he said. He called me a whore, a worse whore than Yamma. He accused me of shameful behavior in his house. He said I was trying to seduce Faid, and trying to place the blame on his son.

"I lost it. I had no way out. I knew the attacks would continue. I knew that if I retaliated I would be the one blamed. I did a very stupid thing that night, Joe." She put her head down to cry.

"You should have called out for help when Faid tried it. We were all there in the house."

"You don't understand," she said. "There, Khaal Abu Faid was police, judge, and jury. Yamma told him and my teacher called him, and he took no action."

"But if Faid was caught in the act—"

"It's not that way over there. Besides, it wasn't always in the house. Many times he followed me when I took walks.

"What did mom and dad do about it when you told them?"

"It may sound strange to you, but what dad did hurt more than what Faid did. Khaal Abu Faid told him that because of my improprieties with Faid and the shame I brought to my family, I tried to do the right thing by killing myself.

"And he begged for dad not to punish me too severely. I was under terrible strain there at school and at the house. My teacher even called to discuss it."

This was beyond anything I suspected from even Abdel. Lies, all of them blatant lies. I knew this not just from what Sue told me but from knowing the type of men Faid and Abdel were.

"Dad turned me out of the house that first year I was home. I stayed with my friend, Lydia, and her family until mom begged us both to make up. We never have but it's at least civil."

For her, being home but not feeling at home was difficult. It was something I would learn for myself. She spooned the macaroni and cheese into a bowl for me. I let her catch her breath then it was my turn. "Sue?"

"Yeah?"

"Adli's dead."

CHAPTER 41

My parents came home while Sue and I were on the living couch watching *Mission Impossible*. She was dozing while I was fully engrossed watching Willy Armitage yank a steel manhole cover out by himself. The back of the couch was to the front door so they walked right past us. It was my mother who came back to send Sue up to bed.

I glanced up at her and I swear it wasn't surprise but non-recognition on her face. "Oh my God, it's you. You're home." She called to my dad. The greeting by him was cordial. I had heard Sue's story; I gave her a pass for not rescuing me. I'm not sure he had a story that would help me get over it. And if he did, he didn't share it with me.

On the trip home, I rehearsed my act of indignation. I envisioned the lukewarm reaction I would display to their hugs and kisses. Their questions—fast, furious, and demanding—would receive only short, cryptic answers. My eyes would focus on the one *not* talking, to create that slow, itching discomfort, and the thought I had gone slightly insane.

But my parents turned the tables. It was they who were lukewarm. They were the ones being short and cryptic. They were the ones who seemed to have gone slightly mad. Had they so much as offered a word, gesture, or look of apology or sympathy, I could have stretched it into a theme. It was those first days at home that set the pattern and rhythm for the remainder of our relationship.

They were looking worn. Like the lawn, things had gone unattended. It was late that night so there was no sit-down to discuss my past three years away. There was none the next night, either, nor the next. My father shot sporadic questions at me.

He wanted to know about his mother but not a word about her death. He asked about the nephews he never met, and his brother, Ramiz. I couldn't say enough good of them, but he stopped the conversation abruptly after my story about visiting Quruntul Mountain on our last day.

My mother wanted to know about the stories Siidi used to entertain us, about our camp out, and the friends he met. She didn't want to hear about his fall on the hillside or how fast his health failed him. Neither wanted to hear about Abdel leaving the family or about the child he gave up to Yamma to care for. Over the next weeks, few questions came up about Palestine. After I gave them the briefest outline of how Adli was killed, they didn't want to hear more.

If I had my doubts about Sue's story of her treatment upon her return, they were gone now. We were sent there to learn and grow, but in defiance of their plans, things turned ugly. They were wrong to have sent us. To find out how wrong, they'd have to delve into our darkest days. They'd have to ask the hard questions, then listen to our answers. They'd have to hear about those things we had to live through, and though there were some magnificent days, there were the painful ones they'd have to absorb.

Guilt. At its onset it is the epitome of empathy. It pulls compassion from deep inside us. Through the years it can lie dormant, seemingly gone, but subtly it becomes the source of all the ugliness around us as it morphs into resentment and bitterness. Like an oxygen molecule, it attaches to other elements. It is now unrecognizable from its former self as it inherits a new function quite at odds with its original intent.

I hated them for depriving me of my grief. This homecoming was supposed to be about me. I was the one to brood. I was the one to wallow in pity. All three of us were coming into this from degrees of guilt. But they were supposed to handle it much better than they did, certainly much better than I could.

I asked about David. Again with the short, cryptic, and non-responses. Finally, about a month after I got home, my mother said we were going to visit him. "'Bout time," I said. It had taken nearly thirty days, but I was comfortable being in my South Chicago home. My English and sass had returned, as well.

"Sit down, Joe," she said.

I complied.

"You're not going to like what I'm going to tell you but there's no easy way to say it."

She had my interest.

"David's in prison."

I was stunned but not surprised. What'd he do?"

"He robbed a gas station with a gun."

"Did he shoot it?"

"No. He was sentenced to ten years. That was last year so he has—"

I finished for her. "Nine to go, not counting good behavior. And it's armed robbery whether he shot anybody or not." I had spent the month catching up with *The FBI* television program.

"Your father and I didn't tell you because ... well, we thought just coming home and all. But you don't sound too upset."

For someone who didn't want to get me upset, she sounded upset that I didn't sound upset. The truth was, I remembered all the bitching she and my father had done about the leather jacket, and the lame reasons he gave for having it. I knew they were right and he was probably heading to the dark side. So I suppose my lack of surprise translated into a lack of grief. That, and I had seen people killed in war. Wasn't much misery left that could shock me.

That Sunday we all went down to see him. It was six hours down to the Southern Illinois Penitentiary where he was being held. My mother was fine most of the trip down. Singing along to the radio, pointing out this sight and that. I knew when we were close because that's when she started losing it.

My father remained stoic. It was partly bravado, and partly his disgust with David and the cops. I didn't have to ask one question and by the time we arrived, I knew the entire story. "He was railroaded," my father said on more than one occasion. "There were others there; they had the guns, not David."

It would not have gone over well for me to remind him that his long ago prediction was correct, that David would end up in prison some day for hanging with such a crowd.

"He wouldn't testify against the others; that was his biggest crime," my father said.

"He should have," my mother said.

"He couldn't. It's the law of the street."

"Of all the childish crap," she said. "He broke the law and his cooperation would have helped him, not to mention the rest of us. Those same boys are still roaming the streets with guns. Probably robbing someone as we speak."

"Yes, with guns. That's why David would be dead if he spoke up."

"So better to obey the laws of the street than the laws of the country?"

"If it means staying alive, yes."

Had I not experienced so much, I may have been overly impressed, or at least fascinated by it all. I would have given all my attention to the moment. My brother, the bad ass. Spit in the eye of authority. Never snitch, never give it up. I wouldn't have appreciated consequences. I wouldn't have understood how dire they could be.

Sam told me I was too young to learn such things. He was wrong. It's something every kid should learn early, that stupid actions like pulling a gun never lead to anything good. The only thing now I could think to say to David was, "What the hell were you thinking, boy?"

We were about ten minutes out when my mother, in tears now, said, "The judge never gave him a chance. The police just wanted to nail whoever they could. David had no record; he should have gotten probation."

"He pulled a gun," my father said. "He got what he deserved."

It was like somewhere along the past hundred miles their brains had been switched. In preparation for seeing her son, my mother went into her "poor baby" mode, while my father reverted to the strict disciplinarian. Hard for me to know which were their true selves in this. But more importantly, it had me thinking about whether there was a true self.

I had my many thoughts about the people back in Palestine. But this was the first episode since being home where I compared the people in my life. I wondered how Yamma would respond. I wondered how her mind would balance her feelings. And I knew. She would have said the same thing leaving the driveway as in the prison parking lot. Nothing would change because she would come to it from a very fine and private place within her heart. There'd come a period in my life where I denied Yamma. I would deny her for the reasons most deny God. Her goodness was inconvenient and upholding it was difficult.

Sue leaned over and whispered. "Here they go. Now they get into this huge fight and we sit in the car until dad stops yelling and mom stops crying. Takes an extra hour because of this."

I had listened to it all with interest and amusement. Nothing they said shocked me. Nothing scared me, or moved me to tears or rage. I was content to stay detached until my father said, "That boy, I swear he's not my son."

"Don't say that," I shouted as I leapt forward in my seat. I was in his ear, nearly sending him off the road.

"Geez, not so damn loud," Sue said.

"Sit back down," my father commanded with that voice he reserved for moments that spun him out of control.

"Don't ever say that," I continued, unimpressed at the tone that once petrified me.

"What are you talking about," he said. "Say what again?"

Sue pulled at my shirt to sit me down. I struggled to stay in his face. "Why would you say that he's not your son?"

"Joe, it's only a figure of speech," my mother said.

"It's not only a figure of speech. It's hurtful and shameful." As enraged as I was, I was very aware of the twitch in my father's face and hands. I sat back down to continue my tirade from a safer distance.

"You can't say such bad things without hurting everyone who hears them. It puts shame on David and Yamma and all of us. And even if you think he brings *you* shame, believing he's not your son is the real shame on you."

In the middle of my rant I saw my mother's eyebrows curl as she looked to Sue. "Who did you say?" She asked.

"Him. Dad."

"No, you said it was shame on David and who?"

"Yamma," Sue said. "It was what we called Amineh."

'It means, 'mother,'" I added.

My mother nodded. "Oh."

"It was more of a pet name," Sue said. "Just to make us ... you know, feel at home."

It was out of habit that I spoke of her. And I know there was a tinge of envy in my mother that we considered her cousin so highly. But more at issue was the heated argument that brought us to this point. These were things I should have said to Abdel, had I the same mind and contempt as I possessed in the backseat of my father's Buick Century. For sure my father's anger had the best of him at that moment. My mother was right; he didn't mean what he said. But nonetheless, he said it.

I hadn't told them how Abdel had cursed Adli the same way. My father wouldn't have been so blatant had he known. Still, I felt no need to enlighten him. Years later I would discuss it at length with my mother but only after her prodding when she wanted to come to terms with my nightmare.

David would spend nine years in prison. That was the one and only trip I made with my dad to see him. I could tell David was shamed for me to see him there. As we grew older and harder, he lost that shame. It was of no use to him in there and no help to me outside. I went from bringing him Milk Duds and Bonomo Turkish Taffy to Winstons and chewing tobacco. We were still growing up together, though much faster and without the innocence. Why should things have been different for me now that I was back home?

CHAPTER 42

From the day I arrived, my transition was not smooth on any level. Socially, scholastically, culturally, even philosophically, I was still thousands of miles away. I was new again. Everyone and everything came back to me in context of Palestine. I waited for new acquaintances to cause trouble and old ones to turn on me. Busy city streets you couldn't haphazardly dash across, sirens and horns day and night, and the endless blocks of high-rise buildings were frightening.

Things once so familiar were either suspect of me or I of them. This was home, I'd tell myself. This is where I was born, where I wanted to return to for so long. I dreamed of it, begged for it, and in a crunch, prayed for it. I was no longer sure of where I wanted to be, or more disturbing, who I wanted to be with.

It was like reviewing Algebra as a parent, that subject that tormented the minds and haunted the nights of many ninth graders and seemed to never go away. But you're older now, more ready to take on challenges. Your mind is sharper, your skills to dissect concepts more acute. But though the terms look familiar, the only details that readily come back are the long hours staring holes through a test paper.

I handled my angst the way most inner city kids did, the way I learned in Dayr Ghasana. I fought it out. My first was with Lennie Borskey, my best friend before I left. Lennie, as I remembered him, was never far from the limelight. If it wasn't given to him, he wasn't shy about reaching out and taking it. It was one of the things from my past that hadn't changed.

While I had grown tall and lean, he stayed short and thick. His reputation matched my own. In Dayr Ghasana, it was my custom to come in with a swagger looking for a fight. Now, I insulated myself to avoid challenges.

Our confrontation started the day he let go a loud and obnoxious fart during art class. The teacher glared at him. "Hey," Lennie said. "Don't knock it. That was the inspiration for jet propulsion."

He let it go as he was dishing out globs of that nasty paste that some kids enjoyed eating after learning it was nothing more than a mixture of flour and water. He waited until he was at my desk. Everyone thought it hilarious but me. Or more accurately, everyone made it a point to act as if they thought so.

My opinion would have been sufficiently made by just continuing on as if I hadn't heard him. But I pushed the issue with a look that had Lennie glowering down at me. Lunch was just fifteen minutes away; I knew that look wouldn't be the end of it.

It didn't take him long to seek me out at recess. Like the first few weeks at The Friends School I usually took recess alone. I sat on a wall of boulders we were not allowed to cross or play on. The rebel in me had me not playing, not crossing, but sitting. It was a technicality I hadn't yet been called on by any of the teachers.

"You got a problem with my jokes?" he said. He was surrounded by kids who weren't living in the neighborhood before I left.

"Not really."

"Then why that stupid look?"

I shrugged. "I guess I didn't find it real funny, Lennie."

He looked at his posse. "They all did," he said. What I saw was a group of kids who would have laughed at Adli trying to write his name straight on the chalkboard.

"I don't know, maybe they were just afraid not to laugh."

He stepped in but I didn't get up. "You did it in front of me," I said. "Like you were trying to get me in trouble for doing it."

"Why would I? I was proud of that joke. I was working my insides up all morning so I could do it." His crew laughed again.

"Then I guess you did it in Katie Loudermilk's face, and that wasn't very nice or very funny at all."

Katie was a shy redhead whose father died when we were in kindergarten. He was well known as a south side drunk who passed out on someone's front yard every month or so. This time he ended up in Grand Crossing Park where he was found beaten to death. Lennie in particular was relentless in his torment of Katie. I admit I laughed back then along with everyone else. It's what you did as a kid. Lennie was cool, Katie was not. But that was then.

"You sweet for Lousy Milk, Khudayer? Are you?"

This was the very place we both knew we'd be in eventually. Though we were friends as babies, it was anything but healthy. I can't ever remember sharing with him, or a kind word passing between us. It was one competition, albeit silly ones, after another: who can hold their breath the longest, climb highest in a tree, stand longest on the railroad tracks at 59th Street. We once dropped our pants and plopped our butts in a snow pile to see who'd cover up first.

He stood in front of me the way I had done in my confrontation with Gamal. His knees flexed, his butt low, as if he was trying to root himself into the ground. I watched him set up. Amazing how good you can be at almost anything with the proper preparation. Sometimes it doesn't take more than a few seconds, which is good because sometimes that's all you have.

He was expecting me to stand and grapple with him. We'd go face-to-face. He would initiate with a shove. I knew it would be him to start; Lennie never followed anyone's lead in anything. Then, like a game of *Simon Says,* I'd shove back. Because whatever it was Lennie did, others did. He may repeat a second time, maybe a third. Small shoves, neither of us making much of an impression. Then he'd tire of toying and launch me over the rock wall.

I stood but didn't give him the opportunity to play his act out. I hit him solid on the side of his head with my right, followed with an uppercut to his jaw. The right tore him from his would-be roots so the uppercut was glancing; otherwise I would have popped out a few of his teeth. He crashed to the ground, conscious but unwilling to get up. I've seen kids dance around after a knock down waiting for the opponent to stand. I found it much more dominating to stand motionless, fists at my side, glaring down, knowing he wouldn't dare.

On a school playground the sound of fist-on-flesh had the effect of chum tossed into shark-infested waters. And such a swarm of kids was sure to be hunted down by teachers. I wasn't particularly afraid of punishment, but I didn't want the kind of reputation I made back in Dayr Ghasana. I needed it back there; I hoped I wouldn't here.

But I was innately aware of a more deep-seated reason for my explosion. A need, a desire, to stand alone from them all. Katie Loudermilk had done so all her life but not on her own accord. And there were others, always there were others. If I was destined to be one of them, eventually, I was determined to make it happen on terms I dictated. If that meant getting a reputation, then I would make that happen, too.

I did get in trouble with a week's suspension. And I got the reputation. I didn't know hockey but there were enough Black Hawk fans in the school to give me my nickname. "The Goon."

***

With us up three to nothing and two minutes left in the game, I figured it was a chance worth taking. I pulled my sweeper aside and told him to stay no more than five feet from me after the next save. He gave me a strange look. "Trust me," I said.

After years of pitiful soccer, our high school was playing for *The Shield* in the semifinals of the Chicago Public League tournament. *The Shield* is the trophy presented to the city champion who also got an automatic berth to the State finals. We had beaten Harrison, the State champs from a couple of years earlier, soundly in the quarterfinals. We were a lock to win *The Shield* and favored to bring the state title home to the CPL. It was a really big deal.

I was a preseason pick for All-State goalie as a junior. At six-two, one-ninety, I was fast and intimidating. An article in the *Sun Times* called me fearless. I always thought of a fearless person as one who cared too much. Never thought of it as a term for one who didn't care at all.

I won the starting job halfway through my freshmen year. Already I had visits from most of the Big Ten schools, to include my choice, the Northwestern Wildcats. My grades would hold me back, I was told. While I worked feverishly on my soccer skills, I let the grades continue to slide.

The right forward for Lane Tech had been in my face all game. He was first Team All-State selection the past two years. I'd never seen such a foot in my life. Quick and deceptive off the dribble, with shots from any angle with either foot, and always with a vicious spin. But I had shut him down with saves I admit were dumb luck. But I'd take that. I gave up just nine goals all year; half of them were dumb luck.

He would charge me from the sides every chance he had, just outside my peripheral vision when I punted the ball away. He did it clean; he never made contact. But he came at me hard and furious to rattle me. It never did, but it did piss me off. I knew his style of play would keep him aggressive till the end. With my sweeper back near me, it would allow him to get closer to me without being off sides.

Lane Tech, however, was losing heart, normally a good thing. I wanted one last push from them, one or two more shots on goal. One finally came. An easy stop for the sweeper but I called him off. He let it skitter by, and as I had directed, fell back towards me. I strategically fumbled with the save as I waited for the forward who was coming hard down the right side.

In my head, the plan was to make my punt seem quite accidental. I would turn casually into his path. But when I made my move he wasn't close enough. So I had a decision to make: let the kick sail over his head, or wait for him to close the gap. With time running out and Tech playing without much enthusiasm, this was probably my last opportunity. I chose to let him close.

Rarely does a plan such as the one concocted go as expected. I figured I'd shave the top of his head, or he'd duck and I'd miss him completely. But he didn't duck and I didn't miss. It couldn't have hit him more square in the face if he had stood and posed for it. It hit him so square that I was forced to make my best save of the game off the rebound.

The shot lifted him off the ground. Blood poured immediately from his face as if his head exploded. He fell, rolled onto his back, lifted one knee, then lay deathly still. I didn't pick up on the gasps from the crowd and my sweeper, the insistent whistle, or the red flag thrown at my leg. I stood unflinching, holding the ball as I stared at the flow of blood coming unimpeded from his face.

A commotion was about him. "What the hell did you do?" the sweeper said. "You almost took his head off. Look at his face?"

I did. Before the crowd gathered I saw that his nose had been split open nearly down the middle. In fact, he had no nose at all, just a seemingly unrelated slab of red gristle plastered on his face. "You're outta here."

It was the ref, up in my grill, his finger in my chest. I maneuvered around him. It wasn't so much to ignore him; I had this overwhelming desire to watch the drama through to completion. "That was an assault, son. You're gonna be charged. Where are the police? Someone get the cops out here."

The moment was a blur to me. While everyone else seemed to have a part to play, I was the actor in a play whose character had been killed off. There was nothing left for me to do but watch and wait in the wings until the curtain call.

There were no criminal charges but I was thrown out of the game. My coach kept me out of the CPL finals, as well. There was no rule that called for a penalty kick for what I had done but the refs were so infuriated they made one up. My coach was so humiliated he didn't fight it. The back-up goalie was a freshman. He let the penalty kick in and another with thirty seconds left in the game. Then we got blown out in the finals.

Despite my body of work, that episode not only vilified me amongst players, coaches, and the CPL, it black-balled me from the All-State team. They did give me the small-print honorable mention. My own coach called that a travesty. "There was nothing honorable about what you did, son."

Losing out on All-State bothered me; the league's censure and my coach's reprimand didn't. I long ago gave up giving a damn about what others thought of me, especially those in authority.

It was my choice not to play my senior year. The forward from Tech, who needed major plastic surgery, went on to become a second team All-American at Ohio State. All my college offers were pulled except one from a community college. Had I gone back to play that last year I could have erased the past. Had someone told me my pride was really ego, it could have been so different for me. My coaches didn't try to persuade me. I don't think my father even noticed until after graduation when I didn't head off the college. It was my mother who brought it up. She was disappointed but said she understood. I don't know what it was she thought she understood. The only lasting result of my almost-stellar soccer career was a son.

CHAPTER 43

The baby's mother was Jennifer Cordella, a university student I met during summer soccer camps at the University of Chicago. The school had no varsity soccer, or even a club team, only intramurals. She was a standout in high school in Altoona, Pennsylvania. She showed me her yearbook that listed her as the team MVP for three years, a record holder for career goals and assists, and second team All-State. She had dozens of scholarship offers. It was unconceivable to me she had given up scholarships for a school with no soccer.

"I've wanted to come here since seventh grade," she said.

"Why?"

"It's a great research school. I want to be a doctor, a psychiatrist, and that's hard to get into unless you have a great undergrad foundation from a great school."

"But no soccer. And no scholarship."

"Soccer won't get me into med school. Matter of fact, the time commitment it would take would hurt me. I've been there and done that. Time to move on. As for the scholarship, I had good grades in high school so I got some academic scholarships, and my dad works for the railroad for not much money so I got grants."

She was three years older than me, an incoming freshman volunteering at the summer camp I attended between my own high school freshman and sophomore year. She was perky and out-going. I was cool bordering on cold, the cock-of-the-walk, or so I felt. Although I knew of her that first summer, it was only by way of the group introduction. She worked with the forwards while I was with the goalies on another field. The closest we got was during scrimmages on the last day.

But deep down something must have clicked. We remembered each other the next summer. We spoke at length after the first day at the refreshment tent. We spoke of conversations and events we had with other people that we swore we had shared with each other. Our imaginations had us together, and that was a good start long before we ever knew.

We had no problem with the age because there was no sexual tension. If there was, I didn't feel it. I don't believe she did, either. There were no hot sparks between us. No electric touches. I didn't steal glances her way. I didn't dream of her, there was no longing. It was a fun, casual friendship. Then we had sex.

The first time was in the winter of my junior year. The events of the city playoffs had me angry and frustrated. Being who she was, a tender woman and budding psychiatrist, she was where I turned. We would meet at the University library, talk, stare, hug, then sneak off to empty school corridors, lounges, or her dorm room when her roommate was sure to be gone for her thirty minute swim.

I guess I fell in love with her. I guess I loved the quiet moments we spent together. I guess the nights we had sex were what they were supposed to be. But it wasn't the type of thing I was comfortable talking about or dwelling on. By that summer we were winding down. She was talking medical school in Virginia, maybe in Oregon. The community college I was planning on attending dropped its soccer program so I spent most our time listening to her with nothing to offer.

I became envious of her. She not only anally planned out her life but enjoyed it along the way. It was one, long inked-in syllabus. I was impressed, yet overwhelmed by her and her talks. We'd make love, or parts of it, then she would discuss obscure and deadly boring topics like Lamarckism, Piaget's Cognitive Theory, and the triune brain, with all the passion that should have been expended thirty minutes earlier. "My head hurts," I would say after a while. She'd laugh as if I said it in jest.

I didn't see any room for me in that neatly packaged plan. If I went to school, we'd be separated. Now that I wasn't, I was further away from her than ever. Hell, there was a good chance I wouldn't even graduate high school.

I wasn't particularly good looking. I wasn't charming, nor was I graceful, social, talented, or witty. If I was a literary character, it would surely be from a Steinbeck novel; she was Fitzgerald, and these thoughts had me spending my senior year wondering if I was her lover or her medical area of interest.

One early Saturday morning she called me at home. She had called me only a handful of times. Whenever we got together it was usually me doing the calling, and I admittedly hadn't done that in a while. Really, I was fine with the idea of quitting her the way my father had quit smoking that year; cold turkey.

My father answered and handed me the phone. I told no one about Jennifer. He was intrigued but played it cool. I thought his curiosity was about this unknown woman calling me, but she was nearly hysterical when I got to the phone. If she was this way with my father, he had a right to be concerned.

I pulled the extension cord to its twelve-foot limit, around the corner and into the hall. My father understood it as the universal signal to back off. "Calm down," I whispered.

"Did you hear me?"

"Yeah, but I didn't understand a word of it."

"I'm late."

"For what?"

"Late. Late, as in not on my monthly schedule."

It wasn't very scientific of her to jump to unsubstantiated conclusions, but then this wasn't a chemistry experiment and objectivity wasn't essential. She needed to be scared, and she needed me to be scared with her. She needed to vent, and she needed me to hate. She needed to cry, and she needed me to listen. I guess I could have done better at doing all three.

"Have you, you know, seen a doctor?" I asked, whispering the last word in the event my father wasn't playing fair.

"I can't do that. I can't afford for anyone to know."

"Well, if you are, you know, that way, people are going to know anyway. If you're not, then there's nothing to worry about. Right?"

She didn't respond but I could hear her despising me on the other end. "Well," I added, "you have to find out for sure before you … start worrying."

"Oh no, you don't get it," she spat. "I started worrying six weeks ago."

That's about where I blew it, if I had any desire to be a man and treat this with compassion. "I don't know why you needed to call and drag me into this. I mean, we haven't even seen each other in what?"

"Six weeks you shit." And she hung up.

That couldn't have gone any worse, or so I thought. I was hoping I pissed her off enough with my insensitive insinuation that she wouldn't bother to call back. But then, it wasn't like it was a *Blood, Sweat, and Tears* eight-track tape I left at her place. And it wasn't going away with skin cleanser. I was a kid and responded like a kid. That was my justification over the next two weeks as I covered my ears and closed my eyes each time I was reminded of the situation by a song, TV show, stray comment, or personal reflection. While the passing days put it further in my rearview mirror, they tormented Jennifer.

She was just a kid herself. While she talked incessantly of her future as a doctor, she was squeamish at the sight of a three-inch splinter I caught in my palm. And her intellect didn't stop her from laughing uproariously at *Blazing Saddles,* even after the third time. But there was nothing I could give her. Or was there?

I knew what it was to be left alone, haunted by the nagging belief it was abandonment. All these years later, it still hurt enough I couldn't confide my past even to her. I knew if I couldn't tell her, I'd probably never be able to tell anyone. And if I didn't, I would never heal. Not a comforting thought.

I couldn't make myself sensitive to what she was experiencing. I've learned that contrary to what pop psychology and T-shirts espouse, it isn't just a matter of falling off the horse and getting back on. Hell, I'd fallen off and got back on some big horses in my days without gaining a clue as to how to hang on. If no one's there to teach you, you learn the best you can, learning bad habits along the way.

At ten o'clock on a Wednesday night, long after our phone activity usually ceased, we got a call. The only one it could have been was Sue who was now teaching at a Catholic School in Cicero and living on her own out there. But I heard my mother talking to her not four hours earlier. I raced for the phone, something I never did, and it had my mother asking if I was expecting a call as I ran to the back bedroom to answer it in private.

I knew instinctively it was Jennifer, and in a young-love way I was excited and anxious to talk with her. I wanted to hear her laughing voice greet me with, "Hey Champ, false alarm, glad that's over with." But she was flat when she identified herself with the officiousness of a political pollster. She paused to catch her breath before telling me she was pregnant.

"You're sure?"

"Yes, Joe, I'm sure," she said, exasperated, as if she had been answering the question all day.

"Oh."

"It was never supposed to be you, you know," she said. There was resignation in her voice.

"I know." Only I really didn't know. On the rare evening when I felt good about myself, I saw us together, living high above The Loop overlooking the lake.

"I'm over being angry about it," she said. "It wasn't in my plans. It wasn't in yours. I'm calling to tell you not to worry. Nothing has changed when it comes to us. There was no way I was going to end up with you."

How she had turned it around. This wasn't what I had been preparing myself for over the past weeks. I was hardening my psyche against her grief, against her attacks on my insensitivity, against her rants on everything from sex organs to the high price of tuna fish. She was either being painfully honest or she was using her pre-psych tools to humiliate and mortify me.

"Anyway," she said, "that said, I'd like to see you one more time."

"Okay. Why?"

"Because this is important even if we won't be together to live it. You'll have a child somewhere in this world. You probably won't ever get to see it. You certainly won't be around to raise it. But as mother and father, I want closure with you. Looking at each other one last time is all the closure we can have."

I was dumbfounded. "You mean, after all you said about me and this ... situation not being in your plans, you're going through with it?"

"Of course."

"But you don't have to."

"You mean an abortion? You've been intimate with me. Joe. Do you truly think I'd ever consider that as an option? Do you think my decision to be doctor was based on anything other than principal?"

"That's the point," I said. "This puts an end to it."

"An abortion puts an end to it?" I had to pull the phone from my ear her voice was so enraged. "Killing puts an end to everything. We're the ones who did this. Maybe we're the ones who should have our lives taken away."

The volume on the television in the front room lowered as my mother, father, or both tried to eavesdrop. "You have choices," I whispered.

"Why do people say that as if they've come across a great revelation? Of course I have choices; we all have choices. I made mine."

"But you have a future."

"I still do."

"Not the one you want."

"You want me to make a choice that affects only me. You want me to make one that fits into the future I created. You want me to make a convenient one. But I can't do that, Joe, because this isn't about only me, and the truth is, I don't know what choice is best. Maybe I am making the wrong one. But I want to be a doctor and for all the right reasons. If I terminate this pregnancy, then I destroy those reasons. And that destroys me."

"You made a mistake, we made a mistake," I told her.

"That's what my parents say. But who's to know if I did? Maybe this isn't the mistake. Maybe the real mistake was made a longtime ago."

"What's that supposed to mean?"

"Not you, long before you. It's hard to explain. All I know is while my body was going through these incredible changes, my mind had to keep up. So maybe I've over thought this thing. We'll talk when you come to see me. I don't expect you to fully understand or appreciate it. Someday I know you will, because I know things have happened to you in your life that you can't yet talk about. Someday honesty will hit you like a penalty kick. I know that because you are a good man Nasser Khudayer. Just … I'm afraid you're going to make the worse mistake a person can ever make."

"What's that?"

"Joe, don't get bitter with life, no matter how it changes for you. Nothing really hurts if you handle it right. And bad things do happen to good people."

She was going to stay at the University to graduate then head back to Altoona to live with her parents. In time, she told me, she would go to medical school and become a psychiatrist. It was her dream, after all. "And Joe, real dreams just don't die."

We made plans to meet at the library, in the periodical section, at seven o'clock that Friday night. I didn't go. I had no intentions of going. Those mistakes she made long ago, I knew what they were. I didn't need to sit and listen to her recite them to me. She should have taken the soccer scholarship at some nowhere state school. She should have taken liberal arts so she had time to hit fraternity row on Saturday nights. She had no business planning out a future in the seventh grade when her friends were getting braces and discussing what to wear to their first junior high dance and playing spin the bottle at the neighborhood park.

She was wrong. I predicted she would be the one to grow bitter. Too much could happen in the years to come. A slob like me could happen, a slob envious and pathetic enough to feign interest in human physiology and menstrual cycles to learn just enough to guesstimate her next ovulation period. Yes, the kind of bitter slob like me who hadn't yet learned shit about the values of life in spite of living amongst the finest examples.

CHAPTER 44

David was released from prison the summer I graduated high school. My father picked him up and brought him home. He was away three times longer than I had been, and like me, in a different world. Though unlike me, in a world where no one much cared if he lived or died.

It was awkward having him around. I couldn't blame my parents for not knowing what to say and not to say to him; I was at a loss myself. Strange. When we visited him we exchanged small talk, with the idea that the deeper subjects could wait until he came home. But now those moments were long forgotten or no longer significant, so we resorted back to the small talk.

Even that got patronizing and insulting. My mother would offer him food with the obligatory suffix, "You get to choose here, you know." And when offering seconds, "There's plenty here, you don't need to fight for it." When he was sent to Greeley's Market she would remind him to talk only to people he knew for sure weren't selling drugs, "because associating with criminals and known felons is a violation of your parole, remember."

"She drives me crazy," he confided to me one night.

"I guess it's her way of saying she's concerned."

"We had plenty of food in there. And I can talk to anyone, just can't hang with them. Shit, nine years from the hacks; I don't want to take crap from my mother. I'm almost thirty freakin' years old. I don't need protection, I need space."

"You need a job, don't you?"

"That, too." He laughed. "Hey, wouldn't it be the shits if I got one before you, and a better one?"

"I might go to school," I told him.

"You? How? You blew the soccer gig, and didn't you flunk home ec or something?"

"It was geometry and I didn't flunk."

"Yeah, well, you're no brain."

He could say what he wanted about how the family treated him, but we never insulted him. Least I didn't. And that flop in geometry is what gave me the impetus to try college. Actually, it was a slick trick by Sue.

She came to the house unexpectedly in the first semester of my senior year. I needed three math courses to pass high school. I barely got by Algebra I and II, but sophomore geometry just never sank in so trig and calculus were certainly out of reach. My guidance counselor challenged me. "Give me a unique excuse for why Joe Khudayer is the one person in the Illinois school system who doesn't need to pass geometry and I'll get you out of it," he said. "And Joe, I've been in this job for twenty-two years so you'll have to come up with something very good."

"How long I got?" I asked.

He looked at his watch. "Fifty-six seconds."

I gave it ten before saying, "I got nuthin'," and right there began to work out my career as a laborer on a road paving crew and a GED at thirty-five.

When she came to the house she had the dreaded geometry book under her arm. I felt no impulse to ask her why she had it so she told me. "I need your help, Joe.

"For what?" I thought she had a couch to move or rodent to kill.

"I'm teaching geometry this year and I'm beyond rusty."

"To fifth graders?"

"I volunteered to do remedial for high school."

"Why?"

"They needed someone."

"But why are you coming to a kid who flunked it once, and is gonna flunk it again?"

"Because something had to sink in and I start in three days."

I shrugged and decided to humor her. We sat at the kitchen table for three hours discussing areas, perimeters, circumferences, supplementary and complementary angles, surfaces, and volumes. She asked what I thought were the most inane questions while I went over the formulas. She flipped through the pages of the book; I barely referred to any. I made up my own problems for her to solve before we went on to the next formula.

"I think I got it, Joe. You've been a doll to help me through this."

It was past nine. The time flew by and I felt bad keeping her there so late. "Kinda didn't know when to shut up, huh?" I said.

She kissed me on the cheek. "You did great."

"Let me know how it goes."

"You, too."

My mother walked her out to the car. When she came back into the kitchen she said, "Your sister, she's a pretty good teacher, huh?"

"Yeah, well, I'm a pretty good one myself."

"Yes, I heard."

I sat there like a spectator at a magic show who just got a quarter pulled out of his ear. Yeah, she was very good. I ended up with a high C in the class and found myself arguing with the teacher for a B-minus. It was at that time that the ill-fated affair with Jennifer was occurring so I made little effort to follow through on other studies.

David was the Encyclopedia Britannica illustration of the lost soul. Nearly the first decade of his adulthood had been spent locked away. I remember looking up to him physically as a big brother. Even in his prison jumpsuit he looked large and intimidating. But he looked frail and puny in loose jeans and a blue-striped Polo shirt. He was a still-life in this world that was thunder and lightning around him.

"I'm gettin' outta here," he said.

"Where you gonna go? You can't leave the state."

"Think Sue will let me stay with her?"

"I don't know. That's a lot of strain to put on her."

"What? You think I'm trouble?"

"Not trouble, just—"

"What? A burden? You think I'm a fuckin' burden?"

It was frightening to see him escalate so quickly but since he was there, I figured to see how high he could go. "Yeah. Probably."

"Yeah, probably is right," he said.

"Hey," I said. "I got one for you. I got a girl pregnant."

He looked at me with a half-smile. "Was she any good?"

David told me I had to broach the topic of his staying with Sue because I knew her better. She didn't flinch at the prospect. She laid heavy ground rules that made the parole board look like neglectful parents. "Shit," David said when she gave him the list, "the whole idea of me coming out here was so I wouldn't be treated like a kid."

"Thanks for reminding me." She took the list from him and scribbled another entry.

"No cursing?" He read aloud.

"That's bad words in general. Too many to list but I'll let you know whenever you hit one."

He continued to read. "Ten o'clock curfew on weekends, thirty-minutes of TV news and thirty minutes of the Trib with discussions on current events at dinner, dinner at home at least five nights per week, a reading list to be provided later, church—" he stared up at her. "Church? You serious?"

"Mine or pick your own. David, you need grounding. You need to know that things go on outside yourself so that you can become part of them. It'll work, you'll see."

I dropped off his meager possessions and left laughing. She'd be good for him; they'd be good for each other. He was a mess. And for all her outward signs of confidence and control, so was she. We were in a time when self-help meant just that. Everything was healed with a Band Aid you put on yourself. A lot of people learned just how tough and resilient they were in those days while many others curled into balls and died.

When I met with Sue to tell her of David's plan she hugged me. "It's a family, Joe, isn't that wonderful?" Poor Sue. I was afraid she was right, that this was the closest she'd come to one. She was only twenty-six, plenty of time, but I didn't see her drawing the boys as she once did. Long ago I called her a drama queen with her folk songs and poetry, a vulnerable girl who'd break into several verses of *Heart's Needle* at the mention of Snodgrass. I hated her for those things as I loved her for them. There were no songs or poetry left in her. Those wrist scars may as well have been carved into her face.

She confided in me one night that it entered her heart to become a nun. It was a decision she made on our bus ride back from Jerusalem. "You remember, Joe, you remember that day?" There was such a mournful way to her asking.

"Course I remember," I said. "You make up your mind before or after they beat that kid to death?"

"We don't know if he died."

"Well?"

"Before. And my heart never changed."

"So why didn't you?"

She rolled her wrists over. "I can't, not after what I did."

I had turned dark and carried a nasty brand of sarcasm with me when it came to things of authority such as school, law, government, and especially religion. Normally I would have cracked about how nuns cause worse injuries than that on kids' hands, but Sue was genuinely wounded by the turn of events in her life. "They'd be lucky to have you, but I think it's a waste of time and life. You're doing better as a teacher."

She smiled and kissed my forehead, something she had been doing since I came home. "Yes, but really, this isn't what I should be doing. I'd like to have children."

"Seriously Sue? Kids?"

"Something wrong with children?"

"No. Something wrong with parents."

She laughed. "I have this bizarre notion," she said, "that children are already there, just waiting to be born. That every day they stand in line waiting for conception, one after the other, and if it isn't their time, they have to come back the next day. So if I don't get involved, it's one more child that has to come back and wait."

Bizarre it was, but it's the logic we use in death, waiting our turn day-after-day, returning each morning for one more shot at it. In the end, I don't know who I felt sorrier for, Sue, who never had a child, or the lost soul still waiting.

CHAPTER 45

I made my first debt collection when I was sixteen years old. Twenty bucks. I didn't even know what it was for. I heard some kid bitching about it with his friend at lunch. "Give me twenty-five percent and I'll get it back," I offered. The kid looked at me puzzled. "That's five bucks," I said, "Take it or leave it."

Anything you can do better than others makes you a commodity. Better still if it's something you alone can do. I had developed such a skill. I was now at my full height, and though I've added fifty pounds since then, I was a solid, intimidating figure. I rarely smiled or spoke, so even those who saw me regularly didn't know how to take me. I had a five o'clock shadow by noon. I was always the last to walk in and out of class. I sat in the back at a forty-five degree angle so the teacher would know I only half gave a damn.

I could approach the biggest, the baddest, or the weakest with the same indifference. It didn't matter to me if they attacked or cried. They owed money, they needed talking to, they needed a reminder, I had a flair for letting them know. The best part was I resorted to violence only on two occasions.

The first time was in my senior year. I was paid to convince a football player to cease and desist in coming on to a cheerleader. It became common knowledge that the girl's boyfriend hired me. As was my policy, I neither confirmed nor denied, but it was actually the cheerleader who paid me by writing my analysis on *The Love Song of J. Alfred Prufrock*. It wouldn't even have come to blows had he not called me "a washed-out soccer wimp."

The second time I needed to use force I was much older and the stakes were higher. After I graduated I found work at a packing house at *Back of the Yards* where I slaughtered pigs. The work was only part-time so I used my experience and contacts to pick up extra money. Gangs were everywhere. They were as easy to come by as pick-up basketball games at Washington Park. I never joined one; I never had to. I was a freelancer of sorts and made money, good money, for doing it.

Some collections were for gangs. Some for individuals. Some, I had no idea. I never paid much attention. Most times, I didn't even know what the collection was for. It made me feel stupid when the guy asked, but I figured it was up to him to know. So I came up with the line: "I collect for drugs, gambling, parking fines, overdue library books, and bad tips. Pick one."

One night I found myself in a bar infested with members of the Hell's Henchmen Motorcycle Club. My wise-ass line wasn't going to work here. I found myself surrounded by twenty of them. They were in a sporting mood and told me I could collect the debt incurred by one of the brothers if I stayed conscious in the backroom against him for five minutes. So for twenty percent of a five hundred dollar drug debt I took on a three hundred fifty pound biker they called "Loco."

I won't say I won the bout, but at the four minute mark Loco collapsed in the corner, not beaten but very exhausted, and the bikers did the righteous thing by handing over the money with an invitation to patch into the club.

When I wasn't butchering dumb animals or collecting debts for and from dumb crooks, I made my way to college hang-outs, primarily at Northwestern University in Evanston. I enjoyed almost belonging. I liked the atmosphere of almost being chosen. I even had a set of clothes, my Wildcats clothes I'd wear so as to fit in. As long as I sat in the corner and didn't try to participate, I was almost one of them.

I invited two older guys I knew from the *Back of the Yards* neighborhood. They didn't work at the packing house; they didn't work at all. But they'd come around to bum money or a slab of pork for their families. I'd give them a buck or two, or a lesser cut of meat that would otherwise go to the owner's dogs. They were decent guys, just not ambitious. I had this idea that maybe I could show them another side, a side that may inspire them to do something with their lives. They wouldn't make it at a place like Northwestern, but there were junior colleges and trade schools. Anyway, it was just a crazy idea.

They got a kick out of driving up in my 1969 AMC Javelin. It was burnt orange, hard to tell where the paint stopped and the rust started. The engine had been souped-up to race as stock but it never made it off the streets before it was rolled. A friend of mine did the body work and sold it to me for four-hundred bucks. It'd been downhill for the car from there. I wasn't a car guy and bought it for one reason; little chance of it being jacked.

I always started my time at the University by parking on the far side of campus so I could walk across it. Occasionally in nice weather there would be outdoor classes. Most sounded to be English, theology, or philosophy, some subject that lent itself to getting acquainted with nature. I'd stop, not so close as to be obvious, but close enough to listen and realize I was enjoying it and could learn this stuff. And of course, I always made it to the soccer fields by the lake to catch a practice.

My friends didn't appreciate it as I did. The co-eds held their interest more than the architecture and gardens. They ogled them, at times without restraint, and wanted to know where they all hung out. When I pointed to the magnificent Deering Library, they said it was the fanciest bar they'd ever seen. It was a Thursday, early May. We got there around four; early enough to see some afternoon outdoor classes but late enough to catch evening activities.

They were beer drinkers, whereas I nursed rum and cokes all night, my one to their three. I wasn't a big drinker; I hated being out of control. But it was high on their list of things to do, the novelty of drinking at a college campus. That, and they really thought it was a turn-on for young girls to see older men drunk. "Hey," one of them said when we got to *Suds,* "here's a bunch of parking spots right here, how come you made us walk all over the damn place?"

The rest of the night was them drinking and me buying in the places where I usually nursed a glass of root beer. The notions I had of arousing their inner muse didn't make it past Shakespeare Garden. The closest it came to a conversation about academics was when they used the tired pick-up line about show-and-tell to a co-ed reading an anatomy book. It wasn't long before we were being summarily bounced from three Evanston bars, a fraternity house, and the Amazing Grace Coffeehouse where they nearly caused a race riot. By eleven we were ordering late night breakfast at The Main Café.

I was now serving as their chaperone. I was just drunk enough to be mellow while they were drunk enough to be stupid. I made them order very strong coffee at the café. That seemed to settle them down.

They sat with their back to the door so didn't see them come in. Two beautiful blondes with two gawky guys. As beautiful as they were, it wasn't the girls I focused on. Visions of those years in Palestine came to me often. So did the nightmares. Many came to me so randomly they seemed to have no origin. But there were times the cause was obvious. Like tonight.

Tonight I was feeling very melancholy. I had spent the night in a place I almost made it to with guys who didn't give a damn. They didn't know my past; they didn't share my dreams. It had been a depressing experience, realizing I was closer to being one of them than one of the gawky kids across the room.

"Whatcha looking at?" One of my charges asked me, then turned around to see for himself while I gazed glassy-eyed.

"Whoa, jackpot." He nudged the other.

"Damn. How's two fags like that hook up with chicks that nice?"

"Money," the other said. "Daddy's got lots and lots of money."

"And a sports car, bet."

Now they were both staring, their chins resting on the back of the bench like boys at the zoo.

"I'd bang the one on the right."

"You shittin', I'd bang 'em both."

"Well, yeah, but you know, with a choice."

I was barely cognizant of what they were saying but I knew this, they were saying it very loudly. The girls were whispering to the guys, trying to get them to leave, but the guys were shaking them off as they stared us down. But my guys were oblivious to the fact a battle was ready to erupt. They were being rude and ignorant, but it was something they came by naturally. In my mind, these two college boys should have been above that. They were in a no-win situation. Beating up a couple of drunks was not a sign of manhood, whereby losing to them was sure to tear it down.

These were but passing thoughts as I stared across at the two guys sitting with the red berets perched jauntily on their heads. They had them pushed back on top of moppy black hair. They looked more like Jughead from the Archie comics than Barry Sadler on the album cover of *Ballad of the Green Berets,* or the Israeli soldiers that killed Adli. Nevertheless, the berets were all I saw, and the dropping of plates became bombs, the clattering dishes gunfire, and the casual stirring of cream in a coffee cup the tapping of a watch against the stock of a rifle.

All around me the makings of a confrontation formed while I engaged in a battle fought over a decade ago, and though I saw the two kids stand, I didn't grasp the drama unfolding. Under normal situation there was no way they would have approached. We were three to their two, we were bigger and scruffier. But the macho side of their egos saw us as easy to handle drunks. "You seem to have a problem over here."

They stood side-by-side at our booth, the midsection of the one on the right vulnerable and within easy reach of my fist. "Yeah," my friend said, "let me ask you, you young fellas like rich or famous? 'Cause you sure as shit ain't got nuthin' else those two foxes could want." He slurred his words, his head bobbed, his elbows slipped from the table. He looked as if he'd fall asleep in mid-sentence. *Yeah,* I could hear these guys thinking, *these clowns will be easy to take.*

"Tell you what, friend. Stand up and we'll show you what we got."

"Friend?" he looked at me. "Joe, look at that. I've been in college less than one day and I already got two friends."

"Get up."

"Okay, but you have to help me." The college kids stood back while the guy climbed to his feet as if he was scaling a sheer cliff, fumbling for finger holds. He collapsed on the floor and lay seemingly unconscious. The two berets stared down at him triumphantly. One tapped him with his foot. "Get up."

My other friend told them forget about it. "He's passed out, go back to your women."

I admit now the kids never touched my friend. He went down on his own. It was the scene I responded to, not the action. The three of them jaw-jacked as I sat looking at the still body on the ground. At one point a kid leaned down and shook the body. "Get up bum, and get the hell out of here." The other leaned across the table to grab hold of my friend's arm. I reached out and grabbed his wrist. "You a Jew?" I said.

"What?"

"You two, you Jews?"

The one whose wrist I held tried to pull away but I tightened my grip. "No," he said. "I'm not Jewish."

"You got something against Jews," the other demanded. He was the mouthier one, the one who led the charge over to us.

I held the one like a bad dog while directing my attention to the mouth. "Those red berets, you in the Israeli army?"

"Shit no." the bad dog said, but the mouth hushed him. He pulled the beret down to his brow thinking the look would intimidate me.

"Yeah. Yeah, that's me, a badass paratrooper."

The bad dog now had a better grasp of the situation and tried to reason his way out of it. "Just berets, man. Just goofy berets we bought in Chicago."

"Then how come he knew it's what Israeli paratroopers wear."

"I don't know. He's a history major; he knows all kinds of crazy crap like that."

The rest happened in a matter of seconds: the girl's scream, the waitress dropping the tray, the manager's threat to call the cops, as I pulled the one guy into my fist before jumping up and battering the other into a bloody mess.

CHAPTER 46

"You've become the very person you hated, Joe; selfish, jaded, insensitive. You could have spent the years learning from so many good people, but you chose to learn from those others."

This Sue said to me after being intensely quiet most of the ride back to my car from Cook County lock-up. I sensed it was the final paragraph of the lecture she worked up in her head since getting my call to come bail me out.

"What happened anyway?' she asked. "They said you went crazy. You said you were drunk. You don't drink."

"You wouldn't understand."

"Were you drunk?"

"No."

"Did you go crazy?"

I looked over at her. "Yeah."

I scared the hell out of everyone there. I even scared the cops who responded. It took four of them to pull me off. My two friends were astonished. "Man, you kicked ass," one said. The unconscious one who came to just in time for the arrest concurred. "No one ever stuck up for me like that before."

I nodded as if they were the reason for my madness. I don't know if the kids were Jewish, probably not. They were just college kids out to enjoy a night with two hot girls and saw an opportunity at manhood. I didn't feel good about what I did. They weren't moving very well when the paramedics took them in.

Sue knew about Adli being killed. But she knew nothing of me being the one who coaxed him out of the ravine then left him behind. Nor did I tell her of being directed by the soldiers to bring him home to be buried. I had told no one of the details of the red berets, tearful shooter, or the conversation between them. No one knew how Adli's head fell apart in my hands or how his defective brain fell to the mud when I pulled him up. I no longer speak his name, even to myself, but in my nightmares it comes to me like the chorus of a television theme song.

"I'll pay you back for the bail," It was a childish approach, to think that was a concern to her.

"You know what people say about it never being too late? That's a bunch of bunk, Joe. It's said by people afraid to say the truth to others afraid of hearing it. You're self destructing fast so you'd better make the grown up decision to get out of it."

"It's not that simple," I said.

"That's right. So why do you act as if it should be? You let your feelings flow like water in the path of least resistance."

"I'm supposed to respond like you, like all in life is good, like God is the answer to all my problems?"

"I handle it that way because it's who I am," she said. "You have to handle it in your own way, but this isn't it. You lived through tragedy, but there are others who live *with* it every day with no end in sight. And I don't let God be the answer to my problems. He's just the reason for how I deal with them."

She was getting dangerously close to my motivation, and I wasn't ready to go there with anyone. "Not everything I do is wrapped up in those years," I muttered.

"But a lot is, for both of us. All we can do is think back on what we should have done, what we should have said. The fact we were only kids is immaterial. We see it in terms of who we are today, that maybe we should have fought back harder."

"Yeah, well, we didn't, did we? And this is who *I* am. Maybe it's who've I've always been."

"You were once too young to know, now you're too old to learn, is that it? Okay, Joe, I won't try. But answer yourself this question: is there anyone in your life whose death you couldn't bear?"

I was about to be a smart ass by saying Walter Payton but she interrupted me. "The thing is, if you have no answer, you have no life. And Joe, I fear you have no answer to that anymore. Me? It's twenty-two, ten–year olds and my family, so as much as it kills me to say it, you can't come to my house anymore. David is trying to get himself together and I won't have you destroying his chances at a future. The life you're living is the only one he's ever known and it'll be too easy for him to fall back into it with you."

When we got to my car she told me, "Those men you associate with have no humanity and until you're away from them, stay away from David."

"That's not very Christian. Those guys are part of the ones you call what? The disenfranchised?"

"Not them. The ones you work for."

"How do you know who I work for?"

"From David. Those guys are trying to recruit him now. He's still weak and those streets still hold him."

I left with nowhere else to go. Home would be the obvious place. My father was dying of lung cancer at Mercy Hospital and my mother was needing someone nearby. But the words "father" and "home" evoked nothing in me. I felt as homeless as any man could.

This had become my sordid life, bouncing between two types of disreputability, crime and the packinghouse. Both would go unnoticed by most were it not for the evening news and Sunday morning brunch. If undertakings such as these had to happen, and they did, better to know where so they could be avoided. Butchering needed to be controlled; it needed its own rules, its own place. And when it was over, it needed to be cleaned before being presented. It was the end product, not the process, that was served up for mass consumption.

But in a perverted way, I liked being where I was. I didn't like these people, but they fit me. It wasn't how I wanted to be known but at least I wasn't anonymous. I wasn't loved but I was respected. All that was expected of me was the illusion of violence. Nothing pretty or fancy, but very real. I saw my life like Lee Remick's character in *Days of Wine and Roses* who tells her husband, "You see, the world looks so dirty to me when I'm not drinking. Remember Fisherman's Wharf? The water when you looked too close? That's the way the world looks to me when I'm not drinking."

I made a turn-around in the Juniper's parking lot. It was an all night diner I drove by on my way home. Nothing ever made me want to stop there. Not much I've done in my life has been proper, but I do eat right. I'll resort to an occasional deep dish pizza or Chicago dog but the idea of dining on pure grease sickened me. Tonight I was tired of driving and could use a cup of coffee. The place looked deserted. Actually, it looked closed. I backed up in the lot and spotted a light on in the galley and a waitress rubbing down the serving counter.

I stood in the small lobby, realizing I looked very much as if I was about to rob the place. The waitress had disappeared. "Got time for a cup of coffee?" I called out to the back in the event she was retrieving a gun.

But she came back with a fresh pot in her hand. "You or me?" she said.

"What?"

"I got all night to make it or drink it. Don't know about you."

I don't think she was afraid of me. We were alone from what I could tell, but as the night girl in this place, in this area, she had to have a backbone. She was petite, nearly breakable, with dark hair and dark eyes, maybe mid-twenties. I took her for Mediterranean more than Italian. She bustled around as if the place was packed. Her hair was long and with bounce when she made her sharp twists and turns at the counter. This impressed me right off. The hair of most women I had seen working places like this was limp and dried out. It hung stiff like its owner, too worn out to show any energy.

I took a seat at the counter. "Not very nice around here," I said. More nervous small talk.

She gave me a severe look. "No one asked you to come in."

"No, not this place, this area. I know this part of town and it's ... you know, not the nicest. No, this place is very nice." I spun on the stool to look around, emphasizing my point. "Are you Juniper?"

She laughed. "I wouldn't admit to a name like that, and I certainly wouldn't put it in three-foot letters."

"I don't know, nice name."

"For a bush."

"What about Donavan's *Jennifer Juniper?*"

"Yeah, what was up with that guy?"

She poured my coffee and slid the creamer and sugar my way.

"So ... you just work the night shift."

She spoke as if it was a prepared speech. "I work whatever shift needs to be worked. I own the place. My night girl got sick. Stupor's more like it. The place isn't dead; my regular night customers work midnights so I get that crowd going in and coming out. As for the name, used to be juniper gardens all around the place till they widened the road. I kept the name because it's been here as long as I've been alive and my clientele like it.

"Speaking of the clientele, they all come from this not-so-nice neighborhood, and they treat me and my place real well. I wouldn't be here if they didn't. Anymore thoughts wandering around in your head that don't involve seeing me naked, I'd be happy to answer them."

"Wow. Didn't mean an insult to the place or the diners. I live in a neighborhood like this; it's not the locals you worry about, it's the strangers."

"So should I worry about you?"

Right on schedule her late-night crowd meandered in, greeting her warmly while eyeing me suspiciously. I left without the only thing I really wanted. Her name.

No one was at the house when I made it there at close to one in the morning. My father's Galaxie 500 was in the driveway. My mother rarely drove it as a result of the abuse she took from my father whenever she did. If she didn't put a ding on it, he bitched about the way it was parked in the driveway. I figured she went out for a late night. She had been spending most of them at my father's hospital bedside and maybe she took a night out with a friend or neighbor. No other possibility entered my mind.

I was asleep when the phone rang at two. It was Sue who started by cursing me for having the nerve not to go right home after what I had just done. Before I could defend myself she told me she, David, and mom were at the hospital. "You'd better hurry; dad's not going to last the night."

CHAPTER 47

My father had been in Mercy for two weeks and I hadn't been there except to drop off my mother and pick her up. "You never gave him a chance," she said, the only time we discussed his health in depth.

"He's had fifteen years to say what he had to."

"Years better left in silence; him screaming, you screaming, and nothing worth a damn being said."

"I went through hell, not him."

"He was afraid, Joe. He tried to keep you safe; it didn't work out as he planned. Isn't that true of a lot of plans?"

"Maybe it worked out exactly as he wanted. Maybe the only part that didn't is that I came back alive."

She slapped me across the cheek. "How dare you? How dare you say such a thing, never mind think it. You're still looking for reasons to hate him. It's your arrogance and stupidity."

"Well, least he passed something down to me. And who was the child back then?"

"In many ways we all were."

I had to ask directions to his room. "You a relative?" the nurse asked.

"His son." I wasn't the least bit embarrassed not knowing where his room was. But my mother told me he was an obnoxious patient so I was a little embarrassed to admit he was my father.

His room was semi-private. They were all three there. The curtain was drawn from the other bed. I could hear the other patient's hacking cough which was already driving me nuts. For a death scene they looked more bored than sad. Sue got up to hug me, Mom put her hand up for me to grasp, David nodded with a "Hey."

"Let's talk outside," Sue said.

I expected another lecture. Instead she said, "What a fucked up family we have."

"I can't believe you just said that."

"What offended you, my opinion or the word I used to describe us?"

"No, really, your opinion was spot on. Just it's only the second time I've heard that word come out of your mouth."

"I use it sparingly and only when appropriate. Mom's in there talking about whether she should sell Dad's clothes or give them to charity. She wants to turn their bedroom into a craft room and sleep downstairs in the dining room. She asked us if she should keep the Galaxie since it's paid for or trade it in and get a newer Buick."

"Whatya tell her?"

"I told her she was talking crazy."

"I don't know. Selling the clothes is a lot of trouble; donation would be a good tax deduction. Sleeping downstairs is more convenient, and the Galaxie's crap. I'd trade it in."

"Joe, this is serious. He's not even asleep in there."

"It's healthy. She's making plans."

"There's an order of things. Mourn first, then make your plans."

"Mourning's no different than facing a danger; you never know how you'll respond to it until you're there. Everybody mourns in due time so don't sweat the order. It's the moving forward that some people never get around to."

"You read that somewhere?" she asked, an air of sarcasm in her voice.

"No. It's mine but I don't even know if I believe it."

"Well, I need to get her out of there, for her sake and his. That makes it your turn."

"I'm not sitting in there alone."

"Joe, he's dying. I'd think you'd enjoy that."

He was asleep when I went in. It gave me the opportunity to look at him without worrying about him looking back. I didn't resemble him. I was taller. My nose was smaller. My eyes weren't as deeply set. My teeth were straighter. I looked for other differences, as many as I could find, as if a sufficient number would break our genetic chain.

The man in the bed was a stranger to me in so many ways. He was dying and I could easily see myself being the one to worry about how to dispose of his clothes and turn a profit on his car. If he was to awake to talk about our times together I'd be at a loss. But of course, so would he, so the point was moot.

I picked up a *Sport* magazine and looked at my watch. It was three-thirty. The patient on the other side of the screen moaned and coughed, I presumed in his sleep. My father was peaceful enough to be dead already. I settled in for a short stay.

My mind couldn't let go of our last conversation. It was not pleasant, not for me. It was two days before he was brought to Mercy, when his mind was set on reflection. "Tell me about her now" he muttered, barely audible. "My mother."

I was hoping he was talking in his sleep. His eyes were opened but staring blankly at the ceiling. He could be asleep, I thought, or in some hallucinogenic state. "Shoulda been me there when she died 'stead of you, Joe."

"What do you want me to tell you?"

"Was she good to you?"

"Very good."

"Did she pay attention to you?"

"She brought me books to read."

"Which?"

"The only one I remember by name is *Little LuLu and her Magic Tricks.'*

He smiled and turned his head to me. "*The Poky Little Puppy* was my favorite."

"I read that, too," I said. "I read while she rocked in her chair. A candle, I remember a candle."

"Where were you when she died?"

"Dad, I told you, I was with her."

"So young for you to see that." He was on the verge of an apology.

"Your uncles, did you see them?"

I reminded him of my drive to Jericho with Nadirah and the mysterious Hatim. Then the week spent with my cousins. I was feeling melancholy enough to share my first day climbing the Zacchaeus Tree. I left out the rumors about Hatim being a criminal, in case he didn't know. But I told him about the wonderful relationship Ramiz and Sureia seemed to have with their four boys.

"He was the sensitive one, Ramiz, the peacemaker. I sent you there for a better life," he said. "I wanted you to become a better man."

"Kinda backfired."

"No, son. You're not done yet."

His stare was once again blank and a thousand miles away. He showed no sign he was giving any of his attention to my stories. I expected an appreciative smile in knowing not every moment was hell for me; that I read his books and ran the same streets, and climbed the same tree. That we spoke of him fondly. But even in death his ego held firm. What I thought was a time of atonement was really just an inventory he was taking. He would rather have been told how Nadirah ignored me; how my uncles mistreated me, and my cousins teased. As Yamma said, the dying didn't have time to romanticize death; they were too busy doing it.

This night he surprised me with a moment I initially mistook for an incoherent utterance. "There's a cobweb in the corner of the room. If I get up to brush it away, it will be gone. If I don't, it will still be there tomorrow," he said.

I sighed deeply. He was never one to be overly concerned with cleanliness of the house. Perhaps in his last days he was feeling the need to not only take inventory but straighten up as well. "I'll take care of it." I got up and looked in the corner. It was there, in a place I couldn't reach without a chair to stand on.

"Listen to me, Nasser. Alive I can choose to do or not do things. That choice makes a difference no matter how small. But when I'm gone…." He stopped for reasons known only to himself. "I can no longer make a difference by what I do or what I fail to do."

I was standing on the chair. From the corner of my eye, I saw him staring up at me waiting for a response. What did he want from me? A new prognosis that he wasn't going to die? A declaration that there was still plenty of time for him to effect change and make differences in the world? Or was he just waiting for me to sweep the damn cobweb out of the corner?

Shit, if he wasn't going to come around even now to apologize he should have had the decency to have gone into a coma. He should have drifted into that good night and left me alone. Instead he came back to life to throw a sorry-ass metaphor at me. *You must change,* he was telling me. *I couldn't. I didn't, but you Nasser, you must change.*

I swept the cobweb away with my hand and hopped off the chair. "There you go dad, we made a difference. Together we made something happen. How about that? I'm glad we had this opportunity to clear the air."

I shook my head, dropped the magazine on the floor, and left his bedside. They were in the waiting room. Sue gasped at my approach. "Oh God, is he—"

"No, he's still here."

"What happened?"

I pushed for the elevator. "We had a moment, Sue. Happy? We had ourselves a moment."

CHAPTER 48

I became a regular at the Juniper Café, to the point people began to grab my shoulder and greet me by name. I still didn't eat the food, but I'd float out the door on coffee, as much as I could hold just to stay and talk with Michie. That was her name, Michelle Regas.

She was second generation Greek-American and had worked in restaurants since she was thirteen. I estimated that to be half her life since she wouldn't give me her age. She bought Juniper's two years ago with her share of her father's inheritance. "You, like, get any time off?" I asked as a prelude to requesting a date.

"Nope."

"Never?"

"Never," she said absolutely as her prelude to refusing me.

But I was persistent to the point I knew when her staff was working so she couldn't duck me by using work as an excuse. She did anyway. "I own the place, I have to be here."

"Bet Walt Disney isn't at Disneyland twenty-four/seven," I said.

"He's dead."

"See."

"This is a restaurant, they'll rob me blind."

"You think that little of them, fire them."

"Can't do that until they do it."

"Is that the game? Hire people you think will rip you off then spend endless hours trying to catch them?"

"It's what restaurant workers do," she said.

"Yes, the good folks of this great neighborhood who are so devoted to you."

But most of the time I just sat quietly at the counter. "You complain a lot, don't you?" she said the one night she was feeling social and I was about to give up trying.

"I'm just sitting here." It came sounding so much like Eeyore the donkey from *Winnie-the-Pooh* that even I had to laugh at myself.

"Oh, yeah?" she said. "And thinking about the wonderful day you had, how blessed, how miraculous."

"Something like that."

"You know what I know?"

"That your employees are thieves and I'm a miserable wretch."

"That the people who come in here and bitch a lot are angry. The ones who come in and bitch just a little are hurt. And those like you who sit at this counter with their heads down and mouths shut, never saying a word, they're bitter."

"Why can't it be I'm just being quiet 'cause I like it that way?" I said.

"Happy people can't do that. The fact you don't know that tells me how miserable you are."

"And this labeling system of yours is fool proof?"

"Has been so far; don't see you being the exception."

"I've been in here like seven times and—"

"Eight," she said.

She'd been counting. I liked that. Then again, I keep track of the number of pigs I've butchered. "Eight times trying to talk to you, trying to ask you out. You got no interest in me so I see no sense in talking."

"I'll go out with you," she said.

"I don't need no mercy date."

"This isn't a mercy date. Just never knew you were asking."

I thought I was home free until she asked me where we were going. "Now?" I said.

"What? You like a relief pitcher, you need to throw some warm ups before going into the game?"

I knew lots of places to go but none that I'd use to impress a woman like her. Something told me that although she worked in a greasy family restaurant, that wasn't the type of place she went for a good time. "I don't know, a movie, maybe," I said.

She shrugged. "Okay, I'll grab my coat. Which one?"

The last movie I saw in a theater was *Dog Day Afternoon.* I thought back on some of the current one's but *Porky's* was the only one I recalled hearing anything about. From what I heard, it wasn't going to work tonight. "I'd like to see *Tootsie,*" she said.

It wasn't nearly as bad a movie as it sounded. Without it being said, we became a couple. It was a different fit than the relationship I had with Jennifer. Jennifer was the one I went to when things became overwhelming which was often until I became indifferent to most things. She was a good ear, a soft shoulder, a gentle touch. But I wanted to be with Michie, no matter my mood, no matter hers, even when she went off on a tirade which she did easily and often. "Feisty," was the word her cook used to describe her, being diplomatic knowing I was seeing her.

"Think so?" I said. "Bitch is closer."

He nodded just slightly in agreement, not wanting to fully commit.

She lived with her mother so the closest I could get to her at night was her living room couch. I quit my job at the packinghouse so I could collect at more reasonable hours, leaving me time to see her. Of course, she knew only of my packinghouse job. "You clean up well," she'd tell me when I got off work. "Yeah, well, you're worth it." So went our sweet talk.

"You should quit there," she told me on several occasions.

"Think so?"

"I do."

"Hmmm. Maybe I will."

She wasn't down on me for the job. "Wasn't for guys like you I'd have no bacon."

"Maybe we should all quit then."

I hated the smell, look, taste, and touch of the stuff, and it started well before the job slaughtering them, though that cemented it. I couldn't separate the grease from the meat in my mind. It seemed as if the meat was an afterthought, something that hung around the pan when the grease was ready to be served.

I told, Michie, "I'll drink your coffee and eat your toast and omelets, but not the pig." She didn't show offense to that, but when I suggested serving a fried cube of Crisco in place of saganaki cheese, she refused to serve me even the coffee. "And if you weren't already sleeping on the couch, you'd be sleeping on the couch." We were both half kidding.

I slept at home when I wasn't at Michie's but had no relationship with my mother, David, or Sue. My mother went from part time to full time as a filing clerk at a Honda dealership. Since my father's death there was a new bounce in her step. I won't say she was happier, maybe more at ease.

David was working at Sue's school as a janitor. He was either being very righteous in his rehab or not hanging in areas I was in. I kept my distance out of respect and anger for Sue's appeal. The fact was it was a matter of time before David went back to his old ways. Nothing I would do, and nothing she could do, would stop this but I was willing to let it play out naturally.

To me, we all start off like balls of mud tossed down a hill. We gain speed, size, and all types of refuse as we go. The older we get, the bigger the ball, the less chance we have of redirecting ourselves. If our course is a good one, so be it. If it leads us toward a fatal crash there's little we can do, even if we see it coming. We're sent on our courses long before we know it. Most of us grab hold of whatever sanity we can along the way. It's all luck. It's why I held out little hope for David and even less for myself. Michie was the sanity I grabbed hold of before my final crash.

I came into Juniper's early on a Wednesday evening. Michie was in the kitchen with a Hispanic man and woman. The man was on a chair, his face in his hands, sobbing like a baby while his wife stroked his back and Michie whispered in his ear. I ordered an apple pie from the waitress while I watched Mama Michie work and all I could think was, the nerve of these two coming in here to unload on her. I was sure their IOU was the topic of conversation. And Michie would be sure to extend their credit until the guy got off his ass or on his feet, whatever his sob story was.

I enjoyed watching her from here, without her knowing, as I supposed many a man had done over the years. But there was nothing sexual in my attraction, not this time. I watched her compassion and gentleness in time of this man's distress. It was something I knew I'd never have, or rather, never have again. In my fantasy, we'd marry and in our vows she would promise to love, honor, cherish, and show me how to have such rahmah.

She had beaten the anger of this neighborhood by taking it in. She didn't criticize or seek change. She didn't pass judgment. She didn't defend. She didn't attack. She didn't organize. She didn't shun. Yet in her cool, subtle way, she did all that by accepting its victims and their world. Of all the skills I had learned, I trade them all for such a gift.

She saw me and the meeting broke up. I think she was somewhat school girl-embarrassed because the first thing she wanted to know when she sat across from me was how long I'd been watching her. "Wasn't watching," I said, "I was leering at you with evil intent."

"Stand in line, mister." She leaned across the table to sniff at me. "You don't smell pig-like. You work today?"

"Could have been I showered before I came here?"

"That's the kind of stink that lingers after the hottest showers. 'Sides," she looked at the clock, "you don't get off work for another half hour."

"Played hooky. But don't tell the teacher, it'll go on my permanent record."

It wasn't George Carlin but I was getting a sense of humor back. Not every look or comment was negative, and not every one was about me. In her disarming way, she taught me that. No other woman could get me laughing in the middle of lovemaking by saying she'd rather smell the actual pig than me.

But actually I was working. I made a collection down in Gary. I got the eight grand from a pharmacist who had become addicted to his own Percocet but didn't dare risk his license by having it prescribed to himself. So he got on the hook with the Chicago mob for twelve grand, a figure they dropped by a third to give him a break, knowing his addiction would keep him coming back for more. In his office, in front of the eight-by-ten of him with his wife and three children, all below the age of ten, he tearfully counted out the bills he took from the three tills in his pharmacy, plus some he had stashed in a locked drawer.

"That an old picture?" I asked, nodding at his wife and kids.

"Huh?' No, last year. Why?"

"No reason." Shame. I was hoping it was about ten years ago and the kids were in medical or dental school by now. But he looked the same as in the photo so I figured it was a recent one. His thing was, he was freaked I was coming after them next. I didn't dispel it. A little bit of fear helps; a lot makes my job brainless.

My take went up to twenty-five percent if I came back with the eight in one trip. I told the guy this as if it was small talk, as if it didn't motivate me in the least, but I think he saw that two grand motivated me a great deal. I knew what I was going to do with part it.

"That guy crying himself out of his tab?" I said.

"He's in a bind is all."

"Hey, get away tonight? I got somewhere I want to take you."

"Where's that?"

"*The Pump Room.*"

"Joe, I've been dying to go there. And you got reservations for tonight? You must have gotten them months ago, why didn't you give me notice?" She was unabashedly giddy. All eyes were on us as if I had proposed to her.

"I have my connections; made the call and made it happened." As it happened, it was the first act of self aggrandizing I had displayed to her. My timing couldn't have been worse.

"I can't," she said.

"Don't say you can't, not on this one. The place will survive without you for the night."

"Okay, yeah, why not? Let me handle a few things back there and I'll be ready in fifteen, no, ten minutes. What time is the—"

"Whenever we get there," I said, it being another part of my deal in collecting the money, having a table set aside for the night.

She hurried to the kitchen but was pulled over by the Hispanic couple who had taken a booth three down and across from us. The man whose back was to me was whispering to her, his thumb pointing back in my direction. Michie stood and stared back at me, her mouth twisted sour and confused. She told the guy to get up; I could hear that angry growl. It pissed me off enough that I started to get up to help, but I had seen for myself Michie's no-nonsense approach with customers and knew I'd just be in the way.

Still I wondered what he could have said to turn her against him so vehemently as she continued to coax him out of the booth. Finally he did, and he and his wife exited quickly. Michie glared back at me giving her a thumbs up. "You know that man?" she demanded, pointing into the parking lot.

"No," I said without looking out the window.

"Look, damn you."

"Fine." I looked but they were in the car speeding out of the lot. "Okay. What did he do?"

"He didn't do shit. What did you do?"

We had everyone's attention again but it wasn't her sweet cooing that captured it. "I have no clue of—"

"He's positive he knows you, Joe. Dead positive."

"How?"

"Did you try to collect money from him?"

I felt it; that *oh shit* look coming on to me. I tried to fight it, tried to reel it back it but it came in on a rip tide. And it was the poster child of *oh shit* faces. I was caught completely off guard. I didn't get a good look at the guy, and the truth was there was a good chance I wouldn't have remembered him. I tried to forget them as soon as the job was done. "No," I said, pathetically unconvincing.

"Oh, Joe, I should have known. How does a stockyard boy get money and connections for a place like the *The Pump Room*? You've been lying to me, Joe. You've been drinking my coffee, sleeping at my house, and lying to me."

We were Juniper Cafe's floor show at the moment so I asked to speak about it in private. She obliged, in part, by storming away to her back office. I followed and had to yell through her locked door. "Let me explain," I said.

"You can't," she yelled back. "My dad dealt with guys like you all the time. You can justify a hit-and-run better than you can extorting money from people."

"It's not extortion. I collect owed money."

I hit a nerve. She threw open the door. "Collect? You collect? Charities collect. Coin and stamp collectors collect. When a big thug like you shows up at the door, no one thinks, 'collection.'"

"I'm not a thug. And call it what you want, these people owe money for legitimate debts."

She put her hand against the doorjamb and leaned on it. "People. Collection. Legitimate debt. See, even you, a thug—and, yes, Joe, you are a thug for doing what you do—have to put a face on it that you can stomach. So you use words that soften it. But the fact is you see it as taking from pathetic slobs who aren't worth shit in your book. You see them as losers, dopers, addicts, deadbeats. And I see them as I saw my father, desperate men who needed a helping hand and when the very banks they used and relied on weren't willing to suffer with them, they turned to men like your boss."

"Don't give drug users that much credit, Michie."

"Tell me, Joe, would your folks give them an aspirin? An antacid tablet? A Band Aid? Or do they only give the highly addictive drugs, the ones that guarantee repeat business? Yeah, I thought as much. You're like them; you only give a shit about the results.

"But collecting the money isn't the end, not for them. Luis Vasquez, that's the man you're leaning on for a thousand dollars, gambled to get money to keep his hardware store going. See, his last few quarters' numbers were down so the bank called in his loan. I don't get gambling but whatever was supposed to happen with the Chicago Cubs didn't. Next thing he knows you're at his store talking about the proper weight hammer to use for beating thick objects. I could use his money a lot more than your people but I told him to keep the fifty he owes me. "

"It wasn't a threat," I said.

"Save it I'm not a cop. You see him the way you're told to; you don't care that he has five beautiful kids. His wife cleans houses. He works fifteen hours a day, seven days a week to barely get by. He goes to church every Sunday. He prays for one thing and it's not world peace or the end of disease. He wants his children to go to college. He has two thousand dollars saved for it, and you told him he has thirty days or you're coming back to take it."

"I didn't know."

"That's no fuckin' excuse, Joe, and I want you to know I never use that word so that's how much I mean it. Don't come back."

I give her credit. She didn't slam the door in my face. Instead she closed it gently and somehow, that had more of an impact. It had me standing there paralyzed, unwilling to recognize the best thing I ever had was over.

"Hey." It was Michie, calling out the front door as I walked to my car. Reluctantly I turned around. "You really work at a packinghouse?"

"Yeah."

"For real?"

"You've smelled me for yourself."

"Quit. And quit your other job."

"What?"

"Can you cook?"

"Yeah. Sure."

"Start here next week. And I want proof you've quit. Both jobs."

"How am I supposed to prove that I left the other job?"

"Don't worry, I'll know."

CHAPTER 49

She was a hard-ass drill sergeant. And talk about threats. But it was good. I quit but found quitting as a strong-arm didn't make me popular. "We know where David's living," they said. It was a warning not to become a snitch. I told them I was quitting because I didn't want to hurt people anymore, not because I'd forgotten how.

While she and her head cook taught me Greek omelets, gyros, and moussaka, I taught them chicken fatteh, knafeh, and qatayef. Some of it I had to improvise, but I surprised myself at how much I remembered from helping Yamma.

I bought the old Ford Galaxie from my mother and not for a favorite-son price. I was living at Michie's house full-time now. Her mother was almost nonexistent in her quiet ways. Still, it wasn't healthy if Michie and I were to have anything more than a employer-employee relationship. We chose to get our own place but near her mother so Michie could be there for her. We couldn't afford much. I had a substantial nest egg from my collections job, but she wouldn't let me use it.

"You know what you're getting into?" she said. "There's not much profit. Everything I make goes back into the operation. Rent and food costs go up faster than my prices. Layoffs out there mean layoffs in here. There's waste and theft under my nose." She was right. There were months I went without pay because there were months she didn't have it. But we did well. We did very well, and money had little to do with it.

"Why did you call me back that day?" I asked her.

"I knew you. There was great potential, and I didn't want to lose you."

I smiled. "You love me."

"That your interpretation?"

"Yeah." It was as close as we got to saying it in those days but it worked for me.

For my birthday she bought me a Garrard GT-10 turntable and Infinity speakers. I went home for the first time in three months to retrieve the collection of record albums I left there. Sue's car, my mother's new Honda, and another car were in the driveway. I hadn't seen or spoken with Sue or David in nearly a year. They could love me for that or hate me. I didn't much care which.

I heard them in the kitchen. It was Sue, my mother, and two others I didn't know: another woman and a man who were speaking in measuredArabic. I eavesdropped from the foyer. The woman laughed. I knew that laugh. My breathing stopped and my heart lifted. I liked where it was taking me, yet it couldn't be, not here, not all these years later.

She was the first one to see me; Johara, older, heavier, but with the same smile that captured me back then. "It's been so long, my dear cousin," she said in clear English. "I've missed you." We hugged. Then we cried. It wasn't a reunion; it was the continuation of our last good-bye.

Standing in the corner beside my mother was Abdel with a wide, yellow smile he expected me to return. I broke from Johara as reality came back to me. "What are you doing here?" I said to him.

"We heard about the death of your father and Khaal Abu Faid wanted to show his respect," Johara said.

That title of deference again brought back my indignation. And if I had ever wondered if the sight of him would soften those memories I could wonder no more. I had to stop myself from throwing him from the house right then. I had no right to do such a thing, yet there was that urge to show him in the strongest terms that I, at least, did not welcome him here.

He was very gray in his hair and his face, and was now as plump as I recalled Yamma being. He came to greet me. I threw my hand out at him. "No," I said. "Don't come near me." He didn't need to know English to interpret the meaning.

"Joe," my mother said. "Our guest."

"Not mine. Johara, it's great to see you, and we've got a lot to catch up on. But keep that man far away from me. I'm not a little boy anymore and I won't hesitate to let him know that. Where are you staying?"

Johara looked nervously at my mother.

"They're staying with me, Joe," my mother said.

I narrowed my eyes and nodded slowly, emphasizing my disapproval.

"Stop this, Joe," Sue said.

My rage surged through a pipe with a closed valve, searching for release but nothing would come. I felt it backing up inside and I was damned if it would explode inside me again. "Johara," I said. "I'll be back in two hours for you. We'll talk then."

***

Michie was not happy with my going out again. She wasn't trusting me completely yet, though it was her strategy not to accuse me. "Distant relatives came in," I told her. "All the way from Palestine. I need to spend some time with them."

"Have you met them before?"

"No." I still wasn't ready to discuss that past with anyone.

"I'll come with you."

"Michie, I'm trying to reach out to my mother. She wouldn't understand us living together and—"

"We won't tell her."

"But I'll have to explain you."

"You're twenty-four years old, Joe. Don't you think she'd welcome a girl in your life?"

"It's not a good time."

"I see. You don't think your mother will like me?"

"No. That's not it. She doesn't even know about you."

"Joe, I realize you're new to this, but if you're ever asked that again by a girl, and I hope you're not, the answer is, 'she'll love you; who wouldn't?'"

It was the second time she almost told me how she felt in spite of the anxiety our conversation caused. It felt pretty good.

I was taking Johara to a coffee and bake shop Jennifer and I frequented years before on the Near West Side. She was initially quiet on the ride, thinking she played a part in my outburst at the house. It wasn't until we were north on Western through the Heart of Italy district that I broke the ice. It was slow going on this warm October night. The sidewalks, street corners, and eventually the intersections were full of restaurant and bar patrons who strolled the area recklessly like hand-fed park squirrels.

"He's your father," I said, "so no offense, but I can't bear the thought of him, never mind the sight."

"I understand, Joe. You haven't had time to make amends with him."

Had we been sitting in a booth rather than navigating crazy streets, I would have given her a mystified stare. To cut to the chase I said, "Are you serious?" Amends? Did he start healing lepers or something? 'Cause that's what it would take."

"He was a young father like you were a young boy. Time has moved on for him, Joe." There was her implied insinuation that I had not, but I let it go.

We sat brooding and licking wounds long enough to make it insufferable. Silence over a plate of food was more bearable than silence at a traffic light. "You like Italian?" I asked.

"Italian what?"

"Doesn't matter. We're stuck in the middle of it so may as well do it."

I swung east onto Oakley to Ignotz's. I got a kick out of introducing her to mushroom pizza. "Makes no sense fighting old battles; too much I want to ask you," I said, "Let's start from the beginning."

"I'd like that."

"I'm glad you're here. I never thought I'd see you again."

"It's why I came, to see you and Sue."

I ordered a draught beer for me, for her a root beer, another first. "No more grape Nehi?" she said.

"God, grape Nehi. No, not in years. Do I dare ask? How's Yamma?"

"I'll give you the skinny on all of them."

"Skinny? Sound like a native."

"I'm addicted to American soaps. So, Yamma is fine. She's painting."

"Really?"

"She's sold a few, too. As far away as Ramallah. But most of them she props on shelves or gives away. She turned the bedroom you slept in into a studio. You may or may not enjoy hearing this but she's doing landscapes again. All of them have two small boys in them."

"Adli and Gamal?" I said.

"Adli and you."

She was right; I didn't want to hear that.

"She's not good with figures, human or animal, so you're always in the distance. In all of them you are running or jumping or playing soccer or basketball."

"She knew about the basketball?"

"Of course. One painting has you playing with a dog. It was Amir, she told me. 'Don't think Joe or Adli would agree with that scene,' I told her. 'It's how I see it,' she said. I swear she's always had the artist in her."

"Are she and Abdel back together?"

"He tried. She still wouldn't take him back."

"That bother you?"

I caught her with a mouthful of pizza, a foot of cheese from her mouth to the plate. I took the slice from her hand and she laughed as I twirled the cheese with it. "Not couth, but very American and effective," I said.

"I see. Fun food, like cotton candy. No, I wasn't bothered. Yamma and I have moved on. And Gamal. Gamal has moved on. He's a very successful chemical engineer in Jordan."

"And Faid?" I almost didn't want to bring him up, not knowing how much she knew about his assaults on Sue. I hit a raw nerve. I saw it right away, the way she fluttered her eyelids just before lowering her head for a moment to regroup.

"He ... he was killed during a raid in Amman where he was working. He was an engineer, as well."

"I'm sorry to hear that. Losing two children, and two brothers, that's hard."

"You lost two sisters."

"Not in war."

"I got the impression talking to Sue that you've been distant from the family."

"We've had issues," I said.

"But you walked out on your father on his deathbed."

"Have you been here for like two weeks without me knowing, or did you and Sue start your re-acquaintance with me and my problems?"

"It evolved into you. That the right word?"

"I guess. A man who lived at our house died. That's how I look at it."

"But, Joe, your father."

"I had no childhood so I have no memories of him as a father. But that's right, you do. You've made amends with the man who walked out on your family and caused the death of your brother."

"Joe, that's not fair."

"He's why Adli begged to go to Ramallah that day."

"My father was heartbroken. He realized what he had done was wrong."

"Too late."

"For Adli perhaps, not for my father."

"We're going sideways again," I said.

"I don't know that phrase."

The question that nagged me most from that day in June was tattooed on my brain. If I were allotted just one question in life, I would ask it. But I feared the answer, and the question made me feel shameful. It sent cold sweats down my back and arms when I brought it into consciousness. "Johara?"

"Yes."

"Adli."

She stopped picking the discarded mushrooms from the pan when I mentioned his name. "Did he ... I mean, his body, was it—"

"Found?"

I nodded.

She slid the pan away and reached her hands across to grasp mine. They were so small now, childlike, but they were the ones doing the comforting. "Yes. It was a beautiful funeral. The entire village was there.

"Yamma asked permission from the imam to have him buried outside a cemetery."

"Why?"

"She told the Imam of Adli's life. His troubles with school, friends, his father, until you came. Until you showed him how to not be afraid."

I started to protest. "But I didn't—"

"No offense," she said as she squeezed my hands, "but you don't know what you did and didn't do for Adli. You were a child. You didn't know him before. Yamma asked for him to be buried in the cave."

I was struck dumb. He was scared to death of that cave. He did his damnedest to avoid it, to go around it as far as possible. I laughed at him, teased him about it, as I reminded Johara.

"Don't you remember that night in the kitchen when Faid called Adli 'Ibn haram,' bastard child?"

"No."

"It was the night we all found out why Ab left us; when he accused Yamma of infidelity. Yamma took Adli outside so he wouldn't hear more, and he took her inside the cave. Yamma was shocked. 'I stood right here,' he told Yamma with so much pride, 'right here the way Joe does. Joe told me it was the bravest thing he'd ever seen.'

"It made Yamma cry to see him proud of himself. He thought Yamma was crying in fear and told her nothing would happen to her in the cave, that he and you would never let things hurt her."

I nodded. "That's not exactly what I said."

"A lot of what makes us who we are our misconceptions, Joe. Good and bad. Yamma asked for him to be buried where he found himself, where he became free. See, Joe, your spirit has always been with us."

When I left Dayr Ghasana I tried to make myself feel such remorse again, such internal pain, yet nothing had the impact. I came to the belief that love and misery were finite emotions most people were able to ration throughout a lifetime. And there were the occasional great loves and losses that depleted us, and made us like the ghost of Jacob Marley, forced to carry around the chains of a heavy emptiness. I was on the verge of begging her to take it all back when I buried my face into her hands. "Tell me Yamma didn't see his body," I pleaded.

"Yes, but it was okay. It was okay. Captain Pfalzer brought him to us."

"Who?'

"The Israeli officer who took you home. He brought him to us about a week after you left. He had him cleaned up. He even stayed for the funeral in spite of the angry words he had to withstand."

"But Adli's head?"

She looked confused. "I don't know what you mean, Joe. He had some scarring but ... he looked very peaceful. He truly did."

Suddenly Adli was in my head sleeping peacefully, his face flushed with color, the black ringlets of his hair folded over his forehead and ears. He had made it home, and though I knew better, I saw him resting contentedly among those who loved him. "That's good, Johara, I'm glad for that. But why did you and Abdel come to Chicago. For real."

CHAPTER 50

I was happy for Yamma and Gamal. I was relieved for the closure with Adli. I had no reason to doubt Johara's assertion he looked peaceful. I don't know how Captain Pfalzer made that happen. Or perhaps I had only imagined the ghastliness and carried it around in me all these years.

I didn't celebrate Faid's fate as it surely added to Yamma's pain. But neither did I dwell heavily on it. I didn't know if he was a combatant, or like Adli, an innocent bystander, but I saw him cowering in the corner of a basement, not leading a night raid.

Johara lit up when talking of Yamma and Gamal; it was quite another matter when talk came of herself. Humility had nothing to do with it. She hadn't gone to college, though she was planning on taking classes in Ramallah once a week. Elementary education, she thought. At thirty-two she was still at home, caring for the olive trees and animals as Yamma had done. And, as she told me, caring for Bara'ah.

I looked at her quizzically. "So much you have forgotten, Joe. Bara'ah is my father's other child."

"You still have her?" I asked.

She laughed. "Is she a car we would trade in? Or maybe like a dog who's passed her life span? Of course she is with us. She's doing wonderfully, a real lady. And so beautiful. But pure in all her ways. I'm hoping she will meet you someday."

I didn't know what I expected. Maybe that Abdel would come back to reclaim her. Such a notion, though, was as farcical as thinking Faid could lead the fight for independence. Johara had become more than a big sister; she had become a mother without the trials and tribulations of love and marriage. Which made me ask about Sam. "I thought he'd be the first one you'd ask about," she said. "I was beginning to think you had forgotten him, too,"

"Is he a journalist?"

She bit her lip and nodded thoughtfully. "Yes. Yes, I guess you can say he is. And his writings have given us quite a bit of popularity."

"Is he a famous writer there?"

"Not famous. What you call ... infamous. And it's us; Yamma, Ab, and me who have become popular from him."

"I don't get it."

"'Course you don't. Why would you way over here? Though we've only been told this by the Israelis, he's a member of the Liberation Organization known as the PLO. Have your heard of it?"

"No. Makes sense though, the way he always talked. I take it the Israelis aren't happy with them."

"Not much. Sam has become quite the propagandist for them, according to the Israelis, that is."

As in my first days in Palestine when I needed her for Arabic interpretations, I found myself needing her for this English one. "What's a propagandist?"

"A journalist, as you said, who writes about a cause for a cause."

"Like a newspaper reporter."

"No, not like that. Reporters look at all sides. They report facts, not conclusions. A propagandist writes to convince the reader of an issue as he sees it. It's good if you believe and want to believe. It's bad if you want to use your own judgment. I wouldn't put it pass Sam to be involved with the PLO, nor would I put it past the occupiers to make it up as a reason to execute him."

"Execute?"

"Men are arrested everyday for much less. They visit us often to check up on him."

"Sam lives with you?"

"He visits on occasion. But they know he is a relative and used to come around often. They think he still does."

"They've followed him."

"Perhaps. But there are many in the village who cooperate with the Israeli occupation forces for money and other favors."

I never did contemplate the consequences of the war. I knew Israel won from Johnny Carson who said Moshe Dayan had to win in six days because he only rented the tanks for a week. But now I knew it had created fifteen years of late night visits, neighborhood snitches, military raids, and subversion. I couldn't see room in there for boys wasting summer days on the Red River, or being so innocent as to be camping on hillsides or tracing constellations from a window sill.

For sure Johara had no time for such days. On the day Bara 'ah came into her life, she gave up whatever youth she had left. And when the war came, her innocence was taken. Like me, she learned of the real world too early. Unlike me, she stayed behind to live in it.

My thoughts turned to Michie who at twenty-six was the sole owner of a restaurant, had been for three years. She had negotiated leases and bank loans. She hired, fired, did payroll, requisitioning, inventory, and marketing. She handled health inspectors, contractors, and zoning boards. She was cook, administrator, arbitrator, and confidante. And there was none of it, not one aspect, that Johara couldn't have done, given the opportunity.

"I like the Italian," she said on the drive home.

"Well, that was one of the most authentic," I said. "Don't think all Italian will be that good."

"I know. We tried Waraq al-'ainib when we got here. Not very good."

I was moved by her story of Adli's funeral and heartened by her update on Yamma, yet I felt much of her talk was a diversion from my original question. I knew my father's death was more of an alibi than a motivation for their visit. Maybe nothing devious, Johara not a having such a mind, but there were no talks of a visit to see him alive so I saw no benefits in coming to see him dead. I knew for sure she was avoiding the subject when she went into tales of the villagers until it appeared she'd take me through the entire Dayr Ghasana phone book if I didn't interject.

I decided on a different tact. "So how long you staying?" I asked, interrupting her story about Rami, a twelve-year-old village boy who was arrested for throwing a rock at an Israeli Jeep that drove past his school.

She sighed. "It depends, Joe."

"On what?"

"I accompanied my father here because he asked me to. Your assumptions are correct. Your father's death was why he came, but it wasn't your father he came to talk about. Or see."

It took a while to sink in, mainly because it was so absurd. I knew it wasn't me on Abdel's agenda. It wouldn't dare be Sue. He didn't know David. We were about a mile from home when I got it. I had three sets of traffic lights and a stop sign ahead of me, but I was back in the house in less than two minutes.

"Now don't go crazy," Johara was saying to me on the way home. "It's just a fantasy to him."

Telling me my mother was Abdel's fantasy wasn't easing my mind. There were the three of them sitting in the living room when I burst in, looking as if I was on a fire run. Abdel was sitting in my father's chair which would have pissed me off regardless because he was sitting in a chair in my house. Knowing he was taking it for a test drive really set me off.

Sue was laughing at something said. Johara must have given her the high sign because she jumped up and bolted in our direction, grabbing my arm as she rushed by. I pulled away easily and took her chair across from Abdel who sat very comfortably, very in control. I was raging inside but used my persona as a strong-arm to break him down. I leaned back and stared into him. I realized my anger made my breathing irregular. Slowly I brought it under control while maintaining my gaze on him.

My mother asked, "What's wrong with you, Joe?"

"Nothing." That was good. Monotone and casual, and without blinking. Abdel was beginning to fumble in the chair.

"Joe, let's talk," Sue said.

"No."

"You're acting very strange," my mother said. "Are you high?"

I ignored her. I wanted Abdel to know he was why I was sitting here, and that I knew why he was here. I crossed my legs to let him know I was settling in for a while. I reached for a roll of butterscotch Lifesavers on the coffee table without losing eye contact. I didn't even like butterscotch. I just wanted him to feel me as I leaned in.

Speaking first would break the mood. I was ready to sit and stare all night, if necessary. Sue attempted to coax me from the room while my mother questioned my sobriety, but Abdel knew what was going on and broke first to show himself the good guest. "Did you two have a nice drive?" he asked.

There was a sick silence until Johara told him she had a mushroom pizza. "What was the place called, Joe?"

"You like sitting in that chair, do you, Abdel?" I said.

Sue was acting the big sister. "Joe!"

"It's very comfortable," he said, staring at and rubbing the armrest to avoid my gaze, and appear as if he believed my question was a serious one.

"It was a father's day gift," my mother said. "Do you remember the year, Sureia?"

"Sue, take mom out of the room," I ordered.

"I will not."

"Fine. Mom, will you leave Abdel and me alone?"

"I'm worried about the way you're acting," she said.

"Don't be. Abdel and I haven't talked in a long while and we both have things to say to each other, don't we, Abdel?"

"I'm sure," he said nervously.

"I do have dinner to prepare. I won't hear any screaming will I?"

"I don't scream," I said.

I waited for her to leave as I eyed Sue and Johara. It was the first time I took my eyes off Abdel. "I'm not leaving," Sue said.

"Sue, you left a situation like this before, you can do it now," I said sternly.

"That was a horrid thing to say," she said. "I can't believe—"

"Do you know why he's here?"

"Yes."

"And how do you feel about it?"

She shrugged, telling me what I needed to know. "It's harmless at this point," she said.

"Harmless. Then at what point did the events in Dayr Ghasana turn harmful to you?"

"Stop it Joe, there's no need to bring that up now. And not here."

Johara's face twisted in a quizzical knot as she tried to think back so her mind could catch up with our conversation. I could tell she never learned about her brother's attacks on Sue. It wasn't my intention to tell her, or even discuss it with Abdel. What I had to say to Abdel involved no discussion whatsoever.

Abdel had become gray and flabby. He was barely five-foot ten, hardly an intimidation to me any longer. His eyes were still dark but no longer piercing. His scowl was gone, replaced by sagging jowls and wrinkles. And he looked scared, as if I was about to throttle him. The running diatribes I had with him in my head over the years involved things I should have said about things that happened back then. I never thought there'd be new situations to confront him on, though in a sadistic way, I'm glad one came along to offer me this chance.

I slid my chair across the floor to get as close to him as I could. "You have some nerve coming into my house like this," I said.

"Your mother could have me leave if she likes." Though his outward appearance had betrayed him he held fast to his pomposity.

"I don't like you," I said. "I never did."

"You made that clear back in my home."

"No. No, I didn't, not as clearly as I wanted to."

"So be it," he said, "that was then. I've come to offer condolences and support for your mother in her time of mourning."

"That's bullshit." I don't think he knew the word but my tone was unmistakable. "My father's been dead for a year. And you never offered a thing. All you did was take their money and give them lies."

"I never lied."

"All you did was lie."

My plan to remain cool and calm was gone. My face was flushed from rage. I was leaning forward into his face. My finger was thrusting him like a dagger. My mother had joined Sue and Johara at the doorway. She held her hand to her mouth as if she was witnessing a murder. "You lied about how I was being treated, about how we were spending money, about how *you* were spending it, about Adli, about why Sue tried to kill herself."

I didn't regret bringing out that truth, but as Sue said, it was a very cruel time and place. I stood and leaned close enough to whisper in his ear before leaving.

"It needed to come out," I said as Sue chased me to my car.

"You did it for yourself, not for me," she said. "Don't try to convince me this was the thorn in your side all these years. It was him, it was always him, and this is your way of getting back at him. And maybe back at me."

I backed the car out but stopped to roll down the passenger window to admonish her, "I can't believe you're willing to let him move in with her."

"It wouldn't have happened. Johara and I both laughed about it. Mom can handle herself."

"Don't you even remember how it felt? 'Cause I sure do."

She ran up to the window and lost it. "I remember, Joe. I remember everything, everyday. And all you've done tonight is forced me to relive it. I have to go in there and retell it. Maybe Abdel will deny it. Maybe Johara will fight for her dead brother's honor. Maybe mom will drop dead of a heart attack. And you ... you just drive away."

"He's a pathetic little man," I said. "He needs to be fronted out."

She opened the side door and sat sideways with her legs dangling out. She took deep breaths to calm herself. "What he is is not the point," she said. "Eventually, it has to be about you, Joe. It took me a long time to learn that. You know the memory I really cherish, the one I cling to?"

"What's that?"

"The closeness we developed there." She shook her head. "We didn't have it before and haven't had it since. God gave us that time to share."

"God," I said it as if I stepped in dog shit.

"Don't scoff. We wouldn't have become close; I wouldn't have had my experience of Jerusalem; we wouldn't have met Yamma; we wouldn't have—"

"Yeah, now my turn. We were abandoned there, Sue. Want me to tell you of the other things we wouldn't have experienced? Your rape, the beatings, the—"

"We don't appreciate one without the other, Joe. Bad things accentuate the good if you see life the way it's meant to be seen. Listen to this, please, and try to understand where I'm coming from. What bothers me most now is not what happened to me, it's how I handled it. How I handled it back then at the cave kept me from becoming who I wanted to be. I understand now that Abdel and Faid were never going to make me a good person, so I've decided not to allow them to make me a bad one."

CHAPTER 51

I married Michie on a Sunday afternoon at a justice of the peace in Shipshewana, Indiana. It being Sunday, the clerk was off so it was witnessed by the justice's wife and a guy painting a barn next door. Other then Fininkia, Greece, her father's hometown, it was the only place she cared to visit. We arrived at six, two hours after the restaurant closed for the day. It was closed on Mondays so that day was our honeymoon. It's been our only one since.

When I recommended we get married she told me, "We'll work six days a week, twelve to fifteen hours a day, to make enough to pay overhead, salary, and a few bucks for ourselves at the end of the month if we're lucky."

"We gotta be somewhere," I said, adding nothing to the romance.

Michie didn't invite her mom who was suffering from a host of ailments including dementia. I didn't invite mine because I hadn't talked to her since the night I saw Abdel and Johara at the house. Neither did I invite Sue or David.

Abdel didn't stay. But Johara did, I heard from David who stopped into the restaurant for breakfast. She was living with them now. Sue was working to get her a visa to attend Morton Community College. "It was pretty ugly," he said when I asked if he heard how the rest of that night went.

"What did Sue tell you?"

"Nothing. I heard it from Johara. She was pissed."

"At who?"

"You. Then Faid. Then Abdel. Then Abdel and Faid. Then Sue. Then back to you."

"Where's she stand now?"

"She's over it."

"Already?"

"Yeah. She wants to be a kindergarten teacher. Can I have a job here?"

He was moving on, too. He wanted to open his own restaurant. It wasn't a résumé highlight but he cooked in the prison kitchen. He was taking business courses at the community college. Now he wanted experience.

We had nothing available, but we hired him for a brief time at our first failed venture on the Loop. When we moved back to the south side he stayed on as a cook for our main competitor, then opened a deli three years later. He's still there today.

I had been pushing to move out of the south side since I began working there. I still had connections downtown where I felt we could make a killing. I didn't tell Michie how I made them, though I'm sure she knew. She scoffed at my ideas. "Family places like this never just take off," she said. "They grow slow. The food is just food. It's really nothing special so you develop your reputation with the neighborhood."

"There's no future here," I said. "It'll be hand to mouth every year."

"These people need a place like ours."

"For free handouts? I know you do it, Michie, I've seen it."

"Not very often, and it's leftover food."

When we began to add Palestinian cuisine I was able to convince her that now the food was special enough to make it downtown with the big boys. The rent was double and the parking limited, but I sank all the money I had into it. Reluctantly, she agreed. The neighborhood rented a VFW Hall and threw her a farewell party. We supplied the food.

The first six months were slow. The next six were slower. I asked my old bosses to throw business our way but Michie didn't care for the new clientele. "They order coffee and tip ten bucks, what's with that?" She asked.

"Told you, big money here."

"They give me the creeps."

But it wasn't enough, and it was highly recommended I get back into doing collections again. In lieu of pay I'd get customers, lots of customers. It was tempting but Michie would figure out the connection between my being gone half the night and a restaurant full of creeps. I'm not saying my refusal had anything to do with the lack of business but the timing was suspicious. Even the "regulars" stopped coming by, which was fine by Michie.

But she wasn't happy. Even if the money was all I expected she wouldn't have been. To her, a restaurant was a big kitchen and dining room with customers like family. She worked incredibly hard to make sure the money came in, but her motivation was not to build as much as to maintain. As long as she could open the next day, she was satisfied. It was the source of many arguments that nearly had me walking out.

One night in August she got a call from the hospice nurse. Her mother had fallen in the bathroom and was rushed to the hospital. I shooed her out the door and told her I'd clean up. We had extended our hours to midnight hoping for some new clientele. I'd even welcome her street bums, I told her, as long they had a couple of bucks left in their pockets. All it did was increase our utility bills.

The café, we called it, *The Palestinian Isle Café,* after both our heritages, was empty. I was closing up early, cleaning the stove in the kitchen when the front bell rang signaling a customer. I wasn't thrilled to stop the process to serve a cup of coffee and a stale donut, but I put on my best face.

He was sitting at the counter, smiling as I came out. I knew him immediately, he hadn't changed a bit. "Hi Joe."

"Sam." Like Ebenezer Scrooge, this was my second ghostly visit. And like Scrooge, I was anxious to be rid of him, but I was intrigued enough not to throw him out.

"I'm cleaning up; I don't have much left out."

"Coffee will work."

He hadn't changed much in appearance. He was still thin and dark with no traces of gray. But he was only in his mid-thirties so I wouldn't expect him to look as haggard as Abdel. In his black slacks, white buttoned-down shirt, and gray Members Only jacket, he certainly blended in with the crowd. Gone, though, was his trademark manic enthusiasm. Liberating a country will do that. Or maybe, like me, he was remembering vividly our last day together. I turned my back which made it easier for me to talk and listen.

"You have a decent place here, Joe."

"Decent as in respectable or decent as in adequate?"

"I guess I mean respectable. I don't know how adequate it is."

"Fair enough."

"I've been in town a while," he said. "I'm almost ashamed to admit I've spent a lot of time at the coffee shop down the street."

"Is it more decent than mine?"

"They don't serve sumaggiya. But now you, owning a restaurant, smiling, serving people, cleaning up their messes. It seems incongruous to me. Like that word? I just learned it. It means inconsistent."

"What's inconsistent about it?"

"From what you used to do to make a living, and I don't mean slaughtering pigs."

"I don't know what you're talking about."

"Relax Joe, I'm not the police. I'm just a visitor. Besides, what you've done makes what I've had to do look civil. Greek and Palestinian? Interesting combination. Surprised it hasn't been a big hit. It has rouhi, right?

I shrugged.

"Soul. You don't remember your Arabic?"

"Not much."

"But you know your salaat still."

"Especially not salaat," I said.

"That's a shame."

"Yeah, well, tell your Allah it's nothing personal, I've pretty much sworn off all religion. You got a reason for coming in so late?"

He jutted his chin towards me. "Can we sit in the kitchen?"

I glanced out the front window to indicate to him I knew his visit carried with it subterfuge. I poured myself a cup and headed back without inviting him. "Johara and Abdel came to visit," I said when he came in and sat on the prep table.

"Yes."

"You know about their visit?"

"I spoke with Abdel when he returned."

"He tell you he wasn't welcome here?"

"Actually, he thought the welcome was quite congenial."

"He lied."

"He said you threatened to slit his throat if he stayed."

"Then he didn't lie, not really. What I told him was I'd have it done to him."

His collaborating with Abdel confused me. Had he been partly responsible for my son's death I'd want nothing to do with him. Unless

Abdel didn't know, or contrary to what Johara had told me, still didn't care. There was a third possibility.

"You plan on visiting with Sue and Johara while you're here?" I asked.

"Probably not."

"Pissing off the landlords over there, I hear. Ironic isn't it? By staying out of Yamma and Johara's life, you've managed to put them in the center of yours."

"It's why I stay away, Joe, to give them deniability."

"Must mean Abdel's in your inner circle."

He cupped the mug in hands too delicate to be staging a revolution. My vision of a revolutionary had a ragged Mexican from a Zapata Western or a greasy politician behind the scenes. I couldn't see Sam as either one. What he was was a trusted advance man sent to deliver a message and take home a response. The people he worked for were not unlike the ones I once worked for. It would be him talking to me but the words would be theirs.

"There's been no change in your uncle," he said. "And there's no room for him in our world, no more than there was in yours. But he's family and we do talk."

"So how much did Abdel tell you about me?"

"Little. And what he did tell us we paid little heed to. Except the part about you wanting to slit his throat."

How did you find me? I mean, here at the café?"

He shrugged. "Like magic, Joe. You want us to destroy the illusion by giving away our secrets?"

"Who's the 'we'? Your band of ... what do you call yourselves? Palestinian Revolution Party?"

He gave me the smile I knew, the one that accompanied his calling me a little boy, too young to know such things. "Why did you leave us alone in Ramallah?" I said.

"I had to go; I think you know why now."

"It took us three days to get back to Dayr Ghasana; Adli never made it home."

"I know; that's too bad."

"He shouldn't have been there. You should have taken us home."

"War started, Joe. Things changed very rapidly for all of us. You survived, you were strong. Adli was not."

"Strength had nothing to do with it."

"There were more important things happening then, and there are now. Joe, do you see how in the Bible and in our Koran the great things that happen upon a mountain top? Moses receives the Ten Commandments on Mount Sinai; Abraham is sent by God to sacrifice his son in Moriah; Jesus is tempted by Satan on Quruntul; Muhammad, peace be upon him, receives his revelations on Mount Hira. It is to the people who brave the climb that great rewards and wisdom are bestowed. When you were in Palestine you needed my help, now we need yours."

CHAPTER 52

Back in high school I interrupted a guy and gal heavily involved beneath a stairwell. Before I could recover my senses, the guy's long-time steady came up behind me. They were together since ninth grade, reigning junior class king and queen, and she was the finest looking girl in the school. The girl he was comingled with was a regular, to put it delicately.

I have rarely seen a person so broken into pieces as that class queen. I could see the struggle between rage and hurt forming in her eyes. But then her lips quivered and her shoulders heaved as hurt won out. She ran off shattered in heart and spirit, and in a voice sincere as could be, her king called out, "Hey, I'll pick you up for the dance at seven."

Sam's request astounded me no less than that insensible remark. Had he forgotten Ramallah, I could have understood where he was coming from, that he was recollecting our talks, the dinners, the camp out, the trips to Jerusalem. But he had not only recalled abandoning Adli to his death, he had moved past it as surely as I had moved past my father's.

I had no such quandary as to which emotion would win out in me, and Sam knew it. He held his palms out to me in a gesture to keep me back. "Hear me out before you blow. Look around you at this place, this life. Your wife, doesn't she deserve better? And you? How about you, Joe?"

"You are no one to talk about making things better for me or anyone else," I screamed.

"Keep your voice down." He paused as if waiting for a train to pass. "Say what you want about me, but I am the same man I was when you knew me last. I have the same convictions."

"Don't brag on that account."

"Do you truly believe I knew what was to happen, Joe? My decision to leave you was based upon a mission I was given. I thought your uncle was home, or would soon be. Knowing the man he was I knew he would not involve himself in the battle. Those were the facts in place for me." He hopped down from the table and walked the floor in front of me.

"Look, you saw this opportunity to move your restaurant up here as an opportunity to advance your cause."

"How do you know that?"

"It was necessary to do background before approaching you."

"You spied."

"I argued against the necessity of it; I see now I was wrong."

He looked truly disheartened that I had not greeted him in a generous bear hug. It didn't sway me. "The point is, when an opportunity presents itself you must act quickly to capitalize on it. That is what I did that day."

"It got you arrested."

He nodded and smiled. "Yes, Joe, another fortuitous event as it turns out."

"What else do you know about me?"

"Enough for a short story but not for a novel," he said with a hint of humor. "Tell me, Joe, were you upset when your father died?"

"Not really."

"I thought not. You see old men who sleep late; who take a leisurely morning at breakfast; who nap frequently, who read and sit alone and content. These are old men sure of what they did as young men, who know that what they did, they did well and the best they could.

"Now watch the old man who wakes early and walks the streets. He sits in public areas for most of his day; not to interact, but to watch others live. He goes home and sits restlessly with his washed-out mind. He knows he has little time left to go, and he has done so little in his life. As a young man he wanted most to live namelessly, to go about his days in the simplest of terms. He will be forgotten for how little he lived. And no man wants to be forgotten. He fears death because it truly is the end.

"My father died shortly after you left, during my last year at the university." He waited the customary time for me to interject my condolences which I never did. "My mother died when I was a boy. My father was all I knew. He was a rug dealer. Nothing like me, but probably much like your father. He showed little concern for religion and none for politics. When I became old enough to notice I asked him why. 'Good men have no time to talk of such things,' he said. Made no sense to me. I was embarrassed by him. I thought everyone in Palestine should raise their voice, if not a gun."

"My old man never said anything worth quoting, or even remembering," I said.

"Maybe *you* should then. Maybe unlike your father and mine, we'll be able to grow old with contentment."

It was like in the past, trying to lecture me. But I was no longer a boy and I was not enamored. "It's late and my … I have to get home." I was sure he knew about Michie, but I wasn't offering him anything. The truth was, I knew the types of people who kept book on you, and I knew how they kept book. They scared me, and now he scared me. "What's this about needing my help?"

"I have this to show you and Sue." He dug his hand into his back pocket for his wallet. He flipped it opened to a photograph which he thrust before my face.

"Damn, get that away from me," I told him.

"Do you know who it is?"

"Some poor bastard's head. What the fuck you carrying that around for? You sick or what."

"Maybe I came to the wrong man."

"For that photo, yeah, you sure did. And why would you even think to show it to Sue?"

"It's Faid El Karim, your cousin who raped your sister."

He was like a beagle, proudly bringing a baby rabbit home clutched in its teeth. "Does Johara or Abdel know about this?"

"Only that he's dead."

"Did you … behead him?"

"No. But I did order it for the honor of your sister. I told him that someday I would so he knew it was coming."

"Is this a threat for me?"

"Of course not. I apologize for bringing it. I thought you'd be … anyway, it's time to get to the point," he said. "Do you remember the man who took you from Yamma that day? That last day you saw me in Ramallah?

"The Israeli captain."

"Yes. Do you recall his name?"

"Cham Pfalzer."

"Ahhh, he made an impression on you."

"Johara told me he brought Adli's body home to be buried." I was still sickened by the photo of Faid, a boy I hated but who now had my sympathy. "Did you even think to go to the funeral?"

"I was not able to. I was still in custody. Had I been able to I could have met Captain Pfalzer for a second time. Maybe … maybe something could have been done then."

Something deeply personal grabbed his attention as his voice trailed off and his gaze drifted. "But that was not possible," he continued. "How were any of us to know at the time?"

"Know what?" I asked.

"Captain Pfalzer was promoted very quickly through the ranks of the Defense Forces. Very quickly. You are no doubt unfamiliar with Mivtza Za'am Ha'el, better known as Operation Wrath of God. Or the Special Forces unit known as Sayeret Matkal. Pfalzer was a senior officer for this unit. He was second in command during the raid on the Entebbe Airport in Uganda."

"Good movie," I said. "Charles Bronson."

"Zion propaganda trash, but no matter. The operation was to assassinate Palestinian patriots who killed Israelis at the Munich Olympics, killings that were necessary to draw attention to Israel's illegal imprisonment of Arabs."

"Saw that one, too. Franco Nero and William Holden."

"I swear you Americans really are simple. You care about nothing outside your immediate grasp. You're even deficient at the two bodies of knowledge that explain life and creation, science and theology. It's a wonder to me how you've managed to stay out of the dark ages while so much of the Muslim world can't manage to get beyond them.

"As I was saying, most of the killings are done by the Mossad," he said slowly to add to his earlier insult. "That's the Israeli Intelligence, like the American CIA. But it was the Sayeret Matkal who killed Mohammad Youssef al-Najjor and two others in Beirut.

"I don't know him."

"Al Najjor was our leader of a group the west calls Black September. They were the patriots of Munich. One of the others was a poet, a very good friend of mine, Kamal Nasser."

"I don't know him, why should I care?"

"Did you need to know the men you threatened for money, or was it enough for you to know the men who paid you for it? I can see, Joe, that there is nothing of our friendship left. And I am truly sorry you cannot see my side while I can surely see yours. So I will talk in terms we could have sent anyone here to talk to you about. Money.

"We cannot easily track Mossad agents; they're very elusive. But soldiers of the Sayeret Matkal do resurface in conventional units, or, in the case of Cham Pfalzer, when they go to Chicago."

"He's here? You sure of that?"

"As sure as we were of you. He left from Israel with his family two years ago. While Operation Wrath of God is their way of never forgetting or forgiving, we have our own ways. Colonel Pfalzer as he eventually became, is high on our list and he is well aware of it."

"So why are you telling me this?"

"We need deniability while at the same time letting the world know our reach. It is a delicate balance."

"Wait," I said. "You want me to kill him?"

"No. We cannot take that chance. As much as you deny it, Joe, you'll always be seen as one of us. I'm sure you've experienced that. What we need from you is your contacts here."

I knew from the start this was not a social visit made by a man trying to make amends. And I knew from Johara's depiction of him that he had indeed grown into the words and ideals of his youth. But the depths in which he immersed himself shook me. He was right; I knew only the orders I was given when I was strong-arming and not because I was naïve or they wanted to keep me ignorant. On several occasions I was asked to join the inner circle. But to do that would entail commitment to people I would otherwise disdain. I was wise enough to never articulate it that way, saying instead that I preferred making money without the obligations of membership.

Sam spoke with such authority and passion that I was sure he was not reading from a script prepared by some puppet master back in the West Bank. I didn't care much about his acceptance, but I still had pride and self respect. He came to me because I was a schoolyard bully, and I considered that a slap.

"I can make an introduction," I said. "But what do I get out of it?"

"No. We give you the information and you must make it all happen. For that we pay you five thousand."

"I don't want that kind of involvement."

He held out his hands. "No, no rouhi here. Think of the rouhi five thousand dollars can make. New equipment, new furnishings, maybe even a better location. I'm close to the end of my visa here. I can't afford to get caught by overstaying, so you have little time to accept this opportunity. I'll stop by for lunch tomorrow. If you accept, serve me a slice of lemon meringue pie. If not, my old friend, you'll never see or hear from me again."

I caught him before he left the counter area. "Sam?"

"Yes, Joe."

"How much if I do it all myself?"

CHAPTER 53

Michie knew only the crumbs of my past, the tiniest specks you don't even take the time to pick up because the foot traffic will obliterate them in time. I told her the morsels such as my dead siblings, my ex-con brother, my "visit" to Palestine. But Adli, the war, Sue's suicide attempt, my blown scholarship to Northwestern, my unknown child, remained my dark-closet secrets, the ones I knew I would have to share if I was to make it work with her. "I had a visit from a terrorist tonight," I told her when I got home.

"Oh? Did you tell him we didn't serve grits?"

"No. No, I'm serious. Not the KKK, Neo-Nazi crap. A real terrorist from the Middle East."

"Okay. So why?"

"Believe it or don't, he used to be a friend."

"How come I feel like I've just come into the middle a Tom Clancy movie?"

I told her about Sam, but only to a point. I wasn't quite sure where that point would end. "You were in Palestine during the Six Day War?"

"Yeah."

"Did you see any of fighting?"

"A little. I was brought home in the middle of it."

"Must have been terrible for a little boy."

"Just like Chicago for a big boy," I said.

"No. Crime is a person doing something crazy; war is a whole country doing it.

We readied for bed but she continued to ask about Sam and his visit. "Joe?" She said as the lights went out.

"Yeah."

"He's not really a terrorist is he?"

"Course not. Wouldn't have told you if he was, would I?"

***

Sam gave me an address in Hyde Park, just outside of the University of Chicago. Thirty grand, I was to get. It was a compromise between my forty and Sam's twenty. I felt a spasm of shame as I drove along the Midway, remembering my days with Jennifer, and wondering if Michie's was just another life waiting for me to destroy.

I thought I was going to a restaurant or maybe a social club, but there were no businesses along the road, only grand old homes and turn-of-the-century row houses. The address written for me on the paper napkin was a cheerful white Victorian, custom made to be a bed and breakfast or a garden club. There was a row of enormous purple, pink, and white Rhododendron bushes shielding the view of the porch which was why I didn't see them until I stepped up on it.

Sam and an older man were sitting on over-sized white wicker chairs, staring at me as I approached the front door to knock. The man was of Arab descent of some sort with a mop of white hair. He was no younger than sixty-five, clean shaven, wore gold-rimmed glasses, and weighed nearer to three-hundred pounds. He sat there grinning and squinting, reminding me of Big Daddy in *Cat on a Hot Tin Roof.*

"Didn't think you'd come," Sam said.

"I served you the pie."

"Hardly a blood pact. This is Marwan Kaddoumi," he said.

"Your house?" I asked.

Marwan Kaddoumi nodded.

"Nice. Don't you think you stick out like a hunk of coal in a snowball?"

"I keep to myself."

"Yeah. Which only makes you more noticeable."

They made no effort to invite me over so I took it upon myself. I figured having a bit of boorishness in me would fit the role. Being a gentleman didn't make you a promising hit man. I took a third wicker chair to complete the circle at a round glass table where a pitcher of iced-tea sweated. Kaddoumi clapped his hands for a young Hispanic woman. "Another glass," he ordered. She was back promptly and quietly to pour for me.

I sat back to sip, letting out a satisfying and bit condescending sigh to show them my smoothness. It left me self-conscious. This wasn't a job interview. I didn't answer an ad in the Trib. They, or at least Sam, came to me. It wasn't as if I had to show them my mettle. Yet I felt as if I was being measured. I sat back up and put the glass on the table. I put my elbows on the arm rests and clasped my hands, awaiting a conversation.

"You have a reputation here, Nasser," Mr. Kaddoumi said.

"I go by Joe."

"Yes. Out there, with them, you may go by Joe. But we need for you to think like and be a Palestinian."

"Fine."

His narrowing eyes, deeply furrowed forehead, and tense jaws let me know my careless response insulted him. Whoever he was, and it was for sure he was somebody, he took this meeting very seriously.

"How is the restaurant business treating you?" he asked.

"It's slow right now."

"Yes. It was slow for me at first."

"You in the restaurant business?"

"I own a chain of bakeries. Jaba Bakery, after my father's village"

"I've heard of it. Matter of fact, I've eaten there. Very good Chnafa."

"Thank you. All old family recipes. As you see, I am a regular customer of mine. Remember Nasser, never trust a skinny baker. Your wife, she is Greek. How did you meet?"

Now it was feeling like a job interview. Or maybe something else. Bringing in family, even obliquely, was a tactic I found useful as a strong-arm. I know now why it worked so well. "She's not why I was asked to come here."

He laughed. "Of course she is. Part of it, anyway. I want to know about you. You are a countryman of mine from the West Bank. And we are in the same business."

"I'm from Chicago. Born, raised, and hope to die," I said with a defiant glare.

"A proud American, as am I. When Samir came to visit me, I asked if he had family or friends here. He gave me your name. I asked to meet you."

"That's fine. And you have, but not my family; you won't be knowing my family."

He nodded more at Sam than at me. "Do you want to know how I know Samir?"

"Not really."

He stood with great effort and a quiet groan. He took a cigar from his pocket. "Smoke it or sniff it; good either way," he said handing it to me. Then he turned and walked down the porch to the front door.

"Hey," I called out to him.

From inside he turned halfway around to look at me from a right angle. "Yes, Nasser?"

"That it? That what I came all the way down here for, iced tea and a cigar?"

"And my friendship, Nasser. My friendship is what you now have."

CHAPTER 54

Sam and I were alone on the porch. "What the hell was that about?" I asked

"Come take a walk with me."

I poked the cigar out at him. "Am I on the payroll or what?"

Sam ignored me as he walked away, expecting me to follow. I told him the only place I was walking was to my car. Sam took my arm and steered me onto the sidewalk. "I have never seen such beautiful homes for such ordinary people," he said. "Remember back in Dayr Ghasana? Remember when grand was on the inside, not on the outside? A man could surely lose himself in a world such as this if he allowed himself. If he were a man unlike Marwan Kaddoumi."

"What's the riddle here, Sam?"

"That cigar that he gave you; it's your lemon meringue pie."

He had me intrigued enough to stay the course with him a few more steps down the sidewalk. He stopped at a house several down from Kaddoumi's. It was a larger home, a red brick Tudor with turret towers on either end whose long windows were stained glass. The roof was gray slate. The lawn was the color of green I had only seen in Disney cartoons; the gardens, too. "In America you can sin just walking down a street," Sam said. "Covet, is the word, isn't it Joe? Americans covet everything, and when they come to own it, they find other things, other people, to covet."

He pointed at the tower. "Point with me, Joe. Talk to me and point. We're probably being watched right now and coveting such a magnificent structure is a good cover. No one will suspect us if we're committing such an All-American sin."

"Who's watching us?"

"The FBI most probably."

"What?"

"I'll explain while we walk and point. But you mustn't look at me. You must look around in awe."

His arrogance annoyed me. He was slapping me in the face for being American. These were his insults to show his disdain. I'm sure inside he felt as if he was crawling through a pile of sludge.

"Marwan Kaddoumi is who he says he is," Sam said, pointing and smiling. "And only wanted to wish you well on your restaurant."

"Okay."

"As for our discussion earlier, here is what you need to know."

He explained the mission to me as casually as he had the history of Jerusalem. He spoke of Colonel Cham Pfalzer, as if Pfalzer was an incarnate of Adolf Hitler. "Doesn't sound like the guy I met," I said.

"Who can you ever meet at six-years old?"

"I was nine by then."

"Only a child. He's a monster now as assuredly as he was a monster then."

He must be stopped, Sam told me. He runs death squads from the safety of America, and with the US Government's tacit approval. Stopping him was what I was being hired to do. "I'm not sure it is a good idea to use someone so close to us," he said. "Maybe you don't have it in you. Maybe I should have seen that when you saw what became of Faid. But the decision has been made. "

I told him I had it in me. I felt as if I was back in grade school, saying things to impress the older kids. I even think my voice raised an octave in pitch as I sold myself. "I have to know," I said. "Abdel, did he leave because I threatened to have him killed?"

"No. Because *we* threatened to."

The mystery that was Marwan Kaddoumi was never explained to me. Nine years after meeting him he was beaten to death on the same porch where we shared iced tea. It was front page news with pictures of the house and porch. A savage attack, most probably when he interrupted a burglary taking place in the swanky neighborhood. I followed the case for months. No one was ever arrested. I didn't see him as the type to intimidate a burglar to the point he'd be beaten to death. It wasn't a stretch to see his relationship with Sam and others from Palestine as a more worthy motive.

***

Cham Pfalzer was standing on the loading dock of Seaver Express on Pratt Street in Elk Grove Village, just as Sam said he would be. He held a clipboard officiously under his arm as a forty-eight-foot Kenworth trailer backed in. I wouldn't have known him by the military photo Sam gave me. Cham was dressed in light Khakis and a dark blue Polo shirt. There was no sign he was anything more than a hard-working stiff.

He was heavier now, and his face deeper and darker in intensity. He was certainly no shorter, but I was taller which made him less physically imposing. The creeping truck missed its mark, nearly tagging a fat Hispanic man who scurried up the flight of steps, screeching maniacally. I laughed; his co-workers laughed; Cham Pfalzer's expression never changed. That's when I was sure it was him.

I repeated this survey twice over the next week. Michie was not happy. "Maybe I've spent most of my life cooped up in restaurants, and I haven't dealt with the types you have, but I know enough to know you haven't been doing volunteer work these last few nights."

"It isn't another woman, if that's what you're thinking."

She shrugged. "Losing you is losing you. Makes no difference how or to who."

"Well, just so you know, it isn't."

"Then it's something worse. Are you back to your old job, the one that makes you stink on the inside worse than on the outside?"

With his background I expected him to be surveillance conscious but he never spotted me, though I sat in the same position all three days. If he had an office he never used it. He was always walking the dock floor, even when no trucks were loading or unloading. He never left for lunch; I never even saw him snacking. He never seemed to take a break.

The next Monday I started at four o'clock in the afternoon with intentions of following him home. By seven he was still at work. I tried again the next night until eight but he still didn't leave. From Sam's depiction, I expected to see him meeting with trench-coated embassy bureaucrats after work to plan their next hit. But he was always the last to close up, and I saw no one come in late to chat with him.

I watched the office and dock workers leave. Pfalzer took a bag of trash out to the dumpster. I used the moment to jump onto the dock and hide myself back in the shadows. He walked slowly back up the steps that all day he bounded up; now he dragged himself. All day he marched the dock, end to end, always being where he needed to be, always in the middle of things. Now he was tired and very old, though he couldn't have been older than mid-forties. He would never let his workers see him this way.

I let him move into the office space before I closed on him. I needed to be sure we were out of view from the parking lot. "Stay very still, Colonel," I said from behind.

He was unarmed but standing at the ready with both arms loose at his sides. He looked every inch the cool, hard soldier who took me from Dayr Ghasana. "Could be a little more discreet," he said. "Didn't even switch up cars, not once. And same location."

He turned slowly. "You've come to kill me, son. You're hardly a pro. Why would they choose you? Family or friend?"

I conceded. "Family."

"Sloppy."

"Like you said, I'm not a pro."

"Not just you, them. Maybe they're not as serious as I thought."

He was unimpressed that a hit had been put out on him. More accurately, that I was the one tasked to do it. He stood casually, almost bored, but he was a soldier, being on either side of death was second nature.

"Certainly don't want it done here," he said. "We have cameras. And if I don't alarm the office by nine, the police call. How much they pay? Five thousand?"

"Thirty?"

"Wow. Don't think I'm worth it but take it if they're offering. You got half up front, right?"

"Nothing up front."

"Trusting or stupid."

"Let's take this into the office, where we can sit," I said.

He walked casually while I followed. Though I was giving the orders, I couldn't help the feeling he was setting me up. His office was all Plexiglas, plastic, and vinyl. He gave me the chair behind the desk and took the one in the middle of the room. Nothing within his grasp, but still.

"So what did I do to earn a thirty thousand assassination?"

"You're part of that Special Forces Group, the Sayonara Mattel."

"Sayeret Matkal," he corrected.

"You assassinate Palestinians."

"I see. All of them?"

"The patriots."

"Yes. Soldiers killing soldiers in war and for that they pay you to kill me?"

"You're controlling it from here now," I said. "With America's help."

"Well, son, you were doing fairly well up until now. Why would I come here to do such a thing? If I was doing so well back there to earn a thirty thousand dollar bounty, why would I go thousands of miles away where I wouldn't be worth nearly as much? And what's in it for America?"

I didn't know the answers to any of that. As with the strong-arm jobs, I didn't think it necessary to ask. I see now I should have. This wasn't drugs or gambling debts. This wasn't just a threat. This was death and politics in a world where I couldn't even pronounce the words.

"Why'd you come here then, to Chicago?"

"What's your name?" he asked.

"Nasser."

He cocked his head and pursed his lips for the briefest of moments that would have gone undetected by anyone else.

"If not you today, someone else tomorrow. Maybe someone better equipped. Family, you said. Let me ask you, what kind of family asks you to do such a thing? No need to answer, just something for you to ponder.

"So you want to know the man first, is that it, Nasser? A good thing, I guess. Why did I come here? I could tell you I got sick of the fighting, but that's only part of it. Yes, I was a senior officer of the Sayeret Matkal. And I was involved in most of their operations. But then I was a soldier so I make no apologies.

"You aren't any more?"

"I'm longer a soldier. My parents grew up in Germany under the Nazi's. My father was an architect. I was born in the ghetto in Lodz, Poland. I was only four when the war ended. Hitler was dead, the Nazis, the real Nazis, were arrested or scattered. We were safe, so thought many Jews.

"But my father, and to a lesser degree, my mother, had such a deep-seated hate for all Germans. We moved to Israel where we were safe from Germans but not from my father's hate. We weren't allowed to speak of it as a place we had ever been, or even heard of. But let me tell you the vile things my father filled us with when it suited him. Rants about the villainous, sub-human creatures they all were. All, not just the Nazi's. And we never went back to visit friends or family. They told us our grandparents died in death camps. As I got older I wondered, why not us too? As far as I know, my grandparents moved to Miami Beach and ran an Oceanside motel.

"I began to ask questions. Never of him, mind you. That was suicide. I asked my mother. 'What he says is the truth,' she would say.

"'Yes, but *all*, mama? All Germans?'

"'It's his truth.'

"'Not *all* could be that way. His truth doesn't mean *the* truth.'

"Then she'd recite the destruction of Sodom and Gomorrah from the old Testament. Do you know the story, Nasser?"

I shook my head.

He told me of angels sent down to Abraham with the message that God would destroy the cities of Sodom and Gomorrah for their cruelty. Abraham begs for the salvation of all if fifty, or even ten, good people can be found within their walls. The angels agree that if just ten can be found they will spare the cities. But not one was found.

"Just prior to the destruction, Abraham and his family, which included his nephew, Lot and his wife, Ado, are led from the city by the angels with the warning not to look back at the cities. Ado turns to look and is cast into a pillar of salt.

He ended it with, "My mother used that story as our reminder to never look back. But, Nasser, that was the point, wasn't it? My parents were always looking back. Forever hating, refusing to recognize even ten good people. That's my memory of their lives." He shook his head. "My father died the year before I came to America. The official cause was heart failure. But he was strong as a horse. It wasn't his heart. Hate killed that man. Hate kills the hater as quickly as it does the ones who are hated. I left before I learned to hate that much. More importantly, before my children learned. You don't want to kill me, Joe. You've seen enough killing in your life."

I leaned forward. "You remember me?"

"Yes, Joe from Chicago. I remember. The years have disappeared from your face as we've talked. In many ways I can see the same small boy who was so upset for the loss of his young cousin, and the hurt he knew it caused. I thought there'd be a chance we'd meet again when I came here. I didn't expect it here, like this."

"Why would you ever expect to see me?"

"Because bringing you home was one of the good things I did in my life."

"And burying Adli."

"Burying children .... He shook his head as his voice faded. "You've grown up hating Israelis, I see. Enough to want to kill them, all of them."

Now I know why people used guns for this type of thing. Cham Pfalzer had a family, and a story I found easy to believe because I knew him. He didn't deny all that Sam had told me, but neither did he wear it as a badge of honor. In truth, he wore it with an admirable amount of discomfort. Like Michie and thousands of other working stiffs I knew, he was trying to get by on a row of unknown tomorrows.

"I'm not here to kill you," I said. "You need to leave. There are others very close by who want you dead. I believe I met the man in charge of doing it."

"Who are they, Joe?"

"Never mind that. There's money to kill you, and to kill others."

"I know that."

"You know?"

"As much hate as there is between the Israelis and the Palestinians, we understand each other. We must in order to be such good enemies. Sometimes I think it's part of our identity, a reason to be us."

"They won't stop. When they find out I didn't do it they'll hire someone else."

"And maybe kill witnesses."

A point I hadn't thought of. Not Sam, I was sure, but as I learned he was only a cog in a much bigger machine. "Maybe we can make it work for both of us," he said.

CHAPTER 55

FBI agents were regular visitors to the diner since Sam arrived. Sometimes as customers, most times as outside surveillance. They approached me twice, very professional, very courteous, and outside Michie's presence. But they were serious and made it known. Samir El Assad was more than he purported to be to me and others. "You familiar with Joseph Goebbels," one asked during our first meeting.

"Just the name."

"He was the Nazi Minister of Propaganda under Hitler. He was responsible for boycotts of Jewish businesses, book burnings, Kristallnacht, all that. That's your cousin's job for the Fatah."

They had a long book on him. And on the organization he belonged to, the Fatah, the violent arm of the PLO. They hit with me stories of bloody raids and butchering massacres by Black September. Sam was a major player and an unwelcomed guest in the United States as a result. Somehow he received a visitor's visa, they explained, and I was listed as a relative he had come over to see. Had I seen him?

The plan to kill Cham Pfalzer was not on their radar screen. I had my deniability and I planned on using it, but I didn't tell Sam of the visits or their interest in him, keeping it as an insurance policy in the event I needed help.

"Haven't seen him in a while," I said. The older agent pulled out a spiral notebook, ready to take copious notes. I told him the last time was when Sam was arrested at the beginning of the Six Day War. That's when the two smirked at each other and the note taking ceased.

Cham Pfalzer had a good job as a warehouse supervisor, secured by family in the area. He loved it in Des Plaines, as did his family. But he knew he was safer in Israel where he had an Army to protect him than on his own in Chicago, an area where he was severely outnumbered by the Palestinian community. His plan was to let me fake his murder while he fled. "Win, win," he said.

I thought about it; I really did. But how would I explain the money to Michie? What if the Fatah found out they were duped? And even though it was a fake, how could I live with exploiting a man like Cham Pfalzer?

I told Sam the truth, that I had met Cham Pfalzer and warned him to flee. That I told him the Fatah was behind it and they knew where he worked and lived. That was three weeks after my meeting with Pfalzer who was now out of the area. Sam was enraged. "I recommended you," he said. "I brought you to Marwan Kaddoumi. Now we are both in danger."

"He saved my life. He buried Adli."

"He saved you to ingratiate himself with the United States. He buried Adli for the same reason."

"What he did, not why he did it, is good enough for me."

"He's a killer. I told you, he's a murderer."

"And I'm not. The FBI came looking for you; they know what you're up to. You were right. They're working with the Israelis and are looking to arrest you." It was a small lie, one easy enough for him to swallow.

I spent the next few years anxiously awaiting retribution. We moved our diner out of the Loop to an area nearer O'Hare. Part economic, part fear. Michie was all for it. The Loop wasn't her kind of place; the people, not her type of people. She rarely mentioned our arguments about my chasing the money. Since none ever materialized she figured it was a passing crisis of a former thug.

In 1999 Sue, Johara, and I went back to the West Bank to attend Yamma's funeral. I was more nervous, more apprehensive, than I was thirty-odd years earlier. The flight was as long, the sky as endless, and the drive to Dayr Ghasana as hard and dusty. But things had changed.

The occupation had torn the heart and soul out of the people. Worse than seeing it, you could feel it. Ramallah was reminiscent of the refugee camp I visited with Abdel and his new wife. A tourist wouldn't notice, preferring to see and know only what was published in brochures. A visitor wouldn't notice, Palestinians the quintessential hosts whose pride and manners wouldn't allow for it. But I considered myself neither. I was, in my mind, coming home.

Life there was now a heavy, wet blanket. The buildings and streets didn't show it. Bustling people bustled, relaxed people relaxed. It was still a mix of quaint European and Palestinian style. A tourist would applaud the brochure's accuracy. But its loss of energy was unmistakable, and the mood was grave. Like Michie picking up on my moods within minutes of them changing, thirty years of occupation was a difficult thing for even the most cordial host to cover up.

It wasn't reflected as much in Dayr Ghasana where day-to-day life allowed little time for global reflection. Some remembered us, or said they did, perhaps to be gracious. Of course all of them remembered Johara. The village was now incorporated into the town of Bani Zeid. The actual village lost population since the war. Johara explained that many villagers had fled to Europe or America, if they were fortunate enough to have the means and family. And of course, few people ever moved in.

As an adult I now focused on adult things. The inconveniences I once saw as adventures, the dirt roads, the water wells, the donkey carts, and even the occasional outhouse, now humbled me as I watched the people go about their work undaunted and with dignity.

We were met at the house by Bara'ah. She was every bit the dazzling lady Johara told me about. She was lively and warm. Her slim build, high cheekbones, radiant smile, and the black eyes that bore into me the instant I saw her, were of her mother. But I could see Yamma in her, too.

She spoke English well. It was taught in most of the schools now, Johara explained. "Joe and Sue from Chicago, I've been waiting so long to meet you. I know you so well from the stories, but I must show you this." She took us into my old bedroom. I knew what she was about to show us, but I wasn't prepared for the scope of it.

The four walls were a mural, a cyclorama, of the world just outside. All had life in them: children playing basketball, feeding goats and chickens, harvesting olives, swimming in the Red River. Beside the window where Adli and I sat to count stars, were the backs of two boys, their elbows resting on the sill. "She finished it two weeks ago," Bara'ah said. "Well, *I* think she did; she wasn't convinced. She was always fiddling here and there. It's truly amazing, don't you agree?"

I did. We all did. "It's us," Sue said as she walked along each wall. The figures were painted in a haze compared to the rest of the mural which was vibrant in its greens, blues, yellows, and reds. Ghost-like figures, they seemed to me, as if they were ethereal visitors to this place.

My first visit was down to the cave. I paused reflectively at the crest of the hill. It was ten in the morning with the sun at the perfect spot for the glistening Red River below. In the thirty years since a nation and a people had been so wounded and disfigured, it was satisfying to know the river held out in defiance, refusing to slow its current or alter a bend.

I recalled how deftly Siidi seemed to glide down this mountainside, perhaps inspired by his youth. But my knees, damaged from soccer, ached, and had me sliding unsteadily and grabbing for even the flimsiest branches. I paused at the grassy landing where we camped out that night I met Sam. My life here revolved around this place, the cave in particular, but while I soaked in the river and drew comfort from the campsite, I dreaded the cave as much as my cousins did when the ghoulies were so in their heads.

They were my ghosts now that haunted it. There'd be no legends growing up around them, but I knew they were there. It held Sue's, as well, and she made it clear she wouldn't be coming down with me.

There was no marker, Johara advised, it being Yamma's wish to let the cave be his headstone. I breathed deeply and entered. The musty air made me feel faint, then I realized I hadn't breathed since entering. I moved cautiously into the shadows. Idiotically, I waited for something unnatural to occur, specifically for Adli to pull me down into his grave. I jumped at the sound of rocks sliding behind me. It was Sue. "You said you weren't coming?" I said.

"I didn't want to. But neither did you."

She walked in to stand beside me. "Johara told me he's over there," she pointed to the corner.

Neither of us approached out of fear and respect. "It was a good thing you did for him," she said. "Johara told me how very proud he was to come in here."

"There's something I need to tell you about that day he was killed," I said.

"No, Joe, you don't need to tell me. Nothing wrong with keeping personal secrets."

"Didn't you tell me I needed to come to accept my past to move on? I have this secret I've been keeping and—"

"You want to know my secret? I hate Faid. I try to accept what he did to me, but I can't. I know it's not right; it goes against all the things I've told you I stand for. It makes me feel like a fraud, but I've come to accept that as part of being human. I thought keeping it to myself would help, but it's making it harder."

"I don't believe there needs to be any forgiveness for things like that."

"Yamma did it. I'm sure she was angry when she was left alone. She was hurt when Adli died. But you saw it; she found her way and celebrated life. You're coming to terms, Joe. You came back to Dayr Ghasana for Yamma. You came for Adli to a place I never wanted to see again. For decades, maybe centuries, this cave was a place for superstition. Because of you, it's now a sacred place for reflection. That's a fine legacy."

Yamma's funeral was well attended, the Imam performing the burial Janazah under the minaret in the village center. As he recited, words came back to me and I mouthed the prayers in unison with him. I was pleased, knowing Yamma would be, as well.

We met Bara'ah's husband of nearly two years. He was an assistant manager at the Al Yaseem hotel just north in Nablus. He followed us around solemnly and quietly, his hands resting behind his back. Perhaps his English wasn't up to that of his wife's or he was just the quiet type. Maybe he disliked us. Whatever his motive, it was obvious Bara'ah was her own woman. They met at one of Yamma's art fairs in Ramallah. She refused his proposals twice and wasn't yet ready for children. Now that Yamma was gone, she would sell the house and farm to a neighbor and get a job in Nablus. "What will you do," Sue asked.

"Anything I want," was her unabashed answer.

The next issue was on all our minds: what would become of the mural? "Yamma told me that by no means was I to stay here to protect the mural," Bara'ah said. "The mural was by her, for her. If the images stay with us for all our days, then the mural lives."

Gamal came back from Jordan. He greeted me first with a hug that was genuine and powerful, as if it was something building inside him for thirty years. It wasn't something I thought would ever happen so I was caught off guard. But it touched me even more so than the mural, and tears welled up in my eyes. This was when I understood what Cham Pfalzer meant about enemies, that as much hate as we suspect is between us, we understand each other better because of it. But I didn't agree with him that it had to stay part of our identity.

Abdel kept his distance except for a non-committal handshake. He didn't even acknowledge Sue. Sam didn't attend, which no one seemed to mind except Sue. "I was hoping to see him, she said. "I'm sure you were, too."

"Yeah, would have been nice," I lied.

"We need to talk later," Johara whispered to us.

"Sam's in trouble," Sue and Johara told me back at the house.

Johara heard it from Gamal; Sam had a contract on his head by both the Jordanian and the Israeli governments. Seems his little failure at my hands didn't hurt his career. He was the leader of what sounded to me like a soccer team, *The Fatah Hawks*.

I listened politely, though not intently. I raised my eyebrows and chuckled when Johara said he was wanted for leading assassination squads against leaders in both countries. "What?" she asked.

"Nothing. Why you telling me this, Johara?"

"I think you can help him."

"Johara, I've learned to make a pretty good Maqluba and a decent gyro sandwich. Rescuing international assassins isn't my thing."

"Sue told me you know people."

I glared at Sue. "Yeah, people I've been warned by her and my wife to stay away from."

The two had concocted a crazy scheme to get him into the United States through Canada. Once here, I was to get him phony identification so he could disappear. Could I do it? No, but I knew people who could. But it was expensive, and dangerous. And illegal. Yes, but would I do it?

Why would I take that chance? I had a family and a business to run. I was glad to be free of my old life, my old demons, at least on some levels. There were times at night I'd wake up and for a happy instant my ugly past was a bad dream.

"He was there for Sue," Johara said. "He was there for you," Sue said. They didn't know. They didn't know he abandoned Adli, that he had Faid beheaded, that he came to Chicago to murder a man. Whatever it was he was doing back here now, he was no doubt wholly responsible, passionate, and proud. He would die a martyr's death.

CHAPTER 56

When Michie picked me up at the airport, I let loose like a lost child with no idea at the time what prompted it or what it meant. I shook uncontrollably when we hugged, as if her touch was an electric shock bringing me back to the moment. It scared her. She didn't know me to be sentimental. Even with our two daughters, I rarely held or kissed them. And the disturbing part, it wasn't an oversight. My lack of contact with them was not only deliberate, it felt natural.

I left Dayr Ghasana knowing I'd never return. The *could have beens* in life get far more attention than they deserve, so I left them there in the cave, in the river, in the olive grove, on the windowsill, and on the overgrown basketball court. All I took back home to my world was a great sense of relief and a piece of Yamma which Bara'ah presented to me before we left for the airport. It was a painting of Adli and me at a bird trap, letting go a white dove. I didn't think the episode made much of an impression on Adli at the time, but it must have. Enough to tell it to Yamma, enough for Yamma to paint it. It hangs alone on the back wall of our restaurant.

"Remember when you called me bitter?" I said.

"I never did."

"Yes. You did. One of the first nights I was at the restaurant. You said people who bitched out loud were just angry but the silent types were bitter."

"I said that? Wow, deep."

"Is it true?"

"I think you were bitter at one time."

"No, not me. In general."

"There's a Catch-22 in there, isn't there? I mean, they're the quiet ones so it's hard to know how bitter they are. But see, you bitch out loud now so now you're just angry."

"I don't want to be bitter anymore. It hurts. I never told you about Jennifer."

"You never told me lots of things."

I stared into my lap, like a kid again, confessing a shame. "I destroyed her life," I said in a whisper. "She deserved better. She was sweet and ambitious and charming. She took our baby and left with such grace. She told me to find something to ground myself or I'd turn bitter. I swore it would be her who'd turn bitter in the end. If what you're saying is true, she won't." I looked up. "I hope you're right because she wasn't anything at all like me."

She wanted to know more but mercifully didn't ask. She knew my head was just passing through these places. "I'll tell you," I said. "I promise. I'll tell you everything. I don't want to keep my past a secret. It's nothing to be ashamed of, right? I made mistakes; it's what happens in life, right?"

She nodded with a queasy smile. She didn't deserve this. She was hurt. But I needed this now, before the moment slipped away. "Remember that visitor from Palestine about fifteen years ago?"

"No."

I reminded her of Sam's visit. Then told her of the mysterious Marwan Kaddoumi, and of Captain Cham Pfalzer, of the meeting on Kaddoumi's porch, of my surveillances of Pfalzer and our eventual confrontation, and of the FBI visits. We were in heavy slow traffic, convenient for the trauma I was putting her through. I watched her palms choke the steering wheel, leaving perspiration marks that showed her concern or anger. She glanced at me with uneasy eyes. But I didn't turn back. I couldn't do that anymore, even if it meant losing her.

"All this happened in our café?" She asked.

"Yeah."

"You didn't know or care how bad it could have been for us?"

"I knew, but no, I didn't much care. Not back then."

"Feel good, getting it all off your chest?"

"I don't expect you to understand. But I've been a miserable person holding onto it, and I can't do that anymore. I've gone through life acting as if that day never happened. It's gonna destroy what's left of me."

"What day?" she said.

"What?"

"You said, 'that day.'"

For all the bluster I was spouting about facing my demons, my one real demon was still rattling deep inside me, desperate to stay there. I would have gone on about Sam and Jennifer and Yamma, convinced I had discovered the causes of all my anxieties and fears. Five, ten years from now, my world still a quagmire of despair, I'd lay the blame on fate.

When the café on the Loop failed, I took inventory of my life. I came away with one shallow conclusion: Failure was my fate, and whether I was master or servant was inconsequential for it would come to pass regardless. I became content in not directing or even trying to understand it. Unlike a jigsaw puzzle, there was no picture to guide me. I had no opportunity to sort the pieces. Yet I was challenged to fit them together into something that made sense.

"Did I ever mention Adli to you?"

"Not consciously, but in your dreams. More like nightmares."

"He was my cousin from Dayr Ghasana. No, he was my best friend. My best friend ever."

"So why didn't you ever—"

"He died."

"Oh."

"He was killed during the Six Day War." I told her the story as objectively as my heart would allow. By the time I was done, we were home and parked along the curb.

"It was war," Michie said. "Horrible things happen."

"He didn't want to get out of that ravine," I said. "I made him get out. For the first time he was challenging me, and that made me angry. The thing was, I knew at the time he was right. I knew we were safer down there. But he made me mad, running off the bus, questioning me, refusing to believe me, refusing to follow me. I knew he was simple, and that I could break him. I could get him to do anything I wanted; I always could. And then I left him behind."

"Joe, you had no way to carry him."

"You don't understand. I left him because I was still angry. His head was blown off and I was still angry that he argued with me. I was his hero, and now he wanted to be the hero. That was sick then and it's still sick now. And you know the sickest part? I'm still pissed."

I'd like to say I felt a great relief in letting it out. That was the way it was in books and movies. But this was Michie I was speaking to; this was a woman who gave away food to homeless and destitute people when we were barely getting by ourselves. When I fought with her she'd smile and say, "You're right. But we're still making it." Telling her of my despicable past had me lower than ever. But I didn't want pity any more than I wanted a lecture. She gave me neither.

"I never said that out loud," I said, "that I still hate him."

"You don't hate him, Joe. You hate what happened; you hate why it happened. If you think this makes you wicked you're wrong. You're a decent man with a good heart."

"What makes you so sure?"

"Because you married a woman like me. Listen, you're doing fine with this, and by fine I mean normal. When I was sixteen I watched my father stumble drunk into the alley behind our restaurant and beat a homeless man with a broom handle for going through the trash. The trash, Joe. I watched from start to finish and did nothing to stop it. He beat him a dozen times, plenty of opportunity for me to step in."

"You were afraid," I said.

"Yeah. To death, like you were. And I knew I was wrong not to grab the broom away. I knew I'd regret it. But when I closed the door and left the man unconscious and bleeding, I fooled myself into believing I could forget it."

"Did you call for help?"

No, I didn't. I told my mother who said the old guy would just keep coming back if my father didn't do something. I thought, 'God, I hope so; I hope he gets to come back.'"

"Did he?"

"No. I don't know if he crawled away or was carried away. I don't know if he ended up in a grave or a hospital that night. It's about breaking the patterns, Joe, when we get the chance."

"Patterns?"

"Any pattern that creates suffering, misery, isolation, fear. And not just in others but in ourselves. I can't pretend to change them all, but I can make damn sure never again is a human being reduced to eating from my garbage."

"It's why you loved Junipers," I said. "Why didn't you tell me? We could have stayed.

"Story isn't one I'm proud of, and it's not as important as the lesson I learned. Like the restaurants I've been involved with, I've learned more from the failures than the successes."

"Glad I could help."

She took both my hands and shook them slightly. "So am I. And the fact is we did go off to the new places. We did it because we had to, and we had to because we did it."

"Fate," I said.

"Call it that. Or just life. We move on, right? We fail, we learn, we succeed, we start over again, if we break the patterns. If we don't, then I guess we just fail."

There were two more patterns from my past I was to break, the first I wasn't so sure I wanted to.

CHAPTER 57

Ralph Waldo Emerson said, "To believe your own thought, to believe that what is true for you in your private heart is true for all men—that is genius." I'm coming to believe that of myself. Hardly the genius part, but that what I know in my heart to be true, is true enough in the heart's of all men. For regardless of religious or political dictates, regardless of heritage or race, regardless of what is spoken outside the private heart, there are fixed truths to our lives.

I knew a thing about patterns. I grew up in one, and into adulthood in another. I knew a thing about changing them, as well. Yamma changed hers. Cham Pfalzer changed his. Michie changed mine. Adli made his own. And Tariq, my cousin, was in the midst of creating new ones.

Saving Sam was the right thing to do. Not because he was the same man I met back in Dayr Ghasana. He wasn't. But because I was. I wiped away all the gray of his idealism, and the religions and politics of that place, to come to my decision. It was their war. It would be senseless of me to pay it homage by letting Sam die.

Always there would be reasons for both sides; justifications and excuses, finger pointing and flag waving. If they found Sam, they would kill him. If they didn't, he would kill them. Either way, the pattern would go on. Like the moving of one grain of sand on the beach, I could change it. The struggle wouldn't stop, but I could save him and perhaps others, and for a struggling restaurant owner on the south side of Chicago, that was good enough.

I didn't offer my help to Sue and Johara right away. There were logistics to sort out, options to weigh, risks to calculate. I had to drop hints around my old haunts and my old contacts, many of whom could have been dead or in prison.

I went to a man who'll stay anonymous as long as I'm alive. He was my first "professional" job and my main employer for half a dozen years. He became a weekly patron to us on the Loop. When I began to tell him who and why he hushed me. "Only tell me the what, Joe."

It would cost twenty-five grand, investment funds I still had left from those dark days which Michie refused to let me use for the restaurant. My part was only ten; Sue and Johara were kicking in seventy-five hundred each. In my head I had Sam coming in through Canada. "Peru,"' my contact said.

"But I don't know—"

"Peru. What else?"

I was short on specifics. I had an alias name, and a date and place of birth given to me by Johara. I had no idea she had stayed in touch with him since coming to Chicago, and had remained fiercely loyal to him, though not to his cause.

I met another man. I was given his name, Roger, and told to meet him at an address up on West Irving Park Rd. I suppose I was given only the address so as not to scare me away, not that I would have been, having immersed myself into this thing. It was the Legacy 21 bar, the legendary gay club my friends often visited back in the day to bust heads. I admit I entered with hesitation, though for no reason as no one threw themselves into my arms, grabbed my ass, or otherwise mishandled me.

I was told a first name was all that was needed. "Roger here?" I asked a very pretty Spanish bartender.

"You Joe?" He asked.

"Yeah."

"Gray-haired guy sitting alone at the table," he said, pointing.

I approached the Desi Arnaz-looking man, very regal and imposing in his crisp gray suit. I surmised he was Peruvian. I didn't dare sit without an invite, not with a man who had his own table and like Madonna, was identifiable by only a first name.

He held out his hand. I handed him the envelope with the biographical information I was told to provide. Oh yeah, and the ten grand cash advance. He dismissed me by turning his attention back to his drink. I saw him slip the envelope into his breast pocket and I gave serious consideration to the notion that I had just been ripped off.

But three weeks later a messenger came into the café with an envelope. It contained an Illinois driver's license, birth certificate, social security card, and even a credit report with scores better than mine. "I'll be back for my envelope tomorrow at two," he said, meaning the rest of the cash.

Right on time, he was back for the money and to give me another curt command. "You have thirty days to get him to that place. You let us know the day and the airline. And no, you don't get the money back."

Johara had the same response I had. "That's not enough time." And I gave her the response I got. "So you'd better hurry."

She got it done. I asked her no questions but the one I needed an answer to: When's he due in?

He flew into O'Hare at eleven at night on January twenty-six. I volunteered to pick him up. I had expectations of having things to get off our chests, but we spent the entire drive without saying a word. The saddest part was, there were issues to talk about but he didn't feel the need to air them, and I was too arrogant to let him know I cared.

CHAPTER 58

I had been forewarned not to be shocked by his condition. His hands shook. His eyes couldn't hold focus, darting about the room as if following the flight of a fly. His walk, if he did walk, had a limp. His voice faded in and out only he didn't know it. He was an old man with an old man's mind, occasionally lapsing into the man he used to be. I didn't want to see him as old and beaten. I didn't want to see him confused and unsure. I didn't want him to ever be ordinary.

In the years since I dropped him off in Peoria, the plight of both the Palestinians and the Israelis have made their impact on me. I consider myself fortunate in having shared life and death situations with both. I've seen their brutality and their humanity.

I drove past the house. Lights were on; a black Jetta was in the driveway. I slowed but wasn't ready to see him. I pulled onto the main street and down to Route 24 that took me back to the lot under the bridge where I dropped him off that night years ago. I parked and rolled down the window to take in the summer noise along the river. I laughed. He wouldn't recognize me if he saw how mindful of life I am today.

We moved the restaurant once again, back to the beginning of sorts, back to the South Side. Marquette Park. We even went back to the original name, Juniper, in the hope fate would recognize our faith in the past. It was a mixed neighborhood, the type that couldn't make you rich like the Loop, but neither would it break you.

It had a large Palestinian population. Being of the descent and the proprietor of a place where intense conversations took place, I was expected to be paying attention to the troubles of those back home. I found that most talk was hearsay, many of the patrons being of second and third generation by now. Those who were direct Palestinians were like Siidi, whose stories were a mix of fact and legend where the lines often crossed.

Where one side of the cafe bitched about the White Sox, the other side bitched about Israel. Old men who hadn't stood in a batter's box since they were twelve-years old complaining with authority that the White Sox had to dump A.J. Pierzynski. Young Palestinians talking about Israeli death squads who snuck into villages to kill male babies in order to eliminate the population. I doubt many of them had ever been over there. Like a good barber or bartender, I knew enough to do more listening than talking. "You got to get out more, Nasser," they told me. "There are things going on outside this café and your kitchen that you need to understand. These are your people."

A lot had changed in Palestine since I was there. But in truth, much had stayed the same. I always sensed their feeling of hopelessness; the belief that this was as good as it got and destiny was waiting for them like a car skidding on an ice patch. It didn't take the physical occupation to make them feel inadequate and powerless; the years of threats were sufficient. I could relate. I rarely had to raise a hand or my voice to get a man to turn his life's saving over to me.

I told no one about my days there. It was no longer because I was hiding them in a dark place. And not because I had come to terms with them. There was still regret at what I did and what I failed to do, still anger at the people who put me and kept me there. But those were my experiences. Those times did not represent what was happening to the men, women, and children over there then or today. I had no more to offer on their situation than African Americans did on the genocide in Kenya. What was changing was the only thing that could. Me.

I left Palestine forty-five years ago, though it never left me. It was always in my rearview mirror. It came to me in Abdel, Johara, Sam, Cham Pfalzer, and my dreams. There would never be closure for me. I don't believe in closure. There is always reflection, and reflection by definition means endless questions with no lasting answers. But it was a journey in the right direction.

I was greeted at the front door by a matronly woman who refused to make eye contact. She was wearing a qumbaz and a colorless headdress. I asked for Sam by the alias given to him. "Rasul here?"

Either she was playing it cool or didn't understand, but I knew she didn't have it in her to dismiss me. "Ask him his name," came a man's voice behind her in Arabic.

"Nasser Khudayer," I called out loud enough to be heard.

The activity behind the door was difficult to witness. The voice was feeble; the movement was a shuffle. I cringed knowing it was Sam. Our relationship had run the gamut of idolization to adversarial. I trusted in him then feared him. I loved him then despised him. But never had I seen him beaten.

His hand fumbled with the door with the dual purpose of supporting himself and opening it to greet me. It was thin and veiny, but as he curled his long fingers to grab it, the tendons tightened and the color returned, giving the illusion I wanted.

"No, not Nasser," he said, his pale face appearing, "Joe. Joe from Chi-car-go." He broke into a smile. We embraced. It was sincere on both our parts. It was a relief knowing our last reunion was either forgiven or forgotten.

He turned from me and his momentum kept him moving into the small living room. It was furnished simply in western style. His chair was a red leather recliner that he sat in upright to avoid the insult of showing me the soles of his shoes, though I'd no doubt he had grown to appreciate the design to its fullest.

Others would have seen an old man who drank a bit too much in his younger days, a man who abused his body with inactivity, or had it ravaged by disease. Few could know him as the dedicated activist, the fanatical militant, the disciplined revolutionary whose broken body was the reward for his choices. "You got yourself married, I see," I said, taking the loveseat across from him.

"What? No." He laughed. "Lama is my caretaker. You are my first visitor in many months, Joe. I'm glad the first one in so long is you. I take it Johara and you talked, to get to me."

"Yes."

"Must be important; she is under strict orders not to give up my location."

"She was reluctant to."

"Don't misunderstand; I'm glad she did. And I'm sure she received clearance to do so."

"I thought you'd be sent further away."

"Hide a feather in the feather bed is the best way. You look good. Healthy."

I palmed my belly. "Healthier every year."

"I know you're too honest to say the same of me. Have you a family, Joe?"

"Two daughters. Teenagers."

"Yes, I know of America teenage girls. So tell me, Joe, why the visit?"

"I want you to come with me," I said. "To Toronto, to see an old acquaintance."

He pursed his lips. "I'm sure I have no one in Toronto."

"Been a long time, Sam, how would you know?"

"I would have been told."

There was satisfaction in his eyes, and such conviction that he was still in the loop, that I hadn't the heart to question his illusion that fighters in Palestine gave a damn about him after all these years. "It's Cham Pfalzer, Sam. He's dead."

So vivid was my memory of his mission to Chicago to have Pfalzer assassinated that I was taken aback by the blank look on his face. Then he smiled. "So, at last the colonel has been killed."

"No, he's dead." I handed him the magazine, opened to the article. He looked at the page for less than a minute before dropping it in his lap. I'm sure he gazed at the photo but paid only cursory regard to the words.

"I see. If you didn't kill him then why did you come?"

He had it in his mind that I had come to remedy our past. As if only death could do so. I expected to see that with his aging body he would rest his weary mind. "I'm going up to see him," I said. "To meet his family."

He cocked his head, genuinely confused. "You wanted me to know that? Am I missing something?"

"You've missed a lot. Why didn't you attend Yamma's funeral?"

"They'd be waiting for that; I couldn't take the chance."

"The old Sam would have defied them."

"Perhaps. But it wasn't a risk I wanted to take. And as I age I don't view death as anything to celebrate, mine included."

"I went to celebrate her life. It's why I'm going to his."

"It's good you've come to accept things, Joe."

"But that's the point," I said. "I haven't. I'm working on it, and this is part of it. Look at you, hiding out here. No one comes to see you; few people even care where you are. The ones who do want you dead."

"Still so little you know. I'm not hiding, Joe. And I'm not running as Colonel Pfalzer did. I'm waiting. Have you been following the war?"

"In the newspapers."

"Don't insult me."

"I hear talk in my restaurant, most of it crap they picked up on the street. And in the papers."

"There are sources, good sources I can send you to."

"I'm not interested in any of that, Sam."

"I should have known it was not in you to do it. As contrary as this may sound, I admire you for it, and in my heart I'm glad you stayed out of it. In the end he was neutralized nonetheless. He had little influence after your visit."

"Because he didn't want to be part of it. He was here to let it go."

"His lips to your ears."

"When does your war end, Sam?"

"You know the answer to that."

"There is no victory for men like you," I said, "only battles. And every one brings about another and another. Like a race horse, only as good as his next race. And when the races are over, the horse has no purpose."

"To breed others of his kind," he said.

"I don't believe the world needs more like you Sam. No offense."

"I don't take it as an insult. You're afraid of me."

"Deathly."

"Well, the world needs men like me."

"Men like me who fought no causes and men like you who live only to fight are malignant tumors this world can do without."

"You talk from a thousand miles away," Sam said. "You're still a child even now. You can't live righteously without fighting."

"Yamma did."

"She was a woman."

"That gave her two battles to fight, then."

"That's the culture. I was not supportive of that way for women, and you know it, Joe. It's changing now."

I leaned in on him. "You said it to me years ago, and I believed it then as I believe it now, someday no one will care what happened between Palestine and Israel."

He shot up in his chair. "But something will happen regardless, and those of us who fight for change will care; those who inherent the change will care. And there will be change for them because we have a cause. The Israelis are like you, like Americans, they have only interests."

"This is about one man, Sam. It's not about a nation or a cause. We both had our relationships with him."

"I had no relationship with him, and yours was minimal."

"He saved my life and you wanted to end his; that's as close as you can get."

"It was what he stood for we wanted dead."

"Kill the man you kill the idea, is that the plan? Take an awful lot of killing."

"Joe, you can't spend youth murdering as Colonel Pfalzer did, then retreat into old age to make it go away."

"I don't know that part of him. I saw him as a good man."

"I am truly amazed at the number of good people who die in this country," he said. "No matter how they lived their lives, Americans believe everyone worthy of sainthood upon their death. This was not a good man. He was responsible for many deaths, as many innocents as soldiers. And then he ran. I would have had more respect for him had he stayed in the fight."

"So you could justify having him killed?"

"His death was certainly justifiable, no matter."

"Like Faid's. You killed him to get to me, didn't you? And Sue? You thought retribution would impress us."

"I admit some killings we did as young men were unnecessary."

"Not 'we,' Sam. There was no 'we.' It was you. Damn it, admit it. Admit it after all these years. Remember you told me that great men climb mountains to receive great wisdom. Going up to get it is the easy part, coming back down to use it, that's the hard part."

He was adamant; he wasn't going. I like to believe he was afraid I'd be right; that I would prove his decades of hate to be misguided and wasted. But as Johara said, he'd admit no such thing. He was man stuck in the past. He held fast to the belief he could right it. As I looked around the small house I saw nothing to suggest he had moved on. No recent photographs. No new furnishings. No updated appliances. There were no flowers and plants. The world here was in shades of gray.

To him, the life he dedicated to changing his corner of the universe was more honorable than my aimless one. In the end, I couldn't blame him. Life has no do-overs, admitting you took a right when you should have gone left makes it painful.

Yet I was glad I came. I could no longer hate him. These were the patterns we were stuck in, and perhaps it was I who was stuck in the past, unable to move myself forward. But there is a truth in our hearts, a single universal truth, often shrouded by what we think we know. It will indeed take genius, and perhaps something a bit more mystical, to find it.

It was a cloudless night. With all the city lights I couldn't see them, but I knew the stars were out there. Adli loved stars for the reason he loved Yamma. "Doesn't matter if I can see them," he said. "I know they're always there."

I pulled down to Water Street before crossing the Illinois River. It was nearing eleven. The traffic rattled the bridge above me. In the grassy park where I stood, only a few street lights obscured the sky. It had been decades since I contemplated it beyond searching out the next storm. The constellations will change over the centuries, obscuring the belt of Orion and the cup of the dipper to the point there'll be no resemblance at all. Yet I suppose as the patterns change, the names will not, so ingrained are they in our legends and myths. I got out and leaned over the hood of my car, imaging the window sill, and the howling pariah dogs, and the smell of the desert. And there was Adli beside me, his finger pointing to a distant spot, proudly calling out the constellations, "Al Jabbar, Ad-Dubb Al-Asghar, Al-Korsi.

About the Author

John Ouellet was born and raised in Massachusetts. After 9 years as a US Army officer, he served 23 years as a Special Agent in the Detroit FBI field office. He has had several short stories published in *St Anthony Messenger,* and professional articles published in financial fraud journals. He still resides in Michigan with his wife and daughter while three other children are now on journeys of their own.

ALL THINGS THAT MATTER PRESS, Inc.

FOR MORE INFORMATION ON TITLES AVAILABLE FROM
ALL THINGS THAT MATTER PRESS, GO TO
http://allthingsthatmatterpress.com
or contact us at
allthingsthatmatterpress@gmail.com

www.ingramcontent.com/pod-product-compliance
Lightning Source LLC
Chambersburg PA
CBHW070307040726
47501CB00018B/383
* 9 7 8 0 9 8 9 4 0 3 2 4 5 *